The Swan Laird

Celtic Hearts, Book 3

Susan King

ARE YOU SIGNED UP FOR DRAGONBLADE'S BLOG?

You'll get the latest news and information on exclusive giveaways, exclusive excerpts, coming releases, sales, free books, cover reveals and more.

Check out our complete list of authors, too!

No spam, no junk. That's a promise!

Sign Up Here

www.dragonbladepublishing.com

Dearest Reader;

Thank you for your support of a small press. At Dragonblade Publishing, we strive to bring you the highest quality Historical Romance from some of the best authors in the business. Without your support, there is no 'us', so we sincerely hope you adore these stories and find some new favorite authors along the way.

Happy Reading!

CEO, Dragonblade Publishing

Additional Dragonblade books by
Author Susan King

Highland Secrets Series
The Scottish Bride (Book 1)

Celtic Hearts Series
The Hawk Laird (Book 1)
The Falcon Laird (Book 2)
The Swan Laird (Book 3)

To Julie Booth and to Jaclyn Reding, two most excellent friends.
Each one hauled around with me on wonderful, hilarious,
unforgettable trips to Scotland.

Acknowledgments

I want to thank the many readers who loved Sir Gawain (the knight, not the goshawk!) in *The Hawk Laird* (originally *Laird of the Wind*) and asked for his story. Heartfelt thanks for the inspiration–you were right, he turned out to be a wonderful hero!

Andy Hernandez and Mike Braid shared archery advice, friendship, and more over the years; and special thanks to Andy for finding a longbow for a short person.

I will always be grateful to Shihan Tim Gilbert, tenth Dan black belt in Shorin Ryu, who shared the secret of catching arrows with me, and then patiently, if exuberantly, shot arrows directly at me until I learned to catch them.

Preface

This beautiful new edition of *The Swan Laird*, previously published as *The Swan Maiden*, is another one of my older novels that I am proud and delighted to share with readers once again. If you read this in its original form, you may be as pleased as I am with this updated version. With all of its original plot, characters, adventures, research, and romance in place, it is now tighter, not as long or as wordy, with crisper pacing and perhaps a bit more plot logic here and there. Trust me, in places it needed some work.

I find, with each original story that I return to, that I have a better grasp on writing now than I did then. I have learned a lot, and I am still learning. Bless digital publishing, which gives authors the opportunity to return to earlier works and improve them for readers and for their own peace of mind.

This book, like others I have had the chance to revise and tidy up, is a better novel than it was, while it is exactly the same story. I'm happy to see, returning to these books years later, that the story holds up well, the characters are ones I am proud to have created, and the research is relevant. All I had to do was tighten extra language and clean up threads here and there. It took time, because I care about my books. What you have in your hands now feels fresh to me.

Whether The Swan Laird is new to you or is like an old friend that you're returning to, I hope you love it.

Happy Reading!

Susan

Prologue

I heard the sweet voice of the swan
At the parting of night and day,
And who should be guiding in front
The queen of fortune, the white swan . . .
> —*Carmina Gadelica*

Scotland, the Highlands
Winter, 1286

"IN THE TIME of the mists," said the *seanachaidh*, "when faeries danced upon the Highland hillsides, a maiden lived in a fortress of bronze and silver on an island in a loch. She granted her heart to no one until a certain warrior wooed her and won her."

Gabhan MacDuff, grandson of the *seanachaidh* and son of a warrior, yawned as he lay on his stomach beside the hearth fire near his parents, kinfolk, and servants, all quietly listening. Resting his head on his arms, Gabhan watched the flames dance.

"Their love was bright as a rainbow," his grandfather went on, "and soon they would wed, he, dark as a raven, she, fair as a swan."

At the mention of love, Gabhan wrinkled his nose. His father, long legs stretched out to the fire, touched his son's head gently to remind him to show better respect.

"But one man, a Druid, wished them ill, coveting the maiden. His heart was hard and dark with longing. He vowed that if he could not have her, no one would.

"On the eve of the wedding, the Druid stood in the moonlight and spoke a spell, then took a faery bolt and shot it into the skies so that a great storm arose. The waters of the loch swallowed the island, lightning struck the fortress, and the walls crumbled."

The bit about magic and destruction was more interesting, Gabhan thought, as he watched his grandfather, a handsome man like Gabhan's father, with blue eyes and black and silver hair. Gabhan's eyes were brown like his English mother's, though he favored his Highland kinsmen otherwise.

"All who lived in the fortress were drowned on the eve of the wedding," Adhamnain MacDuff continued. "And the warrior and the maiden were lost in the loch."

Gabhan did not like that—he had hoped they would be saved. He saw his mother smile at him, then set a loving hand on her husband's arm. His mother had left her English family to marry her Highland husband and live in Glenshie Castle, though her family thought him an unsuitable savage. Yet she was happy, her dark eyes warm and sparkling as she smiled.

"But the lovers' hearts were pure," his grandfather went on, "and such love is strong and cannot be destroyed. Love makes its own magic, you see, and it saved them all in a way. For every soul who drowned that night became a swan."

Gabhan lifted his brows high. This was exciting.

"The maiden and the warrior changed into the most beautiful and most graceful of all the enchanted swans on the loch. When the Druid saw the birds and recognized the lovers, he knew his evil plan had failed, and he fled the land.

"The descendants of those swans live upon the loch still, and their magic and mystery endure. They say that sometimes in mist or sunset, the walls of the sunken fortress appear, but only those who feel great love can see it." He sat back. "That loch is Loch nan Eala, loch of the swans."

"It is near here! What happened to the Druid, Grandfather?" Gabhan asked.

"Some say he will return someday to claim the swan maiden."

Gabhan shivered at the thought. "My father took me to see the swans at Loch nan Eala. There is another castle there now. But my mother and father saw the ancient fortress once, shining deep in the loch."

He saw his mother nod while his father laughed in soft agreement.

"Those who love truly can see it," his grandfather said. "They do say that sometimes the warrior and his lady shed their swan skins and regain their human form for a short while to search for some way to break the spell and free themselves."

"Can it be broken, Grandfather?"

"A warrior who knows true love must catch a faery bolt and fling it into the heart of the loch. That will end the spell at last. So they say."

"*Ach,*" Gabhan said, "I could catch a faery bolt."

The old man smiled. "Faery bolts are hard to find. And remember, the swans on that loch may be content after so long and want to stay."

"I think the warrior and his lady still want to end the spell," Gabhan said. The story was done, so he rested his head while his grandfather and his parents murmured together.

He understood some of what they said—they spoke of the recent death of the King of Scots and the struggle against the English king who was sending his armies north to claim kingship, though he had no right. Rebellion was brewing, and his father intended to fight if he was needed. He wanted to protect Scotland, his kin, and his home.

Soon, the warmth of the hearth and the low drone of voices put him to sleep. He dreamed of a sparkling loch where white swans glided. He too was a swan beside a beautiful female, their white-feathered bodies mirrored in the glassy water. A golden chain encircled his neck, and looped about hers, binding them together. He felt the slight tug of the golden links as he floated on the cool water beside her.

In the dream, he lifted his wings, and the beautiful swan did too. They rose from the water as one, with the chain draped between them like a ribbon of sunlight. A storm chased them with fierce, dark winds; lightning flashed, clouds rolled, and the wind threw them down into the water's darkening embrace.

Gabhan awoke with a cry, and felt his father's soothing hand upon his head.

WITHIN MONTHS, GABHAN rode a pony over the heathered slopes beside his weeping mother, his grim nurse, and an old male servant. They were leaving Glenshie with its purple hills and swift streams, leaving the stone tower that was their home. His mother said they must go England now. His father had been killed when their castle had been attacked, and his grandfather had died as well.

Gabhan could not think of it, for the pain was too deep. They hurried through a desperate escape in the night, with shouts and smoke behind them, and English soldiers in their castle. But his mother was English and they were going to England. His father was dead. He felt so confused.

Yet he squeezed back tears and held his head high, determined to protect and defend his mother, keeping his hand on his wooden sword. His nurse told him to put it away before he hurt someone. But his mother thanked him for his chivalry, and let him keep the sword at his side.

When they reached the border of England at last, his mother traded the red plaid his father had once given him for a brown tunic that fit like sackcloth. She said he must speak only English now, never Gaelic again. He must answer to Gawain, not to Gabhan.

He obeyed, his wooden sword ready, his shoulders straight. He missed his father so much that he ached at night and fought tears. But he loved his mother and would do whatever she asked. The sadness in her eyes matched the hurt in his heart, and he just wanted to see her smile again.

Her English kin were strangers, but kind, and the hills near his grandparents' castle were green and lovely, but not as beautiful as Glenshie. He liked the long-legged English horses and the sleek dogs his uncles and grandfather kept, and he liked to walk along a nearby river to watch the swans. They reminded him of home.

Then his mother wed Sir Henry Avenel, a widowed knight who made her laugh again, and Gabhan—Gawain—had three new stepbrothers. At Avenel Castle, he ran errands for the knights and felt fascinated by their armor, their horses and weapons, and their stories of noble deeds. He yearned to become a knight.

But he thought of Scotland often, cherishing his memories, and meant to return one day to claim his rights to Glenshie Castle, its lands, and his inherited title. That must wait until he was a knight, master of his life, and a benevolent defender of others.

He grew tall and strong in body, heart, and soul, and his boyhood dreams faded. One day he knelt before the king of England to be knighted. Promising fealty, he swore to dedicate himself to the principles of chivalry.

When he returned to Scotland at last, he rode behind the English king and beneath the dragon banner, the sign of destruction.

Chapter One

Scotland, Perthshire
Spring 1300

FLAMES POURED UPWARD, fierce and beautiful, licking at the door frame. Blinking against that brightness, Juliana stumbled back as a web of fire spread over the floor rushes. She ran to the window of her bedchamber and threw open the shutters.

Below, she heard a crash as the blaze engulfed another part of her father's castle of Elladoune. Fighting panic, she recalled coming back inside when her mother had begged her to escape through the postern gate. She was a woman grown at sixteen, she had told her mother. She could take care of herself, and would return quickly.

Now she feared that escape was impossible. She felt the urge to scream. *Be calm*, she thought. She had returned to rescue her birds, and would do so.

She could only pray that her mother and the others were safe in the forest by now. The enemy was at the gates of Elladoune like hungry wolves—English wolves with fire arrows and an appetite for rebel Scots.

Somehow she must find a way out, but first she must free the doves and the little kestrel she kept; she had raised the doves from hatchlings, and had nursed the wounded kestrel until its wing had healed, and she would not leave them. She ran toward their cages as dark smoke swirled throughout the room.

Carrying one cumbersome wooden cage to the window and then the other, she set them on a wooden chest and unlatched the cage doors to urge the birds out. One by one they hopped to the opening and quickly fluttered through the window to freedom.

But one dove clung to the back of the cage. Despite rising panic, Juliana coaxed the bird to the window and merciful release until it flew away, a pale blur in the night.

Heat and smoke seared her lungs, and the wooden floor grew warm under her bare feet. Clad only in the linen chemise she wore when her mother woke her, she had no time to dress. Now, glancing toward the door wreathed in flame, she knew her only choice for escape was the window. She could not fly free like her birds—she would have to chance a steep dive into the loch. Leaning out the window, gulping a little fresh air, she peered out.

The midnight sky, not fully dark in summer, glowed eerily with flame and smoke. The loch was dark and deep below. The castle's back wall faced the loch and sheered downward to a rocky promontory at the edge of the water. Protected by its rear location, her chamber had the luxury of a large window, a tall lancet shape wide enough for her to make a jump.

The glassed arch above her head cracked then, the pieces cascading like stars. Shielding her head, Juliana stumbled away into a side alcove with a tiny window that overlooked the bailey yard. The small space was cool, and fresh air swept through. Hearing shouts, Juliana knelt on the bench seat and looked out to see men in glittering armor filling the courtyard.

"Come down, Lady Marjorie!" one of the men bellowed. He called for her mother. Juliana glimpsed him as he paced the yard. In jet-black armor and a red surcoat, he appeared wholly malevolent.

"Come down to me!" he shouted again. The English commander of the raid on Elladoune Castle believed her mother was still inside. But Juliana knew her mother had fled to safety with her little sons and the servants, and she hoped they were well away.

Not long ago, when her mother had roused her, Juliana had helped to gather her little brothers, a swaddled babe and a whimpering toddler. The English had come to Elladoune to ruin the castle and take Juliana's father—but he had left weeks earlier with his two eldest sons to join the Scottish rebels. Discovering Alexander Lindsay gone, the English commander had fired the castle without a care for Lindsay's family inside.

Her fragile mother had panicked, praying fervently while attempting to soothe her children. Juliana had helped gather them all and with the servants, shepherded them to the back postern gate. Outside, they would flee to a nearby abbey, where the abbot, a kinsman, would shelter them.

"Come down!" the commander shouted again. "Give up your tower to King Edward's knights, or give up your lives!"

Fire-tipped arrows sailed upward, smacking into the walls close to the little window. Startled, Juliana jerked back. She had her own bow, and if it was to hand, she would have aimed an arrow straight into the man's black heart. She had skill enough for it. But she could not harm any creature—her elder brothers teased her for her soft heart. Now, though, she felt as if she could do harm to the horrid man in the bailey.

Coughing, she ran back to the larger window, avoiding broken glass as she climbed up on the wooden chest and stood on the window ledge. She straightened inside the tall lancet like a saint in a niche. A breeze filled with smoke fluttered at her shift.

Below, the loch gleamed, dark waters reflecting the fire. She looked up to see swans winging past, feathered golden in the firelight as they fled.

Perched there, frightened, she suddenly remembered an old tale about a flock of swans that rescued a girl, cradling her safely in a net to carry her home. Another legend claimed that long ago, a hundred people had drowned in this very loch. Each one had transformed into a swan.

The wind batted her chemise against her body and whipped her long golden hair outward. Closing her eyes, she prayed for protection. Then she bent her knees and bounded outward, arrowing her arms toward the water.

HE SAW AN angel fly out of the inferno and sink into the water—a terrifying and strangely beautiful sight. Sir Gawain ran forward, water lapping at his boots as he searched the water for the pale slip of a girl who had leaped from the tower window.

Dozens of swans glided on the flame-bright surface of the loch and rose into the sky, fleeing the chaos of fire, smoke, shouts, and arrows. But Gawain saw no human form among those in the water, though he waded through reeds, searching.

The bellow and crackle of the fire grew louder. He heard the commander, Sir Walter de Soulis, continue his demand that the lady of the castle surrender her home.

Bastard, Gawain thought succinctly. He hoped the lady and her servants, whom he had glanced at through some of the windows earlier, had escaped. But he feared they might be dead inside the blazing castle. He only hoped the girl who had leaped out had survived.

"You—Avenel! Did that girl come out of the water?" A knight ran toward him.

"I have not seen her yet. She may have drowned."

Another knight came near to look at the water. "Drowned or fallen on those rocks—or even killed by those birds. Swans can fight like demons."

"Sir Walter wants her captured," the other man said. "The lady of the castle and others fled into the forest, I hear. The girl is in the water. We must find her."

"We may find her body tomorrow," the other drawled.

Gawain watched one of the swans soaring upward. "Scottish

legend claims that when someone drowns, their soul can enter the body of a swan."

"How do you know that?" one of the men asked.

"When I was a boy, I had a Scottish nurse. This very loch has some legend about enchanted swans, I think. The first swans of Elladoune, long ago, were drowned souls."

"Well, it is likely that the girl is gone," Gawain said. "A swan flew up from the spot where she fell. Could be her soul." He had a wicked urge, just then, to make these two knights uneasy. He felt as if this was his territory. His loch. The girl was his to protect. "This place is enchanted—so they say."

One of them stepped back. "Enchanted swans or none, Edward of England owns this loch now. He wants rebels, not swans. Come ahead. We will tell Sir Walter the girl has likely drowned." He looked up at the birds circling overhead. "Could she really change into a swan?"

"The longer I stay in Scotland, the more I believe such things can happen," his companion said as they walked away.

Gawain remained to scan the water. He was glad the two knights had disliked the thought of enchantment and had left. The girl could have survived—and he wanted to give her a chance to escape with the others. As a boy, he had fled in the night from the enemy; he had sympathy for whoever managed to escape this place tonight.

He watched the burning silhouette of the castle reflected in the loch. Once he had believed in the eternal magic of Loch nan Eala and Castle Elladoune. But the English had destroyed that legend in the space of an hour.

Memories stirred through him wherever he went into Scotland as part of King Edward's army in this Scottish campaign. None of the other knights knew about his Scottish origins, let alone the fact that his birthplace, Glenshie Castle, was not far from Elladoune and the loch. Truth was, he was not sure where Glenshie was located. He had been a boy when he had seen it last, with only a child's understanding of the region.

Glancing toward the black hills in the distance, he knew his boyhood home was hidden somewhere in that direction. Years ago, he had vowed to find Glenshie and claim his inheritance. Now that he was here, a knight serving the English king, that precious dream seemed remote and impossible. Yet whether or not he found his home, he was the rightful laird of Glenshie.

He walked along the rocky base that edged the tower. The water lapped at the promontory and sparks from the blaze sizzled in the loch like amber stars. Searching the loch's surface once more, he wondered if he should give up on finding the girl.

Then he saw the lift of a pale arm and glimpsed a face amid the swans. She was surrounded by swimming birds—but he could not tell if she was alive or drowned.

He yanked off his red surcoat with its English dragon, and pulled at the leather ties of his chainmail hood and hauberk. He laid his sword and belt aside and struggled out of the steel mesh, quilted coat, boots, all the things that could pull him down and drown him in the water. Wearing only his trews, he piled his gear in the fiery shadow of the tower and slipped into the water.

No one watched, nor would he ask for help. His fellow knights were here to claim and conquer, not defend and rescue. His nature leaned to the latter.

Once he had been fiercely proud to be one of them. But he loathed what he had seen of the king's army on its northern trek through Scotland. Chivalry and heroics were replaced by cruelty, lust, and the basest acts and urges of mankind. Witnessing deeds even uglier than the burning of homes, he found ways to avoid committing acts of cruelty directly, stepping aside, fading into the background, even turning his back on an order when he could.

Nonetheless, he had sins upon his soul that bothered him. The thought of dishonoring his knight's vows disturbed him too. Disillusioned and feeling increasingly trapped, he saw that his king claimed to be chivalrous and merciful, while twisting the very ideals and integrity that Gawain deeply revered.

He swam toward the circle of swans with steady strokes. The

birds dispersed, leaving an alley in the water. Treading, turning, he spotted the pale form again. She was moving now, swimming toward the shore. He surged after her.

Swans lurched upward, clumsy in the transition from water to air—grace lost, grace regained. When the commotion of swans cleared, he saw the girl among the reeds near the shoreline. He surged under the water, came up, and grabbed her.

She struggled, but he scooped an arm around her and tugged her toward the shore. When she drew breath to scream, he cupped his hand over her mouth and stilled in the water, hunkered down in the shallows behind the reeds, holding her close.

"Hush," he breathed. "I have you."

She twisted in his arms and gasped out an angry, muffled retort. Shouts sounded on shore. He saw the glare of torches and the glint of armor. Cradling the girl in his arms, he glided deeper the shelter of the reeds, his feet on the soft bottom of the loch. He held her low in the water.

"Let me go," she gasped in Gaelic, writhing. He understood, his mind retaining the language of his childhood.

"Quiet," he hissed in English. "Be still."

"Sassenach!" she spat out. He tightened his hand over her mouth. His arm banded her, encountering soft breasts beneath a wet shift and ropes of wet golden hair.

"Let me go," she snapped in English then, and kicked his shin. Struggling, she sank down, and he tugged her up. She rose sputtering.

"I want to help you," he muttered.

"Then do not drown me," she gasped. As she drew breath to scream, he clapped a hand over her mouth again, one arm securely around her.

"Sweet saints, hush. Be mute like a swan!"

"Not all swans are mute," she mumbled, and squirmed like a hooked fish.

"That I see, Swan Maiden," he grunted, and wrapped a leg

around her thighs, tucking her against him like a lover, with passion the last thing on his mind. "Quiet, if you value your life, or they will catch you."

She went still, then slipped an arm around his neck to cling, hanging on. Her face was silky and wet against his bearded cheek. He felt a fine trembling all through her.

The commander and a few knights walked along the shore and pointed toward the swans, then at the flaming window where the girl had leaped free. A few swans flapped their wings and hissed loudly as the men approached, so that they backed away.

One bird, huge and gorgeous in the fierce firelight, rose from the water and took to the wing, flying so low overhead that Gawain felt the breeze and ducked as it passed.

The girl laughed. "He will not hurt us."

"Hush," Gawain said between his teeth.

Two knights waded into the reed bed and stumbled away hastily as the swan circled over their heads again, fast and low. Gawain watched, astonished. The bird's protective action could not be deliberate—yet it seemed so, and he was grateful.

The girl looked up, hair streaming around her face, her eyes large and dark. She was lovely, delicate, even in this drenched state. Her body was lithe and lean in his arms, her breasts lush against his chest. He held her, water lapping around their shoulders.

"They are gone," she whispered. Her mouth was close to his. Feeling a strong, misplaced urge to kiss her, he pulled away slightly.

"They are just there, on the hill," he murmured. "We should stay out of sight."

"The swans are gone, too. Look."

He turned to see that most of the swans had disappeared. The remaining few glided elegantly over the water as if the burning tower was no distraction. The shore was empty now, though shouts sounded on the other side of the castle.

Waiting another few moments, Gawain cautiously stood,

bringing the girl up with him, keeping an arm around her. He waded to shore, soft mud sucking at his feet. Water sluiced away from him and the girl as if they were kelpies rising from the depths. He picked her up in his arms; sopping wet, she was still no burden.

Glancing warily toward the castle, he ran along the bank, carrying her away from the burning tower toward the forest. People began to emerge from the shadows there. A woman stepped between the trees and opened her arms.

"Mother! Set me down," the girl told him. He did, keeping his arm around her as they hurried toward the trees.

The woman pulled the girl into her embrace and swathed her in a thick plaid. Someone offered a blanket to Gawain. He refused it, stepping back.

The girl turned to look at him. Her eyes were luminous; in shadows and moonlight, he could not tell their color.

"I am Juliana Lindsay," she said. "Tell me your name, so that I can ask the angels to watch over you."

He frowned. If he told her the name given him at birth—Gabhan MacDuff—she might know him for a Highlander and despise him for being with the English. If he told her his English name, Gawain Avenel, she would loathe him for that.

She shivered, waiting, her cheeks pale, hair hanging like strands of honey. He touched her chin with a fingertip.

"Call me your Swan Laird in your prayers, and the angels will find me. And I will call you my Swan Maiden, and pray for you as well."

She nodded. Her mother drew her back. "They are coming this way, sir," the mother said.

"I will lead them away from the forest. Go, all of you—go!" He waved them back into the woodland and turned to run toward the castle, where the inferno raged bright and ferocious. As he went, he could feel the girl watching him.

Running, he felt as if he'd left heaven behind him and was headed into hell.

Chapter Two

Scotland, Perthshire
Spring 1306

QUICKSILVER AND PALE as moonlight, she glided out of the forest into the clearing. Glancing over her shoulder, she heard pounding hoofbeats and shouts that commanded her to stop, wait.

She turned slowly, though her heart beat like a war drum. Lingering was foolhardy, but she always made sure they saw her—she had done so for years.

Nearby, she knew a group of people ran through the forest in another direction. They conveyed a burden, large and cumbersome: a wooden war machine on creaking wheels, partially dismantled, its struts stacked on a pony cart. The engine would be transported along the river by night until it reached the rebel camp.

The king's men must not discover it.

She waited in a beam of moonlight. The knights spurred toward her.

"Swan Maiden!" one shouted. She forced herself to be still as their horses crashed through the shadows.

Then she whirled and ran toward the loch, shedding the white feathered cloak that covered her head and shoulders, tossing it aside. She stepped into the water and crouched, her pale tunic billowing around her, blond hair fanning out as she surged.

She arrowed through the water and neared a cluster of swans and ducks gliding on the loch. When she swam into their midst, the birds ignored her, accustomed to her presence. When a curious cygnet swam too close, she pushed it gently away.

Treading water, she watched the shore. The knights burst into the clearing and dismounted. Running along the bank, they scanned the loch, pointing. One of them picked up a white feather that had fallen from the cloak.

She watched, hidden in the ring of swans. The men walked to the water's edge. One of them picked up a stone and flung it. As it sank near the birds, they scattered with fuss and noise.

Her protective circle gone, she dove under and lunged toward a rocky shelf. Pulling herself along its striated contours, she slid out of the water under the shelter of an overhanging pine.

Friends waited there, holding out a plaid. Juliana wrapped the woven length around her shoulders and slicked back her wet hair. Then together, they ran into the forest.

AMBER FIRELIGHT DANCED over familiar faces. Seated on the earthen floor of the cave, Juliana scanned the group assembled there, then turned her attention to her guardian, seated beside her. Abbot Malcolm cleared his throat.

"At last, my friends," he said quietly. "What we have risked so much to gain may be in our grasp. The report I heard this day will greatly aid our effort." He spoke in rapid Gaelic. "I have a plan, but there is danger. Juliana will risk a great deal this time."

She kept her expression calm. Around the firelit circle, the people summoned by Abbot Malcolm of Inchfillan waited. Her guardian's white tonsure was pristine in the light, his round cheeks pink, his blue gaze keen as he looked at her.

"Father Abbot," she murmured. "If we can win back Elladoune, I will do whatever I must."

"Father Abbot," one of the men asked, "what has happened?"

Malcolm folded his hands. Juliana knew what he would say. She and her younger brothers lived in the abbot's house outside the precinct of the monastery. Malcolm had discussed his thoughts with her earlier.

Anyone who did not know her kinsman and guardian well—such as the English knights garrisoned in Elladoune—assumed that he was a pleasant old man concerned only about his little Celtic abbey and the lost souls he guided along the right path.

Some of his lost souls—rebels all—watched him now.

What Malcolm hid from the English, Juliana thought, was a fierce loyalty to Scotland. He was far more lion than rotund lamb. Years ago, he had taken under his wing several dispossessed Scots and trained them to be forest rebels. Juliana was proud to be among them.

Outside the cave, trees swayed in the night breeze. Inside, Malcolm's rebels listened, and leaned forward.

"I met with the sheriff of Glen Fillan today," Malcolm said. "He asked a favor, and posed a threat."

"Sir?" Juliana drummed her fingers on her unstrung bow, which lay beside her. She felt a desperate urge to act but knew she and the others must proceed cautiously.

"Walter de Soulis has never cared about our interests," Lucas, once her father's herdsman, said. "He will not help us!"

"He did not whine about the renegades and homeless in the forest and glen, as he usually does—though I try my best to help him with that problem." Malcolm held up his hands innocently and smiled.

Juliana glanced toward her two young brothers. Iain and Alec, seven and nine, slept in a corner, curled like puppies on a pile of cloaks. The boys would sleep through anything if tired enough, even a meeting to plan exciting rebellious actions.

"Sheriff says the garrison leader of Elladoune will depart soon," Malcolm said.

"Good!" said one of the men. "Farewell to him who burned our village and the castle, forcing us to live in the forest. But we still must fend against the man who ruined Elladoune, who is now made sheriff over us."

"When the commander leaves, his troops will go with him," the abbot went on. "The English king has ordered them to pursue our new King of Scots, Robert Bruce, and his men, who have gone into the Highland hills in the area north of here. Another garrison will arrive with a new leader for Elladoune."

Red Angus, burly and russet, a former farmer, shook his head. "One English garrison moves out, another moves in. We will have new faces to learn, new habits and patrol routes to watch. It does not help our cause."

"This does. For a few weeks, Elladoune will be deserted," Malcolm answered. "Sir Walter wants the monks of Inchfillan to watch the castle gates and tend the sheep and gardens until the new men arrive."

"Ah, that is what we need," Robert, a blacksmith, crowed. "We will be prepared for it too, with weapons and armor!"

"Exactly," Malcolm said. "God has answered our prayers. We can take over Elladoune."

"And claim it for Scotland!" Angus cried. Malcolm smiled.

Arms raised upward and voices rose. "For Scotland!"

Juliana smiled as hope bloomed within her like a flower. Soon they would live in Elladoune Castle again, and bring the ruined village back to life, farming the land and raising herds in peace once more.

"Juliana," Malcolm said, placing his hand on her shoulder, "will help us carry out our scheme. The soldiers shake with fear when our Swan Maiden appears and disappears as if by magic. She frightens them, and we are deeply grateful to her for creating that illusion these past few years."

"Magic, she has, so say the English," Angus remarked. "Cleverness, say I."

"The silent Swan Maiden of Elladoune, who never utters a

word," Malcolm agreed. "As long as the Sassenachs believe she could be an enchanted swan, that helps what we do. But we cannot allow her to face more risk with a new garrison."

"They will harm her if they capture her," Lucas growled.

"She has a quick and clever game," Malcolm said, "never speaking when English are near, and running away as soon as they see her. The Sassenachs are so anxious about entering the forest that we have been able to do much secret work for the cause of Scotland."

"They are fools to believe she is enchanted." Beithag, the oldest woman among them, snorted her disdain. "That will not last."

Malcolm sighed. "True, and the danger to her is a problem. Walter de Soulis has been sheriff in Glen Fillan for only a little while, but he is not convinced about the enchanted swan maiden. He says she is real, a rebel and a spy. He suspects Juliana."

"What did you tell him, Father Abbot?" Angus asked with concern.

"I said my ward is a simple, pious girl who does not speak because of the terrible loss of her home years ago, with her father dead and her mother cloistered, so that she has not seen her in years." He smiled at Juliana.

She had accepted long ago that she might never see her mother again. Lady Marjorie had put herself and her grief into a Lowland convent shortly after the disaster at Elladoune and her husband's subsequent death.

"If De Soulis believes the girl does not speak," Beithag said, "he has never seen her in a high temper!" Some of the others laughed.

"I told him," Malcolm said, "that when the Swan Maiden appears by the loch, it is a vision, and will bring good luck. I said the locals believe in the legend."

"Still," said Beithag's husband, Uilleam, "Juliana must cease her actions to stay safe." He nodded his gray, leonine head, and others nodded with him. Uilleam generally said little, but when he did, the rebels took heed of it.

"Father Abbot, you must find your ward a husband to give her babes, and you must also stop asking for her help," Beithag said.

Juliana shook her head. "But I want to do this, Mother Beithag. The Swan Maiden helps the work we do. The Sassenachs avoid this part of the forest, and so we have stockpiled weapons and armor, and we have built siege engines that we can transport by darkness. The work is important."

"Mother Beithag is right," Angus said. "You have risked much, lass, and have lost much, and we should ask no more of you. A laird's daughter should wed a Scottish knight and raise sons for Scotland—and stop terrifying the English."

"I am raising sons for Scotland. My brothers." She pointed to the sleeping boys.

"Listen now," Malcolm said. "The time has come to reclaim Elladoune. We must decide how and when. If Juliana is willing, we still need her assistance."

"That devil De Soulis will destroy our plans no matter what we do," Lucas growled. "The man is invincible. They say his black armor cannot be penetrated. He cannot be defeated."

"He can only be avoided, which we do," Angus said.

Malcolm sighed. "We all pray daily about these concerns. The monks at the abbey keep a hundred candles burning day and night to call God's attention to our plight."

"Keep those candles lit," Beithag said tartly. "We need a miracle."

"If we try to take Elladoune, De Soulis and his men will be there," Lucas said. "How can we withstand an attack?"

"Once inside, we will triumph somehow," Malcolm said. "God removed the other garrison leader. He will solve this dilemma too."

"Juliana should keep away from that devil De Soulis," Angus said. "He is the one who ruined Elladoune."

"All the more reason," Juliana said. "My father is dead, and my older brothers are with the new King of Scots. They would help us if they could. Let me do what I can."

"Brave girl," Angus said. "Well then. May our prayers hold sway with heaven."

"My friends, we shall pray now." Malcolm stood and joined his hands together.

Juliana lowered her head and murmured the Latin responses, though her heart quickened with fear. As the Swan Maiden, she stood at the center of the local effort, able to help—or to hinder, if she should err. But more than one miracle would be needed to gain back Elladoune. She could only pray her luck would hold.

One bit of luck she would never forget—on the night Elladoune had burned, an English knight had rescued her. She might have been captured and killed if not for her Swan Laird, as she thought of him still.

Sometimes he appeared in her dreams, nameless and fascinating, a dark-eyed and beautiful man. Of the many Sassenach knights she had seen riding in and out of Elladoune and Inchfillan over the last six years, she had never seen him again.

She whispered a fervent prayer—asking for protection, as always, for her Swan Laird. And she asked for a miracle to assist her.

What she prayed for most of all was the ability and the luck to bring kinfolk and friends, and herself, home to Elladoune at last.

Chapter Three

England, London
May 1306

THE STONE BENEATH his knees was cold and hard, the silence of the courtiers watching him colder still. Sir Gawain Avenel bowed his bare head, aware of King Edward's harsh gaze.

"Sire," Gawain began, "I beg forgiveness of the king for my transgressions in Scotland. I offer renewed loyalty and fealty to my liege lord. I solemnly pledge my heart, mind, and sword to the service of my king." He placed his fist over his heart.

His chainmail hauberk dragged upon his shoulders. In ten years of knighthood, armor had never felt so heavy, a burden of the soul rather than the body.

He must utter this sincere, if humiliating, apology or lose all. His life hung in the balance, along with the welfare of those he loved. He glanced up through the dark frame of his lashes and brows to see King Edward, first of that name, scowling at him.

At least, Gawain thought, the king had not summoned guards to haul him back to prison. He drew breath to continue. "I beg to be allowed into king's peace once again."

The tense silence endured. Gawain was aware many believed he knelt here only to avoid more trouble. He had spent two months in a prison cell and had submitted a request to retain his modest English properties earned in knight service.

But in truth, he subjugated himself to protect his family—mother, stepfather, stepbrothers, and half-sisters—from harm in the wake of what the king termed his transgressions in Scotland. King Edward had a long and vengeful memory. Begging forgiveness was scant price to pay.

The recent death of his stepbrother Geoffrey on a Scottish field still tore at him. Gawain felt sure he had indirectly caused his brother's death by overstepping the boundaries he had danced too near for too long. He had aided Scottish rebels once again, against royal orders.

Worse, he had joined their quest for freedom. To him, those months had been a rare respite of genuine honor and integrity. But his deed was a crime and a breach of faith in the Crown's eyes. And it had brought tragedy.

He had also lost the respect of the Scottish rebels he had befriended. Though the English called them outlaws, he knew them to be righteous folk with noble hearts.

But now all of them—from James Lindsay, called the Hawk Laird, and his wife Lady Isobel the prophetess, to the last man among them—believed that Gawain had acted treacherously toward them. That was not the case, but he could neither correct their view nor regain their trust.

The silence continued. Someone coughed, armor chinked. The chamber glowed with tapestries, painted ceilings and floor tiles, and the jewel colors and sumptuous fabrics worn by the courtiers.

At the center of the brilliance, in black surcoat and steel mail, Gawain felt grim and colorless. He waited, head bowed, for the king to respond.

"This is not the first time you have knelt here, Sir Gawain," Edward finally said.

"Sire, true." A muscle flashed in his cheek. The king had a long memory. "I was knighted here at Westminster Palace."

"I believe you knelt here another time."

"Six years ago, I broke my fealty and begged to be admitted

back into king's peace." *Begged.* He knew Edward wanted to hear that.

"Broke faith in Scotland. Now you are here for the same reason, once again begging king's peace."

"Aye, Sire."

"You aided rebels to escape near Elladoune, I hear. The rash action of a young knight, and you were forgiven." The king waved a hand impatiently. "But this time you deserted your English commander, Sir Ralph Leslie, and joined Scotsmen led by a known renegade. This time, you cannot plead youthful impetuousness."

"Sire, Leslie was a cruel man who served his own needs before those of king and crown. He brought suffering and shame to an innocent woman. May I remind my lord king that Lady Isobel's gift of prophecy is admired in the English court as well as in Scotland. I chose to aid the lady."

"Defending a lady is understandable, but she is the wife of a Scottish outlaw."

Gawain would never regret what he had done, though he had lost friends in Scotland and endangered his family. He could repair the risk to his loved ones and would pay any penance to bring them better peace.

"I upheld my oath of chivalry," he said simply.

"Was that honorable or traitorous? Your father insists you were their prisoner, not their abettor. Shall we believe him?"

"Sire, years ago I knelt beneath your sword blade to be knighted, and swore to defend women and those weaker than myself against cruelty and oppression. I swore to support virtue and honor wherever I found it. Am I to be reprimanded and punished for doing so? I pray that my liege, a paragon of knighthood himself, will trust my integrity and forgive my faults."

"A pretty speech. Do you sympathize with rebels?"

"Sire," Gawain said. "I am an Avenel."

"And they are unswervingly loyal." The king grunted. "You have always shown integrity despite your impulse to help those you should not. The ideals of the courts of love do not apply on the fields of war—especially this Scottish war."

"Sire, I pray pardon." He bowed his head. Near the dais, he saw his stepfather and his stepbrothers. Henry Avenel looked worried, and his son Edmund fisted a hand. Robin, soon to be knighted himself, looked pale.

"Henry!" the king called out. "Your eldest is cut of a different cloth than you and your other sons. He is dark as a raven whereas you three are well-mannered brown wrens. He has a willful nature, which thankfully you lack."

"His mother and I have always been proud of him, my liege," Henry said. "If Gawain has transgressed in rescuing a lady, his mother insists it is due to his pure heart, like his namesake in the Arthurian tales." Henry smiled.

"Huh." The king nodded as if mildly amused.

Gawain lowered his gaze. Few, including Edward, remembered that Henry was his stepfather, nor had Henry corrected that. His gesture of support was humbling.

"Sire," Gawain said, "I can only aspire to be as worthy a knight as Sir Henry Avenel."

"Then aspire to behave yourself," the king barked.

"I offer my obeisance and my pledge." He bowed his head lower.

The king flicked his fingers. "Very well. Your vow is acceptable."

"My lord." He breathed out in relief. This brief royal audience had required two months in prison, three petitions for leniency, and a goodly sum of money. He would not be fully excused even if the king just wanted to discuss the weather.

"We need trained knights in the north now that Robert Bruce has claimed the Scottish throne and hides in the hills like an outlaw," King Edward said. "We must send more soldiers in pursuit. Every capable knight is needed. You are to return to Scotland in a few weeks. My lieutenants are gathering men for the journey north."

"Sire." Gawain swallowed hard. "My liege, if I am to go north again, might I make a request?" Not the best moment, but he would not be granted another audience soon.

"You may try," the king murmured.

"There is a place called Glenshie in Glen Fillan, west of Perth. It was taken from the Scots years ago, burned but never garrisoned. I wish to rebuild the property, sire."

"Why?" Edward demanded.

"I... if I garrison a Highland castle, I can demonstrate my fealty. It would benefit both Scots and English."

The king beckoned to his chamberlain, who summoned an army commander Gawain recognized from among the courtiers. They murmured together.

"That location is remote and impractical," the king replied. "Worthless and abandoned. Still, my general suggests you command a garrison somewhere. If your talents were put to better use, you might be less inclined to behave...so chivalrously."

"Sire," Gawain said, gritting his teeth. The callous denial of Glenshie, his childhood home, cut like a knife. Yet he could never petition for the property as its rightful owner.

"But understand this." Edward leaned forward. "One more transgression and your head—mayhap the heads of your brothers too—will see the cutting block. A bad apple spoils a whole barrel." He sat back. "Let that guarantee your new oath."

"Sire, my word upon it." Suppressing his anger, he felt his loyalty rock beneath him like a boat in rough water.

"We will test the strength of your word," the king said, and waved him away.

Gawain rose to his feet, bowed, and stepped back, filled with a sense of dread. His stepfather and stepbrothers came forward, their faces showing relief and pride.

No matter what he did, their love for him sustained. He could never repay such loyalty, and he must never dishonor it.

But a few months with Scottish rebels, followed by a stint in the Tower of London alone with his thoughts had changed him irrevocably. He was a different man with new ideals. But the Avenels did not know that.

His promise to the king came easily, for he loved his family. Yet he did not know if he could honor his vow this time. He had lost his beloved stepbrother Geoffrey, lost the respect of his Scottish friends, and now he risked more—kinship, the rock of honor and ambition, the calm horizon of the future. He no longer knew who he truly was as a man and a knight. But he had to keep those thoughts to himself.

As he departed the hall with his family, doubt shadowed him, relentless as a hawk.

Chapter Four

A HIGH CRY cut through sunlight and peacefulness like a blade. Kneeling on a sheltered part of the bank, Juliana paused as she tossed bits of grain to the swans and the ducks. She glanced around, knowing that her younger brothers were playing at bows and swords in the forested area between the loch and the abbey gate.

The scream sounded again, more frantic than playful. She rose to her feet, shading her eyes against the sun. Out on the water, several ducks scattered noisily, taking to the air.

Closer to the bank, six swans looked up from intent feeding. Four small, gray-brown cygnets glided behind their parents, Artan and Guinevere—a pair Juliana had named a few years ago when they had first nested on Loch nan Eala. The adults arched their wings and leaned their heads back alertly.

Something was amiss, Juliana thought; the swans sensed it too. Hearing another cry, she turned, recognizing that particular shriek.

"Iain!" she called. "Alec! Come here!"

She waited. A breeze ruffled the pale golden hair that spilled over her shoulders. Her glance took in the water meadow that spread away from the loch, its tall reeds laced with burns and pools, merging with a broad stream where the mill was located. Beyond that lay the ruined, deserted village, where hearth fires had not burned for three years.

She looked behind her. The modest grounds of Inchfillan Abbey, walled and quiet, met the banks of the loch. Past the abbey, the loch was fringed by forest that extended toward Elladoune at its other tip.

The English-held castle was not visible from here, and Juliana was glad. Glimpses of her former home stirred only grief and sadness, even after six years.

She was careful to avoid the English soldiers who rode in and out of Elladoune Castle. They sometimes came to the abbey to meet with her guardian Abbot Malcolm, but she and her brothers kept out of sight whenever possible.

The screams were louder now, and she turned. Her brothers tore out of the woods as if the demons of hell were on their heels. Hair flying, shirts and plaids rumpled, knees bruised and knobby, they pounded on bare feet across the meadow. They gripped small bows in their hands, and feathered arrows—with blunted points—flopped in leather quivers on their backs.

"Juliana!" Alec, the older boy, called. Iain shrieked repeatedly as he followed.

"*Ach*, hush!" she called. "Did you argue between you?"

"Run! Quickly!" Alec called. Iain waved his arms, still squealing, as he rushed toward her.

Seeing genuine fright on their faces, Juliana ran to meet them. Iain thudded into her, wrapping his arms around her waist, burying his golden curls beneath her encircling arm.

"What is wrong?" she asked.

Iain pointed toward the forest. "The black knight!" he yelled. "He is coming!"

"De Soulis?" She looked at Alec.

He nodded breathlessly. "The sheriff and his men are riding through the forest! We were practicing bow shooting, and we saw them! Iain screamed and they followed us. We must hide!"

Alarmed, Juliana took their arms and began to hurry toward the abbey. "They must not see us!"

"I will shoot them," Iain said fiercely. "I am going to win the archery competition and best all the English bowmen!"

"You are not big enough, and hush up," Alec said. "If they see Juliana, they will try to catch her. Hurry!"

Juliana put a hand on Iain's thin shoulder as they hastened toward the abbey gate. Iain had been a babe in arms and Alec a toddler when Walter de Soulis and his men had burned Elladoune. Her brothers did not remember it, but the memories still seared her dreams, and her fear and loathing of De Soulis had not abated.

"How many knights did you see?" she asked the boys.

"A hundred!" Iain said.

"Fifteen," Alec said, glancing at his brother. "They were riding to the abbey."

Iain pointed and shrieked. "The black knight!"

Horses and riders, wearing the red surcoats of Edward's men, burst through the trees and headed across the meadow, hoofbeats heavy, armor and weapons chinking. The leader rode a black horse and wore black chain mail beneath a wine-colored surcoat. Seeing him, Juliana grabbed the boys' arms and began to run.

"There—the Swan Maiden!" someone shouted.

Three horsemen split away from the group and rode toward them, their faces grim. Juliana shoved her brothers ahead of the riders and spun to block the horsemen. One of the knights cut around her and chased after the boys while the other man rode toward her.

She swerved and went down the bank, splashing into the shallows. On the loch, a swan launched into flight, great wings beating. As the huge bird swerved toward them, the horse neighed, but the knight drew closer and reached out. Splashing through ankle-deep water, Juliana avoided his grasp.

"Stop!" he hollered, reaching again.

"Let her go," a deep voice called out. "The boys will pay for her escape!"

With a sense of dread in her gut, she slowed and turned.

De Soulis stared at her from a few yards away, his eyes small and piercing. He was graying but handsome with precise, carefully etched features, and she sensed a darkness about him that went beyond his notorious black armor.

"We have your brothers," he called. "Go into the loch if you wish." He waved a hand to encourage her. "Show us how you turn into a swan. I would like to see it."

Two knights rode behind him with Alec and Iain trapped in their arms. Alec sat quietly, but Iain shrieked and struggled, tossed over the front of a saddle, kicking.

"Juliana!" Alec called. "Run!"

She paused, standing in a cool sweep of water.

"What shall I do with them? Will you speak in their defense, Swan Maiden?" De Soulis guided his horse into the water toward her. She stepped back.

"Do not talk!" Alec shouted. "Remember who you are, Swan Maiden!"

She glanced toward him. Alec bravely tried to protect the ruse they had agreed on, while nearby, Iain squealed and fought. She was proud of both for grit and spirit.

"Shut that boy up!" De Soulis ordered. Iain's captor winced as he was bitten, and smacked the child in response. Iain began to whimper.

Furious, Juliana lunged through the water. De Soulis turned his horse to block her advance. When she stepped sideways, water swooshing, he blocked her again. Her dress was soaked, her breath and chest heaving, her hair hanging down. She stared at him, trapped, wild with a need to free her brothers.

Artan glided swiftly through the water toward them, wings raised aggressively. Nearing the horse, the cob lifted his wings and swatted outward. The bay snorted and stepped back.

Juliana moved again but De Soulis blocked her. Near her, the swan hissed. Reaching down, she touched the taut curve of Artan's neck. The bird settled low in the water and swam away.

"So we see some of your magic, Swan Maiden," De Soulis drawled. In the distance, Malcolm and a few monks ran toward them. "Come here, or the boys will suffer."

She knew it for a genuine threat, and she lifted her arms in passive surrender.

"Well and truly caught," he said. "I am disappointed. I expected more challenge from the Swan Maiden of Elladoune." He grasped her arm to pull her up behind him.

She grabbed his belt to steady herself, head lifted and back straight. He guided the horse to the bank and looked over his shoulder. "No plea for mercy?"

She narrowed her eyes. At close view, he was lean and taut, with sharp features and dark eyes. His chain mail, finely woven and glossy as onyx, draped over him like heavy velvet.

She stared at it curiously. De Soulis's black armor was renowned. Rumor said it was impenetrable, even enchanted. Whatever the truth, she had never seen a war garment like it.

"Juliana!" She looked around to see Malcolm and the monks rushing toward them.

"Father Abbot!" Iain yelled, struggling in his captor's arms. "Help! The black knight has us all!"

"Let my wards go, Sir Walter," Malcolm said sternly in Scots. "You have nae quarrel with them."

"True, though I confess I am curious about the girl. The rumors about her are intriguing."

She twisted, and De Soulis caught her forearm in a steely grip. "You cannot fly away now," he murmured.

"Let them go," Malcolm repeated. "Leave here."

"We have business on the loch." The creamy smoothness of his voice made Juliana feel ill. "King Edward has requested a pair of Scottish swans for a royal feast. He has appointed me his new Master of Swans in Scotland. Part of my duty is to see that swans are captured to stock his rivers and grace his table. My men will take a pair of birds from those you keep."

"We do not keep them," Malcolm said. "The birds are wild. They choose to stay."

"All the swans in Britain belong exclusively to the king," the sheriff said. "That includes swans in Scotland. For now, we need just one more. We have caught a special one already—the Swan Maiden." De Soulis kept hold of Juliana's arm. "The king will find this amusing."

"You cannot take the lass!" Malcolm shouted.

"I can and will," De Soulis answered. "Grab another swan." He gestured to two men who dismounted to take nets and long hooks from their saddles. They walked to the water's edge.

Juliana gasped and twisted in De Soulis's grip. She had known some of the birds since they had been hatchlings, and she could not bear for them to be harmed. But she did not know how to help them here and now.

"Abbot, if the girl wishes to protest, she must use her tongue," De Soulis said. "I am weary of this game she plays."

"Sir Sheriff, she chooses to be silent."

"'Tis said she has some magic about her."

"People say you have magic too. That armor, they say, is impenetrable and under some dark spell."

"Nonsense," De Soulis snapped.

"Then we understand each other."

"Tell me why the girl does not speak."

"She is pious and grieving. 'Tis all."

"Then she should be in a convent."

"She would be if King Edward had not burned most of them," Malcolm said pointedly. "The girl is kind to her brothers and our brethren, and tends to the swans. She is an innocent soul. Leave her be."

"She makes a fine hostage, as do her brothers." De Soulis turned his horse.

"Stop!" Malcolm shouted. "You cannot keep them!"

"They provide assurance. We need the help of the monks of Inchfillan when the garrison at Elladoune departs. I suspect rebel activity in this area. But of course we can trust you, Abbot, can we not?"

"I am trustworthy. No hostages are needed to ensure that."

"Nonetheless, I will have them. The king will want to see this Swan Maiden. As for the boys—what is the tradition among the Scots? Fostering? Consider them fostered by the sheriff of Glen Fillan. My wife will want them in her household." He nodded brusquely. "Good day. Ride out," he snapped to the guards and shifted forward.

Juliana gasped, twisting to look at the abbot.

"Where will you take them?" Malcolm demanded.

"Her brothers will stay at Dalbrae with my wife and my garrison," De Soulis said. "I will take an escort and convey the girl to Newcastle in safety."

"Newcastle-on-Tyne?" Malcolm asked. "Is the king there now?"

"He and his army have been making their way north toward Scotland and have reached Newcastle. 'Tis a short journey from here, a few days at most. She will be in the care of a military escort. The king will decide what is to be done with her."

Panic overtook Juliana then. She could scarcely breathe or think as she twisted against De Soulis's grip in terror. She could not go with these men, nor could she leave her brothers, or Malcolm, or this place. Desperation rose high and quick, and she shoved De Soulis. He wrenched her arm in fierce reply.

"I will come with her myself," the abbot said, "or I will send monks with her! 'Tis not right to take a female like this—the daughter of a laird—"

"Daughter of a rebel, and a rebel herself, most likely," De Soulis corrected. "A priest will be with my troops, and he can chaperone her." He spurred the horse and cantered away.

Juliana looked over her shoulder at the guards who carried her brothers. Alec's eyes were wide and frightened, and Iain emitted bold, earsplitting shrieks. Malcolm and some of the monks ran forward. The abbot ran on sturdy legs, his dark tunic flapping around his muscular calves.

Within moments, he loped alongside De Soulis's horse. "Be strong of heart!" he called to Juliana in Gaelic. "And keep your vow, Juliana—keep silent!"

Tears clouded her eyes as she watched Malcolm. He called out a reassurance to the boys, then stopped in the meadow.

"We will pray for you!" he yelled. "We will ask for a miracle!"

She looked toward the loch, where the two guards stood in the water. One hooked Artan, the large white cob, around the neck, and the other held a net, while the swan beat his wings in a fury.

Juliana turned away, stifling a sob. She too was caught, though her net was woven of secrets.

Chapter Five

A GOLDEN CHAIN encircled her neck, yet it was a captive's chain. Similar links bound her wrists and hands, which rested motionless in her lap. The white satin gown, embroidered with silver threads, was the finest garment she had ever worn. A close cap of white feathers covered her head, and her pale hair spilled down her back.

The precious chains and beautiful costume were meant to transform her into a human version of the swan sitting beside her in the cart. Juliana lifted her head proudly, determined to hide her fear and disgrace from her English enemies.

She swayed inside the pony-drawn cart, feeling dizzy and dull-witted. The watered wine given her by one of the guards had been bitter with added herbs, which sapped her energy and made her feel vague and slow, as if she floated through a dream.

Yet she felt as if she were caught in a nightmare.

The cart rumbled along a torchlit corridor inside the king's castle. Servants bearing large platters of food hurried past. Ahead, two men carried a huge tray displaying a castle sculpted of marzipan and adorned with sugared fruits.

Juliana glanced at the large male mute swan settled beside her in a nest of green embroidered satin. A gold chain around his long neck was attached to an upright wooden post. Artan ruffled his feathers nervously when one of the ponies knickered.

Juliana made a wordless, soothing sound. Artan lifted his

orange beak, its base knobbed in black. He chirred and quieted.

Beyond a set of tall oaken doors, she heard the sounds of music, laughter, and the clatter of dishes and knives. She knew that a banquet was in progress, attended by the king's guests.

Though her head spun from the wine, she sat aloof while a serving woman arranged the sumptuous white gown around her and adjusted the cap of feathers. Artan hissed and the woman stepped back hastily.

"That swan is a beautiful beast, but mean," the woman said. "But ah, the lady looks like a princess. Seamstresses and artists worked day and night to make this gown and the nest. 'Tis a shame, I say, that the king only means to make a fool of her and her Scottish people with all this costly finery."

"Since when are ye the king's advisor?" one of the guards scoffed. "Go tell the chamberlain that the girl is ready to be presented to king and court." The woman hurried away.

"Here, pretty bird," one guard said, chortling as he approached. He reached out and stroked Juliana's shoulder with damp fingers. She jerked away.

Artan hissed and swiped a wing at the guard, who jumped back. "That foul-tempered swan belongs on the king's table," he muttered. "And the Swan Maiden would do well in a man's bed."

"King Edward wants her brought pure and maidensome to his feast, or we will all be blamed," the first said. "Keep yer hands away. 'Tis eerie the way that swan defends her. Chills my bones, it do, and I'll not touch her, king or none."

Juliana fisted her hands in her lap, gold chains chinking. Several days had passed since she and Artan had been captured in Scotland. The journey south to Newcastle had been a blur of rough cart rides and chafing ropes, aching muscles and constant fear, infrequent meals of stale bread and cheese. And too often, she had been given wine mixed with bitter herbs, which induced apathy, compliance, and bouts of heavy sleep.

Walter de Soulis, who had accompanied her south, had ordered the dosings in the wine. She had tried to refuse in silence, but the drinks were forced down her throat.

White satin, golden chains, and the swan Artan beside her were an improvement, but she did not know what King Edward intended for her. She had been told that he was pleased by the capture of Juliana Lindsay, daughter of a Scots rebel and cousin of another. Would she be imprisoned, she wondered, or sealed in a convent—or put to death as a witch or a rebel?

She shivered at her thoughts and turned her attention to Artan beside her, smoothing his feathers.

The Swan Maiden, the English called her, claiming that she knew magical arts. Only fools, she thought bitterly, believed in such things. If she truly had magic, she would have escaped her captivity already.

And if the king discovered the truth about her, she thought, frowning, he would surely order her execution.

The doors of the banquet chamber opened wide, and the cart lurched as the ponies moved ahead. The high-vaulted chamber was filled with torchlight and shadows, voices and distant faces. Clarion trumpets blared suddenly. The swan, startled, ruffled his feathers and hissed again.

She placed a hand on his back and he busked his wings slightly. As the cart rumbled over the floor tiles, Juliana lifted her chin and straightened her shoulders.

A FANFARE OF trumpets accompanied the arrival of servants carrying yet another course arranged on platters. Gawain held up a hand in refusal when a servant offered a tray to him and his stepfather and stepbrothers. Ground pork baked in colored batters in the shapes of fruits seemed highly unappealing, he thought, and turned away.

"No more appetite?" his stepfather, Henry Avenel, asked as he accepted a serving on his bread trencher.

Gawain swirled the last of the red Gascony wine in his silver goblet. "I have little taste for wondrous foods," he said wryly. "I made my appearance here, ate something in good company, and now I am ready to be quit of this feast."

"So early? Look at the marvelous confection coming through those doors now—what… it looks like a girl made all of marzipan!" Robin Avenel, who had been knighted a few weeks ago in London, craned his neck to peer through the crowds.

Gawain did not even glance at the newest wonder being offered. Edmund, Robin's older brother, slid them a mildly interested glance and turned back to the servant girl standing beside him, smiling at her and running his fingers along her arm.

He wondered how Edmund could concentrate on seduction amid the din of musical instruments and the chatter of servants and guests. Most of those attending the feast in the hall at Newcastle were knights and soldiers of the king's army, journeying north to Scotland. They needed a grand celebration, he thought, to relieve the tedium of a military existence.

"Gawain," his stepfather said, "you stayed with the barbaric Scots too long this time. If you are not enjoying the feast and the spectacle here, your tastes have turned far too simple."

"They always were simple," Gawain said. "You forget that before I was counted among your sons, and among the king's knights, I was a lad in those barbaric hills." He rarely referred to that, he thought; the wine had loosened his tongue.

"I have not forgotten," Henry said sternly. "Best pray the king does not remember you are not a son of my body."

"They say King Edward has another surprise planned for the evening." Robin leaned forward. "I wonder if this is it." He seemed frustrated when the other Avenels did not bother to look.

"Another *subtletie* sculpted from spun sugar and almond paste?" Gawain asked. The crowd blocked his view. "Another leaping acrobat? 'Twill be lost on this lot, Robin. Most of them are too drunk to care what else is brought out."

"Grand as it is, this feast hardly compares with the king's

Swan Feast in London last May, when he knighted three hundred men—our Robin among them," Henry added proudly, smiling at his youngest son. "The king threw a sumptuous celebration there. This one is modest, but the food is good. The Plantagenet court, wherever it rests, does maintain quality."

"In London, the king had a pair of swans in golden chains brought to him, and he swore to destroy Robert Bruce and rule Scotland, or die in the attempt," Edmund said. "I did hear that the king will renew that vow on another pair of swans since Newcastle is his last stop before he enters Scotland once again."

"Then I will leave early," Gawain said. "Swan meat is tough and not to my liking." The vow, rather than the meat, was his true objection.

"Aye, swans are out of season now—their flesh is most tender in the autumn," Edmund said. "But the king has talented cooks, and he brings them along when he travels. Each dish here has been more artfully crafted than the last."

"These knights are worthy men, and deserve a feast to lift their spirits," Henry agreed.

Gawain frowned. "The king's true intention is to attract new knights for his army and contributions to his Scottish war."

"'Tis wise to be generous toward the king who has recently granted you king's peace." Henry dipped his fingers in a bowl of rosewater, raising his brow at Gawain.

"I am grateful for the king's goodwill," Gawain said carefully. "I simply wish to leave the feast early. In the morning, I will journey north."

"The king has ordered you to Scotland already?" Robin asked.

"Aye. Gawain has been given a post as a commander," Edmund said, "despite his infamous transgressions."

"The king is desperate," Gawain murmured.

"See, some good came of you bowing that stubborn head of yours and begging king's peace," Henry said. "Your Scottish birth could have cost us all our heads, now that Robert Bruce has so boldly claimed Scotland for his own. Edward is furious toward any who have even remote ties to the Scots."

"Who can blame him," Gawain said, mildly and ambiguously, meaning the King of Scots.

Henry frowned. "I defended your actions in Scotland because your mother was worried about you. She still hopes the king will offer you one of his fair cousins for a bride. But you must behave yourself for that to happen," he added.

"I doubt my obeisance will earn me a bride with royal blood, if that is what you are hoping, sir."

"Whoever you marry, your lady mother will be heartsore if you are not happily wed soon, before she—" Henry stopped abruptly, and took a swift draught of wine.

"I know," Gawain said quietly. For his mother's sake, in her last days, he should marry any suitable lady quickly and find affection for his wife afterward. He had given little thought to marriage, busy campaigning in Scotland for Edward. He had wooed and trysted with high-born ladies and heath-born lasses. But he had never found a love incandescent enough to light his life, and hers, until the end of their days.

Why hunger for something so rare, he thought sourly, the stuff of legends and courtly tales; most of those stories ended badly. He took a swallow of wine and watched the throng.

He had seen true love twice before, seen its power and its grace. The magic between his parents had been a sacred thing in its way. Then he had met James Lindsay and Isobel Seton, and felt the power of that love, basked in its reflected warmth, even envied it. He hoped someday to have a glimmer of that in his own life. Perhaps he had been a little in love with Isobel himself, an ideal lady in an unusual situation.

Months ago, he had spent time with them. The choices he made had resulted in his stepbrother's death, then his imprisonment and a humiliating plea before the king.

Even so, he would give anything to restore that lost friendship. Most likely James and Isobel never wanted to see him again.

He shoved a hand through his thick dark hair. He was more

drunk than he thought. Best consider marriage in the light of a sober day, he decided, when his head was cool and his heart not so aware of what he did not have.

Still, if his mother wanted him wed, so be it. He would fetch down the moon for her if she asked.

"Perhaps the king will grant Gawain some fair demoiselle now that our brother is back in grace," Edmund remarked. Gawain raised his wine cup in salute while the others chuckled. The wine wet his lips, but the smile did not touch his eyes.

"We cannot hope for that now," Henry said. "We can only hope the king will have no cause to doubt your fealty in the future."

"Certes," Gawain answered. "He will not."

"Will you see your mother before you go north? She will be distressed to learn that you are leaving again so soon. She…was not well again last week when I was there."

"I will visit her tomorrow." Gawain stood and stepped outside the bench. "Good night, sir. Edmund, luck to you. Sir Robin, watch your back, lad." He clapped his youngest stepbrother on the shoulder. "New-made knights are not as invincible as they think." He smiled, just as the trumpets blared to announce another course.

"Wait, Gawain," Robin said. "Something magnificent is coming into the hall."

"A few moments more, then," Gawain agreed, aware that his departure might attract the king's unwanted notice.

A pony-drawn cart draped in sumptuous fabrics crossed the length of the great hall, wooden wheels creaking. Guards walked in front, blocking Gawain's view of the inside of the cart. When it rolled closer to where he stood, he drew in his breath, astonished. This was what Robin had urged them to see.

In the center of a lush green nest sat a blond young woman and a large swan. Both were bound by golden chains. On a wooden pole above them, a yellow banner showing the red lion rampant of Scotland fluttered with the cart's movement.

Gowned in white satin trimmed in silver embroidery, the girl sparkled like a diamond. A cap of white feathers framed her face, and her smooth hair had the delicate sheen of purest gold.

"An enchanted swan for the king's feast," Edmund said. "I swear I have never seen a sight so lovely."

The girl and the swan sat so still that, for a moment, Gawain thought they were glittering statues. Then the bird fluttered its wings, and the girl reached out to touch its snowy back.

She turned her head, and Gawain saw her face more clearly. *Perfection*, he thought impulsively. Then he saw, despite the proud tilt of her head, that her eyes were wide with fright. He frowned.

The crowd applauded as the cart rolled nearer. Gawain stood grim and still, watching. The girl's stiff, straight back, her wary gaze, the heavy locks on the chains, and the presence of the guards told him this was not mere entertainment.

She was a breathtaking sight, but Gawain suspected that the king intended to mock Scotland and humiliate the girl. The cart halted near the king's table, and Edward nodded with a smug smile. Gawain stayed where he was and studied the girl from his closer vantage point.

With a shock of certainty, he realized that he had seen her years ago. He would not easily forget that exquisite face. He narrowed his eyes.

Aye, this was Juliana Lindsay of Elladoune, he thought, or else her double. Six years had barely changed her, though she looked thin and fragile. He recognized the oval face, the small, stubborn chin, the wide mouth, the dark-hued eyes, the lean and graceful frame. Her hair was paler than he remembered, like gold washed with silver.

How did she come to be here at the king's feast, dressed like a swan and chained like a captive? He remembered that James Lindsay had once mentioned that he was cousins with the Lindsays of Elladoune. He wondered if Jamie Lindsay knew his young cousin was being offered like plunder to a king who hated

Scots.

"Is she artfully made from spun sugar and almond paste?" Robin asked, staring.

"Far too real," Gawain said grimly. "I know her."

"What! Who is she?" Henry demanded.

"Daughter of a Scottish rebel, cousin to another. I met her years ago." Gawain fisted a hand, wondering if he could have helped prevent tonight's mockery if he had stayed with the rebels in Scotland.

"'Tis madness to chain a young girl so," Henry said.

"Indeed," Gawain growled. He walked around the table toward the open area surrounding the cart. He wanted to help but was not certain what to do, short of grabbing her and carrying her out the door. Surely there was a better solution.

The king stood. The guests rose too, in a rush of movement, dropping napkins and setting down their goblets and half-eaten portions of food.

"What have we here?" the king asked in a smooth, rehearsed tone. "A swan... and a Swan Maiden. Welcome to our celebration." He gestured brusquely. A servant pulled the huge carved chair aside and the king walked around the table.

Edward approached the cart, a tall, thin man, hands folded behind his back. Torchlight gleamed on his white hair and the jeweled collar over his magenta tunic. Age and illness bowed his shoulders.

"The sight of such a beautiful woman will surely stir our knights to thoughts of... victory over Scotland," Edward murmured. A ripple of low laughter followed.

Gawain frowned, watching the king pace in front of the cart. Edward peered at Juliana as if she were one of the strange beasts kept in the little zoo in the Tower of London. The girl straightened her head and back as gracefully as the swan beside her.

The bird moved then, extending its neck and hissing loudly. It batted a wing at Edward, who stepped back hastily. The guards and some of the advisors rushed forward, but the king waved them away and resumed his stroll.

"All the swans in England," Edward said, "belong to the king. No one disputes that. These two *swans*"—he emphasized the last word—"were taken in Scotland. Scottish swans also belong exclusively to the king of England. As does the land of Scotland itself." His voice rose, and he lifted his hand.

"I swore in London weeks past upon a pair of swans," he declared. "I swear again before God and this company, and upon this swan and Swan Maiden, that I will quell Scotland and the rebel Robert Bruce. All men here, swear the same with me!"

Throughout the hall, hundreds of knights repeated the king's words in an echoing, massive single voice. Gawain stood silent while Henry and his stepbrothers made the vow as well.

The king rounded upon the girl, his face flushed. She stared boldly back at him. Gawain watched her reaction with keen approval.

The swan hissed, flapping his wings. Edward raised a hand, avoiding the swan, and stroked the girl's head, cooing. She batted his hand away firmly. The smack was audible.

Gasps echoed around the room.

With a fixed smile, Edward turned to his guests. "The Swan Maiden wants taming," he said. "We shall choose an English knight for the task. She will be brought to rule by him, just as her rebellious nation will be ruled by his king." He looked around the hall. "Whoever can tame this Scottish swan shall have her. Come forward and try!"

Several knights stood, and more followed suit. The king beckoned them forward. Gawain stood not far from the girl's cart, motionless. Even when Henry urged his sons to go forward, Gawain did not move. He had no interest in this cruel game and no desire to dominate or humiliate a woman.

As the men gathered to form a line, Gawain recognized many of them by name or by sight. Some were so drunk that they swayed and stumbled. And some, Gawain knew, hated Scots as virulently as Edward Plantagenet.

He looked at Juliana Lindsay again and saw her face grow pale. Cold fury rose in him. He could not leave now—and could not stand here and watch this.

He stepped forward.

Chapter Six

S HE SAT STRAIGHT and wary, greeting each knight in turn with cool silence. One after another they came toward her, some bumbling and drunken, a few edgy and intense. Despite the haze of the herbal potion, she maintained dignity and quiet.

Most advances or overtures she ignored until the knights walked away to echoes of laughter. Others were bolder, rougher, pulling on her, even caressing her. Laughter rippled out like haunting music, low male voices with scarcely a female titter among them. Her sense of desperation and fear grew.

She batted hands away, turned her head to avoid drunken kisses. Beside her, the swan hissed continually, rocking his head sinuously on his neck, raising his wings to strike blows.

One of the men tried to lift her, and Artan lunged, his wing striking the man's forearm. Juliana heard the sickening crack of bone. The man howled, grabbing at his arm and stepping back.

"My wrist! The bird has snapped my wrist!" he howled. Some of those watching laughed, while some saluted the swan's prowess.

Another knight came forward and yanked on her arm. Juliana shook free of his grip, while Artan flapped his wings and snaked out his neck. The knight stepped out of the swan's reach and stroked Juliana's face, making cooing noises.

In a fury of anger and instinct, she bit his finger.

The man shrieked and jerked back his arm to strike her. At

that moment, a dark-haired knight strode out of the crowd, a hand on the hilt of his dagger.

"Leave her be," he growled.

"Wild swan bitch," the other man muttered. "She cannot be tamed—I leave her to you, Avenel!" He stumbled away.

The knight in black stepped back into the crowd, watching Juliana steadily. She stared at him, wiping the back of her hand over her mouth, her hair wisping over her eyes. His face seemed familiar, yet her head felt fuzzy and she could not place him.

Even without his gallant gesture or familiar sense, she would have noticed him. He was a raven among peacocks, dressed in black amid the brightly garbed knights. Taller than average, broad-shouldered and lean, he was unsmiling, while the others grinned and chatted. His dark eyes were intense, and glossy black hair framed a face of chiseled masculine beauty. Quiet power emanated from him.

Yet he stood awaiting his turn with her. Juliana looked away. His gesture was possessive, not protective.

Another knight came toward the cart and slurred a greeting. He reached out and grabbed her arm.

"One night in my bed will tame her! Come here, little swan!" The audience laughed and called out encouragement.

Juliana kicked and struggled, and Artan hissed, straining at his chain. The knight lifted an arm to defend against a powerful wing blow, dragging Juliana halfway out of the cart.

"Release her," the king ordered. "This grows tedious. 'Tis poor chivalry and poor spectacle. Move on. Next!"

The knight set her roughly on her feet on the floor and walked away muttering. Juliana leaned against the cart, legs shaking.

"The Swan Maiden needs taming, and requires a lesson," Edward called out. "This display has been amusing, but there are priests and ladies among us. We cannot offend them. Who here can win her obedience—and her love?"

Juliana stood straight, though her head spun and her knees

were weak. She waited, proud and still, neck and shoulders tensing beneath the weight of the collar and chains.

A knight stepped forward, a young man with light brown hair and a pretty face that would mature into handsomeness. Artan stretched his neck to utter a snakelike hiss, widening his wings.

"My—my lady," the knight said. "I wish you no harm."

She leaned her head against the cart, feeling dull-witted and weary. Artan hissed. The knight glanced nervously at the bird. "Robin… Sir Robert Avenel is my name. My stepbrother is Sir Gawain Avenel, the man who just championed you. I would be your champion, too." He smiled awkwardly.

Her glance flickered toward the knight in black who watched with a grim frown.

"If you please, come with me." The young knight lifted a hand toward her.

Artan lashed out and bit him. Robert leaped back, shaking his hand.

"Watch, pup, and see how 'tis done," another knight called, this one a broad man in a blue surcoat. He shoved Robert aside and grabbed Juliana's hand. He kissed her fingers, his lips hot and repulsive.

"Sweeting, let me show you the pleasures of captivity." He stroked her feathered cap. "Come with me, and discover delight."

Juliana jerked away from his touch. Artan lurched at him. Swearing, the knight stepped back.

"With that devil swan and a black knight to protect her, no man can gain the lady," he muttered. "Avenel, see if you fare any better!"

The dark knight came toward her. He reached out, as had the others. Juliana expected Artan to lash out and bite him.

Avenel opened his closed fist and sprinkled bits of bread inside the cart. Artan snatched at the food.

The knight cocked a brow and looked at Juliana. "Are you hungry?" he murmured. "I can fetch something heartier than bread crumbs if you wish."

Surprised, she shook her head.

"I imagine you would like to leave all this nonsense behind," he said quietly.

She nodded, looking up at him.

"Come with me, then, and all will be well."

She shook her head. His calm manner was reassuring and soothing, but his intent was no different than the others.

"Lady Juliana," he murmured, "this competition to win you will go on all night, unless you surrender to someone."

She narrowed her eyes. How did he know her name? The king had not announced it. He must be close to the king or in league with her guards. But she would rather live in a prison cell than surrender her body and her will to a king's man. She showed her refusal with a haughty tilt of her chin.

Avenel reached into a pocket and took out a piece of bread, which he tore into pieces for the swan. "Not all these knights share my agreeable nature. A wring of the neck, a twist of a dagger, and your swan will not protect you for long. The only risk is the crime of harming a swan in England. Apparently, it is no crime to mock a Scotswoman. You will want to cooperate with me if you would be safe." He spoke low and urgently.

She slit her eyes at him. He leaned closer, resting a hand on the cart. Artan, busy nibbling, did not even lift his head.

"The king makes a show of chivalry, but he detests Scots. If one of those drunken fools wins you, no one will ensure your safety."

Frightened, she watched him in silence. She had to put her faith in him. He had proven himself capable of decency even if his intentions were no doubt sinful.

"Show the king that I have tamed you. Then I can help you."

She would never submit to him just so he could gain favor with his cruel king. Anger flaring, she turned away.

"Better to be tamed by me," he murmured, "than one of my drunken comrades. Lady, tell me—did you remember the Swan Laird in your prayers, as you promised?"

Gasping, she stared at him. Only the Swan Laird would know that promise.

She looked at him again, and recognition dawned. Years had etched his face and made it leaner, harder, but she knew him. His eyes were just as she remembered, dark brown, deep and warm, framed in black lashes and straight brows. This was the man who had saved her in the water at Elladoune.

He tipped his head. "I see you are still in need of rescue, Juliana Lindsay."

Heart quickening, hope rising, she nodded in answer.

"Give me your hand." He offered his, and she reached out. His grip was warm, dry, strong. "Now do as I tell you," he murmured. "Act heartstruck for love of me." He lifted her hand and kissed it.

A thrill spun through her at the touch of his mouth. Her knees buckled, and he caught her arm under the elbow. His smile was unexpectedly boyish with an easy charm.

Heartstruck was not difficult to pretend. She felt a wash of the adoration she had felt when he had helped her and she had asked his name. *Call me your Swan Laird*, he had said. She had assumed he was Scots, like so many of Edward's knights.

But she could not trust him, no matter if she wanted to do so. He was an English knight, and she was a Scottish prisoner.

She scowled at him. He kissed her fingers again. Applause fluttered amid hoots of laughter. "Smile, lady," he murmured.

The king rose from his seat and came toward them.

The warm cradle of his fingers and the brush of his lips over her knuckles stirred tears in her eyes. She had not felt comfort or gentleness for so long. Her harsh treatment had made her weak and needy, she told herself sternly. Scowling at him, she straightened her shoulders and tried to pull her hand away.

He tightened his fingers over hers. "Look at me as though your heart is mine forever," he drawled, "not as if you want to eat my heart for supper."

She closed her eyes, confused. To get out of there, she reminded herself, she had to cooperate with him. She forced herself to smile at him.

He turned toward the king, holding her hand aloft and bowing. Cheers and light applause swelled through the hall.

Artan, finished with his bread crumbs, hissed and spread his wings. Gawain glanced at the swan, whose neck swayed ominously.

"'Twould ruin the moment if he bites me," he said dryly.

Juliana felt an urge to laugh, until Gawain lifted her hand and turned to the king.

"My liege," he said, "the Swan Maiden is mine."

GAWAIN GLANCED SIDELONG at the girl. Her hand trembled in his, but her lips shaped a beautiful smile that struck him like an arrow shot. He caught his breath.

The king approached the cart. Gawain had to see this through; he could not abandon the girl to the king's game. Once again he had obeyed his impulse to protect others—though that had brought him more trouble than honor in the past.

His greatest flaw, he knew, lay in his tendency to help those who needed assistance, no matter the cost to himself. It was an admitted weakness and one he could not strengthen.

Somehow Juliana Lindsay seemed to draw that out in him. Fate had thrown them together more than once, and each time, he had taken up her cause, though he did not even know her.

King Edward came closer. Gawain bowed. "Sire, I have tamed the Swan Maiden as you requested. I wish to claim her as my own." In truth, he hoped to gain custody of her and send her back to Scotland.

To his relief, Juliana lowered her head demurely. The cap of feathers and her golden hair shone like crown and veil. She swayed, and Gawain tightened his hold on her arm to steady her.

The king scrutinized them. "How did you accomplish it when no one else could? With some magical incantation?" He looked back at his audience, who laughed appreciatively.

"No mystery, my lord. I obeyed the example of my namesake, Sir Gawain, who showed courtesy and kindness to others."

"Easy to be courteous to a little beauty." The king peered at her, lifting her chin with a fingertip. Juliana turned her head aside in a clear, soundless insult.

The king frowned. "And how did you master the swan?"

"With a bit of bread, sire."

"A practical man." As the king turned, the swan lashed out and snapped at him. Edward snarled and stepped back. When he reached out to touch Juliana's arm, she jerked away from him.

"Not tame yet, either of them," the king said curtly.

"'Twill be done, I assure you," Gawain murmured.

"Do it, or the task will go to another knight."

Gawain grasped Juliana's golden neck chain, tugging on it gently. "I assure my liege, the lady will be meek and obedient, and do all my bidding," he murmured. "So will the swan."

Juliana glared at him, while Edward nodded in approval and paced away, lanky and slow.

"Behave yourself," Gawain hissed to Juliana. "Try to act adoring. And keep that swan of yours still." He smiled, wide and showy. She smiled back, her teeth clenched.

The king swung around. "What a pretty pair of lovebirds—the pale maiden and her dark knight. With but a word from him, she turns into his loving leman. One caution, sir."

"My liege," Gawain said.

"Remember the Scots are known for the quick turning of their loyalties. You may lose her devotion without warning. Her countryman Robert Bruce has shown us the bitter side of his fealty lately, even though he renewed his obeisance three times in public audience… ah, much like our good Sir Gawain."

Gawain tensed at the inference. Edward paced away. "What if the Scottish Swan Maiden gave her heart to England?" He looked at Gawain, eyes glittering. "Tame the girl, and train her to your will."

Gawain frowned. "Train her, sire?"

"Surely you need no instruction for that. A woman will do a man's will if he handles her properly." He turned to the crowd, beaming like a jester in a play, soaking in the laughter with raised hands. The king, Gawain realized, was very drunk.

His outraged silence matched Juliana's stillness.

"Take her north with an escort, and display her in golden chains," the king said. "The captive Swan Maiden will be led around the countryside by English knights. She will serve as an example."

"An example of what, sire?" Gawain asked carefully.

"Of the harm rebellion brings to the Scots. Teach the girl about loyalty to England. We may take her into our bosom of forgiveness if she makes a pretty oath like you did. Surely you understand loyalty by now."

Gawain flared his nostrils. "Aye, sire."

"Then demonstrate it. Teach her a pretty speech too."

"My lord," Gawain said, "the lady does not speak."

"'Tis her willful, rebellious spirit. She will surrender to your will. I want to see her in court again when 'tis done." Edward strutted now.

This was a jest to him, Gawain thought, one he would forget by morning. An urge to protest rose in him. Then he noticed his stepfather and stepbrothers watching him, faces somber. His family would suffer if he was uncooperative now.

"As you will, sire," he said flatly.

"Good," Edward said. "She will be ruled by her English husband. Let her be a symbol of Scotland ruled by England." Edward grinned, then waved the applause into quick silence.

Gawain's hand tightened on Juliana's arm, though she pulled away like a jessed falcon. His heart pounded hard. "Husband?"

"You claimed her. Now marry her."

"Sire," Gawain said curtly. "I hoped to win her freedom."

"Your father requested our assistance in finding you a bride. This one will do for you. When she is docile, bring her to Carlisle to prove her loyalty. That will prove yours."

A bride, meted out like a punishment and meant as a test of his loyalty. "My lord, I have renewed my oath to you."

"Your maiden swan is a rebel, hatched in a nest of rebels. This a merciful sentence for her."

"Merciful indeed," Gawain muttered.

"If she proves herself, 'twill be your success. If she rebels, 'twill be your failure."

A muscle thumped in his cheek. "Sire."

Edward's eyes glittered. "Now go and do to her tonight what we would do to Scotland." His grin grew wicked, and snickers rippled throughout the audience.

Gawain felt Juliana shudder. He held her arm without indicating his fury.

"That bird looks to be a juicy one. We will dine on it tomorrow. Tonight you will find your little swan tender and delightful, no doubt." Edward grinned again, then turned to his chamberlain. "Fetch a priest," he directed. "We will end the feast with a wedding."

"Sweet saints," Gawain muttered under his breath.

The king strode away to confer with his advisors, who gathered in a cluster, tall men with long, dark robes, gleaming chain mail, and grim faces. None of them had laughed during the spectacle, Gawain had noticed.

Juliana whimpered, the closest to a sound she had made. "I promised to set you free," he murmured to her. "But as you can see, I am not Edward's most favored knight. My apologies."

She sent him a sour glare.

The knights cleared a path as a priest hurried forward. Gawain felt as if he could hardly breathe. Juliana stood still beside him, tense in his grip. Behind him, the swan hissed.

He saw his stepfather and his stepbrothers at the edge of the crowd. Henry nodded to underscore his support, but Gawain did not feel reassured. He was about to obey the king's drunken whim and enter into a mockery of the sacred state of marriage.

At least, he thought, he could repay some of the debt of honor that he owed her cousin James Lindsay. Juliana would be under his protection now, and he could send her back to Scotland. His conscience would ease knowing he had helped a Lindsay.

Otherwise, his imminent marriage to James Lindsay's rebellious little cousin was plainly astonishing to him. He doubted the girl would ever develop English loyalties. Her kin were rebels, blood and bone, and she seemed to share that. He suspected that her insistent silence was pure stubbornness.

As the priest intoned the marriage text in Latin, Gawain repeated the phrases that bound him to her, legally and forever. He looked at Juliana. She was no loving bride, but clearly furious. Her cheeks were pink, her lips tight, her eyes dark blue flashes. In the cart, the swan hissed. Bizarre wedding music, Gawain thought.

"The lady must speak the vow," the priest said, edging away from the bird.

Juliana shook her head.

"She may nod her agreement," the priest said.

This time her head shake was more vehement.

"Is she deaf and dumb?" the priest asked.

"Not deaf," Gawain said between his teeth. She lifted her chin defiantly. He leaned down. "Nod, Juliana," he murmured.

She glared at him.

"Marry me, and I can save that bird from a roasting pan."

She sent him an intense glance, indignant and yet frightened.

"I swear it." He had promised much to many of late, but would keep this.

The priest repeated the vows. Juliana sighed and nodded.

"Well enough," the priest said, and pronounced the marriage blessing. "Give her the kiss of peace," he directed Gawain.

He bent and touched his lips to hers. Her mouth was still and soft. He felt a swirl of pleasure. His blood surged and his heart pounded as if he were a youth, smitten hard and floundering with it.

The king clapped his hands and came forward. "Well done," he announced. "Now take your maiden swan away, and render her a maiden no more." He walked away with a sly smile.

"Sire," Gawain said. "Might my… lady wife be freed from her chains now?"

Edward ignored him and beckoned to the musicians to play again, resuming his seat while servants rushed to pour wine into his goblet and offer him trays of sweetmeats.

Gawain stood beside Juliana, as silent as she was. The doors of the chamber opened wide as the next cart was brought forward, bearing a huge confection, a fruit-bedecked castle.

The entertainment he and Juliana had provided had ended.

One of the guards approached Gawain. "She's yers to take home, sir, but she is still a prisoner. An escort will go with ye tonight. Orders will be delivered by messenger in the morning. For now, we will wait in the outer courtyard."

As the man turned away, Gawain thought of something and followed him, out of Juliana's range of hearing. She waited for him, standing, wavering slightly.

"Sir!" Gawain placed a gold coin in the man's hand. "Make certain that the swan is taken to the river and released, rather than taken to the kitchen," he said in a quiet, urgent tone.

The guard nodded thoughtfully. "For good coin, anything can be done. I will see to it. The king can eat some other swan on the morrow, eh?" He winked.

"My thanks." Gawain walked back to Juliana and took her arm to guide her out of the hall. She glanced at the swan with a whimper, stumbling, her distress obvious.

"Come, my lady." He urged her toward the door.

She faltered beside him, and he realized that she must have been given some sort of potion to weaken her. He swept her up into his arms and carried her through the huge doorway.

He hurried past servants, past carts loaded with dirty platters and soggy bread trenchers. Striding through a torchlit hallway, he took some stairs that led to the courtyard.

The girl rode silently in his arms. Her golden chains chimed in rhythm with his footsteps as he descended the steps. He walked out into the cool, rainy darkness and set her down, and she leaned against him wearily.

"Not much longer," he said, looking down at her.

A guard appeared, the man with whom he had previously spoken about the swan. He led Gawain's horses, both saddled: Gringolet, a dark bay, a sturdy destrier from his father's stables; and Galienne, a gray palfrey, a temperate mare that Gawain often rode himself to spare the warhorse.

"'Tis done, sir, what ye asked of me," the guard said. "I saw to the matter myself. 'Twill be released in the morn."

"My thanks, man." The guard drew the palfrey forward and Gawain assisted Juliana into the saddle. "She is called Galienne," he said. "Can you ride?"

She slid him a look that said the question was ridiculous, and took the reins in her manacled hands, turning the horse's head. The rain had flattened the feathers on her small cap and turned her golden hair to sopping strands. Draped in the white satin gown, her back was straight, her hands amazingly sure.

Aye, he thought admiringly, she could ride very well.

He bounded into Gringolet's saddle and walked him forward to stand beside the palfrey. Unfastening his black cloak, Gawain swept it around Juliana's shoulders and pulled up the hood.

She looked at him, quick and wary.

"You are wet," he said simply. His stepfather and stepbrothers strode into the courtyard. Gawain waited while they mounted their horses.

All the while, his glance strayed toward his silent, weary, mysterious bride.

Chapter Seven

THE PATTER OF rain and the pounding of the horses' hooves on the cobbled stones seemed loud in the night-dark streets of Newcastle-upon-Tyne. Juliana rode at the center of a group of guards and the Avenel kinsmen. She recognized the younger of the men as Sir Robert—Robin, the others called him.

Gawain rode ahead of her through the Black Gate that led out of the castle and into the walled town, where cobbled streets, crowded with houses, looked slick in the rain. One of the guards led her horse, though she could have handled her biddable mount.

No one spoke to her, and she kept silent. She had not spoken in so long that she wondered if her voice had grown weak from disuse. She shivered in the cool rain, grateful for the cloak that Gawain had given her.

He rode ahead of her, his head bare, his shoulders broad. She glanced at him often, aware of a tenuous bond. Her husband— the word seemed strangely ominous now. Dread sat like a stone in her as she wondered what he would demand on their wedding night.

A guard carried a torch ahead of them, but it scarcely pierced the rain and shadows. The massive bulk of a church thrust into the night, and the river gleamed like a ribbon in the distance.

The riders followed a curving, steep side lane and halted before a whitewashed, timbered building whose third level canted over the street. The door opened, golden light pouring over the wet cobblestones. A woman waited as the men dismounted, and a boy came out of the house to lead the horses away.

Gawain turned to Juliana and held up his arms to lift her down. "This is the inn where my kinsmen and I have been staying. We will spend the night here." His hands braced her waist.

She slid down from the horse, and would not look at him. He led her toward the inn, and the woman stood back as they entered a dim, low-ceilinged room.

"Greetings, Dame Bette," Gawain said.

"Greetings, sir. I see ye brought a guest from the king's feast." Bette shut and latched the door and turned. She was sturdy, with gray hair haloing out from a white kerchief, and a dark gown. She appraised Juliana with a fast glance. "I do not have a free chamber for her. Who is she with? Sir Henry and the rest have gone to an upper chamber. He's called for hot wine, and says he wants to see ye right away."

Gawain lifted his cloak from Juliana's shoulders, hanging it on a wall peg by the door, and then brushed the raindrops from the sleeves of his dark tunic. Juliana turned to face Bette, hands joined in front of her by the golden chain.

"By the saints, she is chained!" Bette said. "And wearing feathers! Is she a mummer? Eek, sir—is she a harlot?"

"She is a captive of the king. We have the keeping of her."

"A prisoner! We've no dungeon here! The crown will owe us for her boarding, and it is the very devil to collect it from the royal accounting clerk at the Sand Gate. That man is a lizard."

"The crown owes you naught for her keep," Gawain replied. "I will pay. She is my bride. A gift from the king."

"Bride." Bette stared at him. Then she peered at Juliana, who stared boldly back at her. "Well, she is not ughsome, and may please a man, but Lord bless us, she is a criminal!"

"She is just a rebel Scotswoman."

Bride, Juliana thought. Scotswoman. Rebel. He had not bothered to say her name, though he knew it. She frowned.

Bette looked skeptical. "Well, she needs a bath. I'll take her to yer bedchamber, and wish ye luck of yer marriage."

"My thanks," he said. "Let her bathe in privacy while I meet with Sir Henry. And bring her a hot meal, if you will." He took the woman's hand, and Juliana saw the flash of a coin. Bette nodded and blushed like a young girl. Gawain crossed the room and went up the stairs.

"Come dear, ye must be tired," Bette said, taking her arm. "And how are ye to bathe, in them chains? We cannot get that gown off ye easily, and 'tis too fine to cut. Well, ye'll wash as ye can. Tsk," she added, scanning her critically from head to foot. "Why are ye dressed like a duck?"

"From what the king's chamberlain said as I left the castle," Henry said, "Walter de Soulis will travel north with you and the lady, bringing an escort of men."

"Walter de Soulis?" Gawain asked sharply. He poured himself a cup of heated wine, watered and spiced, a soothing drink that his father preferred before bedtime. Given the events of the evening, he would have opted for something far stronger.

"Aye, he is the king's sheriff in the shire where the girl—your, ah, wife—comes from," Henry said. "Edmund knows something of it. Ned?"

"I inquired about the girl in the hall," Edmund said. "A shameful farce, that wedding. You saved her from a poor fate if one of those sots had gotten her."

"We know you did not mean to marry her," Robin said. He sat on a stool beside the fire. "Though that may not be so bad. She is a pretty chit."

"Lady," Gawain said irritably. "Demoiselle. Girl. Lass, if you will. She is not a chit. You are a knight now. Act like it."

Robin gaped at him, and Henry held up a hand for peace. Gawain turned away and sloshed more wine into his cup. He did not intend to drink it, but he needed to occupy his hands with the cup.

"At any rate," Edmund said into the tense silence, "this De Soulis has been appointed the first Master of Swans in Scotland—an honorary title, I think, since a sheriff has no leisure to tend royal swans in Scotland during a war effort."

"The king seized upon the symbolic importance of swans last May when he held his first Feast of the Swan in London," Henry said. "No doubt that is behind this appointment."

Gawain downed a long draught. "I know De Soulis. He burned Elladoune Castle the night that I was reported for aiding rebels. Juliana Lindsay lived there. 'Tis where I first saw her."

"By the saints! Did you help her that night?" Henry asked. "You never mentioned that detail before, as I recall."

Gawain shrugged. "Her, and some others—a mother and children who escaped while their home was being torched. I paid for it with a public apology. 'Tis done."

"Not quite," Henry replied quietly. Gawain glanced at his stepfather, whose hazel eyes were piercing, though his manner was calm, as usual. "Now you've met the girl again, and you have married her by king's order—and you must deal with the man who accused you years ago. Not done at all, is it?" Henry frowned.

Gawain sipped. The spiced wine burned a sweet path down his throat. "What else do we know about this girl?"

"She is yours to keep, by legal and sacred bond," Henry said. "That much we know."

"Wonderful news," Gawain snapped. He flickered a glance at his stepfather, who watched him with grim sympathy.

"Some good may come of this."

"'Tis a shock to find myself wed," Gawain admitted. "But if all that comes of it is my lady mother's contentment, then 'tis enough." He glanced around and saw sober nods.

"True," Henry agreed quietly. "Ned, what did you learn about Gawain's bride?"

"She lives in a place called Inchfillan Abbey, under the care of a kinsman, an Augustinian abbot."

"Gawain wed a nun?" Robin asked.

"Nay. The abbot is her guardian. De Soulis took her brothers into custody as well, before he brought her south with that mute swan. King Edward requested a pair of Scottish swans, and his Master of Swans obtained them."

"De Soulis has a poor sense of humor," Gawain drawled.

"One of the guards said that the girl is called the Swan Maiden in the area where she lives," Edmund said, and shrugged. "I do not know why."

Gawain swirled the wine in his cup. He knew exactly where that epithet came from. "Her brothers were taken? I heard there were two Lindsays, older than her, running with Robert Bruce."

James Lindsay had mentioned his cousins. Gawain shook his head slightly as he thought of the irony in this sure tangle.

"Now you have the responsibility of her," Robin said. "But how are you going to transform her into a loyal English lady?"

"I do not think that can be done at all, frankly." Gawain took a stool beside the fire, settling into the slung leather seat and resting his elbows on his knees. "I only meant to free her and send her back to Scotland. I never counted on the rest."

"You will return her to Scotland—and you will have custody of her for the rest of your life." Henry paced the room, rubbing his jaw. His brown hair had grown more gray, Gawain noticed. Henry was a handsome and skilled man, a paragon of knighthood in Edward's court. His advice and friendship were valued by the king, and his military expertise was respected by many. Gawain considered himself fortunate to call him stepfather and mentor.

"But to take her to Scotland, he has to show her in chains the whole way," Robin said. "Is that not what the king said?"

"Aye, so all of England can see the captive Scotswoman,"

Edmund said. "A devilish plan."

"I refuse to treat a woman so," Gawain said. "The king is a madman to expect it."

"He seems so, at times," Henry said. "His hatred of the Scots grows more unreasonable, I admit. But if he issues a writ saying she must be chained, and sends an escort to see it done, there is naught you can do about it."

"There might be," Gawain said firmly.

"Insubordination," Henry said, "does not honor the Avenel name."

"Gold links are soft, and impractical for a prisoner's chains," Gawain replied. "Easily broken."

"You have a damnable habit of helping others when 'twill only bring trouble for you," Henry said sternly.

"Those chains had better hold," Edmund muttered, "or all the Avenels will pay the price of it."

Gawain scowled into his wine, knowing the truth of that. Henry looked out the window at the rainy darkness. After a moment, he reached into his pocket and withdrew a small object. He tossed it to Gawain.

Deftly catching it, Gawain opened his hand. A tiny iron key lay in his palm. He looked at Henry.

"The king entrusted it to me," his stepfather said. "I entrust it to you. Use it wisely."

Gawain nodded and crossed to the door. "'Tis late. I bid you good night. We are leaving in the morn, my… bride and I. Do any of you ride north with us?"

"Robin rides for Avenel Castle tomorrow," Henry said. "Edmund and I must stay in Newcastle for now."

"Ah, then. Good night." Gawain was aware that his family wondered if he would sleep with his new bride this night. He wondered it himself. He opened the door latch.

"Gawain," Henry said. "Thank you."

He glanced over his shoulder in surprise. "Why, sir? I have run the Avenel name to near ruin with all my transgressions.

Even worse, Geoffrey... is gone now, in part my fault," he murmured. "This evening's pageant does not improve matters."

"Geoffrey's death was hard for everyone, but no one is to blame," Henry said. "We know that you have risked much, and given up much, to protect our welfare. We are all grateful."

Gawain began to speak, but his voice clouded. He nodded stiffly, opened the door, and slipped out into the corridor.

THE SMALL BEDROOM was silent and dark but for the low light of a brazier and a single candle. Outside, rain gusted against the walls, making the room seem cozy. The candle's halo illuminated the bed as Gawain crossed the room and looked down.

Juliana lay in the bed against several pillows, with the fur coverlet pulled up to her shoulders. She still wore the white satin dress, although the feathered cap lay on the table. Her pale hair was like moonlight and silk, and her face was smooth and serene. Gawain reached out a hand but did not touch her.

He wanted a wife, he thought, but not like this. When war and traveling were a way of life, knights often craved the peace and contentment of a home and a family, and he was no different, he knew. Someday he had hoped to find a gentle lady to warm his heart and share his life.

Unsure what to make of this marriage, he felt numb, still stunned. He sat on the edge of the bed and watched her. She slept deeply, her breathing quiet. She was a sweet perfection, golden fair and smooth cheeked, with a soft curve to her mouth, her hands curled and slender on the pillow, wrists manacled.

Frowning, he used the little key to unlock the collar. Sliding a hand under her head, he lifted the band away, baring the sinuous curve of her throat. He stroked a finger over the pink crease the collar had made.

Next, he removed the manacles and pooled the chains on the

tabletop. She moaned in her sleep, and he soothed his hand over her head.

He did not dare to touch her further, for desire coursed quick and intense through him. Giving into that was unthinkable. She had been stolen from her home, imprisoned, humiliated, forced to wed. He would not demand marriage rights of her, despite the king's crude suggestion.

He stood, blew out the candle, and walked in the darkness to the other side of the bed. Listening to the driving rain, he removed his boots and clothing, all but his braies. This wedding night was not like most. The girl might wake up and mistake him for a lecher if he kept his usual practice of sleeping nude.

All he wanted was some rest. He felt exhausted from the shock of the evening and the crazy tilt in his future. In the morning he would sort out his obligations. He would receive writs and meet the escort; he realized that he did not even know their destination in Scotland or his military duties yet.

A gust of wind and rain made the closed shutters tremble. The outer world was in upheaval, he thought, like his own world. He eased between the covers. The rope foundation of the bed creaked as he reclined and closed his eyes.

He had much to think about—too much for a weary man to sort through in one night. Listening to the rain, he felt sleep overtake him.

Chapter Eight

Blessed freedom. The chains were gone. Juliana could feel the cool air on her neck and wrists. She wondered, lying in the darkness, if the Swan Feast had been only a nightmare.

More fully awake, she realized that her captivity was still real, for she lay in the bed at the inn. But someone had freed her. Relieved and grateful, she sighed and stretched.

After weeks of straw and thin blankets, the deep, soft bed had felt like a cloud. She yawned and snuggled into its warmth. Just last night, she had curled in a corner of a cold dungeon cell, too afraid to sleep because of the guards outside the door.

Here she had slept undisturbed for what seemed a long while, although the sky was still dark beyond the opaque glazing in the small window, and rain still pattered unceasingly.

She rolled over and squeaked in alarm.

Gawain slept beside her, his shadowed form motionless beneath the covers. She had not realized his presence until now; his soft snores had mingled with the sound of the rain.

She wondered if he had removed her chains—at least he had left her fully dressed. Apparently he had not attempted to ravish her as the king had suggested to him.

Yet. She sat up carefully, watching him.

In the shadows, she saw only the firm gleam of a bare shoulder, the dark mass of his hair on the pillow. He sighed, shifted his head, and resumed snoring. Sure that he was completely asleep,

Juliana leaned closer out of curiosity.

Warmth emanated from him, and he smelled clean and spicy and good. He smelled like comfort, she thought suddenly. She recalled the gentle kiss they had exchanged after the marriage vows had been said. She remembered how he had kept her safe, years ago, in his arms. A subtle shiver traveled through her. She wondered what it would feel like to kiss him again, deep and full, like lovers.

But he was not her lover, and their wedding night was a mockery. A husband had been forced upon her like a sentencing. He had helped her, and she was grateful, but he was an enemy to her people. King Edward had sworn to destroy Robert Bruce and Scotland, and Gawain Avenel had stood with the other knights as they repeated the vow.

She had to get away from him and this place before he awoke and tried to claim his rights as a husband. Best if she escaped Newcastle altogether, so he could not chain her again as his prisoner, albeit his wife.

She eased herself out of bed and stood. Although her satin gown rustled loudly, the knight slept undisturbed. Turning, she wondered what to wear; she could hardly flee through the night in a gown as bright as a full moon. Unlacing the neck, she slipped out of the garment and the thin, impractical slippers she had been given. She stood in her gauzy chemise.

The dark blur of the knight's tunic lay on the foot of the bed. The black serge garment was wide and large, and she tugged it over her head and slipped her arms in the sleeves. Avenel was broad-shouldered and she was slight, but her legs were long. It suited her well enough to flee in it, she thought.

Groping around, she discovered his leather belt and latched it over her hips, but it nearly thunked to the floor and she set it aside. Glancing furtively toward the bed, she snatched his boots. They were heavy and well made, and so big on her feet that she fitted them with floor rushes stuffed into each toe box.

She braided her hair out of the way, although with its fine

texture, it would soon loosen again, lacking a ribbon. Then she tiptoed to the door, eased it open, and slipped out.

THE FIRE IN the brazier must have gone out, Gawain thought vaguely, stirring in the bed. The sheets were cold. He rolled over and stretched out his hand in the darkness.

She was gone.

He bolted upright and grabbed for his clothing. That was gone, too. Standing, swearing, he stepped into a pool of white satin. Juliana had not only fled the room, she had left her gown and feathers behind.

Muttering under his breath, he went to a corner where his saddle pack lay. The previous day, expecting to ride north to fulfill his term of knight service—wifeless, he thought sourly—he had packed clothing, blankets, and other items.

He extracted a brown tunic and yanked it over his head. Discovering that she had taken his boots, too, he swore again and headed for the door, stubbing his bare toe on a stool.

He made his way along the hall and down the creaking stairs quickly. The other bedchambers were occupied by the king's knights, including Henry and his stepbrothers, but no one stirred.

The front door was unbarred, and his cloak was missing from the wall peg where he had left it to dry. Growling in further annoyance, he stepped out into the night.

Rain drenched him within moments. Through the darkness, he saw someone standing at the end of the street. At first, he thought it was a boy. Then he realized that Juliana turned as if uncertain where to go.

Staying in the shadow of the houses, he strode toward her and snatched at her cloak as she whirled to run. "Walking home to Scotland?" he asked.

She fought him, sputtering in the rain. He held her in a fierce grip, while the downpour slicked over his head, ran into his open collar, sluiced cold around his bare feet.

She squealed and tried to stamp on his feet with his own damned boots. He stepped neatly aside.

"You will not get far," he said. "The town is surrounded by a wall several feet thick and more than twenty feet high, with seven gates." He pulled her hard against him and pointed toward the castle that loomed over the city. "Seventeen towers, each with guards on watch, day and night. The outer wall of the town was built fifty years ago to keep the Scots out. 'Twill keep one Scots lassie inside."

He lifted her and dumped her over his shoulder. As he headed back to the inn, he struggled to hold her. She squirmed, her feet beating at his thighs. He smacked the most convenient part he could reach, her small rounded bottom, and received a solid punch in the kidneys.

Inside the inn, he slammed the door behind them and slid Juliana to her feet. Stripping off the sodden cloak, he flung it over a hook. She stared up at him, her gaze livid, her cheeks flushed, her hair hanging in soaking strands over her face. He kept one hand tight around her upper arm.

"If eyes were daggers," he murmured.

"You would feel the prick," she snapped. Her voice was soft and hoarse, and cracked on the last word.

He raised a brow. "Ah, so you do talk. I thought so. Good. You can explain what the devil you were doing out there." He pulled her toward the stairs.

When she dug in her heels like a mule, he yanked, half dragging her up the steps. She shivered in his damp black tunic, which hung on her like a funeral pall.

When they reached the second floor, Henry peered out of an open door. Beyond him, another door opened, and Robin and Edmund looked out. At the foot of the uppermost staircase, Bette stood with a candle in her hand. All of them gaped.

"Good night," Gawain said succinctly, and pulled Juliana

along the corridor. He pushed open his bedchamber door, shoved her inside, followed, and slammed the door, bolting it.

"As if that would keep me inside," she said. She folded her arms and stood staring at him.

"Determined to escape? What about that wall around the town? Do you intend to fly over it, Swan Maiden?"

"You do not understand. I must go home." He heard a plaintive wobble in her voice and frowned.

"I understand well enough that you must stay here."

She turned her head indignantly and did not answer.

"Back to silence, I see. What is this silence of yours all about? I remember having to hush you up, years ago. You were full of speeches when we hid in that loch with the swans."

"'Twas long ago. I scarcely recall." Her English had the airy lilt of a Gaelic-speaking native. It tugged at him swiftly, keenly, a reminder of people and places better forgotten. "What will you do with me now?"

"I have not thought about it. I was sleeping until a few minutes ago." He pushed her toward the bed, and she sat on its edge, sending him a little glare. She was shivering markedly, he noticed. He was cold himself, and damp. "Take off those wet things and get under the covers," he said. He ran his fingers through his hair, shaking some of the moisture out of it.

"I will not." She folded her arms.

He turned to stoke the brazier in the corner of the room, adding dry sticks and coals from a bucket. Juliana stood and edged toward the door. Standing, he spun around and grasped her arm to turn her firmly toward the bed.

"I am a patient man," he said, "but no more. Sit there. And strip down. You are trembling with cold."

"Do not think to warm me!" She sat again, glaring at him.

In answer, he snatched up a blanket from the bed and threw it over her shoulders. She grabbed at it, rubbing at her hair. Gawain turned and stripped off his rain-damp tunic, tossing it over the foot of the bed. Standing before her in his braies, he grabbed another blanket, pulling it without apology from beneath her. He tossed it around his own shoulders.

Her gaze skimmed his bare torso, lowered, raised again. She scooted away on the bed. "I hoped you were a courteous knight who would help me. Instead, you mean to hold me against my will."

"I do not—"

"I heard the king's orders! He may be a king, but he acted like a lecherous cur! I will not be subdued for your amusement. Chain me, ravish me, if you dare! Wring my swan's neck and have him for your supper—or wring my own. But I will not be tamed!"

He stood staring at her. Pale and ethereal as a moonbeam, she housed a white flame of righteousness that would make any rebel proud and strong. She directed it at him as if he were a straw target and she a flinted point.

He held up a hand for peace. "I have no intention of taming you," he said. "Be at ease."

"At ease? In a bed with you?" She pulled the blanket closer. "The king urged you publicly to take me this night—just to show that England can rape Scotland. We Scots know that already, and I will fight to the death if you try it!"

"I do not doubt it," he drawled. "My *written* orders from the king are to take you back to Scotland and keep you for my wife. The rest of his orders I need not obey. He will forget them soon enough, drunk as he was," he muttered.

She slicked her fingers through her damp hair. "And you, are you drunk as well? Every man there tonight was sodden," she said with disgust.

"I am in command of myself, if that is what you ask."

She shot him another glare. He sent one back, then ruffled his hair to coax more wetness from it. "You will stay," he said curtly. "You are my wife now, and my obligation. And a prisoner of the crown. I will not forfeit my life for your escape."

"I am not your wife!"

"We were wed by a priest. Or did you miss that moment?"

She drew breath. "When ice coats the halls of hell, I will be your wife. When the faeries of Scotland serve sweetmeats to the king of England, I will be your wife!" She folded her arms tightly over her chest and lifted her chin.

"You have a talent with words… for a silent maiden."

"Those wedding vows meant naught. I did not speak them."

"But they were legally done, and we are joined in the eyes of God and man. To undo it, we would need a priest willing to request a divorce from Rome. 'Tis easier to remain wed."

"A divorce will not be necessary," she announced. "An annulment will do, since you will never touch me."

"Will I not?" He stared down at her, anger rising. He was tired and frustrated, and he had been more than kind to her so far, yet she treated him as if he were a boor.

"My kinsmen will kill you if you do," she said.

"One of your kinsmen may kill me anyway, if he ever sees me again," he muttered, rubbing the blanket over his shoulders. She looked at him, puzzled, but he was not about to explain the tangle between him and her cousin James Lindsay.

"My guardian is an abbot. I live in his household."

"In a religious compound? You do not behave like a nun."

"If I were a nun, the king's guards would have left me in Scotland. Father Abbot will annul the marriage."

"We will see." He sat on the bed. She scooted away from him. "Go easy, I will not harm you," he said wearily. "And I do not want to discuss legalities, either. I just want to get some sleep." The need pulled at him like a river current.

She looked longingly at the bed. "Sleep on the floor."

"Share the bed with me," he replied. She shivered again. "Take that wet tunic off," he said abruptly.

"I will not."

"'Tis summer, but these rainy days lately have been chilly. You will be ill by morning, the way you are shivering now. Take that off and get warm." He yanked away her blanket, then drew the wet garment from her in one long pull. She twisted and squealed in protest. A quick flip draped the tunic with his other garment, near the brazier where they would dry.

She jumped away from him and stood, dressed in some thin undergarment. He saw firm, pink-centered breasts and lean, graceful curves before she grabbed up the blanket again.

"Take off my boots and get in bed," he said gruffly.

"You do mean to ravish me!"

He sighed in exasperation. "I am too tired to ravish anyone. Least of all a spitting mad lass." Tired, but not unwilling, he realized. The sight of her body had sent a firebolt through him.

She stared at him, her breath heaving. He glanced away to ebb the desire that flowed through him. "Those boots need to be dry by morn," he said.

She stepped out of the boots and kicked them toward the brazier. He walked over to set them to dry properly. When he turned again, she backed away.

"How do I know you will not ravish me?"

"Do you want to be ravished?"

"Nay!"

"Then stop talking about it so we can both get some sleep." He went toward the bed. She watched him warily and shuffled away.

"Girl," he said patiently, "I am a knight sworn to honor, yet you give me no credence. I have proven my worth to you, yet you will not trust me."

"Trust a Sassenach?" she asked incredulously.

"If my word is good enough for the king, 'tis good enough for you. Lie down."

"Go to sleep. I am not so weary as I was." Her eyes darted toward the door.

"Oh, no," he said, seeing her intent. "Do not think about it. A trick done once to me is never done twice." He stepped forward and picked her up, dumping her on the bed. Then he sat on the edge, trapping her with his arms.

"Let me go—you gave your word—" She twisted beneath

him. "I will not be a wife to you, and I will not stay here!"

"Lie still, or I will be forced to chain you here to keep you safe for the night." His blanket slipped off as he half-flattened himself over her to hold her down. His bare chest pressed to the soft globes of her breasts, with only the damp, thin chemise between their bodies. He felt her nipples bead against him, and a shiver went through him.

She bucked beneath him. "Let me go!"

"That would be exceeding foolish of me." More foolish to remain in this position with her, he told himself. He snatched the golden chains from the bedside table.

"You say you are chivalrous, but you lie," she said, wriggling beneath him. "You do mean to ravish your bride!"

"If it would quiet you and please you, I might consider it," he muttered.

"Where is your courtesy?" She torqued beneath him.

"I am summoning all of it just now," he growled. He leaned forward, and she flattened into the pillows, staring at him. "Listen. You must stay here, and I need to sleep. As do you. Can I trust you for the night, at least?"

"I will not stay here with you. I want to go home. I want to be free." Her voice quavered, and he sensed she meant it.

"I will take you home."

"As a prisoner!"

He sighed. "Can I trust you for the night?"

She shook her head.

"Well, you are honest at least. My apologies. You leave me no choice." He slid one of the manacles around her wrist and latched it. Then he looped the chain around the bedpost and locked the other manacle into the links. He stood and looked down at her. "Now we can get some rest."

She fumed, pulling at the manacle, while he plumped a mound of pillows to support her and walked to the other side of the bed to lie down, pulling the covers up.

"I will have the key from you as soon as you are asleep!"

He rolled over quickly and folded her arm firmly against her, holding her wrist against her chest, which rose and fell beneath his hand. "Not unless you want to carry the rest of those chains upon you."

She kicked him. He turned, presenting his back. "There must be tusks on your family crest, for you are a pig!" she snapped.

"And you," he said, "were far more appealing as a mute swan." He punched his pillow.

He heard a husky snarl and felt a halfhearted shove, softened by the bedclothes between them. But she said no more, and he felt himself sliding once again toward sleep.

Chapter Nine

DAWN BROUGHT A thin, clear light and a return to silence. Juliana awoke alone, and found the white gown, feathered cap, and shoes laid out on the bed. The chains, she discovered immediately, were gone. Within moments, Dame Bette knocked on the door and entered carrying a cup of ale and a slab of hot bread with cheese melted on it.

"Yer husband said ye would be hungry this morning," Bette said, grinning with delight. "It stirs the appetite sometimes, when ye've wed one what makes yer heart quicken."

Juliana blushed at Bette's obvious assumption. Just the opposite was true. She and Gawain quickened each other's hearts, but not with loving. She ate quickly, for she was hungry.

"I will lend a hand with yer finery," Bette said. She helped Juliana slip into the gown. "Yer bridegroom and his kinsmen are waiting downstairs. There is a pack of soldiers in the lane, too. Whatever ye did, my lady, they mean to keep close watch over ye. They've brought writs from the king, which yer husband has been reading this morn. He seems none too pleased."

She stood, mute and still, while Bette plaited a single braid down her back and tied it with a bit of string.

"I gather yer husband thinks ye innocent of any wrong, and so do I," Bette continued. "He has been sitting in a dark mood, shifting those chains in his hands until the clinking sound was like to drive me mad."

Sighing, Juliana thought it more likely that her husband was fuming silently over their unwanted marriage, her attempted escape, and their arguments last night. She should never have been so foolish as to break her silence with him.

She sat on the bed and slipped her feet into her flat shoes, painted white leather to match her hated gown. She looked up as Bette approached with the feather cap and settled it on her head.

"There is a king's man, too, wearing the blackest armor I have ever seen," Bette said. "He is the leader of yer escort."

Juliana frowned to herself while Bette adjusted the cap; she remembered the journey south too well. De Soulis had shown no consideration for her, ordering a fast pace, tight ropes, and regular dosing of bitter herbs in wine to keep her senses dulled. Despite Gawain's presence, she dreaded the return now.

"Sir Walter says ye must wear the feathery hat," Bette said. "He says he is the Master of Swans, and ye're the Swan Maiden, and ye're to be dressed as a swan for show, like. Oh my, just awful. And I thought ye were a mummer guised as a duck!"

Juliana smiled despite her somber mood.

"And yer husband," Bette added, "looks like he would like to strangle the Master of Swans. Hurry, now, ye've a long journey."

THE CART RUMBLED over the old Roman road, lurching over pits and stones in the roadbed. Juliana grabbed the edge of the cart to steady herself, chains jangling. She looked out at low, rolling hills and patches of moorland. The driver, a gruff old man called John, said nothing as he guided the two sturdy horses that drew the cart, which was packed with goods and weapons.

A mounted escort of thirty men, with several squires, two servants, and the riderless palfrey she had ridden the night before, surrounded her. Gawain Avenel rode his dark bay horse just ahead of the cart, talking with a knight mounted on a brown horse even larger than the bay. Walter de Soulis, black armor gleaming beneath a wine-red surcoat, rode beside the cart.

Juliana studied her husband's head and broad-shouldered back. He wore a dark brown serge tunic over chain mail, with the heavy hood slid down over his shoulders. His hair was thick, wavy, and glossy as ink in the morning light, and his smile flashed handsomely and often as he listened to the other knight.

The two men seemed to be established friends, she noticed, though appearing to be opposites in many ways. Gawain sat his horse with taut grace and control, while the other had a carefree lack of rhythm. Where Gawain was lean, dark, and restrained, his friend was large, sandy-haired, soft around the middle, and gestured freely with big hands.

In further contrast to her husband's sober nature, his friend laughed quickly, booming out. He even glanced back at Juliana and smiled at her, his face as pleasant as his demeanor.

Though she did not smile back, she found the big sandy-haired knight's confidence and humor appealing. But she was not ready to trust him any more than Gawain Avenel.

Riding near the cart, Sir Walter de Soulis seemed even more severe and humorless by contrast. He said little to anyone, speaking sharply when he did. And he had already forced her to drink from the wine bladder that he kept strapped to his saddle.

Though she had refused at first, he had put it to her lips and poured wine between them, so that liquid dripped over her chin. The bitter aftertaste left a grainy texture on her tongue that she wiped away on the back of her chained hands.

At the time, Gawain had been riding at the head of the escort. He turned to ride back. "Sir Sheriff," he said, "what are you doing?"

"The girl looks pale and nervous. The wine will strengthen and calm her," De Soulis answered. Gawain nodded, glancing at her with a frown before riding away.

That had been over an hour ago, and now she felt woozy from the herbs in the wine. She had swallowed only a bit, but its effect was enough to dull her thoughts and make her feel weary.

She was exhausted already from little rest the night before and for the past several days and nights. As the cart rolled along the road, she leaned her head against a bale of hay and slid into a bleary doze that deepened into sleep.

"LAURIE, I SWEAR I am glad to see you," Gawain said with quiet relief to the man who rode beside him. "'Tis sheer luck you were sent from York with the king's men to ride with this party into Scotland. I had not seen or heard from you for near a year, I think."

"Ha, luck," Laurence Kirkpatrick said. "'Twould have been luckier had I been at Newcastle yesterday. I would have talked you out of staying for the king's feast. Married!" He shook his head. "How did you go into a supper and come out with a wife?"

"I only thought to help the girl. She needed a champion."

"Och," Laurie nodded with exaggerated wisdom. "And of course no one could protect the lass but you. I heard something of it from your stepbrothers this morn. Surely someone else could have stepped in to help."

"Robin tried, but her swan bit him. I brought bread for the poor creature."

Laurence chuckled, then shook his head. "Do what I do, man. Watch after yourself first. Life is more pleasant that way. I am a Scotsman born and bred, but I fight for the English king. The pay is better, and the chances of gaining land and a good life are good."

"And the ale is good too," Gawain said dryly.

"The ale is better in Scotland, I think. But I offer my sword arm and services where my skills will be rewarded best."

Gawain slid his friend a quick look. "Did a certain English girl influence your decision? Maude, was it?"

Laurie's cheeks burned bright. "Maude of Rosemoor. Sir Harry Gray's youngest daughter."

"Ah, Lady Maude," Gawain drawled. "Here you chide me for being a married man, yet I was sure you would wed first. Last we met, you were well smitten."

"Er, uh," Laurie said. "We are wed."

Gawain laughed with delight. "When?"

"Last winter."

"So the fair Lady Maude is the reason a braw Border Scot rides for the English king," Gawain said, grinning.

"Pay and rewards were greatly on my mind." Laurie scowled.

"Oh, I am certain of it," Gawain said. "The lady is accustomed to finery, being Sir Harry's daughter."

"Just wait, now that you are wed!"

"My lady wife does not seem to care for finery and property. She cares only for freedom, and wants to get as far away from me as she can." He frowned, thinking of the unsavory task of restraining her the night before. She had a fresh and wild quality about her and deserved freedom, he thought, glancing back to see her asleep in the cart.

"I cannot blame the lass. Her English bridegroom is a somber sort."

"Aye, and sworn afresh to the king, too."

"Not still torn between Scottish and English? When we were lads and squires together, you used to say—"

"I said naught," Gawain hissed. "And keep quiet about it."

"Many Scots are pulled between two loyalties. Change like the wind, they say of us Scots. But we have kin and property to protect."

"I am not a Scotsman," Gawain insisted.

"Ah," Laurie said wryly. "Then listen to one who admits who he is. This matter is much on my mind of late. Many Scots have lands to protect in England too, as I do, as you do. And some think Scotland is better off under English rule. The English have wealth and military might. Scotland is poor and leaderless."

"Scotland has a bold leader in Robert Bruce, or so it seems."

Laurie shrugged. "I will watch before I decide what I think of that. Bruce was one of the finest knights in King Edward's court, and has English lands and interests, far more than I do. Now he's gone over to the Scots. But following him may not be safe."

"But it may be wise and just. Many Scots care more for freedom than safety."

"I can understand it. But my wife and children, and my gear and my table, are safest in England."

"Children?" Gawain glanced at him.

"We'll have one by the end o' year, Maude says." Laurie grinned, quick and fresh, his cheeks pinkening again.

Gawain clapped his friend on the shoulder. "Good news! No wonder you like to keep on the safe side."

"Aye so. And yourself? I heard you took to the hills with renegades. I thought you had joined your own at last. Yet now you declare anew to Edward."

"Laurie, no one knows of my birth here but you. Better you keep it to yourself. I have kin to protect."

"Pray pardon, Gawain," Laurie murmured soberly. "I know it is a tender subject for you. And you have property in England. Did Henry grant you something more?"

"'Tis not the land that I think to protect, but the family."

"Ah," Laurie said, nodding his understanding.

Gawain rode in silence beside his friend. He had known Laurence Kirkpatrick since they had attended lessons together at an abbey school in Northumberland. They had squired together and had been knighted under Edward Plantagenet's sword in the same ceremony.

Years ago, when they had been boys, Gawain had confided the secret of his Scottish birth to Laurie. At times, Laurie seemed full of bluster and reckless humor. Yet Gawain knew him for an honorable man at heart, and trusted him implicitly.

"What of this new assignment in the north?" Laurie asked. "I hear you have been given command of a garrison."

"Temporarily, while the current commander is out chasing Bruce in the hills," Gawain said. The writ for his assignment had been handed to him by De Soulis that morning. So far, he had scanned it only briefly, but he was stunned by the conditions and restrictions placed upon him.

"Do you know the details of it yet?"

"Not all of them. King Edward wants a written report of the lay of the land. I am to ride about, scribble notes, collect them together, and deliver them to the king's army commander. As for the rest—well, this will not be an easy post."

Laurie chortled. "I hear one of the tasks given to you is impossible."

"The one where I am to tame a girl according to my whim, eke an oath of loyalty out of her, and display her as the captive Swan Maiden of Scotland?"

"Aye, that one. The way to win a lady's affection." Laurie rolled his eyes.

"And I must bring her to court as an example of Scottish obedience, making sure she spits out that oath of fealty for the king. Just as I had to do," he added darkly.

"You did not gain the king's forgiveness this time, my friend. He means to make an example of you."

"It seems so."

"And all this is to be done while you garrison the girl's castle and take the lay of her lands?" Laurie shook his head. "Under the eye of that black dog, the sheriff?"

"I have old arguments with that one."

"Easy to do," Laurie said. "You know what they say of him."

"Only that he is the king's Master of Swans in the north and sheriff of some small Scottish shire."

"They say," Laurie began, leaning sideways and lowering his voice, "that his black armor has some spell of invincibility over it. That he practices dark arts to keep it so."

Gawain wrinkled his brow skeptically. "I have heard no such rumor, and I rode with him years ago, when he wore black armor—this suit, or some other, I do not know. But 'tis absurd."

"Look at that mail—have you ever seen the like?"

Narrowing his eyes as he turned to look at the sheriff, Gawain studied what he could of the chain mail beneath the man's surcoat—the sleeves, hood, lower hem, and leggings. The links shone like polished jet. "It looks blackened with grease and lampblack to me," he said.

"I have heard," Laurie added, "that he traded his soul for that suit, made in some foreign place."

"'Tis well made, and no doubt expensive. But not worth a man's soul. 'Tis a foolish rumor you would do well to ignore."

"They say," Laurie went on quietly, "that never a point can pierce it, or ever has. The man cannot be wounded."

Gawain shook his head. "If such armor were to be had for a decent price, we would all be wearing it."

"Well," Laurie said, "he looks of a size with you. Since he has already paid for it, you should borrow it from him if you ever go into battle. I could not get my arms into it, myself. Pity." He sighed.

Gawain grinned. "Sir Laurie, I have missed you."

"Aye, and now tell me this—is the girl's property worth all this annoyance?"

"Hardly. Elladoune once belonged to her father, but 'twas forfeited years ago. She has no hereditary claim to it since she has older brothers in Robert Bruce's army. 'Twill never be mine, if that is what you are wondering."

"I see." Laurie glanced at him. "So you must train her to speak before the king, or lose your head? Unpleasant."

"Risky, more than unpleasant. She is a bit wild, and comes from true rebel stock. The king's assignment is unsavory and the castle is too damned close to Glenshie," Gawain added in a low voice.

Laurie looked back at the sound of hoofbeats. "Ah. Here comes Sir Soul-less."

Gawain turned to see Walter de Soulis riding toward them,

and he quickly glanced toward Juliana, who still slept despite the jostling cart. She lay curled against a hay bale carried for fodder; stacked around her were sacks of provisions along with a pile of weapons and armor. The girl looked lost and vulnerable amid the trappings of war.

"Avenel!" De Soulis guided his horse to ride beside Gawain. "You have read the king's writ, I trust."

"I have, and I wonder why I am given such an assignment."

"Just be grateful your head is still on your shoulders."

"There is that," Laurie drawled. De Soulis sent him a glare.

"How long will I be posted at Elladoune, sir? Tell me about the garrison."

"Over one hundred men were housed there for five or six years," De Soulis answered. "But at the moment, the castle guard is depleted. The garrison commander took most of his force into the hills when the king ordered a thousand men from local garrisons to hunt for Bruce."

"More than a thousand will be needed," Laurie said. "Two thousand or three. Even then, Robert Bruce will be difficult to track. He vanishes into the mists, he does."

"Kirkpatrick, is it? Sent to us from Sir Aymer de Valence, Earl of Pembroke? Surely you have duties elsewhere, sir, and need not ride with Avenel."

"According to my orders, sir, signed by Pembroke and your-self, sir, I am to guard the lady. As you can see, I am doing just that. I can allow you two gentlemen near her, but no one else can come close." He gave a flat smile.

"I see." De Soulis narrowed his eyes. "No doubt you heard of the defeat of Bruce's troops at Methven a few weeks ago. Bruce fled with only a handful of men. The whole English army in Scotland is on alert to find him."

"I have heard so." Gawain knew that Methven had been a devastating defeat for the small Scottish army assembled under Bruce. "So I am to take over Elladoune until the commander returns from his foray."

"Exactly. Also, De Valence, as the king's lieutenant and commander of his armies in Scotland, will head for Perthshire with near three thousand men. Just now he is at Roxburgh. We will reach there by late today."

"I thought we were going into the Highlands," Gawain said.

"First I will confer with the king's military advisor. De Valence will decide who will hold Elladoune permanently. Until that is settled, you will have to do there."

Gawain flared his nostrils and said nothing, reminded of the value of silence, a weapon Juliana wielded daily. He stared at De Soulis until the other looked away.

"I will be at Dalbrae Castle in Glen Fillan," De Soulis went on. "Near enough to Elladoune to keep an eye on it. And you."

"Sir Gawain will manage well, I am sure," Laurie said. "After all, he has me for his next in command."

"You?" Gawain asked. De Soulis looked equally surprised.

"According to my renewed writ of knight service, I am to be second in command there," Laurie answered. "Aymer de Valence himself gave me the post. Did you not seen those orders, Sir Walter? I have a copy of the writ if you did not." He patted his belt pouch.

"I saw that," De Soulis said. "I was not familiar with the name until now."

"Good to have someone as stalwart and loyal as Kirkpatrick with me at Elladoune," Gawain said, as De Soulis gave them another dark scowl.

"An honor to serve under a knight of Avenel," Laurie said sternly. "They are known for being capable and loyal."

"I hear there is one bad apple at Avenel." De Soulis spurred his horse to ride ahead, falling into pace with the knights in the lead.

"Coward. He delivered an insult and ran off," Laurie growled.

"It was not worth the reply. I did not know you were assigned to Elladoune. I am glad to hear it."

"I was about to tell you when that black crow arrived. My

lady wife is a cousin of De Valence," Laurie said. "When I heard that you were to take over a garrison in the Highlands, I requested the same post and got my gear together fast as I could."

Gawain nodded. "I am in your debt, Laurie."

"You owe me, and I willna be shy about asking for favors. I want to be back home with Maude when the child arrives."

"You will have it." Gawain glanced again at Juliana, slumped against the hay bale, a chain around her wrists, her feathered hat askew. She looked so fragile that he again felt a fierce urge to protect her and get her away from the escort somehow.

His hand drifted to rest upon his belt pouch, where the key was tucked. "I will ask a favor of you myself."

"Certes. Shall I harry a black crow for you?"

"Just help me protect a wild swan."

"Done," Laurie answered.

Chapter Ten

"STILL QUIET, MY lady?" De Soulis murmured as he maneuvered his horse beside her cart. He spoke low so that only Juliana could hear him. Even Gawain, who usually stayed close, was out of hearing range.

She sent him a little glare. Her head felt woolly from the wine. Tempted to point that out to him, she said nothing.

"I wonder about this silence of yours," the sheriff went on. "They say that the Swan Maiden of Elladoune does not talk because of a magic spell over her. But I suspect 'tis a spoiled temperament—or a need to keep secrets. Rebellious secrets."

She turned her head away and fisted her hands in her lap. Silence was the only protection she could provide for herself. No matter what the English did to her, they could not touch her innermost self—nor could they learn what she knew about the rebels.

De Soulis leaned toward her. "Some speak of witchcraft," he said. "Such accusations are best avoided, so I urge you to speak up in your own defense."

She bowed her head and fingered the golden chain. If only she were back in Scotland, she thought. At home in the Highlands, witchcraft was a rare accusation, unlike in England.

"Very well," he murmured. "Keep your secrets for now. Someday we will talk, you and I." His tone was hard-edged. He urged his horse forward to join the knights riding in the lead.

She glanced at Gawain, who seemed deep in conversation with Sir Laurence, the knight who usually rode beside him. Her husband seemed unaware of De Soulis's threats to her—or did he know, indeed, and do nothing?

She sighed. Gawain Avenel was the stuff of dreams for some, she thought—a perfect, courteous knight, handsome and strong, noble and skilled. He had taken risks to help her twice now, and she owed him much for that. But she could not trust him, no matter his courtesy. Their marriage was no more than a mockery.

She looked out over the low green hills of the English countryside. Her natural physical energies had flagged because of the herbed wine and the stress of these last few weeks, and her spirit had weakened too. She felt desperate to go home; only that would fully restore her.

But she wondered if she would be safe at home. Her Swan Laird had appeared twice now—years ago, and last night—to save her when she faced danger. Yet he had chained her last night again, and he had not prevented this humiliation. Somehow it suited his purpose, whatever it was, to keep her a captive.

Perhaps, like De Soulis, he too wanted to know her secrets.

One secret she kept: she had loved the Swan Laird for years. Formed of dreams and long in the weaving, that love would not save her now, nor could she reveal it.

Tears gathered in her eyes, and she bowed her head. Soon the soporific effect of the wine, still powerful in her body, took her into heavy sleep again.

THE ESCORT TRAVELED along the Roman road leading north from Newcastle. As they drew near a town, farmers and harvesters stopped in the fields to stare at the king's knights. Some clustered along the roadside with infants in their arms, and older children ran beside the procession.

Gawain noticed that more people had crossed the fields to watch the military escort pass. They pointed at the strange sight of a lady chained in gold and dressed like a swan.

De Soulis cantered to the head of the train and raised his arm. "Behold the Swan Maiden of Elladoune!" he shouted. "See what befalls the Scots when they rebel against King Edward! The English can subdue even one who is said to have magic about her. Even she has submitted to English justice!"

Gawain swore, low and fierce. "What the devil—"

"Witch!" someone called, and a clod of earth struck Juliana in the back. She looked stunned and confused. Then another bit of mud caught her in the cheek, and she wiped it away with the back of her manacled hand. She lifted her head high.

"The Swan Maiden of Elladoune!" De Soulis called again. "Hooked and netted in Scotland, and taken to King Edward! We have clipped her wings, as you see! Is she magic, as the Scots say? Or is she a rebel deserving of punishment?"

"Damn him," Laurie growled. Gawain turned to see another clump of earth hit Juliana square in the chest. She gasped softly with the blow. He swore and rounded his horse to face the crowd, placing his hand on the hilt of his sword.

"Do not dare disturb the king's peace!" Gawain shouted. A few people stepped back. Two boys stopped, hiding their hands behind their backs. He glared at them and turned Gringolet.

On the other side of the road, Laurie cantered up and down as Gawain did, and other knights soon followed suit. Riding at the head of the escort, De Soulis continued to call attention to the Swan Maiden of Elladoune.

Another clod of mud sailed toward the cart. Laurie swung his horse around and rode back toward some boys who held mud balls in their hands. They scattered, shrieking, as he bore down on them.

"Enough," Gawain growled. He rode hard to the head of the escort. "What the devil is this about?" he snapped as he drew close.

"King's orders," De Soulis answered.

"You are a sheriff, sir, not a mummer with a wandering show. You shame this lady. 'Tis unbefitting to a knight."

"We are not all such exemplary knights as the Avenels," De Soulis sneered.

"That has naught to do with it. The lady is my wife."

"Then you make the announcements. My throat is parched."

Gawain sucked in a breath. "No more of it," he said.

"I am in charge of this escort so long as we are in England. If the king wants her displayed, so be it. According to this writ, you do not have charge of her until we reach Scotland."

"You do not seem to take my meaning," Gawain growled. "There will be no more announcements about her."

De Soulis glanced at him. "A threat? Are you loyal to the girl already? She must have proved a fine morsel last night."

"Have a care," Gawain warned. "You speak of my wife."

"Hot to defend her, are you?" De Soulis slid him a sidelong glance. "You were at Elladoune when her father's castle was taken. Later you were punished for helping rebels to escape. Did you help the girl that night too?"

"I do not recall. 'Twas years ago."

"Has she spoken to you?"

"She does not speak," Gawain pointed out.

"The Scots claim she is a creature of enchantment and can change into a swan when she chooses. What nonsense."

"They also claim," Gawain countered, "that you wear bewitched armor. More nonsense?"

"That idiotic rumor was started by some lackbrain, and haunts me still."

"It is the same for the lady. She was raised in an abbot's household. She leads a pious life, so I heard."

"I know Abbot Malcolm. You will meet him at Elladoune. He seems mild and reverent. He is either a fool—or a clever rebel. Either way, he bears watching. You will need to be aware of that at Elladoune."

"A rebel abbot? Interesting," Gawain drawled.

"Some Scots clergy are more fierce than Scots warriors. The brethren at Inchfillan seem biddable enough, though. I asked the abbot and his monks to tend Elladoune in the garrison's absence, but I told my men to watch them. If there is any suspicious activity, the trap will close on them all." He smiled. "That girl bears watching too."

"I doubt she is capable of much mischief. She seems—fragile." She looked the part, though he knew she had a strong spirit. But he wanted to deflect Sir Walter's interest.

"Besotted already? Beware," De Soulis said. "I pity you, Avenel. Rebel or witch, you will have the responsibility of her once we reach Scotland."

"I am thankful for that," Gawain drawled. He rounded his horse and rode back, and De Soulis followed. As Gawain guided his bay horse to ride parallel with the cart again, De Soulis lingered nearby. Gawain felt as if he had picked up a pesky, biting blackfly that he could not shake.

"At Elladoune," De Soulis said, "you will likely be ordered to pursue the rebels."

"That will depend on how many men are supplied to the garrison."

"When we reach Roxburgh, De Valence will have some news about how many will be sent to garrison Elladoune anew."

An idea occurred to Gawain. "Tell me what you learn at Roxburgh, sir. I will need to part from this escort at the end of this road, and take the fork to Northumberland."

De Soulis stared at him. "I have no orders on that."

Gawain patted his tunic. "I have a safe conduct to visit my family's home at Avenel Castle." He had obtained it before the feast, the wedding, and the king's new orders. "I will stay at Avenel for a few days, and cross into Scotland, where I meet you and the others at another point. The lady goes with me," he added firmly.

"But she is in the care of my escort!"

"She is my bride. I will not leave her in the company of men, without even a woman by her side. Surely you see the difficulty in bringing a female prisoner into a military castle like Roxburgh."

"My orders state that the Swan Maiden is to be chained and guarded at all times. She will be put in the dungeon at Roxburgh until we finish our meetings."

"She will be well guarded at Avenel. King Edward visits there often enough, and would approve his friend's authority, though you seem to question it."

De Soulis groused, then relented. "One day, and no more."

"Four," Gawain replied.

"Two."

"Very well. On the second day hence, at midday, I will meet you at an inn on the Scottish side of the border near Kelso."

"I know the place. Take part of the guard with you when you depart."

"My mother will not appreciate having a military guard at her home," Gawain answered. "Nor would my stepfather, Sir Henry Avenel." He needed to bring up the name again, as the power of it seemed to quell De Soulis a bit.

"I do not like it. But your father can be trusted, of course. Perhaps we should not take another female prisoner into Roxburgh, as you say. There are some Scotswomen held there already. Very well. Midday Saturday, outside Kelso."

Gawain nodded, then urged his horse ahead to join Laurie. He looked back at Juliana. She was still resting, her head tucked in her arms. She drooped like a bedraggled white flower, gown and feathered cap rumpled and soiled. Still, she had a glow about her, a strength of spirit, that seemed always part of her.

He watched the wife he scarcely knew and sensed again the curious mix of fragility and fire in her. Last night, the spark and will in her had intrigued him, and her presence in his bed had heated a passionate urge that he could barely ignore.

He wondered about her chosen silence and the whisperings of enchantment. Had that come from the rumor he had started himself, years ago, as Elladoune burned? He had hinted at a mystery to keep soldiers away from the girl. The legend had grown around her since then. He wanted to know why.

"JULIANA."

Waking as a hand touched her shoulder, she opened her eyes. Gawain stood beside the cart. His face showed concern, his black brows drawn over thick-lashed brown eyes. His hand and voice were gentle.

"My lady. Wake up, now. Come with me." He reached out to help her sit up.

She did so, head spinning. Was he taking her away from the escort? The thought gave her hope. Gawain scooped his arms under her to lift her out of the cart and set her on her feet, chains chinking. The earth felt solid beneath her feet after so long in the rumbling, shaking cart. He kept a steadying arm around her. It felt good.

De Soulis stood nearby, his face a harsh mask. Gawain led her toward the gray palfrey. Then he took a small key from his belt pouch and unlocked the golden collar and wrist manacles. She smiled up at him, glad to be free of the burden.

Boosting her into the saddle, he turned to his horse and stuffed the links into a leather bag behind the cantle. Then he swung into the saddle.

Juliana sighed with relief, looking around, wondering if they were in Scotland yet. The landscape looked flat and green and English, but they had traveled far while she slept. She still felt mildly confused, but the effects of the wine had lessened.

"What are you doing?" De Soulis cantered toward them. "The king ordered her chained at all times. I agreed you could take her to Avenel, but you do not have the authority to free her of her bonds."

"I will not present my bride to my mother in chains."

She stared at him. Mother? But she did not want to go to his English castle. She only wanted to get back to Scotland.

"Take a guard with you," De Soulis snapped. "She is a valuable prisoner and cannot be let loose."

"She will go nowhere, I assure you. She is so weak she can barely sit a horse. A few days rest will not change her captivity but could save her strength."

"You should not have that key. I will report this to the king and his advisors."

"Report it if you like," Gawain said. "Tell them I treat the woman with courtesy."

"You cannot be trusted," De Soulis sputtered.

"The dungeon cells at Avenel Castle," Gawain said, "are in good repair."

Juliana, listening, gaped at that. She was to be transferred to another English dungeon—at the castle where Gawain's mother resided.

Gawain took hold of her palfrey's rein and drew her horse along as he rode ahead. Juliana swayed in the saddle, hands and knees gripping tight. The summer air was sweet on her bare wrists and throat, but her heart pounded.

Soon she heard the escort ride away in the opposite direction. Relieved at that, at least, she still felt wary. Her Swan Laird had rescued her again—only to draw her deeper into more uncertainty.

If only she could run, then and there, she would do so. But her only choice was to follow where her husband—if she could call him that—led her.

Chapter Eleven

THEY LEFT THE stone road and traveled steadily over grassy hills until they followed the path of a narrow river. At last, in the distance, Juliana saw a castle on a green hillock. Gawain slowed to look at it, then started forward, leading her horse at a fast pace as if eager to get there.

The square walls and central keep shone creamy against the backdrop of a dense greenwood, and the calm river flowed past the side of the mound. Juliana gasped at the lovely picture, feeling a sense of surprise. She had always imagined English castles to be brute fortifications teeming with enemy soldiers. Avenel Castle looked like a haven out of a legend, beautiful enough to house faery royalty.

Following Gawain, she rode across the drawbridge, the horses' hooves pounding over the wooden slats, and passed beneath a raised portcullis into the cool shadow of a stone arch. Inside the enclosed courtyard, instead of armed knights, she saw two young pages run forward and wait for them to dismount.

"Gawain!" Hearing a light female voice, Juliana turned, still in the saddle. The square keep, high and massive, dominated the courtyard; stone steps led from an upper doorway. A young girl descended, calling out, dark braids flying out behind her.

"Eleanor!" Gawain dismounted and swept the girl up into his arms. She was slight and tall, and giggled as she threw her arms around him. Juliana saw she was an adolescent, perhaps his sister;

their dark hair and handsome features were similar.

As Gawain set her down, she beamed up at him. "Ah," he said, "not Eleanor, but Catherine!"

"Aye, Catherine," she confirmed, smiling.

"Gawain!" A second girl ran down the steps. She was a mirror of the first, from the long dark braids plaited with red ribbons to the blue gown banded in embroidery. Juliana blinked, glancing from one to the other.

"Here she is!" Gawain caught the second girl as she hurtled toward him for a hug.

"Robin arrived yesterday," Eleanor said.

"He said we might see you, and that you would bring a bride," Catherine said. Both girls looked toward Juliana. "Greetings," they said together in sweet, eerie echo.

"You must be Juliana," one said. "Welcome to Avenel," said the other.

Juliana stared at them, not returning their beaming smiles, for she felt outside the joy on the moment, overwhelmed and uncertain. She did not know if Gawain would introduce her as his bride or his captive. She was so weary, she wanted to fall from the horse, but was uncertain if she would wake in a featherbed or a dungeon cell.

"What did Robin tell you?" Gawain asked.

"That you wed a Scottish woman on the king's command, that you would both be exhausted. And that he was not sure you would stop here at all."

"We hoped you would not be so cruel as that," one of the girls said.

He glanced at Juliana. "My lady, these are my half-sisters. Eleanor"—he nodded toward the one standing to his right—"and Catherine. This is Lady Juliana Lindsay. My bride."

Nodding, Juliana did not speak. The girls bowed and smiled prettily. They were dark, slender creatures with eyes of a startling gray-green. Old enough to display the courtesy and decorum of highborn ladies, they were yet young enough to lapse into bubbly giggles and expressive looks and grimaces.

"Come inside and meet our mother," Catherine said with a dazzling smile.

Gawain went to Juliana and put his hands around her waist. "I beg you show only sweetness at Avenel Castle, if you will," he murmured as she slid down from the horse. His hands lingered at her waist as he made sure she was stable on her feet.

Then he brushed wisps of her hair off her brow so gently that she blinked and blushed. "Your silence," he murmured, "might keep the soldiers away, but it will only make my little sisters more curious. They will pester you. You can speak to anyone at Avenel without fear." He put an arm around her shoulders and turned with her.

Both girls came forward to hug her. Juliana returned their embraces tentatively, still silent, not quite certain what to say.

The twins fell upon Gawain, patting at his arms as he laughingly fended them off. "You did not send word of your marriage, you oaf!" Eleanor said. "When did you wed?"

"Two days ago. It was rather sudden."

"We thought you would never marry," Catherine said. "Mother thought 'twas hopeless. She has longed for this day!"

"I know," he said quietly, glancing at Juliana.

"But we gave up on you—"

"After all that wooing you did, and all those rejections—"

"Hush, Cat, you will frighten my bride," Gawain said. "How is our lady mother? Well enough to bear this surprise?"

"She already knows," Eleanor said. At least, Juliana thought she was Eleanor, trying to keep pace with their chatter and movement. She noticed that one girl's face was a bit rounder and her laugh lower-pitched. "Robin told her."

"'Twas a shock, but she took it well," Catherine said.

"'A Scot,' she kept saying," Eleanor added. "'A Scot,' as if she could not believe you would wed a Scotswoman with the war on. A Scottish bride for an Avenel is not so favorable, but I think 'tis wonderful because you are—"

"It is fine. Do not fret about it," Gawain said brusquely. "Come, Lady Juliana," he said, taking her arm, for she had stepped back at the implication that a Scottish woman might not be welcome here. "I want you to meet my mother. Is she in her chamber, Nell?"

"Where else, these days? Robin was sitting with her earlier, but he left, and she napped for a bit," Eleanor said.

"She is awake now. I just came from there," Catherine added. "She will want to see your bride right away!"

Gawain walked toward the keep, his hand firm on Juliana's elbow. She went silently, slowly, feeling as if her legs had turned to pudding from weariness, the long ride, and apprehension.

"What did you bring us? A book?" Catherine asked.

"If I give you any more books, your shelf will fall from the wall."

"But you bring us a new book every time you come home," Eleanor said.

"Oh!" he said, as if he just remembered, though he teased them. "There is a book in my pack. The tale of Sir Bevis of Hampton, do you know it?"

"Aye, he fought a dragon and saved England, and crossed a desert to find his love." One spoke and the other sighed dreamily. "Like Saint George. Only not a saint."

"A real knight," Catherine said. "I want to read it."

"What did you see in Newcastle? Did you speak with the king? Did you attend a jousting tournament?" The questions came so fast from both that Juliana could hardly follow. "Robin said you went to a great feast!"

"We did," Gawain said, glancing at Juliana.

"Did you bring something for Mama?" Catherine smiled with such charm and candor that Gawain chuckled. Juliana smiled, feeling herself begin to relax.

"Have you been sweet and kind girls?"

"Always." One batted her eyes, while the other giggled.

"I might have something more for you, and for Mama."

"Robin said you attended the king's feast, and there were subtleties and cakes and swans and acrobats, and you met your bride there. Tell us about it!" one said.

His fingers pressed Juliana's arm in a comforting gesture. She knew he would not tell them what truly happened. "There were cakes and sugar castles, and swans and peacocks. The king was there, but not the queen, who is still in London. I rode in a joust and won the day. And I ate so much at the feast that I nearly burst." He grinned. "But I did not eat as much as Edmund and Robin."

"And you won a bride," Catherine said. The girls had shifted again fluidly, as Juliana, despite her fatigue, tried to note who stood where.

"I did meet her there. She was gowned all in white, the loveliest creature I had ever seen."

Juliana blinked at him in surprise. He did not look at her. "I have other news," he went on. "I am being sent back to Scotland."

"Robin told us that too. Mama was distraught about it."

"Then I have no news for you! I did fear Mama might be upset about it."

"You can reassure her. Tell her about your wedding, and tell us, too," the other girl said. "Do not spare the details. Mama loved the splendid celebrations at court when she and Father went there together." The girl—Eleanor?—pouted. "I wish you had invited us. Newcastle is not so far from Avenel."

"And miss the surprise on your silly faces? 'Twas just a wedding. One day you will realize they are all alike." His teasing grin made the twins moan as together they climbed the stone steps to the keep.

Opening the door, he ushered Juliana and the girls into a shadowed foyer with three doorways and another flight of stairs. "Wait here," Gawain told the twins. "This must be a private audience, aye?" He turned them gently toward a bench, and led Juliana up another section of steps.

As she went, she felt her legs tremble. The sound of their footsteps echoed.

"My sisters like you well," he said. "I apologize for their chatter." He glanced at her, but she did not answer as he led her along a corridor that smelled of stone and, oddly, camphor.

At an arched doorway, he paused. "I must ask that my courtesy to you be repaid."

She tilted her head, curious, waiting.

"I want you to act the happy bride when we enter that room."

Puzzled, she folded her arms and looked away. She would find it hard to play a happy bride, after all this.

"You can speak," he said curtly. "Answer me."

She tilted a brow. "Happy bride? Are you daft?"

"You act the mystery maiden well enough. You can do the other now. Coo and smile, cling to my arm, whatever a joyful bride might do." He held out his elbow.

She pushed it away. "I am not some happy new-made wife. I am a prisoner. Not long ago, I was chained and shamed, and will be again, I expect."

"That was not my doing, or my choice."

"So in return for a little freedom from my chains, you deserve a favor?"

He sighed. "It is all I ask."

"Then promise no more chains."

"That is not a bargain I can make."

"Nor am I a happy bride."

"Please," he whispered. That word, ragged and plaintive, caught her sympathy.

"Why?" she asked softly, intrigued.

"Because I am about to introduce you to my lady mother."

"Are you so terrified of her that you must lie to her, and have me lie to her?"

"Nay," he said, lips tightening.

"Is she a virago, that her son begs favors in corridors to avoid the truth?"

He stepped toward her, and she stepped back until her heel hit the wall. "I swear," he said, "the mute swan is sweeter to the ear than the honking goose."

She glared at him. He returned it, full bore, until she shrank back.

"Whatever your opinion," he said, "just do this. I promise courtesy, though I would rather throttle you just now."

"I will not do it."

"Just for my mother. You can despise me all you like in private."

"Your lady mother should know that her son drags a lass across England in chains," she said. "She should hear how he binds her even as she sleeps, and will not let her go, and keeps her captive so he can gain his king's favor."

"I followed my orders and yet tried to treat you gently."

"Gentle for a guard, rough for a husband."

"You do not want a husband," he reminded her.

"Nor a guard," she retorted. "Especially one who keeps my key, locks and looses me at his will, and wants me to play sweet bride to his courteous knight so he will look the perfect son."

He took another swift step toward her, his cheeks flushing, eyes blazing dark. Juliana pressed her shoulders against the wall as he leaned over her.

"I should never be alone with you," he said, pressing a hand against the wall. "It loosens your tongue."

"Better my tongue than my chains. You cannot control my speech or my silence."

He scowled, slanting his weight forward on his hands to trap her where she stood. "Little Swan Maiden, silent and still," he mused. "Delicate lady in need of a champion. Wildcat and hellion who wants help from no one. Sometimes a bitter-tongued Highland fishwife. Who the devil are you?"

"Just a lass who wants to go home. So much," she added in a whisper, and her chin wobbled, tears stinging.

"I will take you there, but first you must play the part of my wife. Please," he added.

She narrowed her eyes. "That is all you ask of me?"

"Aye."

"You do not expect… wifely duties?"

His gaze slowly raked her down, then up. "None," he murmured, his eyes so keen that she glanced away. "Until you want it too, and grant yourself to me freely."

Silence lingered. She watched him. "If I do this, you will take me to Inchfillan?"

"We can stop on our way to Elladoune. That too is home, is it not?"

"Elladoune!" She looked at him in surprise.

"I am to command that garrison. You may have been asleep when it was mentioned."

"It would have been courteous to tell me we were going there. I thought I was going to another prison." Her heart beat hard and fast. She had never thought to set foot in Elladoune again, and now the chance had come. "We will go there as husband and wife? Or as king's man and captive?"

"Husband and wife would be more peaceful."

"Aye," she admitted, then frowned as he leaned close. She could feel the warmth of his breath on her lips. Without thinking, as if she were spellbound, she tilted her head back and closed her eyes.

"I wonder," he whispered, "what a peaceful marriage might be like between us."

She parted her lips, watching him. He closed his eyes, and then gently pressed his lips to hers.

Unexpected pleasure whirled through her. A flash of desire, hot and bright, followed. She almost moaned with the urge of it, nearly cried from the sudden tenderness that tugged at her. But she kept still and passive.

He drew back. "Is it so much trouble," he murmured, "to pretend contentment for a little while? It takes much out of a person to be angry and on guard all the time."

She stared, heart racing crazily, breath deep and fast. She leaned toward him, breathless, wanting what he offered so much—but then pressed to the wall again.

"Juliana, I beg of you to do this."

She sighed. "Will you expect the same at Elladoune? Doing your will."

He growled under his breath. "Please yourself." He stepped away.

"I will think on it," she said quickly, feeling that she had gone too far in her anger.

The door behind him opened, and a servant woman looked out.

"Sir Gawain," the woman said.

He took Juliana's hand. "Act sweetly," he said, and pulled her along with him.

Chapter Twelve

THE BEDCHAMBER WAS shadowed, its windows partly shuttered despite the mild weather. The woman seated in a chair beside the crackling hearth fire wore a blanket over her knees. Gawain walked into the room, releasing Juliana's hand. He looked at his mother, and his heart hurt.

She was thinner than he had ever seen her, though he had visited but a month ago. Dark-haired and brown-eyed like her son, Lady Clarice was still beautiful, though she had lost strength. A slowly progressing disease seemed to clarify her, illuminate her from within. Now she seemed more spirit than flesh, as if she were gradually transforming on the path toward death.

Her hair was leaden in color, her eyes sunken and shadowed, but a light burned bright and warm in her eyes. Her bony frame was yet elegant in her face and in the thin hands draped over the arms of the chair.

She smiled. "Gawain!"

"Mama." He bent to kiss her parchment cheek. "I trust God keeps you safe."

"Safe enough, and better now that we had your news from Robin. My dear, you are too thin. We must feed you well while you are here." She peered past him. "So this is your bride!"

"Lady Juliana Lindsay," he said softly. He walked over to take his bride's hand and lead her forward, praying she would guard her tongue with his mother and not upset her. He feared to stir the shadow of death that hovered too close.

"This is Lady Clarice of Avenel," he told Juliana. She nodded, her dark blue eyes huge in her pale face as she looked from his mother back to him. He sensed her astonishment, for he had not said that his mother was gravely ill. The words were too hard to speak.

"Robin said you had married," Lady Clarice said. "Joyful news, if a surprise. King Edward is full of surprises these days. Henry asked for advice in finding a match for you, and then the king orders you wed to one of his own guests. The Swan Laird and his Swan Maiden. How kind of Edward."

"Aye," Gawain said, understanding the story Robin must have brought his stepmother, no doubt at Henry of Avenel's urging.

"Juliana, my dear, welcome." Clarice tried to stand. "Come here, let me see you."

Gawain murmured a protest, reaching out. The servant girl stepped forward to press Lady Clarice's shoulder until she subsided in the chair. The girl plumped a pillow behind her.

"Oh, go away, Philippa," Clarice said irritably. "Stop fussing. I am not a piece of glass. I want to greet my new daughter, and you only embarrass me. His bride will be frightened if she sees an old lady in a sickroom. Help me up, Gawain." The servant looked at Gawain in appeal. He sighed and assisted his mother to her feet.

She was fragile but stubborn and he steadied her like a worried parent. "Mama, go easy—"

"Oh, hush. Welcome to Avenel, Juliana. Our home is yours."

Juliana moved toward her. "Lady Clarice," she replied, and bowed her head. "I am so honored by your gracious welcome."

Breathing out in relief, Gawain took Juliana's hand and drew her closer. She gave him an adoring smile, sweet and guileless. He smiled in sincere gratitude.

He wanted to kiss her again. The honey taste of it still lingered on his lips, still warmed his blood. He wanted this sweet bride, even if it was just a ruse.

"Come here, sweeting," Clarice said. "Oh, you are lovely, though grimy from the road. Gawain, did you set a soldier's pace? The poor girl looks exhausted."

"We could have been more considerate," he admitted. "Philippa, please order a bath to be prepared in my room for my wife."

Philippa nodded, and at her mistress's gesture, left the room. "Did you bring your things with you, Lady Juliana, or will they arrive later?" Clarice asked. "We can find something fresh for you to wear. That gown is lovely, but it looks in need of repair."

Juliana hesitated. "Ah—my things—"

"Will be sent north," Gawain added hastily. "We can only stay for a night or two. I have a new assignment in Scotland, Mama."

"I heard! Must you go so soon? I hoped you would stay for a few weeks. You have been away from Avenel for years and only make brief visits."

"I know." He felt the loss of those years keenly as he sensed his mother's waning strength. "The king is sending three thousand men to Scotland. His commanders have ordered a soldier's pace for every group. We must depart soon for that reason. But I wanted you to meet Juliana."

"I hoped the king would allow you to stay in England this time or send you to the Welsh border. Not to Scotland again."

"I do not mind," Gawain said softly.

Lady Clarice looked at Juliana. "My husband told me you are a Scotswoman. Lindsay... I know the name." She frowned as if trying to recall something.

"My father was Alexander Lindsay of Elladoune."

Clarice inhaled sharply. "Elladoune?"

"'Tis in central Scotland," Juliana answered.

"I have heard of it." Lady Clarice looked at her son. "Is she a kinswoman of James Lindsay, the rebel—"

"Aye," he said brusquely.

"You know my cousin?" Juliana asked Gawain, frowning.

"I have met him. I am to be constable of Elladoune and its new garrison, Mama."

"Oh, dear," his mother said faintly. "Why would the king allow you to wed the cousin of the man who caused you such trouble—"

"I am sure Edward wants to encourage loyalty among the Scottish rebels by matching a Scotswoman to a loyal Avenel," he said, though he did not believe it.

"Ah. That makes sense. Surely Lady Juliana and her close kin are loyal."

"Surely." He felt Juliana's curious gaze. "Mama, please sit." She did not protest as he helped her back into her chair. Juliana stepped forward to tuck the pillows behind her and spread a blanket over her lap.

Lady Clarice smiled. "What a lovely pair you two make, the lady so pale and delicate, the knight so strong and dark. Swan Maiden and her Swan Knight." She sighed and leaned her head against the high back of the chair. "That reminds me of a legend I heard long agon. But who would want to hear an old woman's rambling thoughts."

"Swan Laird, Mama. And you are not a rambling old woman."

Her eyes sheened with tears. "I am happy for you, Gawain." She reached out for Juliana's hand and took his as well. "For you both. She is kind and lovely, and I see she loves you already," she whispered. "Who would not? The girls who rejected your marriage suits were dimwits!"

"Rejected?" Juliana murmured.

"Mama," Gawain said hastily. "You must rest. I will send for Philippa."

As he spoke, a plump ginger cat slipped out from under the bed in the center of the room and crossed toward them, tail high, followed by three kittens, white, ginger, and a mix of both. The mother cat leaped into Lady Clarice's lap, and the kittens scampered under her chair. The smallest ginger kitten reached out a tiny paw to bat at the blanket.

"What's this? They should not be disturbing you." Gawain stooped to lift the large cat from his mother's lap. "Easy," he said. "This is no seat for a great beast like you."

"I like her company," his mother protested.

He set the mother cat down and stooped again to pick up the little ginger one, boneless and warm and tiny, and gently handed it to his lady mother.

"This one is less burden for you. I will fetch Philippa for you. Juliana—" He turned to see his bride on her hands and knees watching the two kittens beneath Clarice's chair. She cooed with delight and then straightened with the tiny white one balled in her hands. Her pale, solemn face had transformed. She glowed with joy. Gawain blinked. She was beautiful. Happy, he thought.

"Oh, my lady, they are so wee and bonny!" Juliana said.

"Bonny, aye," Lady Clarice said. "Please, sweeting, take the kitten for your own."

"'Tis unsuitable for our journey," Gawain said.

"Nonsense. Pippa can ride in a basket," Lady Clarice said.

"Pippa?" Juliana asked.

"The twins named the little white one after Philippa, even though she dislikes cats," the lady answered. "Or perhaps because she dislikes them."

Gawain chuckled and bent to unfasten the ginger kitten from its grip on the blanket in his mother's lap. The kitten tried to sink tiny teeth in his finger, and he disengaged it gently, allowing it to knead its way up his arm to his shoulder.

"This one cannot stay still," he said, while Juliana and Clarice laughed. Juliana nestled her cheek against the white kitten's head. Gawain set down the tiny ginger, who ran away and came back again, nearly underfoot.

"Pippa is yours now, and you may call her what you like," his mother said. "Gawain may keep his little ginger friend if he likes."

Juliana laughed, an enchanting silvery sound, so sweet that Gawain barely noticed the kitten had dropped down to play with the thongs on his boots. He looked at it. "Ho there, Sir Bevis, do you think me a great dragon?"

Juliana laughed again, brightly. Gawain grinned.

"Bevis is perfect for that one!" Lady Clarice said.

"And Pippa is perfect for this sweet wee thing," Juliana said as she rubbed her fingers over the kitten's head and back, her touch gentle and sure. She glanced at Gawain, her smile dazzling, eyes sparkling like stars in the night sky.

His heart simply melted. He had feared she might be defiant with his mother, yet she played the loving bride so well that he almost believed it himself. Here he saw another facet of her, like a jewel changing in the light. Fascinated, he watched her.

The mother cat came toward them, stepping haughtily, raising a paw as if to declare that she wanted her kittens with her again. Bevis scampered away, and Juliana bent to pet the mother, keeping Pippa curled securely and happily in her hand.

"Do not touch that tabby," Gawain said. "She is a bad-tempered creature. No one but my mother can touch her."

Even as he spoke, Juliana was down on her knees, soothing the mother's long back with her free hand. The cat lifted her head and closed her eyes, purring loudly.

Lady Clarice gasped. "That tabby avoids everyone and barely tolerates me. I have never seen her take to anyone so quickly. Oh my saints, look at that."

Juliana scratched the top of the cat's head gently and smiled. The third and smallest of the kittens, the ginger and white mix with a touch of gray on the ears, crawled out from under the blanket to rub against Lady Clarice's leg. "This wee kitten loves you especially, my lady. May I name her for you?"

Lady Clarice smiled. "What name shall it be?"

"Marguerite," she said. "For she is delicate like the flower and has a soothing temperament." She bent and scooped up the kitten and placed her on Lady Clarice's lap. The kitten curled up and went to sleep immediately, having a quieter spirit than her more rambunctious brother and sister.

His mother smiled at Gawain. "My dear lad, the angels have sent you one of their own for a bride. The kittens love her, and even that disagreeable cat likes her."

Gawain helped Juliana to stand. He raised her hand to his lips and kissed it, filled with gratitude. She had done far more than he had hoped. She had brought his mother a little joy, and he was in her debt for that. He cleared his tight throat and nodded.

"Aye," he said. "An angel indeed—when she wants."

SIGHING LOUDLY, JULIANA sank deeper into the high-walled wooden tub as the steaming water soothed and enveloped her. She wanted to linger here, undisturbed and peaceful, letting the deliciously hot, rose-scented water coax tension and fatigue from her body.

She scooped soap out of a small pot, feeling flecks of lavender and herbs in the slippery stuff as she lathered herself and washed and rinsed her hair. The abbot's house at Inchfillan had few luxuries, nor had there been many at Elladoune in her childhood.

The true luxury was being utterly alone, thoroughly clean, relaxing a little at last after the ordeal of the past weeks. She glanced around Gawain's bedchamber, a pleasant room, not large but furnished with simple elegance. The wood furniture was finely carved and polished, woven rush mats covered the floors, the walls were lime-washed and bordered in a painted diamond pattern, and the window was shuttered below with genuine leaded glass above. A red-curtained bed filled one corner of the room.

She did not want to think about the bed. Its pillows and thick mattress, neatly covered in red brocade, stirred curious excitement in her. She imagined Gawain unclothed with his muscled torso gleaming. Vividly, she recalled the feel of his arms around her and a simple yet astonishing kiss.

Groaning softly, she leaned her head back. Whatever the future held, she would face it when it came rather than fret now. She closed her eyes and tried to clear the thoughts that tumbled through her mind.

She must have dozed. When she opened her eyes, the water was cool and the room was dark but for the low fire in the hearth. Climbing out of the tub, she dried herself with a linen sheet and sat on a hearthside stool. Combing her fingers through her hair, she felt its fine texture beginning to dry in the heat. She began making a single fat braid of its damp golden sleekness.

Philippa had left a gown and other things on the bed. Juliana quickly slipped into the garments: linen hose, tied at the knees with ribbons; a chemise of pale silk; and a mulberry gown of serge that buttoned at the neck and fit her torso closely, swelling full over her hips.

The hem, like the white satin gown, was far too long—perhaps that was fashionable in England, she thought. Her gowns at Inchfillan were practical, simple garments that left feet and ankles unencumbered.

She thought of home and the hills and lochside where she loved to walk. Soon she would see Scotland, but she might never have freedom again. Her life had changed.

Picking up a white veil of sheer silk and a circlet of braided silks, she set it down again, not eager to wear a married woman's headgear yet. Instead, she slid her feet into leather shoes tied with thongs and then explored the room, trailing her fingers over the dark polished wood of such fine furniture.

Avenel was a beautiful home, she thought. Every room was well-kept, and the family was warm and charming. She could see that Gawain loved them. She envied that.

Her family had been scattered far and wide. Her father was dead, her elder brothers were with the Scottish king's troops, and her mother had consigned herself years ago to a religious life, leaving her children in the care of Abbot Malcolm. For years, Juliana felt as if Malcolm and the monks, along with Deirdre, the abbot's sister and housekeeper, were true family to her and her younger brothers Iain and Alec.

At the thought of her little brothers, worry rushed back. She felt anxious again, wanting to return to her brothers and her other kin and friends. The need felt painful and insistent.

Each moment in England felt like another strand of her heart pulling, tearing loose. Scotland was in her blood, part of her soul. She had to go back.

She fought sudden tears and a yearning ache. Deep in her heart, she longed for something more, uncertain what it was. Home, certainly; love, perhaps. Thinking of Gawain, her husband, she sighed.

She was just tired, she thought, lonely and frightened. Covering her face in her hands, she sobbed. When a knock sounded on the door, she lifted her head.

"A moment, Philippa," she called. Sniffling, wiping her eyes, she crossed to the door to undo the iron latch and pin, and opened it to see Gawain.

Startled, she felt her heart bound. He smiled and tilted his head. He looked astonishingly handsome—freshly shaved, cheeks flushed from a bath, hair damp, its waves brushing the column of his neck. His dusty surcoat and chainmail had been replaced by a tunic of dark green. A soapy fragrance, herbs and sage, wafted toward her.

He frowned. "Are you unwell?"

"Just tired," she replied, but his tender question almost undid her, for she was still close to tears. She stepped back, sniffling.

He entered, carrying the pack that had been strapped to his horse's saddle. As he set it on the floor, she heard the harsh jangle of the chains tucked inside.

"Come to chain me for the night?" she snapped.

"Not yet," he said dryly. "If you are ready, my family would like you to join us for supper in the solar. My mother is not strong enough to come to the hall for meals, so we gather in the solar with her. My sisters are hoping to read to us tonight since I brought them a book."

"I must finish dressing. I was expecting Philippa."

"She is with my mother. My sisters wanted to help you dress, but I thought you needed better peace than that. Their little handmaid is as giggly as they are, so I told them I would fetch you myself. They think me eager to be alone with you. It delights them."

"But it does not delight you." She went toward the bed to pick up the white veil.

"If you need help, I can assist. I know naught about weaving odds and ends into the hair, as the twins like to do, but I can fasten bits and bobs."

"I am nearly done." She slid the silk through her hands. "Go on. I will join you."

"My dear wife," he said, folding his arms and leaning against the door, "this castle is a maze of halls and stairways. You might get lost."

"And what a shame if I found a way out and escaped to Scotland," she muttered. She shook the veil, floated the rectangle over her hair, and slipped the braided silken circlet over the crown of her head. "There. A wife for you."

"I see. Lovely. There would be dire consequences if you tried to escape."

"Dire for you, bonny for me."

"Swan Maiden," he said, "do you still think to fly away?"

"They do say I have that power." She adjusted the veil.

He came closer. "It is crooked. Let me—"

Flustered, she stepped away. "I can manage."

"My mother, and other married women I have seen, wear theirs just so." He tugged on the veil so that it cradled the crown of her head. Shivers slipped through her as he picked up the silken ends and tucked them around her throat, wrapping one longer side under the headpiece. His thumb grazed her jaw just above the silk under her chin. "There."

"Thank you." Shivers cascaded through her still, even when

he lowered his hands.

He went to the door to pull it open for her, smiling. Fine lines crinkled around his warm brown eyes.

She tilted her head. "Why are you kind and charming to me at times, and so hard with me otherwise?" she asked. "What is it you want from this marriage?"

He frowned a little. "What does any man want from a wife?"

"Since you have let me be so far, it is not lust," she said boldly. "If you want land, wealth, or title, you will not have those of me. I have no inheritance worth claiming. Perhaps you just want the king's favor."

He closed the door abruptly and leaned a hand against it, his arm above her head. "Each time you see a chance to sting me, you try, lady. My patience grows short with it."

"My patience grows short, too."

"You have none."

"I do, when I want. I just want to be free. I have had enough of captivity."

"But not enough of honing your anger on me. I am not your enemy or your tormentor. I have shown you naught but kindness, and I expect some in return."

She looked away, feeling her cheeks burn. He spoke the truth. She had behaved poorly toward him even though he had helped her. "Likely you just intend to shut me up in Elladoune in a dungeon or a convent, and await new orders from your king."

"If you cannot rein in that damnable temper, it is true you may find yourself shut in a tower somewhere."

She flashed him a scathing look and felt as if it met a brick wall. He stared at her until she glanced away. "But you may keep your kitten in your cell with you," he added when she was silent. "She is in the solar, awaiting you in a basket."

She pursed her lips. "I will be kind to your mother and your sisters too. As for you—"

"Being kind to my mother is more important to me."

"I do not wish to upset her. She is a good lady."

"Aye," he said gruffly. "Juliana—my mother and sisters do not know the full truth about us, or you. And we will not tell them."

"They will cease to like me if they learn the truth."

"I doubt it, but—" He heaved a sigh. "My mother may not live long enough to learn the truth. We will not burden her or the girls, who have enough to bear with our mother so ill, with the poor circumstances of our marriage or the king's orders."

She nodded. "For now. And later?"

"We shall see. We will go on to Scotland and abide by the king's orders."

"Ah. Chains for me and lessons in obedience. Land and accolades for you."

He huffed in frustration and his eyes seemed to blaze. "Do you think I wanted this?" he demanded. "Do you think I like seeing you chained, and displayed?"

"You did not prevent it."

He closed his eyes. A muscle moved in his jaw. "I had choices to make. There are matters you know naught about, and reasons for what I do."

"Tell me, then. Why are you part of this? You do not seem like a man who would play the king's cruel games. Yet you do it."

"I do indeed," he said softly. "For now."

"What do you want from this marriage and this evil scheme to keep me?"

He let out a breath. "What I want," he said, "I gave up on years ago."

Juliana sensed tension in him—and a current of sadness, even loneliness. She tilted her head in sympathy. "There is something you desire," she said. "What is it?"

"Whatever my king wants, of course," he said brusquely and opened the door. "Supper grows cold, and my family is eager to see you. Remember," he said as she sailed past him into the corridor, "for now, you adore me."

"Oh," she said flippantly, "of course I do!" She marched ahead of him and heard his dry chuckle behind her.

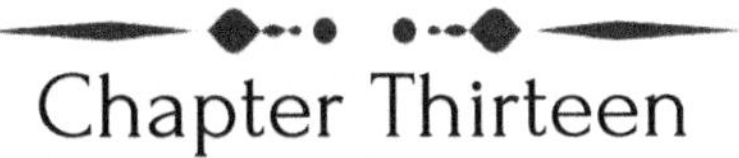

Chapter Thirteen

"A N ELDERLY MAN, a wife he took to hand, the king's daughter of Scotland…"

Eleanor's voice skimmed over the opening passages of the story of Bevis of Hampton. Listening, Gawain stretched out a hand to scratch the ears of the old mixed breed hound that lay beside the fire.

"This maid, I have ye told,

Fair maid she was and bold,

And nobly born."

He glanced at Juliana. Seated in a chair beside him, she held the white kitten in her lap while she, too, listened. Fate had certainly brought him a fair maid of Scotland, he thought. What might come next, he did not know.

At a groan from Robin, he looked up to see his stepbrother seated at a table facing their sister Catherine over a chessboard, lamenting the clever move she had made. Eleanor continued to read, curled at her mother's feet, turning the parchment pages of the illuminated manuscript. Lady Clarice had a blanket tucked over her legs despite the warm room. She stifled a deep cough behind a cloth and took a sip of wine. Philippa looked up quickly while sewing, seated on a chair in a corner, always attentive.

Despite the uncertainty of his mother's illness, Gawain felt content here with his family. What surprised him was how much Juliana's presence added to that feeling. He watched her dangle a ribbon for the kitten's amusement. He wished this peaceful, loving moment—like a little bubble containing paradise—could continue indefinitely.

His gaze flowed over her from head to foot and up again. The plum-colored gown contrasted with her pale golden coloring, and her cheeks were pinkened from the heat of the fire. The cut of the fabric enhanced her lithe body while revealing the grace of her long throat. Profoundly attracted to her, uncertain how she felt, he glanced away. Eleanor finished her passage and she and their mother sat staring at him.

"A fine story," he said hastily. "A good adventure, though lacking the poetry of some epic tales, such as that of Gawain and the Green Knight."

"Few could surpass the Gawain poet." Lady Clarice smiled. "I favor it so much that I gave my son that name." She smiled. "But this is an exciting story. We shall hear more tomorrow evening. Juliana, have you heard the tale of Bevis before?"

Juliana shook her head, her fingers gentle on the kitten. "I have not, my lady."

"No doubt Juliana has heard many other stories," Catherine said. "Scots are said to be fine storytellers. Gawain, surely you remember tales from your earlier days?"

He shrugged. "'Twas long ago," he murmured. "My grand—" He stopped, recalling that Juliana was not aware that he was part Scottish. His mother, who did not like it mentioned, frowned. He cleared his throat. "Er, we had no time for stories. We were concerned with other matters."

"Matters of war," Juliana muttered.

He smiled. "Sweet lady wife." Her answering smile was forced.

"Lady Juliana," Robin said, "do not fret. Ladies can leave matters of war to men who are trained to it."

She scowled at him. "Were war left to women," she said,

"there would be no wars." Robin blushed and lifted a hand in near surrender.

"Well done!" Lady Clarice smiled.

"Juliana, what did you most like to do in Scotland?" Catherine asked. "Where is your castle?"

"I lived in a place called Elladoune. But it was burned by English." Her blunt reply caused Lady Clarice and the twins to gasp. Gawain frowned, almost dreading what might come next, wondering if he should try to stop it.

"My mother told my brothers and me many tales and legends about warriors and their ladies. Wonderful, magical stories," she went on. Relieved, Gawain hoped she would not press the other issue. "Later, we lived in the forest with outlaws and dispossessed families. I learned to hide from English soldiers. But we still heard tales at night around the fire, told by a harper left homeless by the war."

"Oh my," Lady Clarice said faintly. "Homeless! Dear saints. We did not realize that you were a victim of the Scottish war."

"Most Scots are affected by the war in some way, Mama," Gawain said. He felt humbled, for he should have realized that Juliana had lived homeless after Elladoune. He leaned down to pet the old dog at his feet, wishing he had asked her about it.

"I lived in the forest for two years, my lady," Juliana said. "We were safe there with the outlaws and those whose homes had been forfeited or destroyed. We learned to fend for ourselves and avoid the English."

Oh aye, Gawain thought, listening. She knew well how to fend for herself. And he realized more clearly why she did not trust English knights.

"Go on," Catherine said. "What then?"

"My father died fighting for freedom, and my mother entered a convent in her grief. We were taken in by a cousin, an abbot, and we lived in his house on the abbey grounds. His sister lived there with us. My two older brothers went to fight with the rebels. I have two younger brothers too, still with the abbot," she added.

"But how did you come to be a guest in the king's court?" Eleanor asked.

Gawain focused his attention on the hound. Juliana's hands stilled on the kitten.

"She was a guest, Mama," Robin spoke up before Gawain or Juliana could answer. "She was—invited to the king's feast to represent his hope for an end to the Scottish war. She was dressed as a swan, in satin and feathers, and the king himself called her a Swan Maiden. Was she not beautiful, Gawain?"

"She took my breath away, I swear it." That was the truth.

"Swan? Oh, the pretty feather cap," Clarice said, nodding.

Gawain sighed and rubbed a hand over his face. He loved his family, but knew they found it awkward to face hard truth sometimes. If Henry and Edmund had been there, they would have supported Robin's story too.

His family preferred ideals and pretty versions of the truth. They avoided strong emotions. He had seen that intensify during his mother's illness. Henry Avenel was protective of his wife and wanted her to be happy, even if it meant disguising the truth.

And so his Scottish birth and kinship were rarely mentioned. As a boy, he had been hurt by that, but later understood. His mother wanted him to be a favored English knight with no taint of a Scottish name and background. But he suspected she still grieved for his father, whom she had loved deeply.

Yet she loved Henry faithfully, and he adored her. He had provided a luxurious and privileged life and had shielded his family and his stepson well. So if they preferred to embellish the truth about Juliana, Gawain would not correct them.

Yet he never embroidered or denied any matter. The influence of his Scottish father and kin early in his life had given him a hunger for honesty.

He glanced again at Juliana. She had the quick-witted frankness of a Scot, and he found that refreshing, reliable, and familiar. In part, that drew him to her. She would find the unspoken rules within the Avenel family hard to understand.

But she sensed the difference, for she had gone along with whatever was said and done around her. Sometimes her delicate brows lowered over those sapphire eyes, but she kept her thoughts and the truth to herself. He blessed her for it, even knowing she reserved her frankness for Gawain.

"My son was of course a perfect Swan Knight," Lady Clarice went on, still talking about the king's feast. "My family are De Bohuns, Juliana. Swans have been part of our family crest for generations. They say that long ago, one of our ancestors was a legendary hero named Helias, called the Swan Knight."

Juliana looked at Gawain, wide-eyed. He shrugged a little sheepishly; the idea of calling himself the Swan Laird, years ago when he encountered her in the loch at Elladoune, had not come to him out of midair.

"We have a swan on the Lindsay crest as well," Juliana said. "Swans have lived on the loch at Elladoune for longer than anyone can remember. There is an old legend that tells how they first appeared there."

"I would love to hear it," Eleanor said.

"Someday I shall tell you," Juliana said. "Lady Clarice, are you unwell?"

Gawain started, seeing his mother lift a hand to cover her face. She lowered it. "I am fine. And I am sure—that the swans at Elladoune are a lovely sight." Her voice sounded weak. "Gawain would enjoy seeing them." Her gaze met his, and he sensed that her old grief had renewed, hearing of the swans near their old home in Scotland.

"I want my husband to see the swans of Elladoune," Juliana said.

Bless her again, he thought, for being kind to his mother. For a moment, the marriage between them felt real and good, no pretense at all. He could easily imagine loving her. Seated close to her, he reached out to touch her cheek.

She tilted her head away from his touch.

"I am tired and will retire to bed now," Lady Clarice said. "My daughters must go to bed too. Juliana, welcome again to our family. I can see that my son loves you, and I see you care about him too." Tears shone in her eyes. "It makes my heart glad."

Gawain took Juliana's hand and kissed it. She curled her fingers over his.

"We are glad too," Catherine said. "But unhappy that we missed their wedding."

"We can have a wedding celebration here!" Eleanor said, and beckoned to Catherine, who came close to whisper with her sister.

"We had a nice feast at supper this evening," Lady Clarice said.

"But we want the fun of a wedding with dancing, music, and guests," Catherine said. "We have had no guests here for a long while, other than Father's friends, who only come to discuss military policies."

"Juliana and I have traveled far. We are too tired for dancing and too full for more feasting," Gawain said. "We must keep the household quiet for Mama's sake. Later, when she feels stronger, we will have music and dancing, if you like."

Eleanor folded her arms petulantly. "Then you should pay a forfeit for not inviting us to your celebration."

"And keeping us from going to the king's court," Catherine added.

"Forfeit?" Gawain asked. "Shall I dance or sing, as they do in court?"

"Girls, you will regret it if you ask him," Robin said.

The twins laughed, and Eleanor looked inspired. "We shall follow you to the bed chamber with horns and drums, and flowers and candlelight, as they do on the night of a wedding! We shall put you to bed with great ceremony and noise to bless the union, and keep the evil spirits away!"

Gawain gave them a sour look. "That will not be necessary," he said sternly.

"They are too weary for revelry, girls," Lady Clarice said. "And you two do not need to witness a bedding."

"Oh, Mama, we know about such things! Listen to what the heroine says of Bevis—" Eleanor flipped through a few pages, ran her finger down, and began to read.

"Had I taken a young knight,
That was not bruised in war or fight,
As he is,
And would me love day and night,
Embracing and kissing with all his might,
And make for me bliss..."

"Oh, for such bliss!" Catherine cried, clasping her hands. "The joy of true love!"

"Gawain must forfeit kisses!" Eleanor said, and Catherine squealed in agreement. The twins grinned up at him.

He noticed Juliana laughing, her face tucked against the kitten's snowy fur. Grousing for good effect, Gawain rose from his seat and bent to kiss first one and then the other giggling sister on the cheek.

"Nay, silly, not us," Eleanor said. "Kiss your bride!"

"Each time we say, you must kiss your bride!" Catherine said, nodding to Eleanor. "That is your forfeit!"

"You owe us this! We most heartfully wanted to see you wed," Eleanor insisted. "Mama said 'twould never happen, you know, but we were hopeful someone would find you pleasing."

Gawain saw Robin smother a grin behind his hand. His mother's eyes glowed with laughter. In the corner, Philippa chuckled as she sewed a seam.

Juliana smiled, her cheeks pink. He sighed dramatically and turned toward her, bending. She tipped her cheek and he kissed it chastely. She smelled of roses and lavender from her bath. Crazily, he wanted to linger.

"On the mouth, with all your might—just as the book says!"

Catherine insisted.

"Make bliss for her, you silly oaf!" Eleanor crowed.

"Girls," Lady Clarice admonished.

"Oh, let him forfeit," Robin said. "Gawain owes his bride some courtesy, for I would wager her hasty wedding—and what followed—did not suit a lady's dreams."

Gawain sent him a scathing look. He leaned toward Juliana again, meaning only to kiss her cheek, but she turned her head and his mouth met hers. After a dizzying instant of sweetness, he withdrew.

The girls applauded. He smiled, glad to see his mother laughing. He felt responsible, in part, for the sadness that had come to this family lately. None of them had laughed freely or well since their brother Geoffrey had died.

But Juliana did not smile. She blushed and lowered her head to the white kitten.

"There is your forfeiture," he told the twins. "Now go to bed, you imps."

Catherine smiled at Eleanor. "We shall demand more kisses tomorrow. A proper wedding has days of merrymaking."

"You do owe us more celebration," Eleanor told Gawain.

"And Lady Juliana needs more bliss," Catherine whispered loudly. This sent Eleanor into a giggling fit.

"Good night, daughters," Lady Clarice said. "Philippa, take them to find their maid if you will."

Philippa rose from her seat, while the twins kissed their mother. Eleanor picked up the volume of Bevis, and the girls left the room whispering to each other.

"Those two," Gawain said, "are heartily spoiled."

"They are young," Lady Clarice said gently. "Let them have their joy. Too soon, life may take it from them." She stood. "Can someone help me to my bed?" she asked faintly. Gawain took a long stride forward, as did Robin.

"Let me help you, my lady," Juliana said, rising. She handed the white kitten to Gawain, then turned to Lady Clarice.

"My thanks, sweeting," his mother answered in acceptance, allowing Juliana to assist her. "Philippa will come back soon. Then you and Gawain should retire too. You must be very tired after your journey." Lady Clarice moved forward with Juliana and looked at her sons. "Robin, find a page and tell him to bring mulled wine for me, and some for Juliana. Gawain, your bride has dark circles under her eyes—'tis in part her fair complexion, but she is weary. See that she rests."

"I will, Mama," he said softly, opening the connecting door that led into his mother's bedchamber. Juliana guided the fragile lady through. "God be with you."

He turned back to see Robin watching him. "Your bride is not so silent after all," he said. "So that mysterious silence of hers is a ruse?"

"Aye. But we Avenels are not unfamiliar with pretense."

Robin looked sheepish. "Father told me to tell our lady mother that Juliana was a guest of the king, and chosen for you as a favor. He did not think she would react well to the truth about your bride."

"I understand," Gawain said. He looked down at the kitten squirming playfully in his hands and scratched its tiny, snowy head gently. "I wonder if any of us will ever learn the full truth about my bride," he muttered half to himself.

"I will not tell anyone else that she speaks if 'tis a secret," Robin said.

"Good. She has her reasons, whatever they are."

"Good night, then. I will have wine sent up. Blessings to you on your wedding, brother," he added with a smile. "Mother is pleased. That is what matters most."

"Aye." Gawain lifted the kitten and looked into its wide-eyed, innocent stare. He chuckled as the kitten nuzzled his cheek.

"Look, another female who would forfeit a kiss from you," Robin said, laughing.

━━ ◆··• •··◆ ━━

Chapter Fourteen

"SHE'S ABED, SIR. Good night and God bless ye both," Philippa whispered as she slipped out of Gawain's bedchamber. He nodded his thanks, having waited outside the chamber while Philippa had helped Juliana prepare for bed. He pushed the door open.

Candlelight lent a deep glow to the red-curtained bed. Juliana sat propped on pillows under the scarlet brocade coverlet. Her golden hair flowed over her bare shoulders as she held the coverlet to her chest, hands clutching the fabric. The white kitten lay curled in the middle of her lap.

As Gawain came forward, Juliana watched him, eyes wide. He bent to pick up the leather pack on the floor. Chains jangled inside as he moved it. He only meant to extract a clean shirt, but had to remove the chains to do that.

Juliana gave a little gasp as he held the chains and bands. He frowned. The king's orders were clear and he had already disobeyed by bringing her to Avenel unbound. Escape was a possibility once he went to sleep, but he loathed the idea of restraining her.

"Ah," she said. "The golden collar. Will that be the secret of our nights at Avenel?"

"My orders are to keep the Swan Maiden from fleeing."

"So you will chain me like a bird in this fine cage?" She waved a hand at the rich canopy and curtains on the great bed of carved and polished walnut.

"I do not like this any more than you do."

"You could trust me," she said.

"So close to Scotland? I know you better than that, I think."

"And I thought I knew you. I thought you would treat me with courtesy here. Your family has been muckle kind to me."

"You have utterly charmed them. You are like that kitten, there. It is in your nature to be charming, sweet…but both of you have claws."

"And the Swan Maiden has wings, so they say. But you would pinion me."

"I want to trust you." He poured the chains from one hand to the other. He hated them. But he could not risk losing her. Too much depended on keeping her in his care.

Like a bird near a windowsill, he knew she would fly if she had the chance. That was truly her nature, he realized, to seek freedom.

"The chains are heavy," she said. "They hurt."

He had seen the marks and bruises. "I know."

She sighed. "Will you fetch that for me, there?" she asked, pointing toward a pile of folded clothing on top of a large wooden chest. "I cannot get up just now," she said, blushing, a hand to her bare upper chest. "Would you fetch me the white silk?"

Puzzled, he went there to pick up a silk chemise, a veil, a ribbon, not knowing which piece she meant, and brought them to her. The chains swung in one hand.

She motioned for him to turn away. He did. When he turned back, she had already slipped the creamy silk chemise over her head and tugged it down. Then she slid the delicate veil through her hands, rolled its length, and wrapped an end around her left wrist, knotting it. She held the other end out toward him.

"I will prove you can trust me. Tie this to the bedpost. I will not go anywhere, even if I could undo it. I promise."

He realized then she was also offering him her fledgling trust. He did not speak, brows tucked.

"If you please," she said, "the chains are horrible. At least this way I can sleep. And you can keep me captive here, as you intend."

"I hope your opinion of me is better than that." He flung the golden links away, where they fell jangling on the leather bag. Then he stripped off his surcoat and tunic and tossed them after the chains. Kicking off his boots and hose, he turned to the bed clad only in his calf-length braies and climbed in. The feather mattress sank under his weight. He tried not to disturb the snowy puddle of sleeping kitten in the girl's lap as he pulled the coverlet up to his waist.

Snatching the end of the veil, he tied it around his right wrist, closest to her, and held up his forearm. Juliana gaped at him all the while.

"There," he said. "We will bear it together. Should you decide to slip out of the bed while I am asleep, you will have to wake me, or drag me along."

She stared at him.

He folded his hands, silk pulling slightly between them. "Silent again?"

"You would bind yourself for my sake?" she asked hoarsely. Her eyes looked huge, as if she were about to cry. For the love of God, he could not think of a reason for it.

"It solves some of the problem." He settled in the bed, putting his hands up behind his head. Her arm went up. "Sorry."

He lowered his right arm, keeping his left up behind his head, moving to get comfortable against the bank of pillows. Then he leaned to blow out the candles that burned on a small table on his side of the bed. He lay back again.

"Good night, Swan Lady," he said. "Sweet dreams."

Her silence lingered. "Gabhan," she said then.

He had not heard his name in Gaelic in so very long. Whispered in the dark, it was a soft, intimate, wonderful sound. *Gahvahn.* She did not even know it was his original name. No one had called him Gabhan since he was a boy.

He pulled in a breath. "Aye?"

"Thank you. I must ask a favor."

"Ask." He expected a lecture regarding the straying of hands in the middle of the night. But he would never force himself on her, he had already promised her that. If she were to be a true wife, she would have to want lovemaking as much as he did, though he was doing his best to ignore the desire.

But he was sure the chances were scant, judging by her attitude toward him in general. He gazed at shadowed canopy, hoping to seem nonchalant, and waited.

"Take me safe into Scotland yourself," she said. "Please do not leave me in the care of Sir Walter de Soulis."

That surprised him, but this girl was never predictable. "When Sir Walter is done meeting with the Earl of Pembroke, we will have to resume our journey together. All according to king's order," he added. "By week's end, you will be in Scotland. Does it matter how you get there?"

"I want you to take me there," she emphasized. "I—feel safer with you."

He glanced at her sharply. "Has he laid a hand upon you?"

She shook her head. "What I fear is that he will kill me one day. Please do not leave me with him anywhere."

"Kill you? I doubt that. But you are safe with me. I hope you truly know that." He wanted to take her hand to reassure her, but knew better just then.

"I know. And I am not being fanciful. I have reason to fear him."

"He can be an unpleasant sort, but he is a loyal king's man, a sheriff, and now Master of Swans in Scotland. He will visit Elladoune often, but you can avoid him."

"I do not trust him. If you must guard me, then guard me against him."

He frowned. "You really mean that."

"I do. And in return"—she looked at him—"I will stay in your cage. For now."

SAINTS AND MARTYRS, he thought, sleeping with her proved a mighty challenge. Those luscious little sighs, the light bounce of the bed, and the gentle pull of the length of silk between his wrist and hers, created sweet torture. His awareness of her was keen and constant. While he had hardly slept, he knew she did, and deeply.

He tried to turn his back to her but could not, without rolling her with him. He stared at the curtains that enclosed him with her in a warm nest. Flexing his hands, he resisted the recurrent delicious temptation to reach out to her.

He had tasted her mouth more than once. The memory of her sweetness drew him like a bee to a flower. He wanted her fiercely, his body aching.

Perhaps he struggled only against the exaggeration of sensations in the dark. Perhaps it was merely the natural urge that came upon a man at night. In the morning, he told himself, he would scarcely remember how he throbbed for her. This would seem like a dream. But he could not convince himself. He shifted, feeling the tug on the silk.

Honor alone kept him from pulling her into his arms to kiss and caress her as he yearned. Honor kept him still, weighing upon him, keeping him in place.

Juliana turned toward him, sighing long and low. He sensed then that she was awake. Against his foot, through the covers, he felt the tiny pricks of the kitten's claws.

"Must we have the cat in our bed?" he asked irritably.

"Aye," she murmured, her voice thick with sleep.

"I fear I will smash the wee beastie, all unknowing, in my sleep."

"Since you cannot be husband to me," she said, "for that would be ill-done…" Her pause was a reminder.

"Ill-done. We agree. Go on."

"Then I will have the kitten here. A prisoner needs some comfort."

"I hope I suffer so, if I ever fall into prison again," he growled, punching a pillow.

She lifted her head. He saw the silvery gleam of her pale hair and the sweet curve of her cheek in the darkness. "In prison again? What do you mean?"

"I spent two months in the king's dungeon in the Tower of London. I was released about six weeks ago. It is why my mother thinks I am too thin," he added.

"What was your crime?"

"Transgression against the Crown." He did not offer more, for it had to do with defending the Swan Maiden.

She leaned closer, curious. "But you are the perfect courteous English knight. It must have been serious to warrant imprisonment."

"It was." He lay unmoving, aware of his hand beside hers, silk between them.

"What did you do?"

"Betrayal," he said, and turned his shoulder to her. "Go back to sleep."

CAUGHT IN A dream yet on the edge of wakefulness, she summoned back vanishing images, drawing them in to her. The starlit, dark dream world seemed more real just now, a place of love, joy, safety. She heard sparkling laughter and a beloved face streamed past, and she went toward it. She did not want to wake to another day of captivity.

Snuggling into the warmth of the bed, eyes closed, she felt lush and relaxed as the dreams came over her again. Someone caressed her, whispered to her, someone she adored who loved her—he was just there, and she smiled and slipped into his arms.

They floated somewhere, a meadow, an ocean, a bed, heaven. She knew him well, understood him fully, half of her soul.

His hand, slow and gentle, skimmed her shoulder, her arm, her hip. She lay against him, breasts against his wide, warm chest, her knee over his firm thigh, his breath easing sweetly over her hair.

Peaceful, warm, wondrous. In the warmth and contentment of it, she could hardly tell where her body ended and his began. She only knew she loved him. Sinking into his strength, she slid her fingers over the hard, warm contour of his chest, and she sighed as he sought her, his hand gliding over the curve of her breast now, his thumb waking the nipple, sending a starlit burst through her.

Breath soft in her hair, lips warm and gentle on her brow, he bent his head and she tilted toward him for the kiss as his mouth captured hers slowly, sweetly, her lips opening to him. The kiss cherished her, and she returned that, wanting to stay here with him forever in this warm, enveloping joy.

His hand slid from her breast, making her yearn, and his fingers gentled over her throat, thumb tipping her head back for another kiss. Then his head tipped down, his hair like silk, slipping over her skin, and then his lips were warm and exquisite on her breast, seeking, finding as she arched against him.

The dream went on, and she flowed with it, slow, honeyed kisses and sleepy gentleness, warm hands slipping over velvety skin. She wanted to know him, touch him, be touched. Her fingers found the waist of his garment, then found him heated and solid there, rising against her hand. He took her mouth again, firmly now, so that she arched, whispered a moan. He murmured her name, kissed her again.

Catching her breath, the edge of the dream slipped away like the edge of the blanket sliding from her. She opened her eyes to see her dream lover. Gawain.

He stared, blinked as if he was surprised too. Silvery moonlight spilled over his face, his shoulder—and she realized she lay partly on top of him, their silk-bound hands resting between her chest and his. The warmth of the dream vanished. This was real.

His fingers slid away from her breast. Her free hand still cupped his hardness, linen between them. She released him and rolled free, feeling embarrassed, and yet lonely somehow, wanting to go back to him. She felt a little movement, a soft thud as the kitten clawed down the coverlet and slipped away.

"My lass, I am sorry," he whispered, his voice thick with sleep. He half turned away, but his hand still clasped hers against his chest, silk joining them.

"Sorry," she echoed. He was achingly beautiful in the silvery light, perfect, tender, strong. She felt love flow through her, passion burn in her, like light and fire.

Resting with her hand under his, she realized that the man had so much honor, a lifeblood of it in his very veins, that he would not knowingly continue the passion that a shared dream had stirred. For that to happen, she might need to be the one to intitiate—but she must think about it. Yet, lured by the comfort of his sleeping form, she slept too.

When she woke in the morning light, she was alone in the bed. The silk, still tied around her wrist, floated free at the other end. The kitten lay curled at her feet.

$$\text{---}\ \blacklozenge\cdots\bullet\ \ \bullet\cdots\blacklozenge\ \text{---}$$

Chapter Fifteen

MIDMORNING AND HE had not yet seen Juliana, nor had his sisters or his mother. He worried that she had escaped, despite her promise, until a groom in the courtyard mentioned that Robin had taken her fishing. Gawain strode briskly through the open castle gates and over the drawbridge to see for himself.

His stepbrother and a groom sat on the bank of the moat, a favorite spot for fishing, but Juliana was not seated with them. Robin waved, seeing him, and pointed down the meadow toward the river. He hurried there, crushing wildflowers underfoot, scarcely noticing spring air, white clouds, or the perfect sky overhead. Juliana was all he saw, standing beside the calmly flowing river.

She wore the mulberry gown and white veil his mother had lent her, without a cloak, but the sun was warm. As he approached, she noticed him, her face lovely, her smile innocent. The light he saw in her eyes was knowing and pleased and wonderfully sensual. He was glad to see no flash of anger there. He probably deserved it.

Slowing, he felt his cheeks flush as he recalled waking with Juliana in his arms, his lips on hers, his hands—hers too—seeking the joy of each other's bodies.

He dimly recalled apologizing, not even sure either of them was fully awake. He had been caught in the blissful throes of a dream. The very thought of those lush moments threatened to arouse him again. Forget it, he told himself sternly.

"There are swans here!" she called as he approached. "But they are not tame."

"Wild swans often nest near this bend in the river. They say some of the Avenels who lived here long ago tamed the creatures, but no one since." He stood beside her on the bank now. Along the bend in the water course, a pair of swans dipped their beaks into the water and glided in a circle. "They do not come close often. My mother enjoys watching them when they are here. But they are not tame."

"You know how to tame a swan," she said quietly.

He glanced at her. His mind went to the bed. Stop that. "I do not," he said.

"You do. You brought bread to the swan cob in the king's court," she said. "You showed patience and gave him food. It takes little more than that."

"But he was already tamed by you."

"He was a good cob, my Artan." She sighed, folding her arms around herself.

"Artan is free," he said.

She glanced up at him. "Free in heaven. The king ordered him to be prepared for the next day's supper."

"Ah, well." Gawain shrugged. "A little coin invites a favor. I believe the king ate peacock or pheasant the next night."

She opened her lips in surprise. "Artan was released?"

He smiled. "He is swimming the Tyne even now, or searching for a new home. A little bribe to a guard was all it took."

"Oh, Gabhan," she said, raising her arms as if to hug him—but with a glance at Robin and the servant, she dropped them. "How kind of you."

He loved the sound of his name in Gaelic. A secret pleasure. "It was easy to do." "Is it true, not just a tale to ease my mind?"

"The truth, I swear." He held out a hand to bring her higher on the bank. "Shall we go inside? My mother wants to visit with you, and the girls want you to join them to shoot some arrows.

Robin has been teaching them some archery skills."

"I would love that." She looked up at the sky. "Perhaps Artan will be back on Loch nan Eala by the time we reach Inchfillan."

"It is very far. He will find a new home in England."

"He would seek his own home or burst his heart doing so, that cob. His family is there. Besides, he would never be content on an English river."

He watched her. "Nor would you, I think."

"I like it here, but I must go home." Her eyes burned blue. "I feel almost as if I could grow ill if I do not go back home. I cannot explain it."

"I will take you back. I promised that."

She nodded, watching the swans on the river. "You could tame them, you know."

He laughed. "I cannot imagine any member of my family doing that."

"Love and patience will tame any creature."

"Even a Swan Maiden?" He smiled, held out his hand again.

She smiled and put a hand to her brow to shade her eyes. "See down there? They are building a nest. The cob is pulling reeds out of the water, and the pen is taking them from him and tucking them in place. She is making a circle for herself. But she may or may not accept him once the nest is made. Time will tell."

"Time will tell, hey," he commented.

"The pen must be pleased with him. Sometimes a cob will pull materials for three or four different nests before the pen is satisfied and lays her eggs."

"Poor fellow! So his work on the nest is no guarantee?"

"None. She may yet fly away."

"I thought they mated for life."

"Usually," she answered. She walked past him up the bank. "Though it can take a while before they settle with a mate. And," she added, "if he tires of her, or she tires of him, they will separate. I have seen it sometimes among the swans on Loch nan Eala."

"You know swans well."

"I do," she said. "If you bring food—bread and grains—to them every day, at the same time, they will come to you and expect it. They will tame a bit."

"Tell my sisters that," he answered. "They would enjoy it. But the creatures are said to be ill-tempered. So we leave them alone and watch them from afar."

"They only attack when their safety is threatened, or their families or territory are invaded. Treat them with respect and they will be good companions for life."

"So respect is the secret." He twisted his mouth a little, thinking beyond swans.

"Oh, always. Swans take care of themselves. But you can make this part of the river safe from their enemies—dogs, foxes, otters—and ensure that they have food available and good places to nest. Protect them and they will repay you with beauty and loyalty."

"Aye." He no longer meant swans. He wondered if she did.

Perhaps, for her glance flickered away from his. "They would be content here in this beautiful place. Once they are tamed, they might march over the drawbridge and through the gate to pester everyone in the courtyard who might have food for them."

He laughed. "My family would enjoy that."

"There they go," Juliana said, as the swans took a running start and lifted out of the water into flight. "They will not fly much longer. Soon their feathers will molt for the summer, and for weeks they will be earthbound."

"Easily captured," he murmured.

"Aye." She looked at him, then something caught her attention beyond him. "I think you should kiss me now."

He blinked. "What?"

"Here come your sisters. Kiss me and be done with it. This morning they were determined to demand kisses between us all day."

"Well, then." He drew her toward him, and when she lifted

her face, he touched his mouth to hers. She tasted light, good, giving. She curved into him and the dream returned and he was lost. When Juliana pulled away, he looked up to see the twins.

"'Lovelonging has caught me!'—says Bevis's true love," Catherine said. "And true love has found Sir Gawain. We did not have to remind him about the forfeit he owes!"

"Sir Gawain, whom no damsel would have," Eleanor added.

"The Swan Maiden wants him." Catherine smiled.

"Hush," Gawain said sternly.

"Were there maidens who did not want him?" Juliana asked.

"We lost count," Catherine said. "They did not have the lovelonging." Eleanor giggled. Gawain scowled.

"Our lady mother is happy today. She is glad you wed Juliana," Catherine said. "She seems heartier this morning. You are her first son, and your happiness is important to her. She worries more about you than about us."

"She worried you might never wed," Eleanor said.

Juliana smiled. "I must hear more about this."

"Gawain offered for the hands of a few heiresses and even a widow, but each one turned him down," Eleanor explained.

"Why?" Juliana asked. Her eyes were bright with curiosity as she glanced at him.

"My poor behavior," Gawain said. "'Twas long ago."

"A fine knight like yourself?"

"Five refusals. I am no prize."

"Because of his transgressions, Father said. So the women refused."

"What transgression," Juliana said, looking at Gawain.

"Which one?" Catherine asked brightly.

Juliana lifted her brows. "What do you say, sir?"

He shrugged. "I overstepped my bounds in Scotland." He had not planned to tell her yet. "I begged the king's peace. Twice. That is all."

"For what?" Juliana narrowed her eyes curiously.

"Ah, first time," he said, clearing his throat, "abetting the escape of Scottish rebels."

"At Elladoune?" She spoke very quietly. "The night we met? And you were punished for it?" He nodded. "I never knew."

"'Tis done," he said. "I pledged anew, and was admitted into king's peace again."

"The second time?" she asked.

"Similar," he said dismissively. "I helped a Scotswoman in need, and had to petition for king's peace again. My reputation was not the best after that. Rebel sympathizer. Helping Scotswomen is frowned upon in the English court."

"Not surprising. But I am glad you have that weakness," she murmured.

"So I was left to seek a bride, and let it go—until now." He bowed, glad to take the conversation into a lighter vein.

"You can see that Gawain is no prize," Eleanor said, turning from some fervent whispering with her sister.

Juliana raised a brow. "I might disagree."

He gave her the same sour look he had given his sister earlier.

"I wish you could stay longer, Gawain," Catherine said. "Mother is better today. She may not be with us long," she whispered. "The physicians say—" She shrugged.

Gawain touched her shoulder. "She is stronger than you think, and could yet surprise us all."

Juliana frowned, clearly affected by his mother's illness. He was grateful for her tender heart.

Moments later, as the girls ran back toward the castle, Robin and the groom met them and they crossed the drawbridge together. Gawain strode beside Juliana, walking behind them.

"Thank you," he said. "You have done more than I asked. You have brought my family joy." He watched wildflowers dance against her skirts as she walked.

"Do you think Lady Clarice will surprise everyone and recover?"

"She is weaker now. I doubt it."

"Then why did you tell your sisters so?"

He sighed. "What should I tell them? That she will lie in her grave by winter? That they should increase their rosary prayers and buy black silk?" He swore under his breath and halted as an onslaught of grief hit him.

Juliana touched his arm, then kissed his cheek, quick and sweet.

He blinked down at her. "Are the twins coming this way?"

"That was for you," she said. "A seasoned knight who is not afraid to show love for his mother, nor afraid to help Scots in need. Such a man deserves praise and reward, for he is a rare creature indeed."

He felt the heat of a blush. "Ah, well. It is my name, you see. It obligates me to be perfect. Gawain is no easy name to bear."

"You honor it." She smiled gently.

He drew a breath. "My lady mother is one of the finest women I know, strong and kind. We survived—a tragedy together years ago, before she wed Henry."

She touched his arm. "You are fortunate to have such a mother in your life."

"Your mother—you said she is a nun?"

"She chose the religious life after my father died. She left me to watch my brothers while she cared for her own soul. That was more important to her than the children who needed her."

He felt a surge of sympathy. "That was difficult for you."

"Aye, well. Be grateful for your mother's love as long as she is with you."

"I am." He was glad his mother liked Juliana. But he did not know what would become of this marriage once they returned to Scotland.

As he walked on, she linked her arm in his and smiled up at him.

"I must be very deserving today to earn such affection from a swan lass."

"Perhaps." She laughed. "We ought to try to avoid the twins, though."

He laughed too. Had she forgotten what had happened in the night, or was she pleased by it? He did not know how much longer he could pay forfeits without paying a serious price and losing his heart fully in the bargain.

AVENEL WAS PARADISE, a dream world, Juliana thought later. It was not just beautiful and luxurious, it was filled with love and kindness and laughter. The Avenel family, their servants, even their dogs and cats, were attentive and friendly. She could hardly believe how kindly they accepted her, a Scottish rebel in their English nest.

But two dark notes sounded like a knell beneath the laughter: Lady Clarice's serious illness, and the fact that the family was English and enemies to the Scots.

Yet the sweetest note of all in this place was Gawain, a heady and wonderful surprise. Laughing with him, sparring words with him, feeling his touch, his kisses, made her feel like his friend, his lover, his wife. Not his captive. Even if they only played at love for a while, she felt cherished; she belonged.

The grim world of truth waited beyond Avenel, and soon they would return to it when she and Gawain joined the escort again, back to the cart, and silence—and chains.

But the game she played here with Gawain threatened to forfeit her heart and her very soul in the bargain. She wanted that, and could not claim it.

Chapter Sixteen

B Y LATE IN the day, he had kissed her so often at the twins'
urging that he knew the fragrance of her, the taste, the
softness. The touch of her lips even lightly made his body throb,
his heart pound. He did not know if he could endure another
night alone with her in his bed after a day of pretended wedded
bliss. He had to remember honor to master passion. Otherwise,
he would carry her up the stairs and make her his wife forever.

Knowing they must depart tomorrow cooled his ardor. He
dreaded leaving Avenel and returning to the escort. He only
wanted the surprising joy he had found here with Juliana and his
family to continue.

He left his mother's chamber, having read to her until she fell
asleep, and heard laughter as he descended the stairs. He peered
through an arrow slit window. Seeing Juliana and the girls on the
practice field beside the castle, he went quickly through the
courtyard and out the gate to find them.

He could not allow Juliana to leave the castle even with the
girls. His orders commanded otherwise, and he had to balance
those, and that secret, with this pretense of being a happy
bridegroom.

The grassy field, grazed flat by sheep, was used mostly for
weapon practices, with bales of hay set at one end for archery
exercise. The girls stood facing those at a distance now, each
armed with a short hunting bow. Robin was with them, watching

as they lifted their bows to shoot at painted targets tacked to the bales.

"Gawain!" Catherine exclaimed, turning as he walked toward them. She still held the nocked arrow, so he turned her away by the shoulders.

"Careful, Cat. Would you take out the lady's bridegroom so soon?"

"You will owe Juliana another kiss for that remark," Catherine said saucily. She released her arrow, which came down at a crazy angle in the grass barely ten feet away.

"Aha, we will have no problem with field mice with this cat on the prowl," he drawled. Robin laughed outright, and the twins turned mirrored scowls on them. Juliana laughed too, eyes sparkling. She bent to choose an arrow from a pile at her feet, and began to nock it on the small hunting bow.

"Forfeit a kiss for mocking Cat," Eleanor said.

"Oh, come now, Nell, I only teased her."

"You promised that each time we ask, you must kiss the bride," Catherine insisted, "because we missed your wedding."

"Each time you are rude, you must pay a forfeit, too," Eleanor said.

"That was not part of our agreement," Gawain said.

"It is now," Eleanor said blithely.

"We read *The Fifteen Joys of Marriage* and it says kisses make a kind marriage, so a couple must grant them liberally to each other," Catherine said. "You should learn the rules of a good marriage since you have never been wed before."

"I must find a book penned by a nun for you next time," Gawain muttered.

Robin grinned. "Honor the forfeit, brother."

Gawain cocked a brow toward Juliana, who was blushing rather fiercely as she steadied her bow. He went to her and gently kissed her cheek.

Then, because he suddenly wanted to, he kissed her lips. She drifted her eyes shut, accepting it, and his entire being seemed to whirl inside.

"'Oh, that I loved as my own heart's blood!'" Eleanor cried. "Bevis," she explained.

"No more epic romance volumes for you if you insist on quoting from them," Gawain grumbled. The girls chuckled and walked away with Robin for more instruction.

Juliana's cheeks were flaming. "You know you do not have to kiss me each time they demand it," she murmured.

"I know. But we are blissful newlyweds. And I like it. I thought you did too."

"Ah, it is not unpleasant," she admitted. "But if they learn the truth, they will want apologies, not kisses." She made sure to scowl.

"They will not learn it from us."

"Good." She nocked the arrow and tilted the bow, aiming it, her brow furrowed. Extending her bow arm, she drew back the string, relaxed to adjust her stance, and aimed again.

"You know what you are about with that," he said.

"Some," she said.

"Oh, watch Juliana!" Eleanor said. "She is a fine archer."

"Her brothers taught her," Catherine added.

"When will Father let us go bow hunting?" Eleanor asked.

"When you can hit an animal so cleanly that it will not suffer," Gawain said.

"And when you can ride without chattering like magpies," Robin said. "So it will never happen."

"Careful, Robin," Gawain said. "They will demand you marry next and kiss in perpetual forfeit just for that remark." Robin grimaced in mock horror.

"I am sure Juliana's brothers do not tease her so." Catherine tossed her head.

"My brothers tease me horribly at times," Juliana said. She lifted the bow as she spoke. The wind blew her skirts, revealing the lean line of her body and her confident stance. Gawain did not doubt that she was an experienced archer: her arms were steady, her gaze intent. She looked only at the hay bale, drew the string taut, and released it.

The arrow flew true and swift, smacking into the center of the target. Gawain whistled low.

"Another stroke of luck," Robin said. "The wind seems to be with her each time she picks up the bow."

"That looked like skill to me," Gawain remarked.

"Ah, but can she do it again?" his brother teased.

"Move the target back and see," Juliana directed. Robin ran the length of the field to drag the bale back, then returned.

Juliana nocked the arrow again. Gawain watched her raise the bow, sight, draw, and release in a fast, fluid rhythm. The arrow flew true and thunked into the center of the painted target.

Robin bowed with great respect. "If that were a deer, we would have dinner."

"If it were a man, he would be dead." Gawain drawled. "Is that what comes of running with rebels in Scotland?"

"My brothers taught me to defend myself."

"Ah. Ever shot an English knight?"

She looked at him squarely. "Not yet."

"The marriage treatise says a kiss is a suitable reward for a deed pleasing to the spouse," Eleanor prompted. "Go on."

"How long does this continue?" Gawain shrugged amiably and leaned forward as Juliana tilted her cheek as the chaste kiss stirred through him. Her skin was silken, her airy scent intoxicating. He blew out a breath, stepped back, gave her a twist of a smile.

"Little rebel," he murmured. "You have a lethal aim."

"I do," she agreed.

"Straight to the heart."

The others, applauding the kiss, did not hear the exchange. Gawain thought his sisters' sport might kill him before long. He took Juliana's wrist in his. "Come with me. We need to collect the arrows." He drew her down the field at a determined pace, walking past several arrows stuck in the grass.

"Here are some—" she said. He pulled her onward.

Downfield, he snatched shafts out of one of the targets, gripping them in one hand. Then he pulled her behind the farthest, tallest bale and swept her into his arms.

He kissed her deep and hard and full, the kiss that had waited within him all day. With a little cry, she circled her arms around his neck and returned the kiss with clear hunger. He renewed it, sweeping his hands down her back and over the curve of her hips. She pressed against him, moaned softly, pulled back.

"Oh, are they coming?" she whispered.

"Not yet," he growled, and delved again as she tilted her head, her mouth eager, the kiss deeper, longer, open, seeking. She seemed to falter a bit in his arms, but he held her strong and sure.

He knew he must stop, restrain, deny what surged through him. But denial and restraint abounded at Avenel. He craved honesty, truth, passion. He could not stop his thirst once slaking had begun.

His lips lingered on hers, and she pressed against him, so that the next kiss filled him, rocked him, stirred desire, and began to shake down the door to his soul.

Stop, he told himself, or take her in the grass, here and now. Her response told him she was willing. But he forced himself to pull back, hands trembling as he took her face in his hands.

"Pray pardon," he whispered. "These forfeited kisses, a shared bed—too much temptation for a weak man."

"Weak, not at all," she said breathlessly. She leaned full against him, breasts pillowed, body warm through her clothing. He shook his head and stepped back.

"Arrows," he said. "Before my heart is stuck through."

She turned. "Arrows—" She sounded confused. "How many do you have there?"

He looked at the cluster he had dropped on the ground. "Four. Yours, for they were at the center of the target. I could not have done that, and I am no poor archer."

"Robin said you are a fine aim with a longbow. Fast and

sure."

He shrugged. "I have some tricks. And I know enough to see genuine skill." His body, his heart, still throbbed. He needed the distraction. "We must find the others."

"We should look in the grass for the girls' arrows." She walked around the hay bale, tucking loose strands of pale hair under her veil.

Gawain came with her, body throbbing a little less. Seeing a few arrows, he plucked them up. Two more were expertly sunk in the heart of another target.

"Yours?" he asked. "You have an amazing aim." He fisted the collected arrows. "You would be the very devil in a skirmish."

"Good that I am a woman, then." She picked up another shaft. "My brothers and my cousin James are skilled archers. I learned from them." She sent him a glance. "You met my cousin. Your mother said so."

"I have. A fine man. For a Scottish rebel," he drawled.

"Robin said when we were out fishing that Jamie's men took you prisoner but you escaped. But he said you helped them, so you had to pledge new obedience to the king."

"I have not been the most faithful of knights under Edward, I suppose. I think we are done here." He beckoned and she went with him along the length of the field.

The story of his capture and escape from Scottish rebels was the version his family preferred. That kept the Avenel name clean. Men often changed allegiances in the war between Scotland and England, especially those who lived near the border. The Avenels, by tradition, were fiercely loyal to England, and their Scottish-born stepson had broken that pure pattern. But his family loved him regardless.

He wanted to tell Juliana the truth—he was half-Scot and considered himself more Scots than that. But not yet, for he had much to resolve, and Castle Glenshie must remain a secret for now, though it burned in him to tell her.

Juliana swept the grass with her foot. "We are still missing arrows."

"I hope they are not planted in some English knight some-where," he teased.

"If I loosed them, it would be no accident where they hit."

"I have no doubt. There is one."

She fetched it and they walked back. The twins were clapping their hands.

"I apologize on behalf of my sisters, and myself," he mur-mured. "We need not play their silly game."

"It does not bother me," she said. "They are young. And you are a very kind brother to tolerate their fanciful ideas."

"Your brothers taught you to shoot. Which is more useful. Where are they now?"

"My brothers? Do you think to learn where the rebels are?"

"Is that why you do not speak to English soldiers? You know too much?"

"I do not speak to English knights because they are fools! Not you," she added. "I adored my older brothers, though they had scant tolerance for me. Except with the archery. They were excellent tutors. I learned all I could until I began to best them. That pleased them, I think."

"They taught you well."

"They taught me to defend myself. Then they left me to do just that." She hurried ahead.

THUNDER RUMBLING OVER incessant rain woke Juliana. She lay on her side, her wrist tied with the veil, its other end around Gawain's wrist. Snoring softly, he slept beside her. The kitten curled between them, a hillock of warmth against her knee.

Gawain had said little to her, coming to bed late, tying the veil between them, and going quickly to sleep beside her. After the day's closeness—beginning with dreamy kisses at dawn, and passionate kisses behind the hay bale—his coolness hurt. He seemed deliberately quiet and thoughtful around her.

Pale light seared the room and a loud crash startled her. She drew up her knees and winced as flashes and rumbles filled the room. Just a storm, she told herself. But she touched Gawain's arm tentatively, seeking reassurance. He slept on. The next crack of sound and flash of light made her jump and squeak.

"What is it?" Gawain asked groggily. "Oh. Just thunder and lightning." He propped himself on an elbow. When she flinched at a new crash of sound and light, he leaned against the pillows and took her hand, silk draping between them. Between them, Pippa the kitten stretched in her sleep. "Come here. Watch the kitten, now."

"I do not need coddling. You can go to sleep." Too aware of his half-nude presence, she felt a blush heat her from her chest to the roots of her hair.

Thunder exploded again. He circled an arm around her. She relented, leaning against him. He felt warm and good. "It is just a storm. Or is it more than that?"

"I do not like storms. And I do not want to return to the escort in the morning. I am done being the Swan Maiden, I think."

"The king put his Master of Swans in charge of you, not the Swan Laird. I would never have treated you so."

"Why must we go with them? We can ride to Elladoune together." She leaned against him, loving the spell of protection created in the curtained space.

"The king does not trust me to do that."

"Ah. You disobeyed his orders by taking off my chains."

"He does not know that. And we are—bound." He held up the silken veil.

"But he means to test you in Scotland."

His laugh sounded rueful. "I am no prize, and he knows it. Go to sleep now."

"Gawain." She hesitated. "I like it here at Avenel. I like your family. But I want to go home. Just not—the way Edward would send me."

"I know."

"And I think I know why you decided to wed me in the court. For your family. For your mother."

He was quiet. "In part."

This sense of trust and ease might not last, she knew, but she savored it. Yet she wondered what secrets Gawain kept, what other reason he had to marry her and return to Scotland.

A new tumult of thunder made her shiver. "It sounds as if the world is cracking apart. All will be different tomorrow."

"This castle is strong."

"I mean…this peace between us will end." She drew up her knees and rested her arm there. "Avenel is like faery land, lovely but false."

"You are safe with me wherever we are, I swear it."

"But you owe your fealty to Edward. I am never truly safe with you, no matter how—" She stopped.

"Go on."

"No matter how good I feel when I am with you," she blurted. "How safe. How—loved and cared for."

The rumble of the storm covered what he murmured next, as he turned her toward him, his hands on her shoulders heated. A wave of desire flashed through her, and she tilted her head, heart pounding, body throbbing. A force pulsed between them that felt strong and vibrant, impossible to ignore.

"Gabhan," she whispered.

"This is not false," he said low, when she wanted him to kiss her. "You are safe."

"But you obey your king," she said breathlessly. "You are kind to me here as we pretend this marriage. If I follow your will, you will earn favor at court."

His hands tightened on her shoulders. "Obey or not. I am the one caught by the king's will. Not you."

She stared into his dark eyes. "Caught fast. Both of us."

He made a growling sound and pulled her to him, kissing her. She moaned against his mouth for the sheer relief of what she wanted. As he slanted his mouth over hers, slid his hand along her jaw, fingers weaving into her hair, she sighed, accepting it.

She fell into each kiss, lost. When he pulled back, she protested in a silent plea, nudging toward him.

He kissed her again, hands cradling her head. Resting her hand on his chest, she felt smooth, heated skin, a pounding heart. She slipped her arms around his neck, seeking his strength, his embrace, wanting something she could not quite define but yearned to discover.

Bound by silk, his hand entwined with hers, while his free hand soothed over her back and hip. Lush and hungry, his mouth met hers again. When he tipped her back to the pillows and stretched out beside her, she turned into the hard pressure of his body.

The enclosed bed was a haven of privacy, erasing the outer world. She felt the honest, fervent desire between them in this sanctum. Here, she trusted him. Here, she felt safe. Here, she desired him, whatever he wanted, as completely as she could.

His hand gentled over her breasts, his fingers lingering, coaxing. When he settled his lips there, she shivered, gasped. The silk twisted between them as she gripped his hand and wrapped her fingers tightly in his.

Sighing, rolling to allow him greater freedom, she traced her fingers along the hard, sleek contours of his back, sliding lower. Her body craved his fiercely as desire flowered in her, powerful and new. A tiny moan escaped her lips and his mouth captured it as the kiss deepened. She melted as his hand soothed over her breasts.

But he paused, drew back. Cool air filled the space between them.

Then he rolled away, moving so quickly that she turned too, tugged by the silk, her arm over him. She stared at his shoulder, his back, heart slamming, body keen and suddenly lonely, the center of her being somehow aching.

"What," she said breathlessly, "was that?"

"Male weakness," he replied hoarsely.

"It did not seem weak to me."

"Go to sleep."

"I cannot sleep. The storm." That, and her wildly beating heart.

"Good God and all the saints. I must sleep, or I must ravish you here and now."

"I do not want...ravishing," she said plaintively. "I want—" She was not sure what to ask for. A moment ago, she would have pursued it boldly, but now she sensed that he had closed himself off from her. The outside world had come galloping into the gap.

"So be it. No ravishment," he growled. "You swore you would be mine on the day that hell turns icy and faeries serve the king of England, or whatever the devil you said. I will not dishonor you."

"What if I changed my mind?" she asked faintly.

He punched his pillow. "I crossed a border with you today, and tonight. I do not want you thinking poorly of English knighthood. Or me," he added sourly.

Regret poured through her like icy water. Perhaps he was wise to end this now, wiser than she was. The implications for later, in the escort, would be very complicated.

"Gabhan—"

"Good night to you," he snapped.

She sighed, hurt and confused. Her body told her one thing, her mind another. Her heart was ensnared in the middle. He struggled with something similar.

The Church taught that lust was a trap, and now she knew what a sweet trap it was. But passion like this, in a loving union, was a bridge to something beautiful. She wanted to cross there with Gawain. Apparently he did not want that. At least, not now.

Thunder crashed again. She inched closer to him and tucked her fist against his back. He did not turn to take her into his arms, but he patted her hip. Somehow she drifted to sleep behind the battlement of his back. Somehow he managed to snore as if he had mastered what she could not.

Chapter Seventeen

T HE MORNING CLOUDS were leaden gray through the open window of Lady Clarice's chamber, and the air was cool. Gawain turned to latch the window shutters and stopped. There was gloom enough here already, he thought.

He watched his mother murmur to Juliana, who wore the white satin gown beneath a blue cloak, a gift from Lady Clarice. Juliana leaned down to kiss his mother's cheek, holding the white kitten tucked in her arm.

"Aye, I promise," she responded to Lady Clarice's quiet question. "We will return to Avenel as soon as we can." She embraced his mother.

Watching, Gawain felt a tug on his heart and blinked in astonishment at the sheer strength of his feelings. He loved his mother and family deeply and knew it. Now, as he looked at Juliana, something similar stirred within him.

But the feeling had more layers, more texture: affection wrapped with passion and bright hope.

Last night he had wanted her intensely. He had turned away to quell his desire, aware that the boundary he had inadvertently crossed was more than physical desire. The depth of his feelings for her had amazed him, even frightened him.

Love, an inner voice whispered. How could he love her so quickly? Yet it was strong and undeniable. And he did not know what to do.

Juliana held out the snowy kitten to Eleanor and Catherine. "Please keep Pippa for me," she told them. "She is too young for a long journey. Mayhap I can claim her when she is older and we—are settled in our home."

He wished he could reassure her. "Juliana, we must go."

She kissed the kitten's head and handed her to Eleanor. "Keep her safe for me," she said, her voice breaking. She embraced the twins and walked to the door, dashing her hand over her eyes.

Gawain folded Lady Clarice into his arms, careful of her frailty. The tears in her eyes disturbed him, but he smiled and said he would see her soon, though he wondered if this might be the last time. He hugged his sisters and turned away.

Juliana led the way out of the chamber and toward the stairs. They descended the stairs in silence, the hem of her blue cloak sweeping each stone step. He watched its brightness in the shadows and fought grief and regret.

He was leaving Avenel too soon, but he had no choice. Riding beside Juliana beneath the portcullis and over the drawbridge, he turned and waved farewell to Robin, who stood in the courtyard, framed by the stone arch.

Juliana rode silently, fair and perfect beside him. As sad as he felt to leave Avenel, he was aware of the comfort of her gentle strength. And he felt a burgeoning hope: soon he would find Glenshie at last, and claim it.

He urged Gringolet ahead. The palfrey, Galienne, hastened to keep up as they took the road that stretched over the moors.

Just as Juliana had said, their days at Avenel did indeed seem like time spent in a faery land—beautiful and unreal, and flown with the light.

He led her along the road toward the Scottish border not far away, where De Soulis and the escort would be waiting. After an hour, the horses cantered through a stand of trees. Recognizing the area near Kelso, he slowed his horse, and Juliana guided hers to a halt.

He dismounted and reached up, and she skimmed to the

ground in his arms, watching him warily. He turned to take the golden chains and bands from the pack behind his saddle.

He did not speak, nor did she, for he did not know what to say. Should he apologize or beg forgiveness? Should he explain that their marriage, and his assignment to Elladoune, might gain him a long-cherished dream? Should he tell her he loved her?

Husky and quiet, he asked her to remove the veil so he could put the chains on her once again. He felt like a coward.

Juliana unwrapped the veil. Her hair was coiled over her ears, and she pulled the ivory pins free so that the golden sheen spilled over her shoulders. The white silk veil drifted down like a wisp of cloud.

He caught the veil and stuffed it in his pocket, never taking his gaze from hers. He did not want to do this. But the escort had ridden into sight over the rim of the hill. He heard the horses' hooves and saw the men from the corner of his vision.

Juliana lifted her chin, gazing past him. Her eyes were dull, their blue spark turned to smoke. He slipped the collar around her throat and closed it, then lifted the wrist manacles.

She held up her hands passively while he closed the bracelets and attached the chains. She was as cool and delicate and as still as marble under his touch.

Anger at himself, at his king, made his fingers tremble. If he was ever to defy his orders again, he ought to do it now.

Yet he was manacled even more securely than she was. If he broke faith with the king again, his family would suffer. And he would never find Glenshie.

His fingers brushed her slim throat as he checked the collar. "Does it pinch?" he asked.

She did not answer. Chains chiming, she reached inside her sleeve. Drawing out the white feathered cap, she set it upon her head. She acted as if he were not there.

Once again, she was the silent, beautiful Swan Maiden.

She turned and waited. Gawain boosted her into the saddle, then mounted the bay. He took Galienne's lead and rode on. In the distance, he saw the escort heading for the inn tucked at the base of a hill, just over the border of Scotland. He felt as if his heart was breaking. He wondered if hers was too.

When he reached the yard, the party waited there. Gawain tethered Juliana's horse to a tree and turned to see De Soulis and Laurence Kirkpatrick coming toward them.

All the while, he avoided her glance. He felt too ashamed of himself, and the whole of English knighthood, to look in those beautiful eyes.

"SHE IS TIRED," Gawain said to himself, watching Juliana, who sat on her horse out in the yard. He studied the drooping lines of her shoulders and her bowed head and saw fatigue there, and something sad and poignant. He felt as if he had caused it.

"Some of the goodwife's fresh ale and that excellent cheese will revive her," Laurie said, standing beside him. "You speak of her more like a husband than a guard. Is it so?"

Gawain glanced at him. "If so, 'tis my own business."

"I've kept a good hold on your secrets in the past," Laurie muttered, as if bothered by Gawain's reticence. "And my guess now is that you are lovestruck." Gawain scowled to dispel the impression, but Laurie only rolled his eyes.

"Dame," Gawain told the innkeeper's wife, who walked near them, "if you will, bring some ale and food for the lady in our party." He handed her a coin.

"The lady, sir?" she asked, pocketing the silver.

"The king's prisoner," De Soulis said, approaching them.

"The *lady*," Gawain said. The woman nodded and hurried away.

"According to the king's writ, I am to decide what is best for the prisoner," De Soulis said.

"Food and ale are necessities."

"But you spoil her. I allowed you to take her to Avenel to avoid bringing her into a garrison town. But do not fancy yourself her full keeper. We are not at Elladoune."

"But we are in Scotland now. According to my orders, she is now my charge. And she is my wife."

"You wax lovesick. That marriage was no love match. It was the jest of a king."

"A poor joke indeed," Laurie remarked, "fastening two people in marriage to make a dull feast more entertaining."

De Soulis glanced at him. "Go tell the men to mount up. We will be leaving soon."

"Fine. We will depart once the lady has eaten. Surely they can organize themselves in that time." Laurie went to the door.

"Good that he is going to Elladoune with you, and not with me," De Soulis grumbled. "He annoys me."

"He does not bother me," Gawain said. "Tell me, how many men did Sir Aymer decide to send to Elladoune?"

"A few of the men out there will go with you. Later a garrison will arrive, but it is still being debated. You know what to do once you are there. Ride the land, take note of its features, write them plainly for the commander of the king's armies. He is interested in where his armies can set up tents or stage battles, how far apart the villages and abbeys are, and so on. Send a messenger to bring the notes to me."

Gawain nodded. He disliked this, but realized he could search out Glenshie while he went about the task.

"Since you seem inclined to pamper the girl," the sheriff added, "I remind you that she is to enjoy no privileges until she declares her loyalty to King Edward."

"Of course," Gawain repeated flatly.

"I took liberty with the king's orders for you once, but I will not do so again. Was she treated as a prisoner at Avenel or coddled there?"

"She received courtesy from my family," Gawain snapped.

"Even though she committed treason against England."

"I heard she tried to save a few swans. How is that treason?"

"All swans in Britain belong to the king. But truly, I suspect her of rebel activities, which we will have to prove once we are in her territory. Watch her closely. Do not trust her—even if she is a pretty piece."

He would have punched the man then if the innkeeper's wife had not approached just then to give them wooden cups, bread, and cheese. Gawain took a cup for Juliana.

"One thing more," De Soulis said. "I saw a list of Scots fallen and taken prisoner at Methven. Your wife's brothers were captured and will be ransomed. The Lindsays of Elladoune were listed in the notice sent to the guardians of the realm of Scotland. The other two are in my custody at Dalbrae. We took them when we took the girl."

"Other two?" Gawain frowned. Now he would have to tell her that they had been taken. "Where are the ones who were taken at Methven?"

"I do not know." De Soulis slid Gawain a quick look. "Let me give you some advice. Do you hope to hold Elladoune and eventually claim it as the lady's husband?"

"It has occurred to me," Gawain said cautiously.

"Refuse to pay the ransom. Her brothers will be executed."

"Jesu," Gawain burst out. "That is cold."

"Practical. They are rebels, and may never be released or even ransomed. There is no money at Elladoune for that, I am sure. Their kin cannot pay. You are now their brother by law, so you can refuse to pay the ransom. Once their sister pledges to Edward, Elladoune can be reinstated to her family. With her brothers gone, she could be named heiress. That gives the property to you. Practical," he confirmed.

"It stinks of dishonor," Gawain snapped. "What of the other Lindsay brothers?"

"Young scoundrels," De Soulis said. "Rebels in the making."

Gawain frowned, about to ask more when De Soulis took a small parchment packet from inside his tunic and emptied it into the foaming ale in the cup.

"What is that?" Gawain asked.

"A sleeping potion. We will have to carry her in the supply cart, as before."

"Have you given her that before?"

"A few times. The herbal mixture quiets her. She is more docile. You might want to take advantage of that." He gave Gawain a narrowed look.

Oh, to take the man down here and now. Gawain fisted his hands, sucked in a breath. "She was clearly drugged at the king's feast, and perhaps once in the cart."

"More than that. She needs it." De Soulis shrugged. "Poppy and herbs. Give it to her now and she will sleep until it wears off. Otherwise she can be wild without it. You will want to take the remedy with you to Elladoune."

"There is no reason to do that," Gawain ground out, remembering Juliana's plea that she feared De Soulis might kill her someday. Surely this was why. His breath tightened with fury as he glared at the sheriff.

"You are too soft. She is a rebel. If you want a loyal, obedient wife to present to the king, best take a stern hand with her now."

"Kindness fares better with wild creatures."

"Wild creatures see kindness as weakness. She is a volatile female. You should have seen her fight us the day she was taken. Tooth and nail," he went on. "Struggled so that I had to stop along the way and get this mixture from a wise woman I had heard of. The girl is like a bird, impulsive and simple. She would fly away in an instant."

"Birds can be very intelligent creatures," Gawain drawled.

"We tied her and gave her the medicines. The king ordered the golden chains made in Newcastle—he likes that tiresome conceit about the Swan Maiden. Those chains are far more valuable than the girl. Why do you think we have a full military guard for one Scotswoman?"

"Ah. Because she wears a fortune around her neck," Gawain

said. "How foolish of me to overlook that."

"If she escapes, we lose part of the treasury for the Scottish campaign." The sheriff stirred the ale with his finger and handed it to Gawain. "Give it to her. You might like the result, as her— husband."

Gawain lost his hold over his anger then. Snatching De Soulis's surcoat, he yanked him forward. The ale sloshed over both of them. He could smell its bitterness.

"Are you ten fools in one?" he ground out. "A coward in black armor! Are you so frightened of a mere girl that you must use poison to control her?" He let go without warning so that De Soulis spilled the rest of the ale.

"You are the fool." He brushed at his surcoat. "There is no harm in this."

"If that potion harms her," Gawain growled, "your life is mine to claim."

Turning, he stalked toward the door and yanked it open, striding across the yard. He heard De Soulis follow. Laurie hastened toward him, glancing from one to the other.

"We are leaving now—on our own," Gawain said. Laurie cast a grim look at De Soulis and turned to mount his horse.

Reaching Juliana, Gawain handed the bundled bread and cheese to her. "My lady," he said. "There is no ale. We will stop for water from a clean stream."

He took the key from his pouch and unlocked her collar, sliding it off and unlatching the manacles, piling the whole glittering mass in his hands. Juliana widened her eyes.

"Avenel!" De Soulis yelled, coming up behind him.

Gawain spun. "Better take these. They are worth a king's ransom." He dumped them in the man's hands. "I would wrap them around your neck, but I do not think they would fit. This lady is in my safekeeping as of this moment."

"If you take her, I will report it to the king, and you will be wearing chains. Remember that nobles earn the privilege of hanging on golden chains!"

"I will obey my orders, which state she is in my keeping in Scotland. We are there now. I am riding out with her." He looked at Juliana. "We must keep a tough pace. Are you up to it?"

She nodded and took up the reins. He stepped aside and mounted his horse, turning to see Laurie was waiting.

"I would send men after you, but I do not have enough," De Soulis said. "Watch your back, Avenel. The king will not show you lenience again."

Gawain wrapped the reins around his hand. "If King Edward, the Flower of Chivalry, condemns a man for defending his wife, he is not a worthy knight or the leader he claims to be. But I think we all know that by now."

"I will send my report to him as soon as I find a messenger," De Soulis growled.

Gawain inclined his head, lifted the reins, and glanced at Juliana. She sat straight and alert. He blessed her for it.

He urged the bay to a canter, Juliana and Laurie following. They thundered along the road and soon left the inn far behind. Seeing no pursuers, Gawain relaxed a bit.

Soon enough, the air seemed distinctly Scottish—brisk, clean, scented with peat and heather. Riding past hills and streams, he felt the magic of Scotland more keenly than ever. His anger began to clear like fog in sunlight.

Perhaps the devil had possessed him to risk so much to defend Juliana again. By turns, the girl relied on him or did not seem to like him. But he knew the answer now.

He loved her. It had begun years ago, the night he had saved her in a firelit loch, the night he had bound himself to her with a secret—Swan Maiden and Swan Laird. That bond had looped out into time and caught him fast in its net.

Chapter Eighteen

THE AIR HELD the soft promise of rain. Juliana felt the damp breeze caress her bare throat and wrists. She closed her eyes briefly, reveling in freedom. Hungrily, she pulled in deep breaths of Scottish air.

Although they had left De Soulis's escort, she still maintained her silence. Only Gawain had heard her speak, and she felt certain that he would keep that secret. Not knowing his friend well enough to trust him, she stayed quiet.

She drew silence around herself like a cloak, a passive defense. Constant silence, she found, was meditative and protective in the midst of uncertainty. She took peace from it like water from a stream.

She glanced often at Gawain as they rode at a steady pace. As if she had spoken aloud, he seemed to understand her silences, and responded whenever she wanted to go slower, or needed to rest or to refresh herself.

The warmth he had shown her at Avenel had cooled. She missed that easy affection—but Avenel had been a dream, and they were all awake now.

She found his subtle expressions and moods readable, as if she knew him well. Sometimes his dark handsomeness had a hard, compelling edge, when sharpened by anger and impatience. At other moments he seemed more angelic, even boyish, laughing with Laurie or glancing around quickly for her reaction.

Always, though, she saw in him an awareness and concern for others, like a golden thread in all he did. She marveled at it. If his king had been half as decent as this one knight, she thought, Scotland would have no war and no tyrant.

As she rode on, she succumbed further to the charm of brown eyes framed in thick black lashes, to his tilted smile, to the low timbre of his voice, as if—

Her breath caught. As if she were in love. *This is not the way,* she told herself sternly, *that a captive regards a captor, that one enemy studies another.*

Yet it is the way, a gentle voice in her head answered, *that a woman looks at the man she desires. It is the way a wife regards her beloved husband: admiring, fascinated, loving.*

Sighing, wondering if it was so, she rode on.

THE THREE HORSES spread out, spacing one behind another, to follow a narrow drover's track up a long, steep hill. The wind blew harder as they rose higher. Gawain slowed the bay to ride beside Juliana, while Laurie rode ahead, out of hearing.

"I must speak to you," Gawain said. "De Soulis told me news of your brothers."

"Alec and Iain?" She spoke quickly.

"The two with Robert Bruce."

"Niall and Will. Are they—?" Her eyes showed true alarm.

"They live," he assured her. "They were taken at Methven, and may be ransomed for return. All I know is that they were listed as prisoners on the roll sent to the guardians of the realm of Scotland."

She nodded. When she gazed at the purple mountains beyond the moorland, he saw tears gleam in her eyes. His heart turned at the sight. "My kin and I cannot pay a ransom," she said.

"I will inquire and see what can be done."

A fat tear slid down her cheek as she nodded mute thanks.

"What of the other two?" he asked.

"They are young. They would be rebels too, if they had the chance. If my older brothers are released, they will fight the English again. It is a risk for you to help my brothers. Your king would be displeased."

"I have a heart," he snapped. "Though you do not think it."

"I know you do," she said quietly. "That is what frightens me." Clucking to the palfrey, she passed him.

He watched her go, and blew out a long breath in frustration. Spurring Gringolet, he surged up the hill past the palfrey and struck out over the drover's track to catch up to Laurie.

"What does your wee Scots swan want?" Laurie asked.

"To be free. To go home. And wants naught from me, I can tell you." He scowled.

"Ah, but while she may be cool as ice, there is a fire in her eyes for you. A good fire. And you have the same for her. I have seen you besotted, but never in love."

"I am not besotted or in love. Nor is she." He was tempted to ride ahead for a while, needing silence to think. Juliana seemed to need it too. She kept behind them.

"So what do you want? I am a wondering sort of man."

To find Glenshie, Gawain wanted to say. To find my home and the truth about many things. But he guided his horse along the ridge of the hill, its slopes thick with early heather blooms.

Overhead, a flock of ducks arrowed through the sky. "I want to be free as well," he answered. "Free of infernal questioning."

Laurie grinned. "What else to do on a long journey but talk, eh?"

"And free of the ridiculous task the king set for me. The question is what the king wants. We may pay dearly for leaving De Soulis."

"You did nothing wrong. But if you must prepare another apology, we will need to find pen and parchment."

"I am done begging for king's peace."

"You defended your wife. De Soulis was mistreating her. She

will still be in English custody at Elladoune. No harm done."

"If I am lucky," Gawain muttered.

Laurie looked around. "My God, Scotland is a beautiful land. I forget that when I am away."

I have never forgotten, Gawain thought.

PATTING HER HORSE'S neck, Juliana let Galienne stay back. Ahead, Gawain and Laurence Kirkpatrick traveled side by side: one dark, lean, and quiet, the other broad, his laughter rippling, his gestures wide and free.

Rain clouds hovered above as they moved north. Juliana looked around with rapture, as if she saw Scotland for the first time—beautiful, wild, exuberant, and vivid. As they left the rolling Lowlands and moved into the rumpled, heathered skirt of the Highland hills, she regretted her silence, for she could not share her joy in her surroundings so easily.

The horses slowed as they climbed hills thick with heather and yellow gorse and green ferns, past walls of dark rock where bright flowers danced in crevices. Hawks called in high flight, sheep moved like tiny clouds over distant slopes, and red deer skimmed the crests of the hills. She lifted her face to the cool, clean wind and breathed Scotland into her lungs and her soul.

As the sun sank and the sky turned lavender, Juliana recognized the hills and knew she was near home at last. She sat straighter, felt brighter. The wind touched her like a friend.

She urged her horse forward and soon caught up to Gawain and Laurence. Gawain glanced back at her and smiled briefly.

"If an English escort is seen riding here, word will spread," Laurence said.

Juliana liked the Lowland Scot, with his mellow voice and easy manner. She had learned he was a boyhood friend to Gawain, and a Scotsman who sided openly with the English.

"Since we have a local Scotswoman in our company, perhaps we will have no trouble from the locals."

"Unless they think to rescue her," Laurence remarked.

"We are close enough to Elladoune now that someone will recognize her. Look—two children on that hill." Gawain indicated a slope were two figures ran like young deer to disappear. Juliana watched them go and thought of her younger brothers.

"They might carry word that the Swan Maiden is home." Gawain glanced at her.

"You know the area well to know where we are," Laurie said.

"I rode through these hills long ago. I have never forgotten the way."

Juliana frowned. For an English knight, he sounded like a man glad to be in Scotland again.

"I hope we are close," Laurence said. "God gave me a lazy nature. Journeying is not for me. A seat by the hearth, a cup of ale, a soft bed, I am content."

"We shall soon find out if those are available. We will cross a narrow pass between those hills"—Gawain pointed—"and enter a forest. But the paths should be well marked. Aye so, my lady?" His dark gaze swept hers briefly.

She nodded. *Bed*, she thought next, and frowned. What would happen when they reached Elladoune? Would Gawain expect her to behave as his wife, once there? She shivered inwardly, deliciously, at the thought. But too much was unknown.

"We ride northwest for a while," Gawain said. "Then the forest will open into a glen. Loch nan Eala is there. In the Gaelic, that means—"

"Loch o' the Swans," Laurence translated. "I have Gaelic from childhood, man, as you do—my nurse was Highland too."

Juliana frowned. Gawain had a Highland nurse? At Avenel? He had not said so.

"The abbey of Inchfillan, I believe, is at one end of the loch,

Elladoune Castle at the other. Lady Juliana?" He looked at her again. "Is it so?"

She nodded.

"If we go astray, mayhap the lass will speak to us long enough to set us right," Laurence said. He smiled at her, eyes sparkling blue. "Ah, she lifts her head haughtily as a queen. That shows us what she thinks of Scotsmen who side with English."

She sent him a little glare that he missed. Gawain saw, though, and turned away.

Once inside the forest following the muffled path, she knew the track and urged her horse ahead. Gawain and Laurence caught up, each beside her. She peered into the green-shadowed trees and the high green canopy overhead.

The woodland held more than an abundance of flora and fauna, she knew. Men, women, and children lived in the forest and in the glen in caves, forced out of their homes by the English. All were friends, some outlawed by the English, and all were honest men and women, renegades by necessity.

Riding beside Gawain, she fervently hoped the rebels would let them pass without incident. Any party would be noted and tracked. But if she was recognized and they tried to rescue her, it could go badly.

Gawain placed a hand on the hilt of his sword as if he sensed the watchers. The horses filed along the forest track while birds called in the trees. Some of those calls were human-made, Juliana knew.

She had to find a way to signal that she was safe. Reaching out, she touched Gawain's arm. He looked at her, startled, and leaned toward her, riding so close, his thigh brushed her skirts.

"Lady?" Gawain slowed his horse with hers. "What is it?"

She stretched toward him and kissed him on the mouth. He responded, kissing her, though he was clearly surprised. When she drew back, he cocked a brow.

"My sisters," he drawled, "are nowhere near, I assure you."

A blush heated her cheeks. However hasty, that kiss might

have saved his life if there were men with bows and arrows just out of sight. She owed Gawain a rescue.

He smiled. "Are you so glad to be home, lady, that you kiss your new husband for joy?" He spoke loudly enough to be heard, showing her he understood.

The forest opened onto a meadow in a golden wash of sun. Juliana urged the palfrey toward a stream that flowed to join Loch nan Eala, which sparkled not far away.

The silhouette of Inchfillan Abbey was visible past the next hill. She urged her horse forward, sparing no glance for her escort.

She was nearly home.

"IF WE LOSE that lass, the king will be in a temper," Laurie drawled.

"Let her fly. She is nearly home," Gawain said, as Juliana galloped, her white gown rucked up over her slim legs. "We will not lose her."

He could still taste that sweet, unpredictable kiss. He suspected she had saved them from an attack in the forest. She knew a good deal about this place, he thought.

"Look at that." Laurie pointed toward a cluster of fieldstone and thatch cottages as they rode past. Juliana had already gone past, but the men slowed.

Gawain frowned, seeing several fire-damaged buildings along a long earthen lane. The village was deserted, its shared field beyond the last house unplanted and bare, its road overgrown with grasses and weeds. Not a soul, human or animal, stirred among the ruined houses or field. Ghosts might walk here, he thought, but no one else.

"What disaster happened here?" Laurie walked his horse beside Gawain's.

"English."

"No attempt to rebuild has been made."

"If the garrison at Elladoune did this, I should have been informed."

"If they did attack this place, it explains why we were watched in the forest."

Gawain glanced at him. "You sensed it too?"

"I was sure we would be ambushed any moment. But your lady saved it with a kiss. Lucky man."

"There must be a host of dispossessed families somewhere, judging by the number of homes in that clachan," Gawain said. "The last garrison I was with encountered a stubborn faction of homeless renegades whose homes had been ruined."

"Ah, the rebels you joined." He gave Gawain a curious glance. "I want to hear that tale someday, having heard just bits of it. There are rumors about how much of a rebel you might have been."

"And I want to know why you are still in the king's army when you swore you would sail to France."

"Land and title are temptations, my friend. But Scottish ale, ah. I would miss it too much. So I stayed on the chance I could return to Scotland."

"Look there! The lass is riding toward a monastery."

"Inchfillan Abbey," Gawain answered. "Augustinian. She has kin there."

Laurie nodded approval. "Brethren with a practical bent. I will bet they make a very fine ale."

Gawain watched Juliana ride toward the foregate of the small compound surrounded by a wooden palisade. Beyond the high wall, he saw rooftops and the spire of a small stone church with a bell tower that looked partly ruined by fire.

The girl tugged on a bell rope and the iron gate swung open. She rode through, and as a black-cassocked monk ran toward her, she gestured for them to leave the gate open.

Gawain rode with Laurie toward the compound. He

glimpsed Juliana embrace one of the monks, then greet others as if she were indeed home and not visiting. One of them led her horse away, and all seemed excited to see her. Family, he realized, and was glad for her.

Nearing the gate, he noticed the other inhabitants in the yard and reined in carefully. Laurie followed suit.

Swans filled the earthen yard, more than a dozen that meandered and waddled between the gate and the monks with Juliana. The largest swan—and several were of impressive size—turned. With great wings outstretched and necks extended, hissing loudly, they rushed toward the two horsemen entering the gate.

Gawain controlled Gringolet, who snorted and bucked in a yard filled with a sea of white-feathered, irritated birds. Calming his mount, walking him away, Gawain waited for Juliana. Standing in the white gown amid black-robed monks, head high on her slim neck, she looked like an enchanted swan.

"Strange watchdogs," Laurie said, walking his mount to sit beside Gawain. "Those beasties bite, did you know?"

Chapter Nineteen

"T HE WEE LADS are well," Abbot Malcolm answered, an arm around Juliana. She had asked about her brothers almost as soon as she arrived, and then told him, almost blurting it out to have it said, that she had married a Sassenach who sat his horse just over there. The abbot tried to disguise his stunned expression.

"Goodness," he said. "Gracious. Er—your brothers are at Dalbrae. I saw them there last week."

"Pray God they are treated fairly," she said, speaking in Gaelic. She glanced through the gate at the two knights, who had ridden just inside the enclosure and waited in silence, watching the birds in the yard. Gawain glanced at her more than once.

"The lads have freedom there," Malcolm assured her. "They seem fine. There is some news of Niall and Will."

"I heard. Taken," she said.

He nodded. "But we cannot buy their release. The abbey is poor, and even if we had the coin, the Church would never allow us to pay a war ransom with it."

"There may be another way. My husband"—she paused with the word—"may be able to help."

"He would? Tell me about how this marriage came to pass."

"*Ach*, Father Abbot. It all happened so fast." She sighed, and began to explain the basics. As she spoke, Malcolm walked with her toward the gate. The swans swarmed around them, clapping their beaks and extending their necks, looking for attention and food. Juliana knew how often the birds frequented the abbey yard, waddling up from the lochside and through the gate when it was open. One of the monks produced a cloth sack and began to toss out bits of grain, and the swans turned to follow him.

Succinctly, Juliana explained the last few weeks while Malcolm listened, brow knitted in concern. She told him of the royal feast, her display there, the impromptu wedding on the king's order. Then she mentioned the journey, and the time at Avenel, how kind the family was. She kept much to herself, though she blushed throughout.

"Father Abbot, Gawain was with the men who ruined Elladoune. But he is the one who saved me that night."

"Your Swan Laird? Well! God does love irony." He shook his head. "But this marriage need not stand if you do not want it. Perhaps it can be annulled. But we must petition the bishop in Glasgow and he may need to wait for an answer from Rome."

Her shook her head. "Sir Gawain did not want the marriage or his assignment in Scotland, but the king gave him no choice. He must obey."

Malcolm peered at her. "You care about him, I think."

She began to speak, then shrugged to admit that aye, she did.

"You can preserve the marriage if you want," he said gently.

"I—I do not know what I want," she mumbled, blushing. Turning away, she looked around the abbey yard, and suddenly noticed the bell tower.

"What happened to the tower?" Some of the stones were broken and black.

"There was a fire," Malcolm said. "No one was hurt, but we need to rebuild some things. The old bronze bell that Saint Fillan himself once rang is fine. But we must make repairs before the market fair in a few weeks, since many come to Inchfillan then."

She nodded, turning as several swans swarmed toward three of the brethren crossing the yard. One was Eonan, a young lay monk, a dark-haired lad who had come to Inchfillan as a boy. His father, like Juliana's, had been killed by the English. Two elderly monks stood with him, their faces somber.

"Father Abbot, if I may speak," Eonan said.

"You may, Brother Eonan."

"We heard that Juliana Lindsay has married now," Eonan began, nodding respectfully to her. "Greetings, Lady Juliana. Congratulations. Is it possible, Father, that this marriage could be beneficial for those who wish to return to Elladoune?"

"Ah. Juliana, I wonder if you can help the cause since you will be there now."

"I—am not sure." She tried not to glance toward Gawain.

"We will bring the news to those in the forest," Eonan said. "They will be glad to know Lady Juliana is safe. Since you left, mistress," he added, "the sheriff's men have been searching the forest with a vengeance to find any rebels."

"Your marriage might be a boon to us." Malcolm spoke in Gaelic, glancing toward the two knights who waited on horseback. "De Soulis is determined to find any who were outlawed."

She nodded, feeling brittle, unable to refuse, yet unwilling to betray Gawain.

"For now, go with your husband to Elladoune," Malcolm said. "We will talk, and plan. Did you keep your silence, my girl, while you were held?"

"Mostly. Not with Sir Gawain."

"Of course. Will you introduce us?"

Juliana nodded and began to walk toward the knights. The swans turned like a white wave and went with her. Laurie's horse backed away, and Gawain's danced aside. The swans hissed, wings lifted, waddling forward. Juliana tried to distract and move them, but they seemed determined.

Gawain dismounted and walked forward, moving through the feathery surf without hesitation. Small heads wavered on long, taut necks, but no swan attacked, allowing him to stride through the group. They turned, weaving back and forth in his path as he approached Juliana and the monks.

"Abbot Malcolm? God give you good day, Father. I am Sir Gawain Avenel, newly appointed constable of Elladoune—and husband to Lady Juliana."

"Welcome, sir." Malcolm stood placidly amid the gaggle of swans. "She just told me of your marriage. We expected a new garrison leader, and we hoped the lady would return safely. But we did not reckon on a wedding!" He smiled.

"Nor did we." Gawain glanced at Juliana.

"We prayed and entrusted the lady's fate to heaven. God watched over her. But you are an unusual guardian angel, I admit."

"Heaven can be unpredictable," Gawain said, glancing at Juliana.

Malcolm tipped his head. "Do I know you, sir? Your face seems familiar."

Something flickered in Gawain's eyes. Juliana frowned, wondering. "I—was here years ago. Perhaps we met."

"Ah. With the English a few years ago," Malcolm said.

"Thank you for the welcome. We should be going. I must see the castle."

Malcolm clasped Gawain's hand. "Let me wish you good fortune in your marriage and goodwill between us for all concerned here."

"Indeed." Gawain smiled.

Juliana was amazed by the warmth of the abbot's welcome. Perhaps it was part of the plan he had spoken of devising. The swans fluttered and circled, and one of them pecked at Gawain's leather pouch. He looked down.

"She means no threat," Malcolm assured him. "She is greedy and thinks your pouch holds food. The swans are fed here often and are as tame as swans can be."

"I see." Gawain stood calmly amid the birds, while Laurie remained on his horse, looking distinctly unimpressed as he eyed the swans.

Gawain looked up. "You had a fire."

"We will rebuild," Malcolm said.

"Did you apply to the sheriff for timbers? King Edward maintains a policy of support for the local churches."

"So I have heard. We will send a list of our needs to the sheriff. Has he returned from his southern journey?"

"Soon," Gawain said. He turned, as they all did, at a sudden commotion. The largest cob had spread his wings and was charging the horses, causing them to knicker and buck again. Laurie grabbed the reins of Gawain's horse and held both in check.

"Cuchulainn! Stop, you!" Malcolm called to the swan, as one of the monks ran to disperse the gaggle away from the horses.

Malcolm turned to Gawain. "Sir, the sheriff holds my wards, Juliana's younger brothers, hostage at Dalbrae. Can you help?"

"I will see if I can arrange for their release."

"They are good lads and should not be held. Their older brothers have recently been taken as well, kept elsewhere."

"Then I will look into both matters."

Malcolm studied him soberly. "Three years ago, after the burning of the local village, the brethren of Inchfillan came to an understanding with the garrison at Elladoune. We do God's work here and tend to our flock of souls, and they leave us in peace. 'Tis a truce without signatures."

"I respect that and will continue the agreement. I do not yet know my duties at Elladoune, but I do not make war on monks and innocents. Inchfillan and every innocent here and elsewhere will be safe in my regard."

Malcolm nodded his gratitude. "You seem an honorable man for a Sassenach. We will talk again. Juliana, my dear, God keep you safe." He pressed her hands in his. "Come back soon. Go with him," he added, whispering.

"My lady," Gawain murmured. "We must go on to the castle. The horses—and Laurie—are eager to be gone."

The moment to depart Inchfillan and all that was familiar here had come too soon. She had longed to return to Elladoune for years, but she was not sure it would feel like home after so long. She hesitated.

Gawain held out his hand. "My lady."

She glanced at the husband she hardly knew. A few nights together, days on the road—despite his courtesies and the dilemmas they had weathered, she was not yet sure she could trust him. She recalled precious hours wrapped in the privacy of a bed, where trust and affection grew. Yet going with him and away from here felt like a great risk.

But he was her path to Elladoune, to home. He might be the pathway to even more, to love, to a home for her heart.

"Juliana?" His hand was outstretched.

She glided past him through the froth of swans toward her horse, held by a monk near the foregate.

Chapter Twenty

S OARING AND SUNLIT, Elladoune sat high on a promontory of slate that jutted into the loch. Built from honey-colored sandstone, it overlooked the water and the hills. The rounded corner towers were massive sentinels pierced by arrow slits. Juliana felt as excited as a child. For the first time in years, she would enter the castle again.

The gate stood open, its iron portcullis drawn into the overhead arch. Brother Eonan had run ahead to bring word to the garrison of their arrival. Gawain slowed his horse beside hers as the three of them wended their way up the hill.

"I was not certain you would come away from Inchfillan," he said.

"I had to come here," she answered. "I had to."

"'Tis not large, judging by those walls, but it looks strong and built well."

"My great-grandfather rebuilt an older fortress. There have been keeps here for generations. We call it *Dun nan Eala* in the Gaelic, though it became known as Elladoune. Easier for English to say," she added.

"Fortress of the swans," he murmured.

She glanced at him. "You know what it means?"

"I have a little Gaelic." He rode ahead on the sloping track.

She was the last to ride beneath the portcullis, following to absorb the sight. The last time she had been this close, Elladoune had been in flames. And she had taken a terrifying leap into the loch—where she had met Gawain in the water, not knowing until recently that he had pulled her to safety to his own detriment.

The castle was square, with round towers at each corner. The farthest corner tower jutted out to overlook the loch, sheering down to the promontory just above the water. She remembered plunging to the water there.

The fire had destroyed much, though repairs and additions had been made. Living in the forest, she had seen the progress from a distance over time, but she had never set foot inside. Now, in the courtyard, she saw a few monks from Inchfillan, including Brother Eonan, who had run ahead. Two carried buckets and sacks, another shooed goats and chickens out of the way of the incoming horses, and another pushed a wheelbarrow toward a lush kitchen garden.

The garden was larger than she remembered, and so was the kitchen building. But of course, she told herself, more food and more cooks would have been needed to provide meals for a garrison of perhaps a hundred or more men.

Other new buildings clustered along the inside of the high curtain wall, structures of wattle and thatch used for stables and livestock, blacksmithing and armory, for cooking, washing, storage, and garrison quarters. Most of them appeared to be empty. Juliana recalled hearing that most of the garrison had ridden out on extended searches for rebels and the renegade Robert Bruce; some, she had also heard, had been lost in skirmishes and battles. No wonder the garrison had thinned.

Despite the changes, Elladoune looked much the same, and memories assailed her. Yet it was no longer her home. War was conducted here; the enemy lived here. She slid from her horse to stand looking around. A monk led her palfrey away, and Gawain dismounted to speak with Laurence, then came to her, taking her arm.

"Come inside to sit down and rest." He began to lead her toward the keep. But her legs trembled as she climbed the wooden steps to the main entrance of the keep tower, a reaction perhaps to the exhaustion of the day, and the near-shock of being inside Elladoune again. Gawain looked down at her as she paused on the platform to gaze at the compound.

"Is it much changed?" he asked.

"Some things are the same. Other things I do not recognize. There," she said, pointing toward the battlement. "On those stone steps, I see the long crack where I tripped when I was little and broke my arm. My father had the step repaired. I can see the scar on the stone. In that tower"—she pointed again—"we played hide-and-seek and watched the loch for monsters."

"Serious work." A wry smile.

"On the south side of the bailey, we played games and had archery targets. In that corner shed where hay was stored, Niall shot an arrow into my leg as I climbed into the loft. He said the shaft was warped, and he was aiming at the hay."

Gawain chuckled.

"My father's mews were over there. He gave me a beautiful little kestrel to train and fly. She would be gone now—the mews looks empty. And here in this tower, my brothers and I were born. So was my father, and my grandfather."

He glanced at the keep. "What is the plaque above the door? A swan with lifted wings, and an arrow in its beak?"

"The crest of the Lindsays of Elladoune."

"This was indeed a home," he murmured.

"And now it is a place for warmongers. Now there are more buildings, and more dirt in the bailey. The midden pile behind the kitchen shed is too large and needs burning. Harnesses and weapons are hanging outside the sheds, and..." She sighed. "There are traces of the fire."

"Blackened stones along the outer wall," he agreed. "Those should be cleaned. And I can see where stones are a different color where repairs were made. Much rebuilding was done. The repairs and additions look good. Sturdy. They will last."

"Were you here in the garrison, after...you helped me?"

"I was sent elsewhere. To make an apology," he added with another wry smile.

She tilted her head, curious. "I want to know more about that. Why would an English knight in good favor risk his welfare for the Scots?"

"Tell me your secrets, lass, and you will learn some of mine."

She looked away. Though she wanted to know more about him, she could not endanger her friends by revealing what she knew about their lives now.

"You should be glad I speak to you at all, Sassenach." She said it lightly.

"Believe me, I am. Come inside." He opened the door.

GAWAIN FOLLOWED JULIANA past the great hall, where he glimpsed a spacious, white-washed room with a high timber ceiling and planked floor. Tables, benches, and chairs were arranged there, but the room had a starkness that did not speak of home.

The girl did not enter the hall, but silently led the way up the stone turning steps. Gawain paused with her at each level to glance into the rooms that opened off the landings, peering into chambers that were sparsely furnished, some clearly used for military quarters. Juliana said nothing, ascending further.

The uppermost level, he saw, contained a bedchamber, a small solar room, and a garderobe. Juliana entered the main room, the bedraggled hem of her white gown pooling on the wooden floor as she turned.

"This looks so different," she murmured, and went to the window. "Even the shape of the window has changed. But it is the same lovely view over the loch to the mountains."

Gawain surveyed the austere chamber. A bed filled one corner, enclosed by a green canopy and curtains suspended from iron rods attached to the ceiling. It looked lumpy and uncomfortable. The few furnishings—a table, bench, wooden chest, stools, and one chair beside a narrow stone fireplace—were plain. The floor was covered in rushes that needed sweeping out.

"This was rebuilt," he guessed. "The fire in the upper tower was fierce."

"I know. There were mural paintings on the walls in some of these rooms. There were embroidered French tapestries on the walls in the great hall. All gone."

"It must have been a lovely home, but the repairs were done well. It is a garrison now. Not cozy, but practical."

"I had to jump from the window on the night of the fire."

"I remember," he murmured. He felt a fierce urge to touch her, comfort her as she surveyed what was lost, what was new.

"I always hoped one day my family could reunite here. Foolish, I suppose." She shrugged. "But I am here now, and I have you to thank for it." She smiled a little. "What next? As constable of the garrison, what will you do?"

"You need to rest, first. I need to find out about food and sleeping quarters and so on. We will have a garrison here soon, I expect. Laurie and I will look about."

"You need rest too."

"I am fine. There is much to be done here. I will find rooms for us, Laurie as well. He will have much to do as my second in command here."

"Where—will you sleep?"

He glanced at the curtained bed, then through a side door into the solar, which held a bench in a window seat. A man could sleep there if he had to, he thought.

He leaned against the window jamb. "Where do you want me to sleep?"

She blushed. "Do we pretend the happy marriage here too?"

"Do you object to that?"

"It was necessary at Avenel. Here—you have orders to tame me."

"I doubt that can be done. But I am expected to teach you loyalty to your king and show local Scots the proper direction for their own loyalties."

"The proper direction for the English," she said, as if reciting, "is to go south."

"And there is the Swan Maiden I know." Know and love. He gave her a rueful smile. "I do not expect you to surrender."

"No surrender, no taming. No chains."

"That will play havoc with my orders," he drawled. "I gave De Soulis the chains."

"I know. I thank you for that. What if he insists you do as ordered or be reported to the king?"

"He may do that no matter what I do. Listen now. You are not my prisoner but my wife, and you are in my safekeeping." He tilted his head. "Disobeying De Soulis does not trouble my conscience, I promise."

Her cheeks tinted rose. "If I must act the constable's happy wife, then I want the privileges any lady would have. Freedom. I am home, with no reason to run."

"You have freedom, but you must cooperate. Best that you stay between the castle and the abbey, and always with a guard. Laurie will be willing until we have more men."

"Cooperate with what?" she asked carefully.

"Learn a little so you can say an oath of fealty for the king if summoned."

She folded her arms. "I cannot do that."

"Stubborn lady." He nodded. "But the oath must be learned, for you may be tested by someone other than myself. I want your promise to always return to me at the end of the day."

Her eyes searched his. "Aye," she whispered.

"And do not involve yourself with rebels."

"Rebels?" Her blue eyes went wide and innocent. "And what do you promise?"

"To give you my trust." He leaned closer. "Can we seal that?"

She gave a little nod, and he touched his lips to hers, a butterfly alighting. As she curved toward him for more, his heart knocked like a drum. "There," he said.

She slowly shook her head. "I need more than quick promise from you."

With a low murmur, he took her by the shoulders to kiss her profoundly, deeply, just as he had wanted since he had woken beside her that morning in the heavenly quiet of Avenel.

Her hands rested on his waist and tugged him close. Desire poured through him. His mouth upon hers satisfied only the edge of his hunger. Lumpy as that bed looked, he wanted to sweep her up and carry her there.

But he drew back, still holding her. Courtesy. Respect. Always so for him, though more and more it took every fiber of his being to fulfill that with her. She was simply beautiful just then, eyes still closed, her face glowing, peaceful, waiting. Her breasts pressed soft and firm against him. Awareness and sensation drove him toward madness.

"Is that binding enough for you?" he asked hoarsely, thinking he must push away.

"Better than a signature. Better than chains." She sounded breathless.

"Some manacles," he said, cupping her face, so that she leaned into his palm, "are not made of gold or steel. Some chains are invisible."

"And what are those?" she whispered.

"If you do not know, there is no use to tell you. Listen now," he went on, putting her away from him as an alternative to carrying her off, "you are weary. And I must act the constable to see what can possibly be done here."

Striding from the room and closing the door behind him, he let out a long breath. The cool stone stairwell and his forceful steps subdued the heated throbbing in his body. But he felt a deep tug of the heart as if a golden chain spun endlessly out to link him with the lady in the tower.

LATE THAT NIGHT, Gawain stood in the small solar and looked through the window. Entranced by the view—a sweep of lavender sky above dark mountains and the sparkling indigo loch—he stood thoughtful, resting a foot on the stone bench.

In the bedchamber, Juliana slept deeply, as she had for hours. Earlier he had brought her some ale the monks had supplied, and something to eat—burned oatcakes proudly produced by Laurie, and a very good cheese made at Inchfillan. She scarcely roused, swallowing a little watered ale, nibbling a bit of food, then sliding back to sleep. Later, when he came up to the room, he touched her head gently and pulled up the simple woolen blankets.

Though the hour was late, he could not sleep. Laurie had claimed the chamber beneath this one, large but sparsely furnished, and had gone to bed. The monks had returned to Inchfillan Abbey, though before leaving, they had showed Gawain and Laurie various features of the castle, including its stores and livestock. There were a few servants who sometimes helped, he learned, mostly crofters from the glen who came to the castle and usually returned to the hills at night. Tomorrow, the monks promised, either crofters or monks would help gather garden vegetables and bring meat for stew.

Gawain wrinkled his nose at the thought of the burnt cakes. A cook would have to be found; Laurie was willing but not up to the task. Perhaps the abbot could lend a monk or two for a while until a routine and those willing to help could be found.

In the gathering darkness, he saw swans floating on the loch, tiny, pale blurs. He remembered how they had clustered on the water the night Elladoune had burned. But of course they would still be here. Swans were creatures of habit. The garrison would not frighten them away. English knights would leave them be, knowing it was punishable to hunt or kill a swan.

He remembered the legend he had learned in boyhood of a

terrible storm here long ago, created by magic, which had destroyed an island fortress. Hundreds of people had died here, according to the tale, and had transformed into swans.

He frowned, thinking of his grandfather, his family. The ruins of Glenshie were not far from Elladoune. But where? He had been young enough that he was not sure.

Across the loch, mountain slopes thrust upward. He studied each shape, searching for a certain contour, an image that he remembered from childhood: an old woman's face in a mountainside.

They had called it *Beinn an Aodann*—mountain of the face— he remembered. Long ago, a giantess had lived in the mountain. He searched the profiles of the hills.

Yet he knew he was putting off going to his wife's bed. The implicit agreement still existed between them. She was not ready to accept him as her husband, and yet he felt that she was more receptive, wanting kisses one moment, turning cool the next. He was growing deeply fond of her, knowing her moods. Aye, he loved her now. And he had patience when he knew what he wanted.

But the lure of that enclosed bed with her was strong. She slept, and he needed sleep too. And being here at last, so close to Glenshie and yet so far from it, he desperately craved solace. Soon he would tell her the truth. Soon.

He lingered a while searching for the giantess. There he would find Glenshie.

—◆··• •··◆—

Chapter Twenty-One

THEY CAME AS they always had, gliding toward the shore toward her, graceful white forms mirrored in the water. They swam slowly, without flurry, as if no time had passed. As if she had not changed in the very core of her soul since she stood here last.

She tossed grain from a small sack, and the swans fed, heads dipped, bodies spinning as they sought the food. Life was simple and direct for them, peace amid wildness and strife. They accepted the food and her presence as they had her absence.

Though just weeks had passed since she had seen them, she felt different—wiser somehow, kinder perhaps, aware of her deep need for peace, home, love. Gawain had walked into her life, strong and vivid, like torch in the darkness. She needed him.

With an exquisite shiver, she remembered waking in the middle of the night to realize he was there beside her. She had moved closer to him, savoring his warmth and the reassuring cadence of his breathing, his being.

She moved toward the water, careful of the hem of the mulberry gown Gawain's mother had given her. Until she fetched her things from Inchfillan, she had the white gown with its unpleasant memories, or this gown with its reminder of the welcome and happiness she had felt at Avenel.

She glanced over her shoulder, where Laurie Kirkpatrick and Brother Eonan sat on the grass beneath a tree, acting as chaperones of a sort, talking quietly, barely looking toward her. Earlier, when she woke alone that morning, she had learned at breakfast—nibbling one of Laurie's unappetizing oatcakes—that Gawain had ridden to Dalbrae to see the sheriff.

The swans moved about in the water and she strolled there, tossing grain, thinking. Beyond a curve in the bank, she entered a little cove protected by a fringe of reeds and birches, just out of sight of Laurie and Eonan, who did not seem to notice. Here the loch narrowed; across that span, pine trees created a dense cover. Her friends and kinsmen hid there in the vastness.

She felt an urge to cross the loch and go to them. While Brother Eonan knew the rebels' hiding places, it was unlikely that he would tell Laurie where she might be. Stripping out of her gown, she stuffed it under a fallen log, and clad in her linen shift, she slipped into the water, sighing as its invigorating chill enveloped her.

The swans encircled her, a perfect shield as she swam further out, a strong swimmer since childhood. A quick glance showed that the men sat with their backs to her. She shot under the surface like an arrow and came up near the opposite shore, pulling up and out, water sluicing as she emerged under the low eaves of a huge pine.

This very spot had long been used as a rendezvous. Sheltered by the swooping arms of the pine, she soon found the canvas sack that she knew would be there. Inside, as she expected, she found dry clothing: linen chemise, a tunic, a shirt, soft narrow boots. She changed quickly into the clothes she had appropriated a few years ago from her brothers' things. Here she also kept a simple white-bleached gown and a white feathered cape that she had made from discarded swan feathers years ago.

Soon she ran along a half-hidden track, feet silent on a carpet of pine needles.

SHE FELT STRUCK to her soul. Shortly after a reunion near a cave with a few of those who hid in this part of the forest, Juliana stood blinking back tears. Across a wide stream, once feathered by birch and pine trees, charred stumps now thrust upward like black swords.

"What happened?" She looked at two friends, Lucas and Red Angus, who sat by a small fire with some of the others. "That part was all forested when I was last here."

"Sheriff's men," Lucas answered curtly. He stood and came toward her, a dark and powerful man with anger etching folds in his face. "Looking for rebels, though Father Abbot told them only homeless innocents lived in the forest."

"The sheriff is convinced the area is overrun with rebels," Red Angus added. He came forward too, so tall he had to duck head and shoulders to stand near the pine trees with Juliana and Lucas. "He is determined to destroy it bit by bit, either by cutting trees for timber, or burning whole sections. He intends to eliminate any rebel threat in this area, so they are destroying the forest bit by bit. Soon we will have nowhere to live. And these few caves are crowded with families." He gestured toward the rocky hillside studded with a few narrow cave entrances.

"We will be forced to leave Glen Fillan," Lucas growled. "Walter De Soulis will persist until all of this is gone, just to find rebels."

"We have weapons and armor put by, and men to wield them," Juliana said.

"Fight back, says the wee girl with her small bow and arrow?" Lucas asked.

"We cannot defeat De Soulis. Remember what they say. That black armor of his is impenetrable. None of us should risk going against a man who practices the black arts!"

"He is not a wizard. Just a king's man. Remember that they say the Swan Maiden is magical too. It is all rumor," she said.

"We have shot arrows at De Soulis from the trees and hills," Lucas said. "Bolts bounce off his black armor. He cannot be stopped. Some even believe he bought that gear from the devil."

She shook her head in disbelief. "There has to be some way to stop him."

"He will send men to search every inch of this forest until we are either killed or chased off. We have families to protect. We must go elsewhere," Lucas said.

"Juliana," an old woman called as she shuffled toward them, shoulders rounded beneath a plaid pulled high over her head. "I am glad you are back at Elladoune again, even if you came back with an English husband. Now you are back, you can help us."

"Mother Beithag, thank you. But I am not sure," Juliana began.

"My mother is right," Angus said. "You can let our men into the fortress secretly so we can take it over."

Juliana frowned, recalling a scheme she had supported previously. But she shook her head. "I cannot betray my husband. He would suffer greatly for it."

"*Ach,*" Lucas muttered with disgust, turning away.

"Just let us in," Angus said. "We will do the rest. You need do nothing—"

"Please do not ask this of me," she said fervently.

"*Ach*, look at the lass," Beithag said. "She cares for her Sassenach husband. A wife must not betray her man. Find another way of taking the castle."

"Now what?" Lucas growled. "You have kin among us. And we have children here, wives, and elderly folk. You are the only one who can help us, and you deny us now?"

Anguish gripped at her. Beithag set a sympathetic hand on her arm and Angus looked sheepish. But Lucas glowered, and she knew he would not let this be.

"Perhaps you can ask your husband to help us," Angus suggested.

Lucas snorted. "Him? He has already begun a campaign against us."

Juliana lifted her brows. "What do you mean?"

"My sons saw him this morning riding the paths in the forest," Lucas said. "He stopped often as if to memorize what is here. Then he rode out to the hills. My sons tracked him."

"He wants to learn the area. There is nothing wrong in that," Juliana said.

"Likely he will report what he finds to the sheriff."

"I could—ask if he might help," she ventured. Lucas growled his doubt.

"Listen to the lass," said another man, coming close. Juliana turned to see Uilleam, Beithag's husband. Bent and grayed, he always had a wise voice among the families in the forest. "If the new constable cares for his wife, he might grant a favor."

"Then ask him to go to the sheriff and demand that he stop the raids here and let ousted families live in peace. This part of the forest is on Elladoune property. You have the right to ask that."

An idea occurred to her then. "What if you came to Elladoune to live? There is no garrison there now, and there is plenty of space."

They stared at her. "Under the same roof as Sassenachs?" Lucas snapped. "There will be a garrison there soon enough."

"We need help there to maintain the castle and run the household. There is room there for innocent families who can lend a hand."

"Servants to Sassenachs? Bah!" Lucas spit.

"I will need help as lady of the castle, managing a large household, including—hired servants," she said quickly, as the idea grew. "Paid with lodging and needs met."

"If my family could stay there," Angus said thoughtfully, "Lucas and I could be free to join Bruce."

"And nobody would be any the wiser," Lucas allowed, frowning.

"I will simply ask my husband to shelter some made homeless by the sheriff, and bring them in to help in the castle, especially women and children and old ones." Surely Gawain, with his innate kindness, would agree that. "He is an honorable man."

"Bah," Lucas said.

"*Ach*, she is smitten," Beithag said, nodding.

"I must go," Juliana said. "I have been gone too long now. But I will be back."

EMERGING ON THE other side of the loch, sweeping back her wet hair, she reached under the fallen log. Her gown was gone. She groped around, rose to her feet, turned.

"Looking for this?"

She whirled, flinging her arms over herself in the wet linen shift. Laurie stood with her mulberry gown over one shoulder. Brother Eonan stood there too, looking away from her.

"Brother, stay back if you think it a sin to see her thus," Laurie said. "I need a few words with the lass. My lady," Laurie said as he came closer, "where the devil were you?"

She lashed out an arm for her gown. He blew out an exasperated breath and tossed it to her. "Och, here. I have sisters and a wife. A wet lass does not fret me. But Gawain would have my hide if you caught an ague. Get dressed."

As she struggled into the gown, she eyed him in wary silence, heart pounding.

"It wounds me that you do not trust me," he said. "I am not a lecher. You are safe. Fine as you are, you are my friend's wife and a saint to me. Just tell me where you went."

She gulped and watched him, wondering quite what to say. "I went for a swim."

"I see that. Crossed the loch with your swans and ran into the forest. Where did you go? Answer me, lass. Remember I am a Scotsman. I hope it counts with you."

She shivered. A Scotsman who rode with the English, she wanted to reply. But he was Gawain's friend and she wanted to trust him.

Silence rolled out. Birds twittered, breeze rustled the leaves. Brother Eonan stood with his back turned.

"I am dressed, Eonan," she said. "Very well, Sir Laurie."

"She speaks! And?" Laurie asked.

"I like to swim," she explained, turning to walk with Laurie and Eonan.

"And then? You like visiting rebels in the forest beyond loch? You disappeared into the trees."

"I have friends there. Homeless and in need. Good people."

"Ah. No rebels?"

"An old wife and her elderly husband, and their family.'

He tipped a brow. "You need to stay here, lass. If you want to swim, do that, if your husband approves."

She grimaced. "I do not need his approval to swim in a loch that belongs rightfully to my own family, along with that castle."

"Hmm." He pursed his lips, thinking. "I am a lazy man. I will not chase after you like a nursemaid when I can rest on the shore while you splash. We shall have a pact between us. Swim, and stay in sight. Trust me, and I will trust you."

"I would like that." She smiled.

"But do not cross the constable of Elladoune. He is not so mellow a man as I."

Chapter Twenty-Two

EVENING SPILLED AMETHYST color over the loch when Gawain returned to Elladoune. The dark tips of the mountains reflected in the water too. He had ridden past those hills yet had not yet seen the stark profile face he sought. He had ridden to Dalbrae, too, only to learn that Walter de Soulis had not yet returned from his journey. The young Lindsay brothers were inside, the guards confirmed when asked. But Gawain did not request to see them, not keen to raise suspicion.

On the way back to Elladoune, he had ridden over rough tracks and moorland, past long swaths of greenwood and running streams, past hills and distant mountain silhouettes. Beinn an Aodann was there somewhere, but he did not see it.

Perhaps his childhood memory was wrong after all. He was sure Glenshie lay north of Elladoune, but he had been a boy then, after all. He did not have the heart to ask his mother at Avenel and stir her deep grief over the loss. And he could ask no one else or attract too much interest. He could not yet reveal who he was.

But he ached inside to tell Juliana. The need to be open with her, and the need to find his boyhood home and claim his land and title, sat in his belly like a great stone.

Seeing Elladoune ahead, he thought of Juliana waiting inside and his spirits lifted. Being with her was heaven enough to ease this private hell.

A QUICK SUPPER shared with Laurie alone in the great hall consisted of old ale and dried meat, heated and charred. They spoke of what was to be done at Elladoune while Gawain ate sparingly, praising Laurie for the effort. He kept watch for Juliana, but had not yet seen her.

"I offered supper, but she claimed she was not hungry and retired to her tower chamber before you came in," Laurie answered. "You will find her there, no doubt, or elsewhere in the castle."

"You were with her all day?"

"Och, aye. She swam for a bit, said she likes to do that." He cleared his throat.

"She spoke to you?"

"Och aye, the lass trusts me now."

"Good. You can help keep her out of mischief." Bidding him good night, Gawain went in search of his wife, but she was nowhere to be found.

Finally he spotted her up on the wallwalk overlooking the loch. The sky was darkening, but she seemed to hold her own light, pale as a moonbeam, a pale tartan shawl around her shoulders, her blond hair pouring down, free without a veil.

"The sky is beautiful," she said as he approached.

"Aye, and with a peaceful reflection in the loch. I saw the swans as I returned."

"They will swim all day and night, and rest only here and there as they travel the loch and also along the connecting stream that runs by the abbey." She smiled. "They know the monks will feed them. But each evening they find their way back to Loch nan Eala and Elladoune."

"And so did you," he said with gentle amusement.

"My route was not always peaceful," she said wryly. "You rode to Dalbrae? Did you see the sheriff—and my brothers?"

"I went there, but Sir Walter has not arrived yet. I was assured your brothers are there, and well. But I thought it best not to ask to see them yet. Then I rode through the hills and the forest."

"Searching for rebels?" she asked tartly.

"Learning the land. And you? I heard you went swimming."

"The water is nice this time of year. I often swim the loch."

"I know. I pulled you out of there once."

"I would have made it to shore on my own that night." She folded her arms.

"To shore, but not past the English. But promise me you will stay near Laurie. He seemed concerned about that. Though he was pleased that you spoke to him." He chuckled.

"I like him well," she said. "But I will not disrobe near him if I feel like swimming."

"Best if you keep away from the water for a while. De Soulis and his men are still a danger to you."

"So I am still a prisoner?"

"I only ask that you stay between the castle and the abbey for now, and stay safe."

She nodded, and was silent for a bit. "Gabhan, I must ask a favor."

When she softened his name in the Gaelic, she could not know the effect on him. He was ready to grant her anything. "Aye, ask."

She hugged her arms over her chest as if she guarded something. "There are people living in the forest near here. Some are my kin, the rest are friends. They are homeless since the English destroyed their village. You saw the ruin of it."

"Aye. Not well done by the garrison. No need," he murmured.

"The sheriff's men have been burning and cutting through the forest looking for them. I heard it from the monks, and I saw some of the damage today—whenIswam that way. They need shelter and safety. I want to bring them here to Elladoune," she said quickly.

He looked at her in surprise. "You want me to harbor Scots rebels here?"

"I thought you would act the charitable knight, not the king's man," she said curtly. "They are good folk in need of help. There is plenty of room here. This was once my family's home. I want to help them."

"I understand you are loyal to your friends. But soldiers may be here soon."

She looked away. "They are in dire straits. The men need not come with them if you think they are rebels, but the families are truly in need. There are women there, and elderly, and children. De Soulis would rout them out like rodents—"

"Stop—children, elderly? You weaken me, and you know it."

She tipped her head. "Please," she whispered.

He blew out a breath, unable to refuse her even if he wanted. "We can shelter the neediest of them here. Certainly no rebels. I do not even want to hear if they number among these people."

Her smile flashed. "Then I will not say. Gabhan, thank you. You will not regret it."

"I will if I lose my head for it."

"They will be a great help here. They can be servants and stable grooms and so on. The women can clean and bake and cook—"

"Cook! You should have said that first," he drawled, then he laughed, just to see her smile again. In the moonlight, she looked ethereal and magical. He found it easy to believe that some believed her to be one of the enchanted swans of castle legend.

"I am grateful to you. I knew you were the Swan Laird, re-member?"

"Swan Laird?"

"Chivalrous and compassionate. Willing to help those in need, just as you have saved me."

Her words touched him deeply. "You did need saving now and again."

She tilted another glance toward him. The pull between them felt strong and clear, like golden links or a rope of silk, drawing them. He wanted to take her into his arms and kiss her. But he would wait, wanting to be sure. So very sure.

He looked out over the loch. "Those mountains—what are they called?"

"Those are just hills. The true mountains are in the upper Highlands. But they may look like mountains to a Sassenach used to low green hills." A little smile played around her mouth.

"Ah, you have not seen much of England. What is that peak called, over there?"

"That we do call a mountain. Beinn Beira."

"Mountain of Beira, the old Celtic goddess of winter." He turned to stroll the wall walk, and she turned with him.

"You have a little Gaelic, I have noticed."

"Some. Is there a mountain near here called Beinn an Aodann?"

She shook her head. "I do not know that one. Why? Are you ordered to claim a new property for your English king?"

He shot her a frown. "Just curious. I had heard the name."

"Tell me how a privileged English knight knows Gaelic."

"It was—spoken by some in my household as a boy. What of you? Your English is very good."

"I was born at Elladoune. The monks taught my brothers and I English and Latin." She paused. "Gawain, can you help my brothers? All four of them?"

The wallwalk ended at another tower. He stopped in its shadow. "I will do what I can. The two in De Soulis's keeping— what were their misdeeds? You have not said."

"The sheriff took them hostage to keep a tight fist on the abbot. They are scarce more than babes. Seven and nine."

"God save us, I did not realize they were so young. I will do what I can, I swear." A breeze rose up, and he reached out to brush a windblown lock of hair from her brow.

"And help my kin and friends?" She watched him, her eyes

gleaming like the night sky, indigo sparkled with stars. Her chin lifted, her throat lengthened.

"Kin and friends too." He skimmed his palm along her sleek hair. "You remind me of a swan, beautiful, graceful. Passionate and loyal."

"If I am like a swan at all, it is in my need for freedom, and my fierceness to defend my home and family. *Ach*," she said. "But you have never lost a home."

"More than you know. Juliana—" It burned in him to tell her.

In that moment, she leaned close, face lifted, and rose on her toes. He felt her breath touch his lips. He felt his heart, his body, begin to pound within. Wanting desperately to pull her close, hard against him, he knew she must begin this first. He would stand in shadows and moonlight forever to wait for her if he must.

A tilt of her head, and she nudged her nose to his, seeking, and her lips touched his in a faery-like caress.

He leaned down and kissed her full on the mouth, the taste and feel of her blissfully familiar now. She opened to his lips with a breathy little moan, a sound that made him throb, surge, made him pull her tightly against him as he kissed her again.

Passion laced with tenderness filled him, and a sudden sense of love—powerful and real—rocked him. She was haven for his spirit and heart. He knew that now. He would do anything for her—yet he must guard his secrets. And for a moment, he was glad that the kisses had stopped that urge to share too much, perhaps too soon.

The evening wind blew through his hair and hers, weaving dark and light strands together. She pulled back.

"Come away from here," she said breathlessly. "We will be seen."

"We are wed," he murmured, seeking her lips again.

"Come away," she whispered. She took his hand turned toward the door of the tower, where moonlight poured over the stone. He opened the door and guided her inside.

SHE FELT AN utter calm and certainty, his kisses sparking a hunger that had lingered in her for days. She wanted to be with him inside the sanctuary of the curtained bed, wanted to let passion burn clean between them, dissolving the knots and tangles that surrounded them in the outer world. When she paused beside the bed to unfasten the brooch that held her cloak, Gawan stepped back. His stillness gave her the chance to change her mind—to end this, or continue.

Her gown was a simple thing, easily removed as she drew it over her head and cast it to the floor as her answer. Then she drew back the curtain in the shadows. A low fire burned in the hearth, a little warm, a little golden light spilling over the plain woolen blankets. He stepped toward her and reached out.

Cradling her face, he kissed her again, slowly and thoroughly so that she felt herself melt like honey in sunlight. She wanted to sink into his arms, into his skill and surety, into the allure of what was to come. Her knees felt uncertain, and the floor seemed to drop away beneath her feet. She moved back toward the bed, silent, waiting.

The small gap between them felt too wide, tugging at her heart. She yearned for his strength, his warmth, his vibrancy. She leaned back on the bed, her invitation clear. The silence seemed natural to the moment, to who she was here, who he was.

He undressed, the belt, the boots, the long tunic, the shirt beneath. She sensed that he still meant to give her time, but she did not need it any longer.

His body gleamed golden in the fire's glow. She had never seen him fully nude, and she drew in a breath, stunned by the elegance and strength of his body. He stepped into the shadow of the curtain, a knee upon the fat heather-stuffed mattress, making it sink.

Desire took sure form in a man, and she studied him, intrigued, her body responding, heart thumping. She shifted, drawing her chemise away, letting him see her in shadows as she saw him, though her breath quickened, hands trembled with the boldness of it. He drew the curtain shut, darkness enveloping them, a trace of light seeping through the weave of the cloth.

Inside that sanctum now, he took her in his arms, sank with her, pulled her toward him, her body pressing against his. His skin was firm and warm, and felt so good that her fear was chased away. She only wanted to be closer as she looped her arms around his neck and leaned into him, breasts against his chest, heart beating faster.

His kisses were rich and potent now, exploring, his hands skilled and gently teasing as he ran fingers down the sinuous curve of her spine to rest on the slope of her hips. She curved against him, warm to hot, soft to hard, and shifted her hips to deepen the cradle that formed for him. He groaned low, and as his hand swept her breasts, she felt herself pearl beneath his fingers even as he kissed her. She arched her back, shivering, as he supported her with a hand at the small of her back, kissing, teasing, his touch new and alive and astonishing, touches that stirred every urge her body had, questing and insistent. She learned quickly, loving—needing—more from him.

He stretched out fully on the bed with her now, and she felt wrapped in his embrace, enveloped in a simple, surprising, fiery ecstasy as his hands found tender places. As he kissed her again, she slid her hands over his shoulders, his back, his torso, skin heated smooth layered over taut muscle.

She sank her fingers into the thick silk of his hair, glossy and dark, and his lips were the only softness she found in him. The rest was hard strength tempered to velvety tenderness, like the quiet hallmark of his character. He explored her, lips and fingers cajoling, until she sighed and arched and sought his body with her hands and lips, savoring its power and grace. Touching him, being touched, was as potent as dark wine, and she ached deeply inside for more, opening widely to him.

He cupped her hips, found her as she found him. Wild yet gentle, rapture stirred and flashed, and she cried out, urging him toward her. And carefully, he covered her, sought her. A breath, a pause, and she felt him there, steady and rigid. The small pain passed, and he eased into her as a sweet, wild storm took her, filled, flowed with her.

Kissing her, separating, he held her, then reached for the curtain. Murmuring a protest, she drew him toward her again. She did not want their sanctum breached, even by a thread of moonlight.

◆┅● ●┅◆

Chapter Twenty-Three

GAWAIN STOOD IN the bailey yard of Elladoune, facing the open portcullis as a group of people moved up the hill to pass under the entrance arch. Juliana walked with them, her hand tucked in the arm of an elderly woman. Beside her, a young man, large and soft-bellied, carried a basket filled with ducks.

Behind them, Laurie led a horse on which a young woman perched, pretty, dark-haired, great with child. Four children walked behind them with an elderly man. Still others followed after them, led by Brother Eonan. They carried bundles and herded chickens, goats, a few sheep, a shaggy ruddy cow, two small ponies, and three dogs.

As they came through the gate, Juliana approached Gawain. "Husband," she said, "Sir Gawain, this is Beithag. She would like to be our cook, if you will have her." She murmured to Beithag in Gaelic, low and rapid. *Daimheach*, he heard: friend.

"Welcome," he said in Gaelic, smiling.

Beithag peered at him warily, eyes keen, face wizened over strong bones. A plaid covered her head to foot, a rich weaving of red and earthen colors. He frowned, the pattern suddenly familiar, but the thought was gone. Juliana beckoned to the others. A tall old man came forward, surrounded by children and dogs.

"Beithag's husband, Uilleam MacDuff," Juliana said. "And their grandchildren."

Dumbstruck by the old man's name, Gawain hardly took in the names of the children. Uilleam, too, wore that same pattern in his belted plaid.

MacDuff. Were they kin to him? Had they known his father?

Smiling, greeting all who came through, Gawain welcomed them. The old man peered at him intently, almost as if he knew him and would speak. But in the commotion of the arrival, the man turned away to help others. Gawain petted the dogs, distracted by striving to seem calm.

"Here is Mairead," Juliana went on, as Laurie helped the pregnant woman down. "She is wife to Adhamnain MacDuff, Uilleam and Beithag's son."

Adhamnain. Both his grandfather and father had been called that, a common baptismal name among MacDuffs of Glenshie.

"Her husband has gone away for a bit," Juliana said. "This young man is called Teig." She pointed to the smiling youth who carried the basket of young ducks. He waved to Gawain and grinned at the children, who ran back toward him.

"Another MacDuff?" Gawain asked.

"A nephew to Uilleam. Beithag is married to a MacDuff, but is of another clan. My mother was her distant cousin. Teig MacDuff is a simple lad, and the children love him. He is strong and will work hard. Uilleam knows all there is to know about horses and livestock. Mairead and Beithag and the other women will work in the kitchens and in the household with cooking and brewing and cleaning. Do you approve?"

"I do," he said. He still felt stunned. More people came through the gate, along with a few monks from Inchfillan. The chatter in the yard rose to a crescendo around him. He stood watching, not sure what to say, with so much to ask.

"They will help all around, inside and outside the castle," Juliana was saying. "They have been living in the forests or on the charity of others. They are glad to be able to help here. None of them would accept charity. They want to work."

"They are welcome here, and we are grateful for the help.

Are they all MacDuffs?"

"Some. Not all."

He had to know. "Was Uilleam a laird near here before they lost their home?"

"He and Beithag had a fine stone house in the hills, where they raised sheep and cattle and garron ponies. Years ago, Uilleam had a brother, another Adhamnain, who was laird of a fine castle near a tall mountain. I think he said he was a bard, that laird."

"Aye?" Gawain asked casually. His heart pounded.

"I have heard him mention how dear he held that kinsman. The family was killed and some escaped in a battle with the English, years back, when the trouble with the English started in Scotland. The laird's son was killed and his little grandson was taken away by the mother, who was English. Years ago. The property was ruined by the English."

His fists clenched so hard that he set them behind his back. Silent, in turmoil, he watched Uilleam, then turned to stare toward the mountains well beyond the loch.

All unknowing, Juliana had brought his own kin to Elladoune, and they needed his help. Sometimes the world turned neatly on irony, but this turn astounded him.

He did not know how to tell them that he was not just a Sassenach commander, but Gabhan MacDuff, born among them, grandson of the laird who had once held Glenshie. A lost son returned more than twenty years later.

He watched his elderly great-aunt and great-uncle climb the steps to the tower. And he remembered, then, that red, brown, and purple tartan. He had worn it himself on the day he had left Glenshie with his mother. She had traded it away to a farmwife for a dull brown tunic for him to wear as she took him into England. She had changed his name from Gabhan to Gawain, altering his life forever. All to protect him.

Inside an ivory box at Avenel Castle, tucked away in a storage chest, was a piece of that plaid, a small scrap that he had clutched when he had slept as a child, until he set it away and turned his thoughts and his life to becoming an English knight.

He stood awhile longer in the bailey, watching them, silent. Juliana looked at him, questioning, and went to help the others.

BY WEEK'S END, Juliana had ushered a few more people through the gate, including two orphaned boys named MacDuff, an old man whose name Gawain did not learn, but suspected was also MacDuff. He led a straggling line of greylag geese.

"The geese have lost their mother," she told Gawain. "One of the older men is a blacksmith. His wife will tend to them with the chickens and ducks."

"This place is like a Lammastide market now," Laurie said, joining them. "We are replete with food, and help, and companionship. And I do not need to cook."

"Excellent," Juliana said.

Gawain suppressed a smile, glad of the friendship blooming between his wife and his close friend.

"We have much to do here now, it is true," Juliana said.

"Tell me this, lass," Laurie said then. "When will you learn that oath o' yours, so you can go to the royal court and prove yourself, so we may all live in peace here?"

"When hell turns icy, and the English king eats sweetmeats served by Scots faeries," she answered over her shoulder, walking away.

"What the devil does that mean?" Laurie mused.

Gawain groaned. "It means never. I cannot get her attention. She will not repeat even the simplest oath for the king," he said. "She is too busy, she claims, and will attend to it later. Not that I blame her."

"If she does not do that soon, it could be unpleasant when you are summoned to explain yourself. She is a stubborn lass, your wife."

"With no intention of becoming a loyal English subject," Gawain muttered. "But it is no surprise. We can only hope that Edward has forgotten all about it, with so much else going on."

"He well might. But Walter de Soulis will not." Laurie turned to survey the yard and the castle walls. "This place has changed quickly. Stables swept out, outbuildings repaired, animals penned in or grazing in the hills with shepherds to watch them. The gardens trimmed and growing again. Savory cooking and sweet baking in the kitchen. And brewing begun, thank heaven. We will have good ale before long."

"That is the reason you returned to Scotland." Gawain chuckled. He pointed toward a corner of the curtain wall where two men worked with brushes and buckets. "My bride has them whitewashing away traces of the old fire."

"I wonder," Laurie said, "if your wife will allow a garrison in here."

Gawain frowned. He was glad of the changes at Elladoune, clean linens, clean rushes, good food, steaming baths in the bedchamber for he and Juliana to enjoy the other night. Together—and that was one of the best changes here.

After supper, one of the women had played a small harp. The poignant tunes that had made Gawain's throat constrict. He remembered them from childhood.

Riding out each day, he had not found Glenshie yet, but he was not yet ready to speak to Uilleam MacDuff. But he would. Soon, he would. Now and then, he caught the old man studying him, though neither of them spoke their thoughts.

He did not have enough Gaelic, and they did not have enough English. It would have to wait, though the urge at times was overpowering. He had to tell Juliana first.

He wanted to find Glenshie before that. It seemed important somehow.

"Aye," Gawain said at last. "I do wonder how she will greet the garrison."

Laurie huffed. "Not well. And how you will explain all this to

De Soulis, I cannot imagine. The place is filled with Scots."

My own Scottish kin as well, Gawain thought. Yet another secret. "I will think of something. De Soulis will be at Dalbrae by now, and I must meet with him soon."

"I will go with you. Well, my friend, a week has passed and the world of Elladoune has changed. Will your lady rest on the seventh day from making miracles?"

Gawain snorted at the pun and went in search of his wife.

Juliana lay enveloped in silence, warmth, and darkness inside the curtained bed, listening to the easy flow of Gawain's breathing. Cuddled beside him, she felt his arm tighten around her, even in his sleep. His whiskered chin lay against her cheek as he slept on.

Gray light filtered through window and curtains, and she sighed. With dawn, there was often much to do. Some planned to scrub floors, sand away the marks of boots, spurs, charring from old flames. There was more whitewashing to be done, while others were returning to the caves to bring lengths of plaid and weavings stored there that could be hung on the walls again. While Elladoune was no longer the home she remembered, she began to hope a home could be made here after all.

A home, with Gawain. Children, family, her brothers here again. She snuggled against her husband, considering. Fanciful thoughts, but here in the enclosed bed, her dreams seemed possible, if fragile.

And easily shattered if the king's commanders sent a large garrison here. They could even send Gawain away.

She wrapped her arms around him in the dark as wave of love and desire poured through her—edged with poignancy. She had fallen in love with her Swan Laird after all, and though she wished he was Scots, and at times she felt as if he could easily play that role and never look back, he was yet a Sassenach.

Yet here, she could hold and keep him. Here, she was home, and he had become a home for her heart. She kissed his cheek and woke him slowly with gentle hands.

Chapter Twenty-Four

DALBRAE, HIGH ON a grassy hill ringed by a ditch and earthworks, was a fortress, its gate sealed, its battlements guarded. Gawain had been admitted without question, and he and Laurie now stood in the great hall waiting for the sheriff.

For a moment, he startled, hearing high screams emanate from above, near the gallery, a narrow loft area that protruded over part of the great hall. He glanced up but saw no one. Another scream sounded, followed by thunks and shrieks.

"God save us, they are tormenting the laddies," Laurie muttered. "We should have come sooner."

Gawain frowned in silence, for Walter de Soulis entered the room, dressed in a long black tunic with silver trim. He greeted them perfunctorily and indicated seats on a bench beside a large oaken table, where he sat down in large carved chair. He narrowed his eyes as alarming noises sounded again in the gallery.

He beckoned to a servant near the door. "Wine," he snapped. Soon pewter goblets were filled with claret. De Soulis drank, wiped a hand across his mouth. Gawain sipped, cast a look at Laurie, and cleared his throat.

"Sir Sheriff," he said. "We are here to discuss several matters, but first I must ask after my wife's brothers... What is that noise?" he added abruptly as a horrifying scream rang out.

"That," Walter said, "will drive me mad if it does not stop."

"Are you dragging children on a rack up there?" Laurie asked boldly.

"That is the sound of my wife's indulgent nature," De Soulis muttered, and downed wine again. Now a clacking sound echoed through the hall.

"Apparently you are holding two young boys hostage," Gawain said. "I am now wed to their sister. I ask that you release them into my custody."

"I cannot do that. Much as I would like to," the sheriff answered.

"They are babes, not criminals. Give them to me in a show of mercy."

"Babes! You have not met them, I think."

A shuttered window in the upper gallery, meant to allow musicians to be heard playing, smacked open. Gawain looked up.

A small, blue-covered behind emerged from the opening, and a small body thrust outward as a wiry little boy in a blue tunic and bare legs clung to a rope knotted to a rafter in the hall. Its length had been pulled over the gallery railing.

But the boy wrapped arms and legs around it and pushed outward to swing out over the hall. He dangled for a moment waving a wooden sword at the men gaping at him from below. Gawain stood in alarm. On the return swing of the rope, the child smacked the soles of his bare feet into the gallery wall, landed deftly, and looked up.

"Three of them," he called, "armed and ready!"

Gawain sat, seeing that the lad was safe on the gallery platform. But Laurie jumped up.

"Saints in heaven!" he cried, crossing the room to stand under the gallery. The boy had disappeared through the window, but then a second pair of arms appeared in the window. This boy, clad in red, was smaller than the other. He peered over the gallery railing, holding a little bow and nocked arrow.

"Get back," Walter drawled. "He will shoot."

"English dogs! Surrender!" the small bowman cried.

"Come get me, Highland pig!" Laurie boomed.

Stunned silence. Then the boy laughed and the shutters smacked shut.

Laurie returned to the bench. "A good game," he said. "Played arrows in the hall with my own brothers as bairns. But swinging over the hall—that's bold, that."

"I take it my wife's brothers are allowed some freedom here," Gawain said dryly.

"As I discovered when I returned," De Soulis replied. "You, boy," he told the page, "find my lady wife and tell her to bring the Lindsays here." The boy hastened away.

"How goes it at Elladoune?" De Soulis went on. "Have you prepared notes on the territory for Sir Aymer de Valence?"

"I am working on those."

"We need them soon." De Soulis poured more wine and quaffed it. "I hear you have allowed a bunch of ruffians and rebels to enter Elladoune. Why?"

"We allowed some of the locals to find shelter in the castle. They provide willing hands for the many daily tasks—chores, livestock, cooking, and such. They are not rebels. Mostly women, old men. Children."

"Huh," De Soulis answered. "I must report your activity to the king. Do not think I have forgotten that your behavior was out of bounds."

"Out of bounds! I took my wife away for her safety. I am cooperating with the garrisoning of Elladoune."

"Then why have you let rebels inside?"

"They are homeless locals, not outlaws or malcontents," Laurie said.

"But they have connections with those who are just that. My men have spent weeks searching for rebels, burning them out, and you take them under your wing."

"Where are people to go when you destroy their homes?" Gawain snapped.

"They should flee, but not into one of our castles. You have to turn them out."

"They are servants. Every garrison commander must rely on the local populace to maintain the castle. Surely you have Scottish servants here."

De Soulis grunted. "Not rebels. At Elladoune, you have invited the same folk who have been running about the forests and hills. We found a site where they were constructing a war machine. Your servants are not simple, I promise you."

"I have to disagree." In truth, he did not find it hard to imagine at all.

"Some of my men have reported that the monks at Inchfillan may not be entirely trustworthy either. They asked for funds from us to repair their bell tower. Outrageous. The Scottish Church should maintain their own parishes and abbeys."

"The king encourages good will with the Church here, so I hear," Gawain said.

"But some of those clerics are rascals despite their robes and vows." Walter waved a hand, as if it mattered little to him. "Either way, allowing too many locals inside Elladoune is foolhardy."

"Better to have them where I can keep an eye on them," Gawain said.

De Soulis frowned. "You need a force of men there to do that."

"They are good folk, glad for food and shelter and eager to help. Sir Sheriff, the other reason I am here is to receive orders regarding the garrison."

"That decision has not been made yet. Ah, my dear!" He rose to his feet.

A woman entered the hall, short and plump and pink-cheeked. She ushered two boys with her. They were dressed in matching blue tunics and red surcoats, their hair short, their knees knobby in stockings. They both had the pale blond coloring that their older sister shared. He would have recognized them immediately.

Both had short wooden swords stuck in their belts, and both scowled furiously.

With a boy's hand in each of hers, De Soulis' wife bowed her head. "My lord," she said, "you summoned the lads."

"Lady Matilda," De Soulis said. "This is Sir Gawain Avenel of Elladoune. He is wed to the boys' sister."

"Greetings, my lady." Gawain stood. "What are your names?" he asked the boys.

"Alec Lindsay. This is Iain," the older one said. He eyed Gawain suspiciously, setting a hand on the hilt of his little sword, the gesture of a knight more than a child.

"I am Gawain." He half sat on the edge of the table to be closer to their level. "I am your sister's husband now."

"She does not have a husband," Alec said. Iain half hid behind Lady Matilda's hips and eyed the sheriff nervously, Gawain noticed.

"She does now," Gawain said. "Are you well, lads?"

"Well enough with the Sassenachs," Alec said, chin high.

"She makes us wear pretty gowns," Iain complained. "She took our plaidies and cut our hair, and said we were savages."

"But she gives us sweetmeats and lets us play at our games," Alec added. "How fares our sister, sir? Is she well?"

"Very well. She wants you to come home to Elladoune."

"We do not live at Elladoune. The Sassenachs have it," Iain said.

"You, both of you, come here." De Soulis beckoned. Alec stepped forward, pulling Iain by the sleeve. "Frightened of me, are you?"

"Aye." Iain's voice quavered. "You have invisible armor."

"Invincible," Alec hissed.

De Soulis glared at the boy. "Swing in my hall like that again, and I will have you caught and skinned."

"Walter!" Matilda exclaimed. She surged forward to wrap her arms around the boys. "Do not scold my dear little puppies!" She kissed their heads. Iain gazed sweetly at her, and Alec turned a beaming smile on her.

"These Scots brats are doing whatever they please. Shooting the garden vegetables with arrows. Tying knots in the harnesses. And this—" He waved a hand at the gallery, where the rope was slung.

"They are high-spirited," Matilda said. "They will behave." The boys nodded vigorously.

"They had better," De Soulis growled.

"Walter, I wrote to my lord father to tell him of your kindness in fostering two little ones here for me. He will tell King Edward how courteous you are."

"My dear, how good of you," De Soulis said smoothly.

Gawain sat with arms folded. Then he saw Alec reach inside his tunic to pull out a tiny wriggling mouse, which he slipped to the floor. As it ran in front of the woman, she shrieked.

Alec drew his sword. "I will defend you!"

"I will! Me!" Iain yelled, running after the mouse, which disappeared in the shadows. Alec ran after him.

The sheriff glowered at his wife. "They should be punished."

"I longed for children and I am grateful you decided to foster them. They are like my own now." She clasped her hands.

He waved her away. "Go. Keep them out of my sight."

She gathered her skirts and ran sniffling from the room, calling the boys.

Gawain returned to his seat and picked up his goblet. The three men quaffed their wine all at once.

"Fostered?" Gawain asked. "Hostages!"

"She cannot accept the truth," De Soulis said. "I could foster them so they can become knights of England, if the wildness can be tamed out of them."

"I will take them back with me to their family," Gawain said. "Your wife treasures them, but you can arrange to give her a child she can treasure—you can do it, or find a young orphan to take in. Let the boys go."

"I will keep them," the sheriff said, waving his hand in the dismissive gesture that seemed common to him. "My wife will soon return to England. She does not care for Scotland. They will go south with her."

"You have no right," Gawain snapped.

"Their sister is a prisoner of the king, let me remind you. And your tenure here is undetermined. So I will keep the boys. But if they do not behave, I cannot guarantee their safety."

"Guarantee it or give them up now."

De Soulis slid him a dark look. "I do not mean to harm them."

"And I will be back to ensure it," Gawain said, staring steadily at the man.

"The abbot seems a capable guardian," Laurie said. "Give them back to him."

"I do not trust him," the sheriff answered. "Or you two."

"One last matter," Gawain said. "The two older Lindsay brothers taken captive."

"What of them?"

"My lady wife wishes to know the ransom. She seeks to pay it."

"How? Will you pay it and free two Scots? I know nothing of a ransom for them. Though I am beginning to wonder if your last oath of fealty was sincere."

Gawain rose to his feet. "I think our business is concluded for now. Good day." He stalked out of the room, Laurie behind him.

He strode through the busy yard, heading for the stables, simmering over the meeting. His future at Elladoune seemed uncertain. At least he could report that Juliana's younger brothers were holding their own under the circumstances.

"Hey, look there," Laurie said. "A warning did not go for those rascals."

Gawain glanced over to see Alec and Iain in the garden, shooting vegetables lined along a low stone wall. A young servant boy ran from the garden, arms waving.

Wheeling, Gawain headed for the garden at a stiff pace and stomped through the gate. Greens fluttered around his booted ankles.

Iain pointed his weapon at a head of lettuce and pulled back the bowstring as Gawain angled through the planted rows. Striding toward the garden wall, Gawain took note of the boy's aim and his target. Just as he heard the arrow leave the bow, he lashed out his hand and snatched the arrow in midair. He brandished the shaft.

"Come here, Iain Lindsay," he growled.

The boy gaped at him. "You caught that?" Alec stared too.

Behind Gawain, he saw Laurie step forward, hands on hips.

"Is this how you behave at home?" Gawain asked.

Iain gulped. "N-nay, sir."

"And you," Gawain said to Alec, "do you set a good example for your brother?"

They way Alec lifted his head reminded Gawain of the sister. "I do, sir."

"Swinging on ropes in the hall, shooting vegetables, letting mice out to scare ladies—you call that good?"

"We would not do so at home. But these are Sassenachs," Alec said. Laurie snorted, listening.

"And we are rebels," Iain said. "If you please, sir."

"We cannot waste in prison," Alec added. "We must fight!"

"Then consider this." Gawain waggled the arrow shaft in his hand. "As hostages, you are guests rather than prisoners. Play as you are allowed. But do not harm property or frighten anyone. Especially not a lady who treats you well."

"We let the wee mousie go to show we could protect her," Alec said.

"Show a lady gentleness, and you will be all the stronger for it." The boys frowned as if puzzling that out. Gawain handed Iain his arrow. "Next time, ask before you shoot."

Iain stared at him. "But sir, how did you catch it?"

"I practiced it. If you both behave here, I might show you someday. But do not try it on your own. There is a secret to it that only I know. Promise me."

The boys spit on the ground to fix the promise. Gawain

touched Iain's head, the pale curls baby-fine. "I will tell your sister you are well and show courage. I will see you again, and bring you home to her as soon as I can."

"Promise?" Iain asked.

Gawain spit on the ground.

HE COULD NOT stop searching the skyline. As he and Laurie rode back from Dalbrae, his gaze continually strayed to the hills.

"I forgot about that trick of catching arrows that we used practice years back as young squires," Laurie said. "That gave those two a startle!" He laughed.

Gawain grinned. "I should not have done it, for now I fear they will try it. But in the moment—ah well. They will think twice about misbehaving, I hope."

Laurie nodded. "What gave you the urge to ever practice such a thing?"

"A legend I heard as a boy. Something about a faery bolt. I always wanted to master the trick."

"And now you can frighten wee boys with it." Laurie grinned. "They are good lads, those two. They will be fine rebels one day, too. Years from now."

Gawain nodded agreement, his gaze scanning the distant slopes again. He sighed, wondering if he would ever have time to find the landmark and the ruin of his family's castle. He had been scarcely older than Iain when he had left Scotland with his mother.

They rode over a meadow beside the loch. Buttercups and bluebells scattered over the grass, and the water sparkled blue. Far out, swans flowed elegantly over the surface. He remembered this loch and its swans as a boy, and remembered his father telling him the legend.

He remembered a small waterfall where they had stopped to

drink. He looked around. He had felt so proud that day, riding out with his father over heather-deep hills.

"What's caught you so deep in your thoughts?" Laurie asked.

"Memories," Gawain answered. "Being a boy in Scotland. Thoughts of home."

Through a fringe of trees, he saw the stone walls of Elladoune, and rode quickly.

THAT NIGHT, SILENTLY, gently, he took Juliana into his arms again. Each kiss, every touch, was deep and sincere, fluent with feeling, profoundly comforting.

He cherished their secluded chamber and the privacy of their bed. The freedom there with her, without words, without explanations or questions, was bliss in itself. As before when he loved her, he was aware of natural concordance and deep mutual passion. He followed its compelling course like a swan on a stream.

Exploring her, he let her discover him, body, heart, soul. He burned for her until the brightness of it took him into itself. From the simplicity of a perfect kiss to a sensuous, incandescent ending, he savored it all, and gave all he could, and held her close afterward.

He wondered how he could ever have bound her against her will, and he knew that he would never be able to let her go if he was ordered to leave Elladoune. Uncertainty whispered to him constantly from the shadows. He did not know what was to come. He only knew, now, how much he loved her.

Resting in her arms in the quiet and the darkness, he thought about her silences and his own reticence. They had discovered the honesty of their bodies, but a host of secrets still lay between them. Yet inside the refuge they had found with each other, none of that seemed to matter.

Chapter Twenty-Five

THE FIRST RAYS of the sun lifted over the slopes beyond the loch. Standing on the bank, Gawain watched mist ripple over the water, and with it came swans.

Juliana walked past him, rosy dawn light glowing over her long, fine-spun hair. Although a married woman now, she preferred not to wear a veil here. He was glad; he liked the soft gold of her hair, braided or free.

Swans arrowed through the water toward them as Juliana tossed barley grains into the water. The birds dipped, found, dipped. She threw another handful, stepping backward so that they followed her, toddling comically, losing the grace of the water.

Soon Gawain was surrounded by a wave of white swans too, bumping against his legs, snapping at the air. Juliana handed him the little sack of barley, and he filtered some of the grain to the birds.

"If we do this every day at the same time," she murmured, "they will meet us."

"A bit later in the day would be nice. Must we leave our bed so early?"

"Have I married a lazy man?" She smiled.

"Just a man who finds his bed a fine place to be." He twitched a smile in return.

A blush colored her cheeks. "We can come out here a bit

later, always together, so they learn to accept you too."

Together. "That would be fine."

"You should make the same call when you feed them. They will wait for you." She scooped barley from his hand and dribbled it downward, cooing softly.

"What sound should I call?"

"Anything you like."

He nodded. "Your cousin James has a goshawk that he sings to. A kyrie—and the bird flies straight to him each time."

She looked at him curiously. "I did not know that. I have not seen him for quite a while. How do you know that?"

"I met the man. Saw the goshawk he trained. But the swans come to you without a call. They know you by sight. And you are often silent. Juliana," he said. "Explain to me the reason for the silence."

She shrugged. "I cannot explain that to a Sassenach who holds a Scottish castle and looks for rebels."

"Ah," he said.

"The swans are as familiar as kin to me. That cob, there, is the oldest of this group. I call him Cuchulainn, after the hero of the ancient tales. His mate is over there—Eimhir *alainn.*"

"Eimhir the beautiful," Gawain said. "The strong-willed wife of Cuchulainn."

"You know the old tale? Your nurse? She must have been quite a storyteller."

He shrugged. "They all have names?"

"Aye, many from the legends. That one pulling at your tunic is Fionn, and his mate is Grainne. Those two at the water's edge are Naoise and Deirdre, from that sad tale. And that couple out on the water Aenghus and Caer. And the cygnets are Fionnghuala, Aedh, Fiachra, and Conn."

"Caer, who turned into a swan, and Aenghus who searched for her for years. They cygnets are named for the Children of Lir."

She studied him. "You *do* know the old tales."

"Some. The sons and the daughter of King Lir were turned into swans by their stepmother," he said. His grandfather had told the story many times. "Finally the pure note of a bell rang out and broke the magic spell. But they were so old by then that they died as soon as they became human again. Tragic."

Juliana stared at him. "How does a Sassenach know that?"

He did not answer, but watched the golden-pink sun rise up behind the highest mountain. He wanted to tell her the truth. The news might upset her deeply—or please her. He was nearly ready to tell her he was, in fact, a MacDuff from the mountains.

But his private quest was to find and claim his home. He had his own reasons for silence.

The swans wandered back to the water, lowered, swam out. One female kept herself distant from the rest. He remarked on it.

"Poor Guinevere," Juliana said. "She is lonely. Artan was her mate. He has not returned, though I hoped and prayed he might."

"Perhaps he found a life in Newcastle."

"Not he. He would do anything to get home if he could."

He smiled. "Come back to Elladoune. I must ride out and will meet you later at Inchfillan Abbey if you like. I need to see Abbot Malcolm." He walked with her across the meadow.

As the sun rose higher, he glanced over his shoulder once again. He stopped suddenly. Juliana rounded with him.

Mist sat in fragile rings around the mountains, and light touched the tallest slope. A face appeared near the summit in the black rock. Eyes, a nose, a mouth, a straggle of hair in a wave of rock: an old woman.

"Look there," he said hoarsely. "On Beinn Beira. Do you see a face?"

"That?" She shaded her eyes. "Aye, we say that is the queen of winter, trapped in the mountain. She escapes once a year and brings winter, then must be sent back to her prison by spring. Sometimes we can see her face."

Gawain took her hand, watching as the sun shone on the mountainside. Then the brightness washed away the image in the rock. It vanished.

"It is a good omen to see her," Juliana went on. "It means summer will continue." She smiled at him.

He leaned to kiss her. "My thanks," he whispered.

"For what?" she asked. "I am surprised you never heard that tale, Gabhan."

"That one," he said, taking her hand, "I did not know."

HE LEFT THE forest track and headed into the foothills, making his way carefully along the steeper slants where rock was more prevalent than turf. Wildflowers bloomed yellow, blue, and violet in crevices. Sunlight highlighted the old woman's countenance once more as he made his way slowly upward.

This was what he had been seeking, thinking it a different mountain altogether.

But he saw no castles or ruins. Only few homesteads or shepherd's huts were located here. The area had been overrun by English years before, just as lower down by Loch nan Eala and Elladoune.

After a while, he dismounted the bay, for Gringolet had faltered once, and Gawain did not want to risk an injury for the animal. He secured the reins to a bush and left the horse grazing near a burn where water was available to him.

He followed the track of water into a narrow gorge, where the rock walls were covered with twisting vines and bracken. Beyond the burbling burn, he stopped to better survey the view. Wearing a tunic and surcoat rather than a heavier hauberk, he sweated freely in the summer's heart, and stopped to scoop a drink from the dancing water.

He paused with a booted foot on a rock ledge. He could see his horse grazing lower down. Far beyond, he saw the smooth blue sheet of Loch nan Eala, and the honey-colored walls of

Elladoune on its promontory. All looked perfect in miniature.

He rounded and looked up the slope. A narrow waterfall trickled among dark rocks above a line of scrub. He remembered that white frothing tail.

Then, not far past the waterfall, he saw a square thrust of stone. High, gray, a broken remnant of a tower. Its shape struck a deep chord in his memory.

His heart lurched. Climbing with new fervor, he pushed his way through the skirt of bracken and scrub until he burst through and found what was left of Glenshie Castle.

—— ◆┄• •┄◆ ——

Chapter Twenty-Six

WALKING ALONG THE bank of the loch, Juliana wanted to check on a nest that might have been plundered again by otters. To her relief, she found the nest unharmed; the pen perched calmly on four eggs, and the cob pulled at the reeds nearby. She turned back, and looked up to see Brother Eonan and Laurie hurrying toward her.

"Father Abbot says he must see you," Eonan said breathlessly.

"Is something wrong? Alec and Iain—"

"They are fine. Abbot saw the sheriff, and the lads." Eonan stopped. "I do not know what else has happened, but Abbot seems very agitated."

"We should go there now. Laurie, when Gawain returns, tell him I went with Eonan."

"Aye. He planned to meet you at the abbey later, but he will be anxious to get there sooner now. I will—what the devil!" He stopped, glancing across the meadow.

A man melted out of the forest and walked toward them. Laurie put his hand to the sword sheathed at his belt. Juliana gasped and put out a hand to stop him.

"*Ach Dhia,*" she breathed. "James!"

Dressed like a pilgrim in a brown cloak with a scallop shell pinned to the shoulder, James Lindsay might look nondescript to some, but he was recognizable to her. Tall and strong, he moved with agile grace. Sunlight glinted off his dark gold and brown wavy hair. He lifted a hand in greeting.

"Jamie!" she called out, running toward him.

"Pilgrim," Laurie greeted him, walking with her. "If you seek the abbey of Inchfillan, it is that way. They will admit a pilgrim who wishes to pray and rest."

"This is my cousin!" Juliana told him, and ran to embrace the pilgrim.

"Cousin!" Laurie echoed.

"Aye, sir," James said. "I am glad to see Cousin Juliana is well protected." He pushed back his hood, his keen glance the same dark blue as Juliana's, a legacy from a shared grandfather.

"I thought you were a rebel come to challenge us," Laurie said gruffly.

"Rebel? Oh, never that," Juliana said earnestly.

"I travel in peace, on pilgrimage," James said. "I was on my way to Inchfillan Abbey. What a pleasant surprise to see my cousin before I reached the abbey."

"He is a pious man anxious to be at prayer," Juliana added.

"Och, no doubt," Laurie drawled.

"I must speak with my cousin and tell her news of our kin," James said.

"If you keep in sight," Laurie said as they moved away.

"Did you really come here to see Father Abbot?" she asked him.

"He sent word to me." James glanced back. "He said you were taken by the English, and the wee lads too, and he needed my help. I came as soon as I could. I have another mission near here on King Robert's behalf. But I am glad to see you are fine."

"I am back. The wee lads are held by the sheriff at Dalbrae. And—well, I was taken to King Edward, who—had me wed to one of his knights. The new commander at Elladoune. The king is expecting my pledge of fealty."

"Wed?" James looked astonished.

"To Sir Gawain Avenel—you may not know the name. He is constable at Elladoune now, although no garrison has been sent yet. Jamie, what is it?"

"Gawain? I know him well."

"He mentioned he met you."

"Met me? He ran with us for a few months."

"He fought with Scots rebels?" Juliana gaped at him. "He is Edward's loyal man!"

"Not quite. Though I heard that he pledged his oath anew." James frowned. "He was a good comrade. But some must change their loyalties in this war. We are all challenged to choose between head and heart sometimes."

"But Gawain is English… he never—" Juliana felt stunned.

"He sided with the Scots for a while, lass. He never said?"

Juliana stared, her head spinning. "But—"

"A solitary man. A noble spirt, and courteous. But he has some secrets. He must have had good reason to side with us and then change back. Inheritance, perhaps. My wife liked him well, and she has a fine eye for character."

In spite of the distracting revelation about Gawain, Juliana gasped. "Wife? You do have news! The Hawk Laird is wed?"

His smile was quick and charming. "Caught fast. My wife is Isobel Seton of Aberlady."

"The prophetess? I have heard of her! So the rebel softened enough to take a wife." She smiled. "And you were nearly a monk!"

"True." He laughed ruefully. "You must meet her."

"I want to, and soon. But tell me more of you and Gawain. He never said he ran with rebels."

"I doubt he wants it known if he swore fealty again. He helped Isobel and me in a bad situation and stayed for a while. He fought at my back. A man to trust." He frowned. "One day the English camped nearby, and there was a skirmish. He helped us. The next morn he was gone. We saw him riding with the Southrons."

"*Ach Dhia.* Did he…betray you?" she nearly whispered.

"I doubt it, though some thought so. He returned to England,

I heard, and knelt before the king to beg forgiveness. Thrown in prison for a while, we heard. But he is in favor again if he was given Elladoune—and a bride."

"I did not know—he did mention a transgression," she murmured.

"Quite. He was a good friend. I can never repay what he did for Isobel. I did not think him a traitor, so his abrupt departure surprised me. We liked him well." He looked at the loch and watched the swans.

Tucking her brows together, she recalled that Gawain had mentioned being imprisoned for betrayal. He had not explained it, but she wondered now if it had to do with the time he spent with James and the other Scots.

"Cousin, I have news of your older brothers," James said then.

"We heard something of them. But I cannot pay a ransom. The two young ones, Alec and Iain, are in the sheriff's keeping, and he refuses to give them up. I do not know what will happen to any of my brothers."

"I am heading to the abbey to discuss these things with the abbot. Come with me, aye?"

"I will. Jamie, Gawain intends to come to the abbey later to see Abbot Malcolm."

"Indeed? I would like to see him after all this time."

GLENSHIE BURNED BRIGHT in his mind even as he sat in De Soulis's hall beside Laurie. As the page poured cups of ale, he thought of the sunlit stones of Glenshie. While De Soulis complained about a delayed delivery of wine and salted fish, Gawain thought of the long view from Glenshie down the hills to Loch nan Eala and Elladoune.

The place was a stone shell, choked with ivy, though its

foundation walls looked sound enough. An abundance of ferns and grasses filled the inner bailey and the steps leading to the tower keep had collapsed. But he saw his childhood home in that shell After he had explored some of it, he was sure it could be rebuilt. In his mind, he could already see Glenshie as a strong stone tower again.

When he met Laurie for the ride to Dalbrae, he said nothing of his discovery, though he was bursting to reveal the news. But he must explain all to Juliana first.

Now he fixed his attention on the conversation, for he had come here to ask about the boys and to learn more about his orders. He needed to know where his future lay.

"Has De Valence decided what to do with Elladoune?" he asked.

"There is some news, but others matters need addressing first. I have here writs from Aymer de Valence and from King Edward to be conveyed to you."

The sheriff reached toward a small wooden chest, which he opened to remove a few folded parchments with broken seals. He looked through them, then looked up.

"I believe you have a report to deliver to me?"

"It is almost complete." Gawain had the parchments tucked inside his surcoat, and he had intended to turn them over. But something urged him to hold off until he learned what the king and his lieutenant in Scotland had in mind.

The sheriff scowled. "De Valence wants that information from you." He flapped the parchment in his hand. "I suppose you should know—as the king's Master of Swans, I am obliged to capture swans to populate the king's rivers in England. The swans of Elladoune are some of the best known. Soon I will send men to capture some of them."

"The swans' feathers are molting just now," Gawain said. "They are unable to fly."

"Which makes them more suited for upping. They can be hooked, netted, and transported more easily. The younger ones are easier to catch than more aggressive adults. The men will snare cygnets and young swans and send them south."

Gawain narrowed his eyes, knowing how deeply this would upset Juliana, especially considering her own capture weeks earlier. And he recalled the pen Guinevere's four young cygnets—and her strong protective urge. That proud and beautiful female swan had endured the loss of her mate, Artan. Her offspring should not be taken from her, too.

"King Edward has more than enough swans on his rivers, I am sure," he said. "Why does he bother to sign writs for Scottish swans? He has a war to think about."

"The king has a special fondness for swans, and he had already held a swan feast to dedicate his efforts to capture Scotland. The birds are good omens of victory."

"Not content with claiming to own all the swans in England, now he has to grab Scottish swans," Laurie muttered aside to Gawain. Then he sat forward. "Sir Walter, where are the young lads? Their sister is anxious to know that they are well."

"Her kinsman, Abbot Malcolm, was here this morning and saw that they are well. I asked to meet with him to discuss the orders for Elladoune and the loch, which will also affect the abbey."

"What are my orders—and how would they affect the abbey?" Gawain asked.

"You will know shortly. Just now the boys are with the priest at prayers and lessons. They have been better behaved of late. Though I have decided to send them with my wife to England when she leaves this week. It is best—"

Gawain leaned forward. "You have no authority to take them away," he growled.

"On the contrary, they are in my custody. Now, about your orders." De Soulis opened two documents and pressed them flat in front of him. "This writ is from the king," he said, displaying the red seal and trailing ribbons. "'Greetings,' etcetera." He waved his hand impatiently as he skipped ahead. "The king requires that a written statement by Lady Juliana Lindsay be sent to him at Lanercost Abbey."

"Lanercost?" Gawain asked. "He was expected in Carlisle, I heard."

"He has been ill—just temporary, I hear—and will rest briefly at Lanercost. The journey from London was long and draining for a man of his age and responsibility."

"A written statement?" Gawain asked then. "What does he expect to see?"

"He wants her sworn fealty in writing, and an affidavit signed by witnesses. She is to pledge…ah," and he began to read. "'Her loyalty and that of her kin and acquaintances and all those attached to the lands of Elladoune, pledged in full fealty to Edward, King of England.'" He passed the parchment to Gawain.

He studied it and read further. "'If the lady cannot write a fair hand, she is to make her mark upon a written oath, and two witnesses, civic and religious, must swear that she has said the oath aloud and with good intention.'" Gawain glanced at Laurie.

A written oath was unexpected luck. Still, he suspected Juliana would likely refuse. Laurie's skeptical frown said he had the same thought.

"At least he does not demand she come to court," Laurie said.

"Indeed." Gawain looked at the sheriff. "Is Edward very ill?"

"Not at all. He is simply attending to more important matters," De Soulis said. "Once the lady's oath has been accepted, the king will release her from formal captivity. I will witness the oath-saying personally, as sheriff of this glen. Her kinsman the abbot will do to represent the clergy. Can the lady write an oath? Is she educated?"

"I am certain she can handle a pen for her name at least. When will this signing take place?"

"I will be at the market fair soon. We can meet there. She must read the oath aloud. If she refuses, she will not fulfill the king's demand."

"I will explain that to her," Gawain said carefully.

De Soulis lifted one brow. "Does she insist upon her foolish silence with you?"

"She communicates with me," he said evasively.

"No doubt," De Soulis drawled. "Tell her to comply or be at the mercy of the crown—both of you, perhaps. Bring her to the market fair next week, where she will say her oath before witnesses." He gave a flat, sly smile.

Narrowing his eyes, Gawain doubted Juliana would do any of it. "We shall see. As for her brothers, if you try to take them away, be assured that I will come after them."

"We shall see, as you say. Now, for the second writ, brought by a messenger yesterday. De Valence has decided to close Elladoune."

"Close it." Gawain clenched his jaw. He sensed Laurie's quick, shocked glance.

"You knew it was possible," De Soulis said smoothly. "You are there temporarily."

"I expected a garrison to be installed, since you suspect there are rebels nearby."

"I can deal with the rebels from here, through my own authority."

The decision stunned him. Consequences rattled through his brain. He would have to turn out his own kinfolk—and take Juliana away from her home again, away from the home they were making together. He might be sent elsewhere in England or Scotland, even Wales or France. What would become of her then? And the swans—no wonder they planned to snare the swans. His heart slammed in his chest.

"Why close it, when you could add forces there?" Laurie asked.

"De Valence thinks a garrison is unnecessary there. Extra men will be sent here rather than Elladoune. We will extend patrols along the loch and into the hills. It can be managed with fifty extra soldiers here at Dalbrae."

"Ah," Gawain said bitterly. "Fifty to Dalbrae rather than a

hundred to Elladoune. Save men, time, supplies, and coin."

"Exactly," De Soulis said.

A muscle bounced in his jaw as he restrained his anger. He merely nodded, but every part of him tensed. His mind whirled.

"What, then, for the rest of us?" Laurie asked.

"You may both be useful here. Or wherever Sir Aymer posts you. I can inquire on your behalf."

"And Elladoune?" Gawain said. "Closed for how long?"

De Soulis slid another parchment page across the table toward Gawain. "These are the orders for Elladoune."

Gawain scanned the neat script until he came to the lines that contained the orders he sought. He stared at it, then read it again.

Until no stone remains.

"What is it?" Laurie asked.

"Elladoune," Gawain murmured, "is to be burned, and every stone torn down."

Chapter Twenty-Seven

"F RIEND OR FOE, he is your cousin's husband and so your kinsman now," Malcolm said. "Tell me, Jamie, do you trust Gawain Avenel?"

Juliana caught her breath, watching James seated beside her in the small, sun-washed solar of the abbot's house. He sipped ale and considered the abbot's question.

"Gawain is a man of integrity," James replied. "But I do not know where his fealty lies, with England or Scotland. The man would help anyone who needed it. But I understand that he renewed his oath to King Edward. Even so, I would trust him with my life."

"He ran with your men, then rejoined the English. Is he still the man you knew? That is the question," Malcolm said.

Juliana listened, still a bit stunned to learn through James that Gawain had been with James's men for a while, a crucial help to them. He had left suddenly without explanation. She knew little of it from him, but had begun to piece it together.

His transgressions, as he called them, must have included helping James Lindsay—and likely helping her and others at Elladoune years ago. She could easily believe that Gawain had risked his life to help Isobel and James. She could even imagine him declaring for the rebel cause. Why he had gone back to Edward was another matter.

Yet, like James, she believed utterly in his core of integrity.

Though if he had stayed with the Scots, she would feel obstacle between them now, she thought sadly.

"Is he a spy?" Malcolm asked then.

"It could be," James admitted.

Juliana gasped softly. "But you said he sided with the Scots."

"He is English, and would inherit there. He chose the safer course," James said. "Many caught between the English claim and the Scottish cause have done that."

"Gawain has been very helpful to the Scots here," Juliana said.

"There is something else I must tell you," Malcolm said, his tone grim. "I met with the sheriff this morning. The king has demanded that Juliana declare her loyalty to him before the sheriff and witnesses. She may do it here, but it must be done."

"Can we find a way around the oath?" she asked.

"Perhaps, but listen. De Soulis will send Alec and Iain to England with his wife."

"*Ach Dhia!*" Juliana felt the news like a blow. "He has no right!"

"He says they are in his custody and that gives him the right. He also said that Elladoune is to be closed. The king's commander in Scotland has decided it does not serve them to garrison it again."

Juliana set a hand to her chest. "Shut down? Will Gawain be sent away?"

"He is a king's man." He frowned. "Very much so, apparently."

"What do you mean?" James asked sharply.

"De Soulis said Gawain has been preparing a report for Edward's commanders on the lay of the land here—the terrain, where troops can camp, water sources, and so on."

"I did not know." She felt her heart sink. She was aware that he patrolled daily and wrote sometimes at night, locking the parchments away in a wooden box. He had said the pages were only thoughts he wanted to save, and she assumed he had some scholarly habits because of his upbringing and education.

What a fool she had been. She cupped a trembling hand over her eyes. When she looked up, James was watching her, and reached out to touch her arm in sympathy.

"We have seen him riding out in the forests and hills often," Malcolm said. "He has been collecting information for the English to use in fighting the Scots."

"But he would not—I am sure he would not betray us." She wanted to defend him, but doubts flooded her. There was much she still did not know about Gawain Avenel.

"If Elladoune is to be closed," James said, "Gawain will be the one to shut its gates. His report and his actions will gain him favor with the king. He may need that."

"I find this very hard to believe," Juliana said. She felt betrayed, ravaged, fearful. She would lose Elladoune again. She would lose Gawain, and all her hopes and dreams.

"Cousin," James said, "we will find a way through this."

"But Jamie, he would not be so traitorous as to do this, toss everyone out of Elladoune when he has just welcomed them in, and then desert us just to gain the king's favor. He would not do that!"

"He may have to follow his duty. He may have no choice," James said.

"What can we do?" She worried at her lower lip, thinking of all those who had found shelter at Elladoune and would be homeless again. "Where will we go?"

"We will find ways to help them," the abbot said. "As for Gawain, there may be naught we can do. Only he knows what he does and why."

Tears welled in her eyes. She took in a quavering breath and nodded.

"My dear girl, this is hard, I know," Malcolm said gently. "There is much to do. We also have to gain back Alec and Iain, and find a way to help Niall and Will."

Jamie leaned forward and began to discuss that with Malcolm. While they spoke, Juliana looked down, twisting her fingers anxiously. She would lose Gawain—but perhaps she had already lost him, if indeed he was capable of these actions.

But he was not gone from her heart. No matter what, she could not stop loving him. Her cheeks heated as she thought of the kisses and caresses and comforts in the privacy of their bed. She had been so content, so foolishly in love, tumbling ever deeper, racing toward dreams of a future with him.

Had she been so misled by her dreams and her heart? Tears slid down her cheek. She dashed them away.

"We will pay the ransom ourselves," Malcolm was saying.

Juliana looked up. "How?" she asked. "We have no coin!"

"I have a scheme," Malcolm said. "And a scheme to fetch the wee ones back as well." He smiled, but she saw effort and sadness in it. He, too, was affected by the devastating news about Elladoune—and Gawain.

"We have a source of gold," Malcolm continued. "The archery competition."

"A contest?" James asked.

"It is held each summer at the midsummer market," Malcolm explained. "The prize is an arrow—the Golden Arrow of Elladoune, 'tis called. Good quality gold, worth much. The competition has been held for years. The Lindsays of Elladoune have often won the arrow, but not for years. The arrow used to be kept here, locked away. It is with the last year's winner now, and I did not think of it as available—until just now."

"I have heard of it," James said. "Juliana's father won it more than once, and his father before him."

Juliana nodded. "But for the last few years, English bowmen from the garrison have taken the prize." She looked at Malcolm. "Even if we could win that arrow back, it would not be not enough gold to pay two ransoms. And we would have to melt it down and destroy it."

"The sheriff has it at Dalbrae. I am thinking he might pay good coin to keep the Elladoune arrow in his garrison's possession," Malcolm said.

"Ransom the arrow to pay the fee?" James asked.

Malcolm nodded. "De Soulis has boasted all year that his men have the arrow and will keep it by winning again. He says it will always be kept at Dalbrae. That pride could cost him."

"Interesting," James said. "Win the arrow and charge him to get it back—enough for two ransoms."

Juliana sat straighter. "My father often won it. My brothers won it more than once. I wonder if I could take it."

"You?" James tipped his head, considering her. "It is possible. I remember you had some considering skill."

"She does." Malcolm smiled broadly at her.

"I have the skill," she said, "but I am a woman in the custody of the crown. De Soulis would never allow me to compete."

James shrugged. "You could pass for a youth if you hide that hair and…your shape." He lifted a brow expressively. Malcolm cleared his throat.

"I could do that. But it is an unusual contest. The shot is difficult, impossible for some. I have never mastered a similar shot. And the fair is but a week from now. Even if I enter the competition, I may not take the prize."

"You could though," James said, and Malcolm nodded agreement.

"Jamie, could you compete?"

"I would if I could stay. But I only came through here to see that you were safe and to meet with the abbot. I am obligated to see to a matter for Robert Bruce. I should not stay long, for I must go west to meet our king, and then back to Wildshaw Castle. My wife's child will be born in a few weeks. I intend to be there."

"A child!" Malcolm congratulated him, and Juliana smiled at Jamie's news. Inwardly, her heart pounded. Did she have the courage to pull off a ruse and attempt to win the arrow back for Elladoune?

"Well, cousin?" James asked. "What will you do?"

She nodded. "I will try."

"Good," Malcolm said. "Now, here is my scheme to gain back the wee lads. The sheriff said his wife will bring the boys to the fair. We must snatch them away then."

"That could be dangerous and might cause a skirmish," Juliana said. "Could we use the Golden Arrow to get them back?"

"We must try to use that for the older lads. It is possible to just steal the bairns, easy enough if we are there, and prepared. You know it is held not far from Inchfillan. We will talk to the forest folk, and those at Elladoune, and form a plan."

"The rebels will not go against De Soulis in public," Juliana said. "They fear him and his black armor. They will not risk his wrath directly. It is far too dangerous."

"Black armor! Ah, then I have heard of him," James said. "But I doubt that garment is as frightful as rumor says."

"If the man would take a wound wearing that armor, the rumor would disappear fast enough," Malcolm said. "Just a wee wound. It might be arranged."

"Father Abbot!" Juliana pretended shock at his suggestion. James looked comically astonished.

Malcolm shrugged. "We must show the men of the forest that they need not fear De Soulis. And we will ask for their help in stealing the lads away. For now, we agree that Juliana will take the Golden Arrow."

"Let us hope she can," she added.

"One last matter," James said. "King Robert will be disappointed if my mission here is not successful."

"Mission here?" Juliana asked, puzzled.

"I was sent here to inquire about a war machine," James said. "Your forest men sent him one before, secretly and in pieces. It was assembled elsewhere and greatly aided the rebellion. But Abbot Malcolm tells me that the sheriff's men burned the site where the rebels were building another engine."

"True, but I have good news on that," Malcolm said. "We have another one nearly finished, hidden where the sheriff's men will never find it." He gestured toward the window, where a summer breeze entered.

Juliana looked out, puzzled, seeing only the new bell tower under construction. "Will the bell tower be ready in time for the market? The bells call people to the fair and we hold the contest close to the abbey church each year," she told James.

"My girl," Malcolm said. "Look again."

She stood to gaze out the window. A wooden scaffold had been erected beside the broken bell tower. Two monks had climbed up to hammer on the timber framework that surrounded the broken tower. She gasped. "The scaffolding?"

Malcolm grinned. "And we did it with timber the English brought us, according to Edward's decree that the English must support Scottish churches in need."

James joined her at the window. "By the saints, I see it now. A siege engine! Father Abbot, you are a bold fellow." He grinned.

"If Bishop Wishart can build one and take it against the English, I thought I might do the same." Malcolm beamed. "It needs wheels and the catapult arm. Those are hidden in the dormitory. Tell the King of Scots he will have his engine. We will transport it in pieces, by night, when it is completed."

"This is brilliant," James said.

"And foolhardy." Juliana said. "What if De Soulis recognizes it?"

"He has seen it, and so have his men," Malcolm said. "No one seems to have noticed what we have done with the timber the sheriff's men brought us for our new bell tower and the scaffolding needed to rebuild it."

"Ingenious," James said. "But Juliana is right. You take a great risk."

"Rebels," Malcolm replied, "risk all for the Scottish cause."

"This secret must be protected until the machine can be moved," James said. "The English must be kept away."

"They do not come here often, but they will be around for the market fair," Malcolm said. "We may be able to move it at night when there are fewer patrols at night, with sheriff's men closer to the town and not so much in the forest and hills."

James nodded. "Good. And Juliana, what of Gawain? Will he be here today?"

"He said he might after he sees the sheriff."

"We must know how the wind blows with him."

She sighed. "I do not know if I can ask him just now. I am—not ready to accuse him, and I do not know how to ask."

"I will speak with him myself," James said. "It is time, I think."

"Wait here, Sir Gawain." Deirdre, the abbot's sister, who kept his house and helped look after his wards, showed him into a small sunny side room that held a table and chairs. "The abbot will be with you shortly. There is ale on the table."

"My thanks." He waited there, noting a few cups on the table beside a jug of foamy ale. He poured out some ale, swallowing quickly. It was cool and light, well-suited to the summer warmth this late afternoon.

Riding here from Dalbrae, his head was filled of troubled thoughts, his heart filled with torment. He did not know what he would do. There was so much to sort out.

He looked out the window at the repairs in progress on the broken bell tower. Something seemed odd about it. Tilting his head, he could not quite discern what it was, and so he did not hear the door opening behind him.

"Gawain." A man spoke.

He turned, expecting the abbot, and saw instead James Lindsay. He stared, heart slamming. Recovering himself, he set his cup down.

"Jamie!"

James shut the door and sat on a bench, indicating Gawain to sit too. He did so in silence, then picked up the jug of ale to offer it.

James shook his head. "I had my fill earlier."

"Ah." Three cups here were used, he realized. Presumably James had met with the abbot—and Juliana, who was expected earlier. "I am surprised to see you, James."

"Bruce sent me here to see to a couple of tasks. Can I be sure that information is safe with you?"

Gawain sipped his ale, but it tasted dull now, no longer quenching. He set it aside. "Of course you can. I owe you an explanation."

"I think so. You left us abruptly to ride with the English. And we heard you made a new obeisance to King Edward." James's tone was cold and flat.

He remained cool himself. "Your spies are always about, even so far as London."

"They are," James agreed. "I am not here to confront you. Every man must make his own choices in this war. I made mine. You have had to make yours."

"I have." He frowned slightly. "You saw your cousin? My wife?"

"I came here for Robert, and also because the abbot sent word that my cousins needed help. I am thankful that Juliana is safe, though the lads are in custody. She told me much of what has gone on." He watched Gawain steadily.

Gawain realized that James's eyes were the same dark, rich blue as Juliana's. He had not noticed that color in his friend's before—he wanted to think of him still as his friend. And with his mind so constantly on Juliana, he now saw the familial resemblance in their eyes, their coloring, their fine and handsome features.

"Felicitations on your marriage," James murmured. "I will not congratulate you on your post. It might please a Southron, but it poses difficulties for me and mine."

"I just learned today that I will be released from my duties at

Elladoune all too soon. The abbot spoke with the sheriff earlier today too, so you may have been told."

James nodded assent, studying him in the quiet, serious manner Gawain remembered well. "What of your obligation to my cousin, your wife?"

"I will always honor her. Though I cannot say what will happen. I do not yet know where I will be reassigned. She may not want to come to England with me."

"Ask her," James said. "Though be warned, she is rather upset by what she has learned of you today."

Gawain played a finger along the rim of the cup. "I am not surprised, and I am sorry about it. I wanted to tell her myself. I want to tell her…many things."

"Some you could have told her already, lad. She did not even know your involvement with us."

"I waited for the right moment, which never came. If I told her that I ran with you willingly, she might believe I would work for the Scottish cause here and change allegiance."

"Oh, well, cannot have her thinking that," James drawled.

"The marriage came quickly for us," Gawain snapped. "There is much left to explain between us. And much to guard. She keeps her secrets too."

James scowled. "She has not guarded much from you."

"What do you mean?"

"She loves you. I see it plainly. She has already given you all of her heart, all of herself. This revelation about you is hard for her. I warn you, do not hurt her—"

"I never would. No need to warn me."

"Ah, I see. The feeling is shared between you," James said slowly. "You love her. This is a tangle indeed."

"Well and truly knotted." Gawain stared out the window, where the scaffolding of the bell tower topped the abbey wall. "That scaffolding," he said. "It looks odd."

James chuckled, paused, went on. "Juliana said she met you six years ago, when Elladoune was burned and she and her kin were cast out. She said you saved her life, and were the first to call her Swan Maiden."

"True. An odd coincidence, since it brought about her capture, where I met her again in Edward's court."

"I do not believe in coincidence," James said. "I believe in a world directed by God and his angels with great purpose and intricate connections. I believe fate is created through those means. I have been its victim and its beneficiary often enough."

"Then I am a victim of fate."

"Or its beneficiary, in the long run. As I discovered for myself."

"Is it so? To be honest, sometimes I feel caught in a purgatory of ironies with no escape." He shoved a hand through his hair and exhaled in exasperation. "I have new orders that my wife will not like at all. It could shatter the marriage. It could shatter… the lass. I do not know how to tell her."

"Be honest," James said quietly. "The abbot told us both that your orders are to close down Elladoune. If there is more, tell her."

Gawain tightened his mouth. "The truth is not as easy as that."

"The truth can seal where we think it will sever."

"Not this."

"Did you know," James said, "that I fired Lady Isobel's castle on the very night I met her? Something tells me your orders are similar."

Gawain raised a brow. "Did she forgive you for it?"

"Once she understood why I did it, once she knew me…aye. She did."

"I have much to explain to Juliana before she would understand any of it."

"Such as your betrayal of me, her cousin?"

"I thought you did not care to bring that up."

"I think I must." James fisted his hand on the table, knuckles white, wrist strong.

"Say what you will."

"The morning you left," James answered, low and fierce, "the Southrons hunted us in the greenwood. You know that. You were with them." His eyes went cold.

Gawain nodded, remembering that day. His stomach clenched. He swung the cup like a small bell, listening.

"Patrick was wounded, Quentin nearly captured," James went on. "We lost one of our own that morning when you disappeared," he added. "We were concerned about you. And we did not care to lose more."

"I am glad none were killed." Gawain drew a deep breath. "You know my original fealty was to King Edward."

"You were working with them when Isobel met you. Then you helped her and defended her. For that I will always owe you, no matter the rest. But you deserted us."

Gawain studied the flecks of ale foam as if it contained a map of life's mysteries. The air in the room felt oppressive. He could relieve it with the truth.

His stepfather and stepbrothers would have mollified James. They would have apologized, soothed him with apology and logic, screening what they wanted to hide.

But he was not like that. He knew that now. He wanted only clear, refreshing honesty. The truth had to be known. Withholding it roiled within him like bile.

The truth could seal what was severed, as James had pointed out.

"We skirmished with the English the day before," he said. "Do you recall?"

"I do. You fought well. And left before dawn."

"We saw the faces of some of the men we killed, from the trees where we hid."

"English deaths could not be helped."

"One of them was my stepbrother Geoffrey," he said bluntly. "I saw him fall. So I went to their camp to find him, and found he had died." He drew a breath. "I hope it was not my arrow."

"Jesu," James breathed out. "Why did you not come back and tell us?"

"Geoffrey came to Scotland to search for me," Gawain said. "My stepfather sent him. I was welcomed back as if I had escaped from the enemy. I could not go back without leading them straight to you. My brother was dead, Jamie. I took him home."

James rubbed his fingers over his brow. "And you stayed to make amends."

"I did," Gawain said curtly. "I was punished by the king for betrayal, and was lucky to escape with my life. I gave up nothing to harm any of you. I stayed in prison for a while, then was allowed to request king's peace again. Edward always had a soft spot for my stepfather and his sons, and fortunately that included me."

"Isobel swore you had good reason for what you did. Her gift of Sight told her that you left to protect us. I assumed it was some dilemma of loyalty and inheritance. A question of convenience."

"Guilt and obligation. And grief."

"And loyalty to us, if you did not betray us."

"Never that. I gave naught away. I had two months in the Tower of London for aiding the enemy. My stepfather began the rumor that I was taken captive. He wanted to spare the family any disgrace."

"So you stayed with the English."

"I had no choice. King Edward has a formidable temper. I had already helped rebels by helping Juliana and others at Elladoune, years before. I did not want my family to suffer. My mother is ill. She took Geoffrey's death hard."

"How much does Juliana know?"

"Not much of this." Gawain sighed, fearing the damage to his marriage might be irrevocable. "I should have told her sooner. I have been remiss. Secrets...are hard to relinquish. There are other things I must tell her as well. She deserves the truth."

"Truth and cream," James said, "rise to the top. She has a few confessions to make to you, too, I think."

"I suspect so."

"Talk to her. She is here in the abbey."

Gawain looked down. Relief and shame mingled. The urge to tell Juliana the truth was strong, but his secrecy could hurt her. Nor did he know if his marriage could be saved if he must ruin Elladoune.

"I must leave soon," James said. "King Robert awaits my report. Though you, Sassenach, do not know that."

"I never saw you," Gawain said quietly.

"Isobel sends her love. She never doubted you. I was wrong, and I apologize."

Gawain nodded. His throat tightened. "Send Lady Isobel my love in return, my friend," he said quietly.

"We will meet again soon, I hope. I would stay if I could, but Isobel is expecting a child soon. I do not want to linger anywhere when I can be on my way back to her."

Gawain smiled. "Of course. Give her my congratulations and my apologies."

"She holds no grudges. I think you will find Juliana can do the same."

"She will have to decide that."

"Gawain, I must ask a favor." James leaned toward him. "It is another question of loyalty. You made a pledge to your king, but you also made an oath with Juliana."

"I did." Gawain frowned, waiting.

"That makes us kinsmen now, and makes you kin to her brothers as well. They need protection."

"I mean to remove them from the sheriff's custody somehow. Children must not pay when men create war. Even if those lads are ruling the roost at Dalbrae," he added. "Ha, with their spirit, I am not surprised. But listen. If an attempt is made to snatch them at the market fair, Elladoune's constable should look the other way."

"Is it so? I will."

James took his hand with warm sincerity. "Farewell, then." Opening the door, he looked back. "Had you stayed for the Scots—*ach*, what a warrior for our side you would have been."

Chapter Twenty-Eight

SIGHTING THE CENTERMOST circle of the target—a painted cloth nailed to a tree—Juliana raised her bow, arrow nocked. She adjusted her stance, squaring shoulders and hips, and went still. Drawing back the string, she released.

The arrow whistled away and struck the target's center. Leaves spit downward with the force against the tree.

Applause sounded from above. Angus, Lucas, and Lucas's three sons peered from the leafy canopy. Seated on a log nearby, Mairead's four small children giggled and clapped. Juliana plucked an arrow from the quiver beside her.

"By Saint Fillan, the girl never misses!" Angus called out. "Try the wands on that other target. Split them if you can."

"Step back more," Lucas advised. "You are too close."

"Though nothing challenges her," one of Lucas's sons said. "Next year I will win the Golden Arrow from her, but this year, she will surely take it from the Sassenachs!" Laughter echoed among the trees.

"Hush, you," she said, "or the Sassenachs will take you instead."

Walking toward another target, she stepped back farther to please her critics. She adjusted the leather band wrapped around her wrist and shifted her balance. Then she eyed the target—four stripped saplings stuck upright in the ground in front of an earthen mound. The game was to nick a wand as the arrow went home to earth.

This time, she chose a steel-tipped, pointed war arrow, a type she rarely used, preferring the wedge point of a hunting arrow or a blunted practice arrow. But they would not do for this. Nocking, lifting, tilting, she drew back the string in one fluid movement that came easily to her after years of practice, needing little thought. Archery, after all this time, was a natural and exhilarating. She had the skill and strength, even the grace, and allowed instinct and intuition to take over rather than logic. That was the only secret she knew.

Gazing at one wand, then the target, as if nothing else existed, she lifted and tilted, pulled the string to her jaw, sighted down the shaft to the arrow's deadly point and beyond. When she let go, the arrow struck the wand in passing, biting it, the stalk wavering as the point embedded in the center of the turf mound.

The next shot split the wand in half and soared past. Whistles filtered through the treetops. She missed the third and set herself to shoot again.

"Wait," Lucas called. "Practice overhead shots again, straight up into the trees. You need that to win the gold arrow."

"Not while we are up here," one of his sons said, laughing. Seated well away, Mairead's children laughed too. Both of Lucas's sons dropped down as Juliana walked to the tree fringe, loaded her bow, and looked up to assess the difficult upward shot.

As she readied to pull the string, she heard an owl's call, a hiss of warning, a rustling. She straightened and glanced around.

The men had disappeared. The trees seemed silent. Mairead's children sat on their log, looking past her with wide, uncertain gazes as Gawain stepped out of the green light of the forest and into the sunny clearing.

Juliana stared, propping her bow upright. Days had passed since she had seen Gawain and Laurie ride away from the abbey. She had not gone back to Elladoune since then, sending a message that she would stay at the abbey for a few days. Gawain returned to the abbey gates to ask for her, but she sent her refusal to see him through the monks. She was angry, even devastated. James had urged her to talk with her husband—but she was not ready.

But seeing him now, she only felt relief and joy—he was so handsome, strong, confident. He was all her dreams realized. She wanted to go to him, but reminded herself that she was angry. He only got an aloof look from her as he came near.

Lush summer light glossed his raven-dark hair and his brown-eyed gaze was warm and compelling. She melted a little, but would not relent. A brown surcoat draped over a lighter tunic where his upper arms bulged at the fabric, and a leather belt hung low over his lean hips. He moved with ease and power all at once. She went still.

"My lady," he said. "I am glad I found you."

Tipping her head, she turned away to nock a blunted arrow. Love rushed in to drown out reason, and she fought its pull.

"Silent again, Swan Maiden?" he murmured.

All she wanted was to drop the bow and run to him, kiss him where his cheeks were pink above the day's dark whiskers, kiss his bow-curved lips. Most of all she wanted to forgive him and be happy again.

But she had questions and she felt hurt, even furious. She had wept in her narrow bed in the abbot's house. He had come to the gate once, but she had pride, and so did he, so he had not returned. But he was here now.

She raised the bow again and spread her feet wide, pointing the arrow upward.

"An unusual shot," he said. "What are you after? Birds? Squirrels? Rebels?"

She glared at him, aimed again.

"If you want to hit something up there, I suggest you get down on one knee and lean back. You will be more stable that way, less likely to waver in your aim."

She lowered the bow, deciding not to shoot at all. "What do you want?"

"She speaks," he bit out. "Eonan said you might be here. We must talk."

"You have no time for that. You have a castle to empty and Scots to harry," she snapped. "And territory to explore for Sassenachs so they can take it away from us. Be sure to lead them to that beautiful mountain you were so curious about."

"God save us," he growled, "your tongue is as sharp as an arrow sometimes."

She jammed the arrow in her hand into the quiver. Setting the bow tip on the ground, she stepped through the arc to push down on the bow and remove the string, all in signal to him that she was done. Holding stave and quiver, she stepped away.

"Children," she said in Gaelic to Mairead's brood, waiting there, "come with me."

She did not glance up at the trees where the men and boys might yet be hiding, but beckoned the children to follow her along the forest path to a place where birches edged a wide overhang, and a curve of the loch spread below, water sparkling in the sun. She leaned her things against a boulder and sat, the children gathering around her. As the smallest boy scrambled up, Gawain lifted him to her lap.

"You can go," she told Gawain. "I do not need a guard. Ah, pray pardon, I am still a prisoner of your king." She slid him a glare.

"Juliana—" he began, then shook his head, setting a booted foot on the boulder.

She fought tears for a moment and circled her arms around the children, who were exclaiming, pointing toward the loch, where in the distance, swans looped in lazy paths on the water.

"They cannot fly," she said after a moment, aware that Gawain listened. "Their wing feathers have molted. They are helpless. Earthbound. I feel like one of them sometimes."

She slid a look toward Gawain, who stood staring at the loch. Her heart felt taut. She sensed sadness and loneliness in him, and it hurt her in turn. Somehow she had become part of him, woven together, linked. Her anger began to drain away.

"Tell us again about how the swans came to Loch nan Eala," asked Ailis, the oldest girl. The others nodded.

Juliana smiled. "Long ago in the misty time," she began in Gaelic, "a beautiful maiden, lovely as a swan, lived in a fortress on an island in that loch. She loved a warrior who was as dark as a raven, handsome, and strong…"

She told them of the lovers who planned to marry, and of the Druid who summoned magic to destroy them; of the faery bolt he shot into the clouds to raise a storm. She told them how the island and the fortress sank and everyone drowned.

The children listened intently, the smallest one staring at her in fascination, his blue eyes wide.

Gawain listened too, watching the loch, the wind pushing at his hair, his cloak.

"But the Druid's magic failed, for the warrior and the maiden, and all the people, changed into swans," she said.

"But sometimes the maiden and the warrior swans come out of the water," the older girl said, "and leave their swan skins to look for a way to break the spell."

"Sometimes," Juliana agreed. "Most of the time they stay on the loch, happy in that world—" She caught her breath, glancing at Gawain.

"How can they break the spell?" another child asked.

"There is a way, but I have forgotten," she said. "Let me think—"

"Only a warrior whose heart is true, a man who has a love like theirs, can free them," Gawain said softly in English.

She stared at him. He glanced at her over his shoulder.

"Tell them in Gaelic. Mine is not strong enough, and they do not have the English. Tell them that a warrior who knows true love must catch a faery bolt and fling it into the loch. That is the only way to break the spell and free the swans."

"How—how do you know that?" she murmured.

He turned away. "I know the old tale. Tell them."

She did, her thoughts tumbling. Ailis sighed, but her oldest brother snorted.

"No one can catch a faery bolt," he insisted.

"Some have tried, just to prove it can be done, hoping to break the spell one day." Gawain looked at Juliana. "Tell him what I said."

"You understood his Gaelic."

"I did. Tell him." His dark eyes were keen. Full of golden light somehow. "Just to prove it can be done. Just in case the spell could be broken someday," he added, his eyes penetrating.

Astonished, Juliana finished the story. Then she lifted the smallest child to the ground, stood, and ushered Mairead's brood toward the forest path, asking them to wait there. She walked back to Gawain.

"Tell me how you knew that. Tell me how you understood the old tongue. That is an ancient local legend. Few outside this glen would know it."

"Someone told me the tale, long ago."

"'Twas not your nurse," she said.

"Nay," he said. "My grandfather." His profile was spare, elegant, troubled.

"You have secrets, Gabhan—and I want to know what they are."

"I will tell you. What of your secrets?" He glanced at her. "I want you to listen—and I want you to talk to me."

"I will tell you all. But I know you have been keeping something from me, and I know it eats at you. If we are to be together, we need honesty between us."

"We do." The wind whipped at both of them as he turned and took her face in his hands. His eyes were deep and steady and warm. He kissed her, soft and slow, then pulled back.

"My God, do you know how much I love you?" he whispered.

Her tears welled, lip quivered. He kissed her gently, and she gave a small whimper of relief. Tears slid down her cheeks. He brushed them away, kissed her again. She moved into the circle of his arms. "Gabhan—"

"Juliana! Juliana!" The children's voices sliced anxiously through the trees. She broke away and ran to them. Gawain grabbed her bow and quiver and followed.

"What is it?" she called, alarmed.

"The swans! They are hurting the swans!" Gilchrist said, pointing.

Juliana whirled to look toward the loch. Gawain came toward her, turning to see the water and Elladoune on the promontory in the distance.

Soldiers swarmed on the bank near the castle, holding nets and long hooks. Some were knee-deep in the water, surrounded by a froth of white as the swans struggled and flapped wings that would not fly. On the shore, a man in black armor watched.

"The sheriff's men," Juliana said as he joined her. "They are upping the swans!"

ONCE THEY REACHED the meadow that edged the loch near Elladoune, Gawain set down the smallest boy he had carried. Running across the meadow from the direction of the castle, two women came to shoo the children with them. He turned back toward the lochside.

Several knights, the sheriff among them, thundered across the meadow in the opposite direction, away from the loch and forest toward Dalbrae. Secured in baskets on packhorses, several white swans were netted and tied.

Juliana ran after them, but stopped, for it was futile. The summer wind dragged her gown against her legs, whipped her pale braided hair in a long rope. Gawain joined her. "My love, come away—I will go after them—"

Them, from Elladoune's entrance, he heard shouts, and

turned to see some of the MacDuffs waving the children and the women into the gate. They were safe. Good.

Juliana bent to retrieve a few white feathers that lay in the grass. Out on the water, a few swans circled, agitated, necks attended, wings busked in white arcs. A pair of females curved their heads to nudge at their offspring, while one of the larger males, patrolled the outer cluster in wide circle.

Cuchulainn, the oldest and largest, was in a fury, driving across the water, wings out, broad chest lifted. He charged a group of hapless geese, clearing them away, then turned his temper on a flock of mallards, who skimmed away as well. He orbited the other swans, neck curved, wings slightly lifted, a proud and angry guardian.

"They took Eimhir," Juliana said. "I do not see her. Cuchulainn is in a rage over that, and the invasion of his territory."

"What others are gone, can you tell?" Gawain asked.

She shaded her eyes, fingers trembling. "Some older cygnets are missing. And a female with no mate—a maiden swan," she said. "I called her Etain, after—"

"After the princess transformed by magic into many forms, including a butterfly," Gawain said. "Until her lover found her and brought her home." The story bubbled up in his memory.

Her shading hand hid her expression. "Who are you, Gawain Avenel?"

"Later for that," he murmured. "How many more are gone?"

"Too many. I do not see Guinevere and her babies either."

He scanned the loch, then turned at the sound of voices as some of the Highlanders who now lived inside Elladoune— mostly MacDuffs, his kin—hurried toward them. Laurie and Eonan were ran with them.

Uilleam was shouting and pointing, and Teig waved his arms. Juliana ran to meet them, then returned.

"Guinevere is in the cove," she said. "Something is wrong."

Turning with her, Gawain went with the others, his long running stride carrying him ahead with Laurie and a Highland man. They crossed through trees to emerge on the narrow shore of a little cove.

Guinevere swam in anxious circles, wings halfway up, neck stiffened. Cuchulainn glided in from the loch, both of them sliding back and forth. As the people appeared on the shore, the birds swam toward them, hissing in distress.

"Where are her babies?" Juliana stepped down into the water, her gown floating around her as she surged toward the swans. She turned.

"There!" She pointed. "One of them is caught!" She swam with fast strokes, the swans with her.

Gawain ran on land, followed by others, to find a bed of tall reeds where netting floated. Caught in a tangle of rope, a small gray-brown cygnet splashed, flapped, giving a gurgle that pulled at Gawain's heart. He saw quickly that its struggles could drown it. He approached the bank, about to step into the water when Juliana pushed through with swimming strokes to enter the reed bed and stand breast-high beside the little bird.

Examining the netting, she sank under the water, then rose again. "His legs are caught in the net!" She pulled frantically at the trappings.

Unable to just pace on the shore, Gawain kicked off his boots, dropped belt and cloak, and stepped into the loch himself, waist high and surging to reach the reeds.

"This is such a tangle," she said as he approached. "Help me!"

Feet in the mucky bottom, he found the knots under the little bird and began to work at them.

The water seemed to be getting deeper. At first at his waist, it was approaching his chest, and Juliana's shoulders were nearly submerged. He realized they were sinking in the soft silt beneath their feet, as she did too, for her eyes were wide with alarm.

"We will get the little one free, and get out of here quickly," Gawain reassured her. She held the cygnet while he pulled at the interlaced roping. Finally a knot slipped free and the net loosened.

Juliana released the little bird, and it scrambled and then

swam toward its mother, who swept her long neck down to push at him with her beak. Then she sank her tail until he clambered onto her back along with his three siblings that had found her. She glided away toward Cuchulainn, circling in the water.

Gawain laughed and pulled Juliana into a wet embrace, recalling another time when he had hidden among the reeds with her on the night Elladoune had burned.

"Come, we must get out of this muck," he said. The water was already lapping at her throat. He felt the silt sucking at his stockinged feet.

"Gawain!" Laurie called. He looked toward the shore as Laurie stepped into the water followed by Eonan, and then others—Teig, other MacDuffs, even old Uilleam and Beithag. They made a line as Laurie stretched to grasp Gawain's extended hand. Eonan grabbed Laurie's belt, and one by one each grasped another until the last one—Teig, with his solid strength—pulled on Uilleam's belt and moved backward.

Holding Juliana, Gawain felt them being pulled out of the muck to more solid ground under their feet as the living chain of friends and kin connected them to the safe shore of Loch nan Eala.

WET, RELIEVED, JOYFUL for the moment, Juliana wrapped her arm around Gawain's waist as they walked with the others toward Elladoune. She laughed at some remark Laurie made. Her wet gown slapped against her legs, the grass beneath her bare feet felt soft and good, and the sunshine was warm. She felt healed and renewed.

Whatever their secrets, they would share them and peace would return. He had come for her, they had saved the cygnet together. They could resolve their differences.

She smiled up at him, but he slowed beside her, looking

ahead. His arm tensed and dropped away. She glanced toward the castle.

De Soulis and a few knights waited on horses at the rise of the hill outside the front gate. Dressed in black armor, the sheriff pointed to Gawain and beckoned.

Gawain looked at her. "Go to the abbey," he growled. "Take the others and go."

Heart pounding, she turned so that De Soulis would not see her speaking to Gawain. "Are we to be expelled from the castle today? Will he shut it now?"

"I wager he is displeased to see me consorting with the locals. Let me deal with this alone. The…castle will be closed later. I wanted to explain all you—but go now. Hurry."

"So you can give him more secrets? Another piece of our life taken away?"

"Go or he will snare you too," he snapped. "I will come for you later."

"If you only mean to follow your king's orders, do not bother," she retorted.

Whirling, tears in her eyes, she ran across the meadow even as he walked toward the sheriff.

Chapter Twenty-Nine

S HE IGNORED THE noise of the crowd behind her. Feet planted firmly, Juliana raised the bow and drew the string taut, balancing the arrow shaft, intent on the upright wand a hundred paces away. The crowd urged her—or rather, the hooded, cloaked youth they thought she was—to take the shot, as she was the last to do so in this round.

When she released the bowstring, her arrow chipped the wand and sank into the straw target behind it. A man approached, a merchant and contest judge, to offer her the prize, a tiny silver bell. She had won two already that day, which put her nearly in the lead in the contest. Now she was placed with three archers from Dalbrae.

The next contest would be shooting to win the golden arrow now held by Dalbrae. She knew De Soulis was loathe to give it up. Bow fisted her hand, she shouldered her way through the crowd in the market square. Brother Eonan and Teig, acting as her guards that day, hurried beside her.

A crowd of children and youths followed; some were part of the rebel forest band—Mairead's oldest children, Lucas's sons, a few others—and the rest were from the surroundings of the town, located in the triangle of territory between Dalbrae, Inchfillan, and the loch.

The village had a spacious market square with a tall carved stone cross. The square was dusty and busy, full of people wandering past cloth-draped booths where farmers, wives, and merchants offered a variety of goods from weavings and leather to ironwork, knives, hot food and cool ale. Juliana walked past, hardly looking.

Soon they would close the booths and most would walk or ride the short distance to Inchfillan Abbey for the final contest.

She had bells enough, and handed this latest one to Teig, who looked pleased. She wanted only one prize, that golden arrow, to use toward a ransom.

"Now for Inchfillan," she told Teig and Eonan. They walked together along the earthen track that led toward the abbey. When a thunder of horses sounded behind them, they stepped aside.

De Soulis was in the lead, scowling and intent on hurrying. He rode with a few knights, the three archery contestants, a woman in a red gown—and two boys riding pillion on a horse led by a guard in chainmail.

Juliana gasped at the first sight of her little brothers in weeks. Disguised among the crowd, she could do nothing to catch their attention. They looked healthy. Happy, with no idea that they were about to be caught in a struggle over them.

The last two riders went by: Laurie, riding a black horse, and a lean, dark-haired knight in a deep brown surcoat and leather hauberk on a bay horse. He stared ahead.

Gawain riding Gringolet. Her heart leaped. She pulled the hood of her cloak over her brow, but he did not glance her way.

THROUGHOUT THE DAY, he searched for her in the crowd—sunlit hair, the face of an angel. He never saw her. But he was not sure she would attend. Perhaps she would remain in the abbey. Perhaps he would see her there. She tugged on his heart, his thoughts.

Riding toward the abbey, he saw Eonan and Teig standing

with a youth in a dark brown cloak and hood that obscured his face. Heavy clothing on such a warm day, he thought. Perhaps this was one of the forest rebels that Juliana protected in her way.

Outside the abbey palisade, spectators gathered. A table for the sale of pies and ale sat to one side of the clearing with a platform erected nearby for the sheriff and his party, including the merchant judges and the abbot.

Gawain dismounted and assisted Lady Matilda and then the Lindsay lads to the ground. Alec and Iain were whisked away with the sheriff's wife, who seated them with her on the dais as De Soulis and the abbot joined them.

He narrowed his eyes. If the boys were to be taken back today, the situation did not favor it. Hearing a shout, he saw Laurie coming toward him carrying two wooden cups already. "Excellent Scots ale!" he crowed, handing Gawain a cup, then slurping his.

Gawain sipped, watching the archers from Dalbrae gather near the wooden palisade. They set down quivers and tested their bowstrings. He frowned, calling on a dim memory of this contest in his boyhood. He had been very young then.

"I hear that Sir Soul-less is determined that his men will take the prize again," Laurie said. "A gold arrow. Knights from Elladoune or Dalbrae have won the contest for years. Generations. He intends to keep it."

Ah, the gold arrow. Now he remembered his father claiming it once.

"The shot, they say, is toward the bell tower," Laurie went on. "But the tower is being repaired. The scaffold would be in the way."

"It is not toward the bell tower," said an old man standing near them. "It is that bell up there." He pointed toward the palisade, where a tall, sturdy pole extended upward. At its height swung a bronze hand bell.

"That?" Laurie asked.

"It is tradition," the old man said. "The archers must shoot straight up and ring the bell. Whoever does wins the Golden Arrow of Elladoune, so they call it. Real gold, a fine thing," he added.

"Curious," Laurie said.

"It is to honor a legend. Long ago, they say, an evil wizard shot a faery bolt into the clouds to raise a storm that sank the first fortress that was on the loch. The archers try every year to ring the bell in remembrance of that."

Gawain stared upward. "The faery bolt," he murmured, half to himself.

"And in honor of those who drowned and were enchanted into swans," the old man said. "A good tale, eh?"

Gawain nodded. "Dangerous to shoot straight up. An archer could be killed."

"Aye so. Ah, here comes the fourth archer. The contest will begin."

The last archer walked across the field, and Gawain recognized the youth who had been with Eonan and Teig. He scowled, deep in thought. The lad looked familiar.

"That lad won three silver bells today," the old man said. "A fine shot."

Gawain narrowed his eyes. The youth loaded his bow, smaller than the knights planned to use. In practice, the lad bent back to tilt the bow toward the sky.

"God save us," Gawain muttered, seeing the long legs and the graceful curve of that slender back.

PURPOSE AND VENGEANCE should have kept her cool and deliberate, but her hands shook as she stood watching the other archers. Like the two who had gone before him, the knight spread his legs wide, leaned back, and aimed upward.

"De Lisle will do it," one of the sheriff's knights said.

The archer, who had a powerful build, assessed the shot, loaded his bow, and then placed a knee on the ground and reared back with his upright bow. His blunted arrow went straight up, chinked against the bell's rim, and came down to the grass near the archer, who scuttled away from the danger. He bowed and left the field, nodding to Juliana as if the wish the next man luck.

"Close," she heard a man say. "But the bell must ring out clear. If the lad misses, the arrow goes to De Lisle."

She walked forward, hands shaking as she withdrew a blunted arrow from her quiver. In a moment of cold fear, she wanted to run. She did not fear the shot, but the consequences if she failed and De Soulis claimed the gold arrow for Dalbrae.

Her forest friends were ready to snatch the boys if the opportunity rose, but they were sitting with the sheriff and the guards were thick there. The rebels could be caught and hung for their crimes. Something would have to change.

Nor could she appeal to Gawain, who was following orders. Soon he would close Elladoune and leave, perhaps forever, if she could not go with him. She felt empty inside. But she had to push all that from her mind. The bow shot was paramount.

Steeling herself against heartache, she looked up at the little bell suspended from the tower. Her hood dropped back, revealing only the snug leather cap that covered her hair. She hoped no one recognized her otherwise.

Nocking the bow, she spread her feet, leaned back, sighted along the shaft. The little hand bell far above her head shifted in a slight breeze, making the shot even more challenging. Shooting upward into trees was scarcely enough practice for this. The arrow had to hit under the rim to strike the hammer and ring the bell.

Gawain had told her to get down on one knee, as the archer had done ahead of her. His shot had grazed the bell's surface. If she did not do better, he would have the prize. Dropping to her knee, she aimed, paused.

Too much thought. Just send it up, straight and true, with

will and heart.

She curled forward, and on a deep breath, swung upward to aim the arrow tip toward the bell in the clouds. Heart and soul moved within her as she released.

The bell rang out sweet and clear.

HOLDING HIS BREATH, Gawain had never loved her so much as he did in that moment. Grace, she was, beauty, perfect skill. The dull clothing she wore disguised her to others, but to him, she shone like an angel—one who had just rung a bell in heaven.

He suspected she was doing this to gain back her brothers, but he could not guess how. As her arrow hurtled down to slam into the earth by the palisade fence, the crowd cheered. Gawain stood without moving, his heart leaping with love and pride.

Back on her feet, Juliana nodded, slung her quiver over her shoulder, and stood looking around. Alec and Iain were hopping up and down on the dais, yelling, heads bright in the sunlight. Gawain wondered if they recognized her, for she gave them a private little bow.

Gawain smiled, while Laurie whistled loudly beside him. Her gaze swung at the sound and her eyes met Gawain's. He smiled wider. She looked away.

His smile faded. But some instinct told him to stay close. He moved quietly toward her, a hand on his sword.

SHE LOOKED AWAY, searching the crowd for those who stood near the boys ready to reach for them when she gave the signal. But if she did so, all might be lost. De Soulis was with them, and too close. She had to change the plan.

De Soulis rose to his feet, glaring at her, the young archer who had just rung the bell and taken the prize from him. As Abbot Malcolm took a leather case from the glowering sheriff and walked toward her, she waited.

"My dear," Malcolm murmured, knowing her. He held out the leather sheath. "A beautiful shot. We have our arrow back again. Felicitations to the winner!" he said loudly then, turning as people cheered. He opened the leather wrapping.

She took up the arrow. Shining bright, shaped like a short, thick war arrow with winged fletching etched to resemble feathers, it was cool to her touch. She held it aloft, then handed it to Malcolm.

"Father Abbot, please take this for Inchfillan. I am pleased to donate it."

Then she drew off her leather cap and shook her braids free in a flaxen spill. The cheering was replaced by gasps.

De Soulis stood, shouting for his guards. Gawain took a long step out of the crowd, Laurie with him. Eonan and the monks came toward her, along with several locals, many of them cheering even more joyously than before. She heard her name among the happy shouts. But the Dalbrae guards advanced.

"Oh my dear, you had best run," Malcolm said as De Soulis barreled through the crowd. As Malcolm took the golden arrow she pressed into his hands, she turned to face De Soulis.

"Take the lads—no one is looking in this chaos," she told the abbot. "Go inside the church for sanctuary. Please—go!" He slipped away through the press of people.

Juliana reached into her quiver and snatched an arrow, nocking the shaft quickly and raising the bow.

"Walter de Soulis!" she called. The crowd went quiet. Those near backed away.

Coming toward her, he froze in the clearing. "So the Swan Maiden has a voice after all. Put that thing down," he said, indicating her bow. "You do not dare to harm me. Are you ready to give your oath of fealty, Lady Juliana?"

She trained the arrow tip toward him. "Release my brothers

to the custody of their own kin," she called out. Beyond the crowd, she could see her friends moving toward the boys. Lucas reached out and took Iain, while Angus took Alec. The abbot was just there, too, and directed them to run to the chapel, even as the guards looked around and De Soulis called out again.

"Take the girl! And do not let those boys go!" The knights turned one way and the other. Angus and Lucas had disappeared into the density of the crowd, but two knights appeared beside her now, reaching out.

"Stop! I will shoot him if I must!" she said. They halted uncertainly. She flexed her fingers on the bow wood. "You know I will not miss."

Silence descended as she felt a hundred and more gazes upon her. Then Gawain stepped away from the crowd and came toward her.

"Stop. Please," she told him, still staring at the sheriff.

"My lady," Gawain said, standing close, speaking quietly, so that only she could hear. "You have never shot a man."

"I have never shot a bell before either," she said. Her arms were beginning to tremble. "But I struck that and I can strike him. And he knows it. That black chainmail he wears will not stop my arrow. There are seams and laces, small openings—I can hit him." She kept the arrow trained on De Soulis, who stood stiffly, glaring.

"But what will it prove?" Gawain asked.

"That he can be stopped. That he cannot be a tyrant here. I will not kill him. I only want to show his armor can be penetrated."

"Jesu, I thought you had gone mad," he murmured.

"It is time we of the glen resisted him. He had my brothers. He was willing to ruin the forests to find a few men. He will close Elladoune and cast the people out. And he was the one burned Elladoune years ago—you were there."

"Avenel!" De Soulis yelled. "She is your wife, man. Take her down!"

"My wife is in earnest, sir. And she has a deadly aim."

"Get back. Go," she told Gawain. He did not move. "Leave this to me. You are one of them. If you help me, you endanger yourself."

"Juliana—"

"Gabhan," she murmured. "You cannot save me this time. Look after my kin."

"Jesu, lass, this is madness after all."

"Go," she said bluntly.

He stayed there, one long step away. She felt his gaze touch her to her soul.

"Sir Sheriff," she called out. "These people fear you and that accursed armor you wear! No one will fight you, despite your cruelties. If my father were alive, if my older brothers were here, they would not fear you. Neither do I!"

"You do not fear me, Swan Maiden," he said, "because you understand magic."

"Magic! I understand illusion. You do too," she said, realizing it was so. "Rumor gives power to magic, even if it is false."

De Soulis smiled flatly. "Just so."

Admittance enough, she thought. But if she lowered the bow now, his guards would leap upon her, and anything gained here would be lost. Her arms ached. The tension in the weapon demanded release. She breathed hard, fast.

"Juliana, give it to me," Gawain said low.

"What do you want, lady?" De Soulis called. She felt a shift, as if she had won.

"My brothers have the safety of Inchfillan now. Do not try to harm them again."

He shrugged, his eyes flickering toward the guards ready to pounce on her.

Keeping the arrow aimed, Juliana saw out of the corner of her eye that her brothers had reached the church, ushered inside by the men with them.

Tears welled in her eyes. She blinked them away. Her arms,

her legs trembled as she kept the arrow directed.

"My love," Gawain said low.

She wanted to turn to him, give up, but could not. Would not. The king still wanted her pledge, and De Soulis would want more than that in his fury. She had not thought through this plan born of desperation.

She slid her gaze around the crescent of people. Some were familiar faces. Others were knights of Dalbrae. They had drawn apart, both groups. She saw a narrow aisle of escape—and beyond that lay the sparkling surface of the loch.

Between her and that freedom stood Gawain.

She pulled the bowstring taut, aimed, and let go. The arrow arced and stuck in the ground at De Soulis's feet. He roared for the guards to take her.

She threw bow and quiver away and launched into a run, streaming past Gawain. He winged out his arms to stop the guards as they rushed toward her.

Running fast, she cleared the opening, the gap closing behind her. Her feet pounded the grass, quick and sure. Behind her, De Soulis screamed orders amid a chaos of shouts. Moments later, she heard horses' hooves thudding behind her. The meadow leading to the shore suddenly seemed impossibly long. She was an easy target for bow shots, for a man on a horse to snatch her up.

To her left lay the blue expanse of the loch. To the right was the copse surrounding the cove, past that, a meadow, and Elladoune. She ran for the trees just as an arrow thunked into the ground near her. She zigzagged between tree trunks. Another arrow split the ground ahead of her. She stumbled through a green skirt of ferns, boots crushing and cracking through the undergrowth.

Shadows enveloped her as she swung toward a thicket of trees, and arrows zinged past her, smacking and whizzing. She glanced back. Guards followed on horseback and on foot. She never slowed, skittering sideways and heading down a slope. Her footing slipped, and she slid on her bottom into a bed of ferns.

Rising to her knees, she was ready to bolt when powerful arms took her from behind. She kicked fiercely, and he grunted and dragged her into the shadows.

Chapter Thirty

"IF YOU KICK me again," Gawain muttered, "I may just leave you here."

She twisted, staring up at him. "Oh, Gawain!"

"Hush!" He glanced up the slope, but saw no knights. Holding her, he pulled her down into a nest of ferns. "Be still."

She wrapped her arms around him, her breathing fast and ragged. He held her, touched the tangled silk of her braid, relieved to have her safe in his arms for now.

He leaned back, tense and motionless, to listen. Guards shouted, moved around as he held Juliana close and waited, his hand protective on her head.

After a while, he let out a long breath as the knights began to depart, calling out to each other, swearing, walking and then riding away.

"There, my wee swan lady. It seems you needed just one more rescue."

She tightened her arms around his neck, and her little sob tore at his heart. But she pulled away. "Go," she said, pulling back. "I can get away."

"Come back here." He yanked her toward him. "We must be certain they are gone." He kept an arm around her.

"Leave me here," she said fiercely, "or they will hunt you too!"

"Leave you in danger to save my own hide?" he growled.

"Just wait."

She relented and he sat with her, listening warily. After a while, certain of the quiet surrounding them, he exhaled. "They went elsewhere looking for you."

"If they find me," she said, "what then?"

"What did you think would happen when you did that?"

"I hoped De Soulis would let my brothers go, and we could live in peace."

He wanted to laugh. "My sweet dreamer. This is a bit of a tangle. But we will get through it."

"I could not think what else to do."

"You could have let me help."

"I…was not sure you could do that."

Gawain blew out a breath, pushed fingers through his hair. "You have to trust me. You can," he said hoarsely.

"It is hard to trust any Sassenach, even you."

He felt a punch to his gut, and pressed his brow to hers. "I owe you—the truth."

"You do. What would you have done if I had shot De Soulis? Would you have arrested me or let me go?"

He drew back. "He would not have been shot."

"I never miss my aim. Well, almost never."

"I would have snatched the arrow before it hit him."

"You cannot do that."

"I could." He shifted to his feet and helped her up. "Come quickly now."

He led her along a fast course and angled toward the loch. The castle rose in the distance.

"Elladoune?" she asked. "We cannot hide there."

"We cannot. We must go to the other side of the loch. There is a place we can rest and be safe. No one would find us there."

"Across the loch? I have a better way. Come." She grabbed his hand and turned for the little cove that they had passed. Above it, she stopped among a stand of birches.

"Quick, take off your things." She fumbled at the leather

thongs that tied his hauberk. "We can swim from here."

"You are mad," he said.

"It is not far across from here." She yanked at his belt. He sighed, realizing he had lost the argument, and began to remove his heavier things. She pulled on his shirt. "Can you swim?" she asked. He nodded.

"Good." Then she stopped. "But the sheriff will hunt you and arrest you this time. The king will have your head. Better you stay, protect your good name. Leave Elladoune." She looked up at him, her hands on his shirt. "Leave Scotland."

He took her face in his hands. "We will cross this loch," he said, "and I will show you something."

Frowning, she nodded and turned away. Gawain removed all but his braies and his shirt, and knelt to shove sword, boots, clothing, and hauberk under a patch of heavy bracken, where it all but disappeared.

He turned to see that she had stripped down to a long shirt, her bare legs lean and beautifully shaped, her single braid near as long as the shirt. She ran to the cove bank where tall reeds verged, and slipped into the water. He came after her.

The cool shock of the water faded, refreshing after the frantic running. He treaded water past the reeds, and Juliana surged ahead, quick and sleek. A group of swans came toward them. Just as he glanced back to see men and horses near the shore, the swans glided nearer and surrounded them.

They knew this girl, he remembered. They knew how to protect her. Juliana dove under, came up in the midst of the swans, and he skimmed under water too, emerging inside that extraordinary ring of guardians. They swam together—somehow the birds knew what they needed. Sooner than expected, they reached the other shore.

Juliana led him along the shore to an overhang of huge pines, and climbed out. He went too. The swans skimmed away, and his wife led him under the branches.

"We keep things here." From a hiding place, she produced a

cloth sack, and Gawain, sopping wet beside her, saw her pull out dry clothing and a blanket.

Stripping out of her wet things, she knelt, nude and damp, under the piney eaves. She tugged at his wet shirt. Stripped down, he took her into his arms and gave her a breathless kiss. Somehow it was the finest, the most passionate and yet pure kiss he had ever shared with her. His hands skimmed the curve of her back, her hips, and he felt her breasts, nubbed and firm, against his chest. He nestled to her, rising hungry, kissed her again, wanting her fiercely. Yet he inhaled and forced himself to turn away. This was not the time. Snatching up the blanket, he wrapped it around her.

Then he handed her a dry gown of bleached linen that lay within the cloth sack. He drew it over her head and arms, tugging it down, dressing her like a child. He kissed her chastely, quickly.

"Later," he said, "when we have time, this secret place of yours could serve a fine purpose for us."

Her teeth chattered. "Dress now, and hurry. They may try to cross the loch."

"Your swans hid us well." He grabbed the blanket, a tartan length, then stopped.

The plaid was the earthy pattern he had seen the MacDuffs wear. He had worn it himself, long ago. Slowly, deliberately, he spread it out on the ground. He had seen a leather belt in the pile of clothes, and he grabbed it, sliding it under the cloth.

He pleated the plaid carefully, leaving a length free, as his father had showed him so long ago. He thought he had forgotten, but it came back, all of it, in full, as he pleated the length and wrapped it around him, over his damp shirt and braies. They would dry. He had to do this.

Juliana watched in silence. He lay on his back, knees up, wrapped the gathered plaid around his waist, then stood, head and shoulders ducked under the pine overhang. He fastened the belt quickly and flipped the extra cloth over his left shoulder.

"Where did you learn—only Highlanders know the proper

way to—"

His heart slammed. "My father taught me."

She gaped. "Henry Avenel?"

"My own father. Adhamnain MacDuff of Glenshie."

"MacDuff? Oh," she breathed out. "Glenshie! There was a lad Uilleam spoke of, a wee lad who left here long ago…Gabhan. He went south with his mother—his English mother!" She set shaking fingers to her mouth in astonishment.

"Aye," he said. "I am he, come home again. I could not say. How I ached to tell you." He held out his hand. "Come. Let me show you something, *mo cridhe.*"

My heart. The words came so easily.

SHE STARED AT him. Somehow, in the space of a few heartbeats, he had transformed from a king's knight to a Highland warrior.

"Gabhan MacDuff? Truly?" she asked. Blinking, she wondered suddenly if he had gone mad, surrounded by Highlanders and legends for so many weeks at Elladoune.

"I am he," he repeated. "The one who left here years ago." He drew her out of the sheltering pine into the forest. Heading out, he strode so fast, barefoot and plaided, that she could not ask the host of questions that rioted through her mind.

She followed him through the trees and up a hill. He slowed, wincing.

"I am not used to bare feet," he confessed.

She laughed. "You will toughen up, Gabhan MacDuff of Glenshie."

He took her hand and helped her over rocks, past wildflowers tumbling in crevices where heather swayed, intensely purple in the twilight.

They passed a rushing burn, and she paused to catch her breath. Gawain—*Gabhan,* she corrected, as she called him without knowing—looked back.

He belonged there on that rugged hillside, with heather cushioning his feet, and the dark craggy mountain behind him. The setting sun touched the mountain's face, and for a moment, she saw winter, old Beira, gazing down from the high slope.

"The face," she said. "She is there again."

"I know. Come." He held out his hand and led her upward, placing a hand, warm and strong, at her back to make her safe. They passed a trickling waterfall and stopped to drink its clear, cool water. Gawain led her up a grassy slope, and stopped.

Looking past him, she saw a high broken wall of gray stone.

"What is this place?"

"Glenshie. I was born here."

She stared again. But he was not mad. He was in deep earnest. The missing heir to Glenshie, the kinsmen of many here, had returned. And he had been here all along.

When he drew her by the hand inside the perimeter of the ruined keep, she sat on a fallen stone. Around them, the gloaming descended, soft and purple, like a veil.

Propping a foot on a stone, he stared out where a long bluff overlooked the loch far below, and her own castle beside it. And he began to speak.

"I BETRAYED THEM all," he said, after telling his story—his childhood, his secrets, his disillusionment as a young knight. Even his mother's grief and reticence. He added some of his sojourn with James Lindsay and his rebels.

She had listened patiently, accepting all of it. He was grateful for that. The night darkened around them, and still he sat with her among the broken walls of Glenshie as they talked. Each revelation lifted a burden from him, heart and soul.

"I betrayed those who had faith in me, those who had helped

me. My stepfather was a good man. My stepbrothers, all good men," he continued. "I went over to the Scottish side with rebels. I broke the word I had given King Edward—and I swear to you now, I know he does not deserve our loyalty. But one of my stepbrothers died because of choices I made." He had explained what happened to Geoffrey.

"You betrayed no one," she said. "You acted out of honor, which flows through your veins. True honor, even if it goes against the rules others make. Now you have uncovered Glenshie and found the part of you that was lost. You can have peace at last."

He stared at his hands in the gathering darkness. "I cannot redeem what happened to Geoffrey."

She set a hand on his arm. "Death is a risk of war. We all know that. You think about others but forget to tend to yourself."

He smiled a little. "I tended to what I needed. I looked for Glenshie. And I allowed myself to fall in love with you."

She lifted his hand, kissed it. "I am glad you did. And now you must tend to the rest of your sense of honor."

"My allegiance," he said softly.

"You love Scotland."

He looked at the mountains. "I always have," he murmured. "And I love England, the best parts of it. My family there. The kindness and beauty in the land, the people, who rise above the king and his obsession."

"Then you must choose what suits your heart best."

"I know what you want to hear. But it is not easy to cast off all that I am, and take up the plaid and the cause of Scotland."

"You are one of those who are sore caught in this war. You care for both sides. The Avenels love you truly. They would tell you to go the way of your heart. The Scots who know and love you will tell you the same. Only you can decide."

He slid his hand over the satiny crown of her head. "You sound like Laurie."

"Laurie is another with a foot in both lands. He just will not admit how much he cares for Scotland."

"His wife is English, and he likes life to be easy. But he does love Scotland. It would not take much to sway him to the Scots one day. He knows what is right, as far as the king's war goes."

"You wanted to tell me all of this before. Why did you wait?"

"I am not sure. I had to find out who I was on my own. I had to find Glenshie. I wanted you to know all of it. Including what I am ordered to do at Elladoune."

"Close it," she said.

"Raze it. That is the full truth."

She gasped, sat up. "Not that," she whispered.

"It torments me. With you there, with my own MacDuff kin—I cannot do this. Yet my orders will hold. Naught will change just because I put on this plaid. My chainmail still exists. My orders still exist."

"Perhaps," she said, "you have made your decision for England."

He let out a sigh. "That does not sit well with me, truly. But I am a knight of King Edward, and I have a chance to gain Glenshie by that means."

"Ruin my family's castle," she said, "to save your own."

"I will ride out to see the king's commanders and argue against ruination. They may listen. De Soulis will not. He will do whatever he can to ruin me now."

"I hoped you would choose for the Scots. I think your heart lies there."

"It may," he allowed. "I need to serve those I love—my family in England, my kin in Scotland. My honor as a knight. You," he whispered fervently. "You. I can keep you safe here if I side with the English. Do you not see that?"

"Safe perhaps, though without you if they move you. I love you," she said fervently. "But a Sassenach who rides through Scotland ruining it for his king—that is hard."

He stood abruptly and stepped away. "So you cannot love a Sassenach."

She came toward him. "You I love. You. Not who you side with. But the rest of it, where you go, would I go? I cannot say," she whispered. She touched his arm.

He turned with a low groan, held out his arms. She tucked in under his chin.

"What if there was another way to claim this place?" she asked. "Claim it through your king—the King of Scots. You were born a MacDuff. Not an Avenel. He is your king."

He looked over her head at the night landscape. She spoke irrefutable truth.

"Robert Bruce will take Scotland back one day. We will all be free, I feel it in my heart. Glenshie is yours by right. Your Scottish king would never dispute that claim."

"Unless the claimant fought for the English." He sighed. "I have seen that Robert Bruce is a true king, noble with it, dedicated to this land and the people. Dedicated to gaining it back in his sure fist. Would I change my allegiance?" He looked away.

"Would you give your fealty to a man who has transgressed against King Edward too, and made obeisance three times? So I have heard. Would you pledge to follow a rebel king?"

He huffed a flat laugh at the irony. "Understand this. I obeyed my heart once, and went over to the Scots. It ended in disaster."

"Then try again."

He stared out at the mountains and the land. "'Tis a beautiful place, this," he said. "I remember it well. I always wanted to come back. I have family here, the MacDuffs. I need to tell them."

"Someday," she said, taking his hand and placing it on her abdomen, "there will be others who are kin to you, and who you will want to protect."

He kissed her temple. "Would you want that with a Sassenach knight?"

"I want that with you."

"Would you go with me to England if I asked you?"

"To visit your family, aye. But not to stay."

He nodded his understanding. "You bargain hard, love."

"I will not give up."

"Give up for now, here in this place with me," he murmured. "Where we only have loyalty between us." He touched his brow to hers.

"Just here," she whispered. "Hidden away."

The night wind was soft around them, and stars glittered in the indigo sky. He slipped his hands into the silk of her hair and tipped her face upward. He kissed her tenderly, and drew her down to the cool grass. While the cool wind caressed his skin, he bared hers gently, and surrounded her with his plaid.

With slow, deliberate, gentle caresses at first, he skimmed his hands over her body, cherishing her, feeling her warmth surround him, succor him. Kissing her deeply, luxuriantly, he groaned low when her knowing touch stoked the fire within him.

Unable to hold himself back any longer, he felt an urgent need that was more than physical. The sun would rise soon, and the outer world would return with it. When she arched in sweet, silent ecstasy, he filled her, loved her, lost himself within the boundary of her soul.

As the morning sky brightened, they walked together down the mountainside, following a rough track. Earlier they had foraged berries and nuts and Juliana had found nettle and dandelions to boil up in clear water for a light but fortifying meal, and they had decided to return to the abbey to see her brothers and confer with the abbot.

He paused for a moment on the long slope that overlooked the loch. Long ago, he had stood here with his father and heard for the first time the legend of Elladoune. For now, a sense of peace enveloped him. She had been right about that. No matter what he had done or decided to do, she loved him. And he loved her to the depth of his soul. Nothing would alter the core of what they felt. But soon they would cross the water and face what had been wrought around them. The morning was cloudy with a soft drizzle, the loch below silver where the swans floated on the on breast of the water. Mist slipped around the banks of the loch.

At the heart of the loch was a shimmering veil of gold. Frowning, he pulled Juliana close, wondering at it on such a peaceful silvery morning.

"Look," she whispered. "Do you see it?"

A wash of gold hovered on the water and took the shape of windowed walls.

"Is it Dun nan Eala, the old fortress of the swans? The sunken castle?"

He blinked, unsure. A moment later, the image vanished. He wondered if it was ever there. Juliana turned in his arms and he kissed her, held her close. Now he looked past the loch to movement far off, on the opposite shore. Something moved in the forest. Figures, and something large, awkward, a structure of some kind. He narrowed his eyes.

"What is that?" It moved away from the abbey toward a deeper part of the forest.

"*Ach,*" she said softly. "You do not see that."

"I see it. It looks like a tower," he muttered, as the tall thing swayed as if in a cart. Or on wheels—"God save us. It looks like a siege engine."

"It is naught. Come away." She pulled at his arm.

"Naught? A siege engine in the forest, propelled by robed monks, naught?"

She looked up, earnest then. "Gabhan MacDuff, do not think on it. You wear a Highlander's garment, and stand on your Highland property speaking to your Highland wife. So you do not see that, down there."

"Juliana, why are the monks moving a siege engine?"

She sighed. "They are taking it to the King of Scots."

"Ah! The scaffolding. I thought there was something odd about it. They have been building this right under De Soulis's nose, and mine as well."

"De Soulis burned the other one the rebels made and promised to the king."

"What rebels would those be?"

"The ones in the forest. The ones in your own, ah, castle."

He rubbed a hand over his face. "Let me guess. James Lindsay came here to claim that machine for the king."

"Partly."

"And I have been harboring rebels under my roof and consorting with them. And I married one of them."

"That is—all true." She winced a little, glancing up at him.

He stood taking it in. Then he shook his head and began to laugh. Setting a hand over his eyes, he gave a disbelieving chuckle that ended in a groan. "Dear God, wife."

She smiled a little. "Heaven will play these games in your life until you give in."

"Give in to what?"

"Being the Scot you were born to be."

He groaned again. He had no good answer to that, but his feelings were becoming clear. He had followed heart and instinct before when he had gone over to the Scots under James Lindsay. And he had held himself back from doing so ever since because of the consequences to others. What if he followed his heart again?

The upper sky filled with heavy gray clouds. Rain would come soon, cool dampness in the wind. He looked across the loch, and drew his brows together.

The golden image of the castle showed in the water again. This time, the image was brilliant orange-gold, floating on the surface of the water.

"Juliana," he said. "Elladoune is burning."

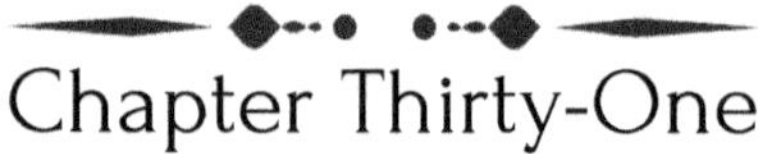

Chapter Thirty-One

"I S THERE NO boat?" Gawain asked when they reached the pine tree at the edge of the loch. "We would cross faster."

Juliana nodded, breathless with running. She only used the little boat in cold weather, but it was needed now. Turning, she led him along a forest path until they reached a bit of shore under the trees. Hidden in shallow water in a reed bed was a small round hide boat with one cross seat and a triangular paddle. Gawain helped her into it, though it spun as they stepped inside. Once settled, he took up the paddle.

"I have never rowed a curragh, though I remember riding in them as a lad."

"Rhythm," she said as he began to move them out on the water. "Rhythm and stroke will balance it."

He nodded and thankfully mastered the vessel's crazy wavering by the time he struck out over the loch. Soon the swans glided out of the mist to surround them like an escort again as the little boat skimmed toward the opposite shore.

Juliana watched Elladoune, heart sinking as she saw flames lick the inner side of one wall, smoke billowing from a corner of the bailey. "I think only the kitchens are on fire. Not the keep."

"We will be there soon enough," he said, rowing. "Whoever is there, Laurie or the MacDuffs, will fight it the best they can. If it is just the kitchen or another outbuilding, the blaze might be put out and the place saved."

"Look!" She pointed. "Sheriff's men on the hill, just watching."

"De Soulis must have ordered the firing of Elladoune in my absence."

"They will be patrolling the forest too. They might see the war machine!"

"I pray your friends have sense enough to abandon it and find safety and sanctuary in the abbey."

"Hurry!" she said. "There might be a way to help them!"

"We can help with buckets of water. And I will fetch my sword and your bow and arrows."

"You showed me your secret." Her heart slammed. "Now I will show you mine. But you must never tell."

"I am a keeper of secrets," he said.

He slid them smoothly into the sheltered little cove, leaped out to beach the small boat on the pebbly shore, and helped her out. She ran toward the hidden cache of belongings beneath the fallen tree. With shaking hands, she pulled out his gear and her own clothing and reached for another cloth sack.

Gawain pulled on his hauberk and strapped his sword belt over the leather protective gear, then pulled on his boots. There was no time to change out of the plaid.

"Now you look even more the Highland warrior," she said.

He slid her a wry glance. "You will not stop, will you, now that this possibility exists."

"Never, *mo cridhe.*"

He looked toward the castle, where a rim of flame edged along one wall. "We must hurry." He held out his hand.

"Wait." She fell to her knees and reached into the other sack, drawing out a white cloak, and then a shoulder cape made of swan's feathers sewn to a linen lining.

Standing, she draped the cloak and capelet over her shift of bleached linen, tied the strings and the neck, pulled up the white hood.

"So the Swan Maiden does exist," he said, sounding awed.

"And she has been seen before in this area. So this is your secret."

"Part of it. We use the ruse of the Swan Maiden's magic to trouble the king's men and keep them away from certain places in the forest and along the loch."

"So you could move siege engines."

"And to keep the king's men away from our forest homes. When De Soulis captured me and then you brought me back here, I thought I need not do this again."

"And your silence goes with it?"

"That encourages the legend and confuses the Sassenachs. Gawain—"

He set a finger to her lips, touched the same finger to his lips. "I never saw this."

He turned at the sound of horses thudding along a forest path. In the distance, he saw them move in two. One split toward the abbey, the other toward the castle.

"We must hurry," she said. "I will meet you at Elladoune." She stretched to kiss him. "Put out the fire and save our friends and our home if you can."

"I will do my best. But I cannot let you do this."

"I must," she said. "Just as you must choose. We are both too stubborn to change easily. Go. I will find you later."

He pulled her to him roughly, kissing her again. Then he moved back, and she whirled away. Gawain turned for Elladoune.

IF SHE CUT across the meadow toward the abbey, she knew that the knights might see her out in the open and pursue her—she would be too clear a target. Instead, she made her way along the fringe of the forest by the meadow. She could hear hoofbeats along another path. The route led behind the abbey grounds and onward, the way the monks were taking the war engine. If the knights were not stopped or diverted, they would soon discover the machine, the monks, and the rebels.

She wended her way through trees and undergrowth, through light and shadow. Her white cape nearly glowed and was easily visible. Soon they would see her. She prayed they would pursue her from here, where the trees could shield her as she led the men away from the rebels.

Then she saw the knights. Six; seven. De Soulis rode in the lead, his black armor and black horse like heavy shadows.

The forest path forked, and she paused at the top of a slope, waiting, watching. When she saw the horsemen on the track, she leaped down, far ahead of them to let them see her.

When one of the men shouted and spurred forward, she whirled and took the fork toward the village. Without looking back, she ran as fast as she could, hearing the thud and snort of horses, the shouts, behind her. Looking over her shoulder, she ran on.

Dashing sideways into an area where leaves shielded her, she looked back, but stumbled on a hidden root. She fell to her knees, the breath knocked out of her.

As she rose to her feet, a shadow emerged from the trees and a man lunged toward her. She backed away, but his hand whipped out to grab hold of her cloak. Pulled forward, she fell again. Black gauntleted hands grabbed her arms, dragged her up.

"Ah," De Soulis said, "the Swan Maiden is mine."

"It was the sheriff, sir," one of the Dalbrae soldiers admitted to Gawain as he approached the castle. The man eyed the Highland plaid, but said nothing, respecting Gawain's office. "We were to use fire-tipped arrows to set the outbuildings aflame. But there are people in there, sir." He gestured toward the walls. "I, for one, disagree with the order."

"Aye, with the place not even cleared," Gawain said. "There are women, old ones, and children, for love of God." Up on the battlements, he saw heads, shoulders, saw one pause at an opening beside a merlon. He recognized Laurie and shouted, waving. He pointed at the massive wooden doors. He wanted to go inside.

"Sir, we were told 'twas empty."

"I understand. I am going in to vacate the castle. This ends now. You and the others can return to Dalbrae. Where is the sheriff?"

"Rode out after rebels, sir."

"You have met your orders. Now be on your way." He strode past the guard and headed toward the gate. The massive doors parted slightly and he slipped through the gap into smoke and shadows. Coughing, Gawain turned to help the man shut the doors and turned in search of Laurie.

He paused to stare at the blaze alive in one corner of the yard, consuming the thatched roof of one of two kitchen buildings. A few MacDuffs—Teig, Uilleam, others—ran with sloshing buckets of water drawn from the well by the garden plot. He saw Laurie then.

"Jesu. Is everyone safe?" Gawain asked.

"So far." Laurie wiped a hand across his brow, his face streaked with soot. "We moved everyone into the farthest tower and wet down the doors and walls as much as we could. The horses and livestock were moved outside the castle walls. And we created a wet earthen gap between the kitchen and the rest of the outbuildings."

Gawain raised his brows. "You have experience with castle fires."

"In the Lowlands, a man gets used to it. The Southrons and the Scots are forever burning each other out. The kitchen may burn to cinders, but the rest could be saved."

"Stone will not burn, but will only turn to glass in the hottest of fires. That will not happen here, with luck. Most of it should survive, with what you've done." He hurried toward the steps to go up to the battlement, Laurie with him. Together they strode along the wallwalk, Gawain keeping a long-legged pace. They encountered a few Highland men armed with bows and arrows behind the merlons, occasionally aiming through the crenel space. Two or three gave Gawain curious glances.

He stopped to search the meadow for any sign of Juliana.

"Man," Laurie said then, "what are you wearing? Where is the rest of your gear?"

"We swam the loch. When we came back I had no time to put the rest on. I took Juliana away for safekeeping for the night. They were searching for her."

"The sheriff was in a high fit over it, though he only deserved it. His chainmail is just common blackened steel, I hear now." Laurie laughed. "Why a Highland plaidie?"

"I had naught else," Gawain replied.

Laurie grinned. "You are dressed like a MacDuff now. They wonder at it."

Gawain sighed heavily, watched the fire, saw men working there with buckets, saw that it was under control. Soon he would lend a hand. But first, this.

"Laurie," he said, "did I ever tell you my name—my birth name?"

Laurie scratched his whiskered chin. "Scottish. But I do not recall hearing it."

"I was born Gabhan MacDuff. Only days ago, I discovered my grandfather's castle, Glenshie, along that mountain beyond the loch. It is in ruins now."

"By heaven! Will you claim it as your own?"

"I have the right."

Laurie's grin shifted to a frown. "Edward would never grant it. Though I heard before I came here with you that the king's military advisors do not see much advantage in keeping a tight hold on Highland areas. It is costing too much effort."

"Aye, when they have fierce rebel opposition and want to

find Bruce."

"If you want Glenshie, you may have to change your fealty. Edward will not grant that land even if you were born to inherit it. Go over to the Scots, man. Many do. More and more, if you ask me."

Gawain frowned, turning to look down at the sheriff's men, still there. An attack did not seem imminent or even likely now, the way the knights peered nervously up at the battlements where Highlanders kept bows trained on them. "'Tis no simple matter."

"Your English family? Henry Avenel is in Edward's pocket. They will be fine. They may have to deny you, but will not condemn you for it. Look at me. I cannot save the world. I know it. Sometimes we must do what the heart wants, and let the world fend for itself."

Gawain cocked a brow. "Uncommon wise, sir."

"You have done all you could to make up for transgressions that never seemed very serious to me. Do what you need, what your wife and new family need. I always thought you would jump the border sooner or later."

Gawain huffed. "Between you and my wife, I am surprised to be given a choice. You sound as if you lean north yourself."

"Me? I am content enough. I come north for the ale, and south for my wife."

"The MacDuffs are fighting the fire. I must go help them."

"A moment. There are MacDuffs up here you have not met." Laurie moved along the wallwalk. "This is Angus MacDuff," Laurie said, indicating a brawny red-haired man, who turned and nodded. With him were others. "These young men are MacDuffs too, the sons of Lucas MacDuff, who is with the abbot, I hear."

"Ah. I know what he is doing."

"Aye? I just found out myself. I feel the fool. That scaffolding! Rebels all, from the monks to the forest folk, the abbot himself, and your own lady. Making a war machine under our noses."

"Aye so." Gawain nodded a greeting to each Highlander and

ran toward a section of wall that overlooked the gate. "Keep watch for Juliana," he said. "She should come to the gate soon. We must get her inside quickly."

"And if she does not come?" Laurie asked.

"Then I will go out after her." He scanned the meadow and forest again. Dread turned in his gut and a prickling ran along his neck.

Chapter Thirty-Two

"Pity I do not have the golden chains with me," De Soulis murmured. "But this will do." He finished the last of the knots and stood back. Juliana turned her head away, standing still and silent.

Her neck and wrists were bound with loops of rope, attached by a length of hemp. A long tether stretched to the sheriff's hand. She was caught fast.

"I know you can speak. I suppose it is contrary female temperament that keeps you silent."

She glared at him, knowing he had no idea how contrary she felt just then.

"The king wants an oath of fealty out of you. But that looks pointless. So you will be tried for treason, and for threatening a sheriff's life." He tied the tether to the back of his saddle and mounted his horse.

Waiting for him, six guards sat their horses in silence. She expected no help from that grim quarter.

De Soulis tightened the knots. "So the Master of Swans has caught the Swan Maiden. Now he shall catch a Swan Laird. There is some legend about that, I think."

"There is one part of the legend you should know," she said clearly. He raised a brow, looking pleased and snide. "One day a warrior will defeat the evil that keeps the swan maiden and her swan laird apart."

"How will he do that?" De Soulis pulled on the tether, walking his horse forward. "Tell me. I am interested in such things."

"He will fling a faery bolt into the loch. It will release the spell that holds the maiden and her lover trapped."

"Impossible! Good. We are safe."

"You are not safe. But I will be set free." Her heart pounded. If only she had an bow and arrow, she would send her shot true without hesitation this time. Now she had only words to defend herself. And trust, a steady shield.

Somehow, she felt sure she would escape this. The first time De Soulis had caught her, she had been terrified and helpless. Now she felt some inner certainty, some sense of courage that diminished fear.

De Soulis yanked on the rope and stepped his horse ahead.

She stumbled after him. The horse walked ahead and she walked with it, holding her head high. Behind her, the other knights did not ride after them.

De Soulis stopped and looked back. "Come ahead," he snapped.

"Sir," one said. "It is not right to treat a woman thus. None of us liked it the first time, but the king wanted the girl. But we will not watch this again." The others nodded agreement.

"This girl tried to kill me," De Soulis growled. "She is a rebel, a traitor, likely a witch. I arrested her, and she will go on trial. This is a just treatment for a criminal."

"She bested me at archery several times yesterday," another knight said. She recognized one of the archers in the competition.

"She won that damned gold arrow. You let her take it from you—Sir Rolfe de Lisle, the captain of the sheriff's archers! You should be ashamed."

"The king's commanders will not look kindly on this," the first knight said. "We could all be condemned for it." The other men muttered with him.

"As sheriff, I have every right to arrest her. Enough! We must hasten to Elladoune. Her husband will be there by now. He must be apprehended as well. King Edward will be more than pleased. Remember that, all of you."

The archer dismounted and walked his horse forward. "We do not dispute her arrest. But there is no cause to humiliate her. She is no witch. That is but a mummer's costume she wears. Naught to fear. Something to admire."

Juliana stared at him, surprised, filling with gratitude.

"The lady does not deserve this. She is the wife of the constable of Elladoune, who is a son of Sir Henry Avenel. She deserves courtesy until the king decides."

"What," De Soulis snarled, "all of you, as one?"

"Sir," Rolfe de Lisle said, "she can ride my destrier. I will walk."

Bold and quick, he reached out to untie the knot from De Soulis's saddle. Then he turned to lift Juliana up to his own horse. She put her roped hands on the man's shoulders and looked into a pair of steel-blue eyes.

"Thank you," she whispered.

"It is all we can do now. He has the right to charge you with a crime. But few have your skill with a bow. To my mind, you are a comrade in arms." He gave her a crooked smile. "The rest you must face on your own."

"Sir Rolfe," De Soulis said, "mount up. You will pay for insubordination later."

"Aye, sir," Sir Rolfe replied. "When the king's general inquires into this matter, if he learns of the lady's fair treatment, it could look well for you."

De Soulis growled something and guided his horse ahead.

Sir Rolfe shifted Juliana sideways on the saddle and swung up behind her. They cantered along the path behind De Soulis.

Captive again, she felt strangely safe, as if she had an honor guard this time.

THE DAY HAD brightened, but the sky above Elladoune was dull as old pewter due to the smoke. But overhead clouds promised much-needed rain soon. Gawain wiped his forearm over his sweaty, sooty brow. He had taken over from Uilleam to carry and dump water buckets on the blazing kitchen garden, after working to wet the thatch on another shed.

Flames still burned in the kitchen buildings, but the blaze was lower, closer to embers in places, though it could burst out at any time. Stinging smoke trailed upward. Two buildings and one garden were ruined, but sparks had not spread in the damp air.

He glanced up at the wallwalk, where Laurie watched for Juliana. Too much time had passed, Gawain thought. He could only hope she was with the monks, all of them safe. But he felt another spin of dread in his gut.

Laurie shouted, pointing outward. Gawain tossed the empty bucket to Lucas's eldest son, then ran to the stone steps.

"Your bride comes at last. But she has an escort. You will not like it."

Gawain took the steps in twos and strode to stand where Laurie looked out. Then he swore under his breath and smacked his hand against stone.

Knights headed across the meadow, De Soulis in the lead. Juliana, in white, her hair a pale glow, rode with one of the men.

He swore again. "I should never have let her do this." He grabbed the bow and quiver nearest him and loaded the bow.

"Surely you did not expect her to listen to you," Laurie remarked. "Let them inside. We will kill the Soul-less one and be done with it."

Gawain slid him a sour glance. Laurie shrugged. But the same thought had crossed his mind. "Open the gate. Take Angus with you, he is a big man in a fight."

"I know what to do." Laurie took up a bow, jammed arrows into his belt, and ran down the steps to the bailey.

Gawain hurried along the wallwalk for a better vantage point over the gate. The sheriff's men who had been waiting outside the castle walls came forward to meet the sheriff and the others. While they conferred, Laurie and Angus ran inside the entrance arch and unbarred the wooden doors beyond the portcullis.

Gawain watched from above as De Soulis motioned to the rider who carried Juliana. That one, he realized, had been in the competition against Juliana. Studying the scene below, he drew arrows from a nearby pile, stuck a few in his belt, took up a nearby longbow, and loaded it.

The sheriff and the knight riding with Juliana came through the gate, and a few others followed inside. Gawain swiveled and trained his bow down toward the bailey, coldly prepared to kill on an instant's decision if needed. He waited.

The groan and slam of the iron portcullis, followed by shouts, told him that Laurie and Angus had successfully trapped some of the riders inside the entrance arch. Only the sheriff, the knight, and Juliana rode into the bailey. Laurie and Angus ran toward them.

Laurie raised a nocked bow and big Angus set one hand to the great sword sheathed at his back. Keeping his own bow steady, Gawain looked at Juliana. The ropes tied about her neck and wrists only heightened his fury. But the pale look on her face, the stubborn chin—that near broke his heart. This should have never happened to her again.

He sighted her captors, each one a pull of the bow away.

A damp wind touched the back of his neck, stirred his hair. He stood like stone.

"De Soulis!" he shouted from above. "Let her go now!"

The sheriff looked upward. His black armor was like jet in the smoky light. He motioned to the second knight, the archer, to release Juliana. The man slid her carefully to the ground and dismounted. De Soulis swung down too and took Juliana's elbow. Gawain saw her wince. He tightened the string.

"Avenel!" The sheriff looked up. "This place was to be razed by king's order. But your men are working to save it."

"It was to be cleared first," Gawain said. "You ignored that part of the order."

"Burning sufficiently clears rodents."

"Hey! My wife's Cousin Aymer will want to hear about this," Laurie called, his voice carrying.

De Soulis turned. "Aymer?"

"De Valence." Laurie grinned.

The sheriff snarled and turned back to Gawain. "You have committed another transgression against the king. Come down from there. I am obligated to arrest you."

"What is your accusation?"

"Protecting Highland rebels. Aiding your wife in assaulting me. Aiding her escape. She is fond of that swan legend," he added, stroking her shoulder in its feathery cape. "But we upped her." She flinched her shoulder away.

Suppressing fury, Gawain lowered the bow he held, biding time. He was sure Laurie and Angus would rush the men if any move was made. Setting the bow upright, leaning on it, he stared down at De Soulis.

Elsewhere in the bailey, Uilleam, Beithag, and others came closer. Behind them, the fire burned like a hearth, but less now. A damp wind whisked through Gawain's hair and stirred the plaid around his bare knees. He heard distant thunder.

"Why are you dressed like a Highlander?" De Soulis asked. "And how do you explain your actions? You, an Avenel! You should beg mercy of that fine man."

"I did not assist my wife in her assault. She handled it nicely on her own," Gawain said. "And she freed her brothers from your custody." Beside De Soulis, Juliana stood slim and straight, the rising breeze ruffling the white feathers against her throat, where the rope was noosed.

He narrowed his eyes. The blond knight standing with them was an expert bowman, he knew. The man had taken his longbow from his saddle, but made no move with it.

"Secondly," Gawain said, "her escape. She had good reason, with armed men in pursuit of a helpless girl."

"Helpless! Have you seen her shoot?"

"I have," Gawain said.

"You aided her before. Years ago," De Soulis growled.

Gawain shrugged. "Possibly. As for abetting Highland rebels…" He looked at the MacDuffs standing in the bailey. "It is no crime to shelter one's kin."

"Kin? You take your marriage too seriously. They are savages."

"My marriage has naught to do with it. I was born here among these savages," Gawain said. He looked wholly at Uilleam now. "My birth name is Gabhan MacDuff."

In that instant, saying it aloud before witnesses, his decision was made. A burden, long carried, lifted from him and fled with the wind. He heard another crack of thunder.

Juliana widened her eyes. The MacDuffs, beyond, whispered urgently. Uilleam stared up at him, unmoving.

"You have gone mad," De Soulis said. "Mad, thinking yourself one of these rebels. Thinking this is a noble cause. They are in the wrong. Edward has the right in Scotland."

"Let my wife go," Gawain said.

"If you want her," the sheriff said, "you will have to join her. Come down from there." He pulled her in front of him. "Sir Rolfe," he barked, "take him."

The blond knight took up the longbow, quiver over his chest, and began to stride across the yard. Juliana looked at Gawain, her eyes large, pleading.

Gawain narrowed his eyes and scanned the whole of the bailey. He could demand her release, but little would come of it. If he used one swift arrow to take down De Soulis in cold blood, he risked hitting Juliana despite his good aim. If he let Laurie or Angus take the sheriff down, Juliana could be hurt. He could not live with himself if harm came to her through his actions.

He moved slowly toward the battlement steps. The sheriff's knight reached the middle of the yard. Gawain lowered his bow, judging what might come next.

Juliana cried out and twisted violently in De Soulis's grip. She broke free and ran for the steps, launching past the knight. He reached for her and missed.

Gawain saw De Soulis spin and grab a bow from his own horse. He snatched an arrow from the quiver, but needed time to set the arrow and aim.

Standing on the stone walk, Gawain raised his bow. But Juliana leaped onto the steps, bolting up, not looking back, though she ran between three bows—his, the knight's, and the sheriff's.

De Soulis straightened his aim. Seeing the angle, Gawain knew.

Time slowed and his vision sharpened even as he lengthened his stride toward Juliana as she mounted the stone steps. De Soulis drew back the string. Rage and hatred darkened his face as he sighted the arrow tip on the girl.

In that instant, Laurie roared and raised his own bow, the blond knight swerved, and Angus slid the great sword free. Juliana reached the top step, her back to the bailey. Gawain lunged for her, lunged to stop what was about to happen, bow lowered, hand out, eyes keen as a hawk's.

He heard the twang of the bowstring, the only signal he needed. The resonant had him reaching out, stretching toward her, arm, hand extended.

The arrow arced upward. Gawin felt, body and soul, as if he were a bolt leaving a bowstring. He angled into the arrow's curving path and his hand closed around the shaft.

He slammed into her, knocking her down with him to the walkway.

She gasped beneath him, and he lay over her, heart thundering. He gripped the arrow shaft. Then he heaved to his feet and dove for his bow. De Soulis yelled out and lashed another arrow onto his bow.

Juliana began to get to her hands and knees. The sight of her, roped and crying, snapped his control. Gawain snatched up his bow, nocked the arrow he had caught, pulled the string back, all while De Soulis readied another arrow. Gawain aimed—

And stopped. De Soulis fell hard, dropping the bow, dropping to his knees, slumping forward with an arrow in his armpit, the gap in any man's armor.

The blond knight lowered his bow and looked up at Gawain. Then he nodded just once, and walked toward his fallen commander, sinking to a knee.

Laurie rushed forward to look down at the sheriff, then turned away. "That accursed black armor," he growled, his voice carrying, "did not protect him, did it?"

Juliana was on her feet now, bound hands raised to her mouth. She ran toward Gawain with a little cry.

He still held the bow, the tension enormous in his hands, the bow shaking for release. He turned to face over the wall, angled high, and let the shaft go.

The arrow sailed upward, its soaring arc long, long, and perfect. The bolt came down in the center of the loch.

He spun as Juliana reached him, threw the bow aside, and swept her into his arms. After a moment, he pulled back to loosen the rope, dragging it away from her. Then he untied her white cape, fingers shaking, and tore it away from her shoulders. That, too, he flung over the wall. It sailed out like a bird.

"*Ach Dhia,*" Juliana whispered. "The legend. Gawain, the legend! The arrow in the loch—my swan cloak—as if the old legend came to be!"

"Just an old tale," he growled, as he untied the rest of her bonds. He pulled her into his embrace, free and unencumbered. "What is real is this. We are together, you and I, and we will stay here always, if that is what you want. At Elladoune."

"Home," she said, looking up at him. "Here, and at Glenshie too."

"Aye, love," he said, touching the silk of her hair. "You are home to me." As he spoke, the rain began, pattering at first, then refreshing, cleansing. He kissed her.

"Gabhan," he heard moments later, and turned.

Uilleam and Beithag stood down in the bailey by the steps to the upper walk. Teig and others were with them, all of them soot-darkened. They stared up at him.

"Go on," Juliana said. He took the steps downward, giving her his hand as she came after him. The rain came down in earnest, cleansing the yard now. The knight with the longbow stood with Laurie and Angus. De Soulis lay in the dirt as the rain muddied the yard.

He moved toward Uilleam and Beithag. The old woman reached up to touch his face.

"Gabhan, is it you?" She repeated his name, lips trembling.

Uilleam grasped Gawain's hand in his, leathery and strong. So like his grandfather's hands. Gawain looked into the old man's eyes. So like his grandfather, for they had been brothers.

"I am he," he said in Gaelic. "Gabhan, Uncle."

"Welcome home," Uilleam said. "We have missed you, Gabhan our own."

He smiled, felt his throat tighten. He reached out and drew Juliana with him into the heart of the gathering.

Epilogue

JULIANA STOOD WITH Gawain on the shore of Loch nan Eala at sunset, beneath a pink and brilliant sky. The autumn leaves in the forest were masses of gold and wine and flame. Their colors spilled into the loch, where the swans glided, part of a perfect mirrored reflection.

The castle rose on its promontory, solid and sure. Beyond the loch, the face in the mountain appeared again, touched by the changing light. She could not love this place more. She could not love this man more.

She looked at Gawain. "Soon old Beira will be let loose from her prison, and winter will be upon us. And the swans will fly south again."

He smiled as he studied the mountain. She loved seeing those quiet expressions of contentment that he showed more often now. He took her hand.

"Not all of the swans will fly away," he said, and lifted her hand to kiss it.

The sunset grew vivid, a fiery poem of a sky. Shadows deepened. The wind took on a crisp edge. Gawain turned with Juliana to walk back toward Elladoune, her hand tucked in his.

"Gabhan," she said. "I have something to tell you."

He slanted an affectionate glance at her. "We both know you are quick with child. Is there some other surprise?"

"I have decided to take my oath."

He raised his brows. "You have nicely avoided that for months. I expected you to sidestep it indefinitely."

"I wanted to, but with a new sheriff at Dalbrae, the matter will come up again. I will say the words, the new man will sign the affidavit, and 'twill be done. Peacefully this time. He has no grudge against us, I hope."

"He does not. What caused this change of heart?"

"I will not declare for the English, if you wonder that."

"I am certain of it," he drawled.

"My thought is that this will keep you out of prison. Charges of treason could come from Edward. I am surprised he has not sent some nasty message to you about that. But they say he is ill again."

"He is distracted by his fury toward Scotland. I am small to him now. So far I have stayed out of his dungeon and I may be free of yet another oath of obeisance."

"If my oath will help, I will do it." She looked up at him earnestly. "I would do anything for you."

"Offering me a rescue, my swan lady?"

"If you need it."

He cupped her chin in his hand. "Your loyalty is all to me. But there is no need to take the pledge."

"I made up my mind to do it. Send word to the new man that we will come to Dalbrae this week. What is his name? You went to Dalbrae this morning."

"I did. And I can tell you that the king has been informed that you took the oath."

She felt confused. "But I did not."

"The new sheriff saw to it when he came to Dalbrae. First thing. He told me so this morning."

"Tell me," she said impatiently. "What sort of man is he? Why did he send that writ out?"

"I think you will like him." His eyes twinkled. "Sir Laurence will make an excellent sheriff for Glen Fillan."

"Laurie?" She laughed. "You knew and did not tell me?"

"I wanted to surprise you." He smiled. "He was appointed sheriff by his wife's cousin, Aymer de Valence, and came to Dalbrae just yesterday. He found the writ for the oath among the documents De Soulis had prepared. You never took the oath, but Laurie sent a note out saying it was done and is no longer a matter for the crown to bother about. His gift to us, and he says do not forget it. And he offered another. The first thing he did was release the swans De Soulis had taken. I would not be surprised if you were to see them again soon."

She laughed in pure relief and stretched her arms toward him. He gathered her in and she closed her eyes for a moment. A chilly autumn wind cut past, but his arms were a shield around her.

"Laurie will make an excellent sheriff," she said. "But what of Gabhan MacDuff? Will the king pursue you for treason over that?"

He tucked her hand in his arm and strolled up the hill toward Elladoune. "By Scots law, if a man is born in Scotland, he is obliged only to the King of Scots."

"I thought so. Only Edward would dispute it."

"I pledged to Edward and broke that vow. There is not much to be done about that," he explained. "But the king is ill. And his advisors care little about small matters of justice. They will leave such things to regional sheriffs and lords."

"What will the new sheriff do about your case?"

"Nothing. He says Glenshie is impossible to find and it is too much trouble, to his thinking, for knights to ride out in search of a renegade when there are other matters to concern them. Market fairs, crofter disputes, ale rights. Much is on his mind."

She laughed, then tugged on his arm to pause their stroll. She leaned up to kiss him on the mouth. His hand pressed the small of her back, his other hand brushed along her jaw. Warm, hungry, his lips slanted over hers.

"So you approve of the sheriff's decision," he murmured.

"Very much," she whispered.

"There is one thing. He has offered to foster Alec and Iain at

Dalbrae, if you are ready to let the young ones out of the nest after keeping them close these months."

"Not yet," she said, thinking ahead to the spring, when their child would be born at Elladoune. She wanted her younger brothers to have a sense of family. "But when they are ready, that would be a good place for them. They adore Sir Laurie."

"They will have the run of Dalbrae," Gawain drawled. "Laurie's wife will come north soon. She sent word to Laurie that she is healthy, now that their son has been born, and she wants them to be a family. Maude will be a good friend to you, I think."

She held his hand. "Sometimes I wonder if I can hold any more happiness inside me. Life is better than I could ever have dreamed."

"And one matter more," he said softly. "The ransom for Niall and Will has been paid. They will come home before winter."

She gasped, tears springing to her eyes. "Paid?"

"I asked Henry Avenel to pay it from my revenues. I have some land in Northumberland farmed by tenants. It produces well. He said the coin was available."

She took his hands, their fingers wrapping together. "I can never thank you enough. You just released two rebels, you know."

"We are surrounded." He shrugged. "I want your blessing. I want to send word to James Lindsay to request that he come here to meet with me."

"Jamie? Of course you have my blessing for it. Why?"

"I want to offer my services to the Bruce. I have contacts and influence as constable of an English-held castle."

"Gabhan, it is a great risk."

He nodded. His gaze swept the castle, the loch, the mountains. "I think it is something I must do."

"And Laurie? You might place him in the position of being your enemy."

"It was his suggestion. I told you he leaned that way. He says he likes Scots ale too well to be unkind to those who make it. And the sheriff gets the best ale." He laughed and put his arm around her as they climbed the hill.

Hearing a fast and rhythmic sound, Juliana looked overhead. Gawain did as well.

A huge white swan flew toward the loch, its great wings beating in a steady cadence. Dipping, sinking, the bird landed on the loch with a flurry and a splash. Then it settled on the water, curving head and neck in a graceful arc.

"*Ach Dhia,*" Juliana breathed. "Look!"

"What is it?" Gawain asked, glancing where she pointed.

Guinevere glided across the loch with her four cygnets, now grown larger, their grayish feathers mingled with white. They streamed in a line toward the newcomer.

"Artan," she said. Tears pooled in her eyes. "He is back." She looked at Gawain. "He found his way home after all."

He drew her again into the circle of his arm. "I knew he would, even if it took him all his life to find his way here."

Juliana tilted her head and he kissed her, a familiar comfort. The child within her flitted, the tiniest movement. She looped her arms around her husband's neck. "Whatever happens," she said, "we will be together here."

Gawain nodded. "Aye so, my love. We will be here always."

Author's Note

Swans and swan lore are shining threads in the Celtic, as well as the medieval fabric. The history, the legends, and the natural care of these beautiful birds, who lend themselves so well to imagery and metaphor, were a pleasure to research. As early as the twelfth century, swans in Britain were regarded as the exclusive property of the English monarchs. Masters of Swans were appointed by the crown to care for the birds, and to raise them for table and captivity on rivers and lakes. Today, swans in Britain are carefully tended and protected.

Symbolism was never far from the medieval mind, and swans have always lent themselves to that. Medieval chronicles record that in May, 1306, Edward I of England held a grandiose feast at Westminster, in which he knighted, en masse, three hundred knights. Later in the festivities, two captive swans were brought into the great hall, where the king then vowed revenge against the Scots he so despised.

The link between swans and Scotland exists in the rich Celtic tradition of swan legends and tales; the Lindsay crest features a swan with wings raised. For purposes of the story, the legend of the swans of Elladoune was invented, and a second Feast of the Swans was created in Newcastle, where the English king stayed in 1306 while gathering his armies.

Readers who are familiar with my previous novel, *The Hawk Laird*, will recognize Sir Gawain Avenel from his introduction there, and will know James Lindsay and Isobel Seton and their involvement in the cause of Scotland.

Finally, while arrow catching is possible to do, it is best left to experts! I was fortunate to be instructed by a tenth-degree black belt who had trained for years to master the technique. (Definitely it should never be done except under the supervision of a tenth-degree black belt!)

If you'd like to know more about my print books and ebooks, please look for me on social media or visit www.susan fraserking.com. I'm also part of the Word Wenches blog at www.wordwenches.com.

Happy Reading!

Susan

About the Author

Susan King is the bestselling, award-winning author of (so far) 28 historical novels and novellas, a hefty nonfiction history, and dozens of magazine and web articles on education and the craft of writing. Her books, including mainstream historicals Lady Macbeth: A Novel and Queen Hereafter: A Novel of Margaret of Scotland, have been published by Penguin, Random House, HarperCollins, Kensington, ePublishingWorks, and Dragonblade. Praised for historical accuracy, lyrical writing, and storytelling quality, she is a USA Today bestselling author with numerous awards, nominations, and career achievement awards as well as starred reviews from Publisher's Weekly, Booklist, and Library Journal. Most of her books are set in Scotland ranging from the 11th to the 19th centuries.

Susan is a former university lecturer in art history, a private school teacher, and a founding member of one of the longest-running author blogs, "Word Wenches" (wordwenches.com). She holds a Bachelor's in studio art and English literature, a Master's in art history, and completed most of her Ph.D./ABD in medieval art history. Raised in Upstate New York, she lives in Maryland with her husband and three sons in an ever-growing family.

Website – www.susanfraserking.com